# THE LOST LETTER FROM MOROCCO

Adrienne Chinn was born in an old paper-making town in Newfoundland, and grew up in rural Quebec and Montreal. She retraced her English father's footsteps back to England, where she now lives and works as an interior designer.

When not writing or designing, she can normally be found in the queue at Gatwick heading off somewhere new; she travels all over the world, but most often to her beloved Morocco, which she has been visiting regularly for over ten years.

# ADRIENNE CHINN

# THE
# LOST LETTER
# FROM
# MOROCCO

**avon.**

Published by AVON
A division of HarperCollins*Publishers* Ltd
1 London Bridge Street
London SE1 9GF

www.harpercollins.co.uk

A Paperback Original 2019

A catalogue copy of this book is
available from the British Library.

PB ISBN: 978-0-00-831456-9
TPB ISBN: 978-0-00-833243-3

This novel is entirely a work of fiction.
The names, characters and incidents portrayed in it are
the work of the author's imagination. Any resemblance to
actual persons, living or dead, events or localities is
entirely coincidental.

Typeset in Minion Pro by Palimpsest Book Production Limited, Falkirk, Stirlingshire

Printed and bound in UK by CPI Group (UK) Ltd, Croydon CR0 4YY

**MIX**
Paper from
responsible sources
FSC www.fsc.org    FSC C007454

This book is produced from independently certified FSC™ paper
to ensure responsible forest management.

For more information visit: **www.harpercollins.co.uk/green**

*For H.*

# Prologue

## Marrakech, Morocco – March 2009

Addy steps away from the window and runs her hand through her short red hair. She looks in the mirror and rubs a finger along the downy gingery growth of her eyebrows. She'll need to pencil them in, but she's used to that now. An expert.

The hotel room could be in London, Montréal or Philadelphia, the walls yellow-white, the furniture cheap wood, the bedcovers brown nylon. Only the framed desert print of a palm tree and a camel hints at the exotica outside in the Marrakech streets. Addy grabs her new digital camera off the chest of drawers and leans on the windowsill. Several storeys below, the hotel's swimming pool shines like a turquoise kidney in the spring sunshine. A hotel is going up next door, the steel frame silhouetted against the blue sky. Men lean from scaffolding and shout as they haul up plastic buckets and pieces of metal. Addy focuses her lens and snaps several photos. Warming up. Getting into the groove. So many more images to capture in her camera before her visa expires in three months' time. Then the book will be done and it's back to London, God help her.

# Chapter One

**London, England – January 2009**

Addy watches the crimson poison run down the plastic tube that loops like a roller coaster through the disinfected air. Over the green vinyl arm of the chair, over her father's old navy cable-knit jumper that she's pulled on, until it disappears down the roll-neck to a tube inserted in her chest. She's named it the Red Devil. Killing everything in its path. Good cells and bad cells. Hopefully more bad than good.

The chemo room is full today. The girl, Rita, lies back in her chair and watches a nurse insert a cannula into her hand. Her long curly black hair twists around her earbud wires and bunches on her shoulders where she leans against the beige vinyl. Addy grimaces and turns her face away. She raises her arms and examines the purple bruises yellowing like spilt petrol on her arm. Collapsed. Every single vein. They've had to insert a Hickman into the veins leading to her heart. She hides the tubes inside her bra. So much easier than the cannula. She'd recommend it to anybody.

'Jesus fuckin' Christ!' Rita howls. 'That fuckin' hurt!'

Rita is only nineteen. Breast cancer sucks.

'God, the lift was out again. I mean the one for normal people.

Visitors aren't allowed in the sick people's lift, apparently. Where do they get these orderlies, anyway? Rude little bastards.'

Addy's half-sister, Philippa, drops her Louis Vuitton sample bag onto the mottled green linoleum and dumps a stack of magazines onto Addy's lap as she leans in to air kiss Addy's cheeks.

'You're wet, Pippa.'

'Yes. Blasted English weather.'

Philippa shrugs out of her Burberry raincoat and flaps it around, spraying Addy with the winter damp. She drapes the raincoat over the back of Addy's chair and drags a metal-legged stool across the linoleum. She perches on the stool, her slender knees neatly together.

Philippa rifles through the magazines on Addy's lap. She folds over a page of *House & Garden* and hands it to Addy.

'I'm in it this month. That place I did for the Russians in Mayfair? God, what a trial. Your photos don't look too shabby either.'

Addy examines the plush interiors – an artful mix of bespoke English sofas, pop art, Gio Ponti originals and Georgian antiques.

'Well done, Pips. It's good publicity for you.'

Philippa wrinkles her elegant nose. 'Don't call me that. You know I hate it. Your pictures are in *House & Garden*, Addy. Do you know what that means? It's a fresh start. You should thank me. That little photo shop of yours was bogging you down. Just as well it went bust. I don't know how you could stand doing those dreadful kiddie and doggie pictures.'

'We can't all be David Bailey.'

'Well, indeed. I don't understand why you feel so terrible about it closing. It's a bloody recession. Everyone's going bust. Even my dentist is downsizing, which tells you something. He's had to sell his Porsche and buy an Audi. Not even a sports model.'

Addy stares at her sister. 'It's hard out there.'

'Absolutely,' Philippa says, missing the sarcasm in Addy's voice. 'There's no shame in your business going bankrupt, so I wish you'd stop fretting. Frankly, it's getting on my nerves.'

Addy drops the magazine into her lap and picks up *Heat*. She flips through the flimsy pages trying to spot a celebrity she's heard of.

'It's easy for you to say, Pippa. You've got Alessandro's divorce settlement to live off.'

Philippa folds her arms across her chest. 'Money isn't everything, Adela. Status and reputation are much more important.' She draws her groomed eyebrows together. 'Well, at least as important as money.'

'I'll tell that to the supermarket cashier next time I try to pay for my groceries with my reputation.'

Philippa takes the magazine out of Addy's hands and places it neatly on top of a tin of Cadbury's Roses chocolates someone has left on the metal table beside Addy's chair.

'I was reading that.'

'Don't be absurd. There's nothing in there but tat.' Philippa brushes a stray hair out of her eye with a pink lacquered fingernail. 'Didn't I tell you I'd set you on the right track, Addy? What good are strings if you can't pull them?'

Philippa perches on the stool, straight-backed and attentive like a fashion editor in the front row of a catwalk show. Her grey tweed suit hugs her yoga'd and Pilate'd body, every dart and seam tweaked to perfection. How is it possible that they share the same DNA? Addy wonders. The pale, curvy, ginger-haired Canadian and the stylish English gazelle.

Addy taps her chest. 'I was the one who got us the *House & Garden* gig, Pippa. I'm the one who sent the photos in on spec.'

Philippa's eyebrows twitch. 'Oh. Did you?'

'I did.'

Philippa purses her lips, fine lines feathering up from her top lip to her nose. 'Well, anyway, you're finally getting somewhere with this photography lark.' She picks up the *House & Garden* and pages through the article. 'I do have a knack though, don't I? I'm not one of Britain's top-fifty interior designers for nothing. My psychic told me the Russians would be good for me. Thank God someone's got money in this godforsaken recession. All it took was blood, sweat and tears.'

'Your blood or your clients'?'

'Mostly the curtain-maker's this time. The builder told me they call me Bloody Philly.'

Addy shakes her head. At forty-six, Philippa is six years older, a successful interior designer, a short-lived marriage to an Italian investment banker behind her, a tidy divorce settlement in the bank. A stonking big house in Chelsea. On all the charity ball committees. In with the 'in crowd'. Busy, busy Philippa. Nothing like herself – the gauche one at the party in a cheap dress from the vintage stall in Brick Lane and flat shoes from Russell & Bromley hanging out by the kitchen door to grab the canapés. The grit in Philippa's oyster.

Their father, Gus, couldn't leave Britain behind fast enough after his divorce from Philippa's mother, Lady Estella Fitzwilliam-Powell. The 'Ethereal Essie' as Warhol christened her in the Sixties when she'd become a fixture at Warhol's Factory in New York after the divorce.

Her father had told her once that he'd met Essie on a July afternoon in the Pimm's tent at the Henley Regatta in the summer of 1962. Addy had seen pictures of him at that age – handsome in the fair-skinned, black-haired Black Irish way. Like Gene Kelly or Tyrone Power. Essie was eighteen, famous for her boyish figure and pale beauty. You could find pictures of her online now. Impossibly slender in minidresses and white go-go boots, her thick dark hair in a geometric Vidal Sassoon cut. Their father was fresh out of Trinity College with a degree in geology, the first of his working-class family to earn a degree. Philippa came along six months after the wedding. The marriage lasted a year. After the divorce, their father headed to Canada to find oil for a big multinational. By forty, Essie was dead on the bed of her rented flat in New York. Drugs overdose. Withered and desiccated. No longer ethereal.

Now their father was dead, too. Alone in his garden on the coast of Vancouver Island, on a bed of his favourite dahlias.

'Pip, I've been thinking—'

'Thinking? What do you mean, you've been thinking, Addy?' Philippa waves the magazine at the plastic bag of Red Devil hanging from its drip stand. 'You've got enough on your plate right now with all this palaver. Nigel's chosen a wonderful time to run off on you. You have to stop expecting men to be there for you. They'll always let you down.'

'Don't go there.'

Philippa holds up her hands. 'Sorry.'

Philippa's words stick into Addy like pins in a voodoo doll. She hasn't told Philippa that she's been scrabbling to cover Nigel's half of the mortgage as well as her own share for the past four months while he 'recovers from the cancer trauma'. Didn't they say disasters come in threes? They were wrong. A break-up, a bankrupt business, cancer and her father's heart attack – four things. More than her fair share.

Addy rubs her hand over the short red wig, reaching a finger underneath to scratch her sweaty scalp.

'I've only got one more chemo session, Pippa. Then some radiotherapy for a few weeks. They told me that's a doddle. Then Tamoxifen for five years. If I can stay clear for that long, I'm back to being a normal human being. Even the insurance companies say so. That's assuming I'm not dead.'

'Don't be so dramatic.' Philippa tosses the *Heat* magazine onto the metal table and prises the lid off the tin of chocolates. 'Someone's taken all the caramels. Sod's law.' She drops the lid back on and reaches into the pocket of her suit jacket, pulling out her cell phone.

'You can't use that in here, Pippa. It interferes with the equipment.'

Philippa slides the phone back into the pocket of her tailored grey jacket. Her body is tense with what Addy takes to be the desire to leave and get on with the job of being Bloody Philly. 'You were saying?'

'It'll be the spring when the radiotherapy's done. It's been a long year. I'm tired.'

'Of course you're tired. You have cancer.'

'I *had* cancer.'

Philippa gestures at the women in various stages of baldness flaked out in vinyl hospital chairs the colour of dirty plasters. 'What's all this? Performance art?'

Addy rolls her eyes. 'It's insurance. To make sure there's nothing hanging around.'

Philippa adjusts her grey wool skirt to rest just so on her kneecap. 'Fine. You *had* cancer.' She folds her arms, her lips in the tight line that sets Addy's teeth on edge. The lipstick is leaching into the fine lines running up to her sister's nose. 'What's this big idea of yours?'

Addy clears her throat. The Red Devil has created a hunger inside her. With every drop the hunger has sharpened until she's become ravenous for life. Time is short. You hear it all the time. But now she *knows* time is short. She's not going to waste one moment longer. Faffing around with a cheating boyfriend while working in a failing photography shop. No. She'll become the photographer she's always dreamed of being. Travel the world and capture it in her camera. Leave her footprint on the earth before it's too late.

'I've been thinking of working on a travel book. Julia at the photo agency thinks it's a great idea. A "Woman's Guide to Travelling Alone" kind of thing. On spec but if it's good enough, Julia's got contacts with some literary agents. Travel stories are big right now. Everyone's trying to escape the recession one way or another.'

'Seriously?'

Addy thrusts out her lower lip. 'I'm not an idiot. I've thought this through. I need to get out of London for a while. I'm worn out. I just need to decide on a country. It needs to be exotic. And cheap.'

Philippa shudders. 'Exotic? That sounds hot, and . . . un-hygienic. Your career's doing beautifully here. *House & Garden*. Do you know what that means? It's a calling card. All my designer friends will be clamouring to have you photograph their work. And you want to leave on a silly jaunt to some hot, dirty, dusty, filthy fleapit? That can't be good for you in your weakened condition. Do have some sense, Adela.'

Addy glares at her sister, knowing from countless past stand-offs that arguing is pointless. 'Perhaps you're right.'

'Of course I'm right. And how on earth are you going to afford something like that? Your money's all tied up in your flat.'

'I can manage a few months if I'm careful with the money Dad left me. I'll find somewhere cheap to travel to. Then, when the book sells—'

'*If* it sells.'

'—*when* the book sells, I'll have some money. It might even lead to another commission.'

'Obviously you know best. Heaven forbid you listen to your sister.'

Philippa rises and smooths her bobbed hair, a sleek sheet of brown silk. She reaches for her raincoat and rests it over her shoulders like a cape.

'Must go now. My Russian clients are taking me to lunch at The Wolseley. They've just bought a house in Berkshire from some impoverished earl.'

'I thought you hated the Russians.'

'Don't be daft. Of course I do. Pushy, gaudy nouveau riche with more money than sense. Which is why they're perfect clients. I'm hardly going to let my feelings stand in the way of decorating a stately home. I'll do a fabulous job and get you in to do the photos. I won't even charge you a finder's fee.'

Addy smiles feebly, wishing that Philippa wouldn't try so hard to impose her idea of what her life should be.

'Oh, mustn't forget.' Philippa picks up her sample bag and pulls out three tattered photo albums and a bulky manila envelope, adding them to the magazines on Addy's lap. 'It looks like you're not the only photographer in the family. Father's solicitor sent these to me with a stack of documents for me to sign.' She rolls her blue eyes. 'Like I have time. I've had a quick look. Tourist photos, mainly. More your kind of thing.'

Addy clutches at the albums as they slide off her lap. 'I never knew Dad took photos.'

Philippa leans in for a quick air-kiss. 'Who knew?' She grimaces. 'I hope they don't charge the estate for the postage from Canada. Those albums weigh a ton. I've asked the solicitor to clear the house and sell off the contents.'

'I might have liked to go out to Nanaimo and do that myself. I did grow up in that house.'

'In your condition? Don't be ridiculous. Trust me, I did you a favour. I've asked her to send me anything else she finds of value, though I can't imagine there'd be much. Once the estate clears his debt, we'll split anything left. Enough for a meal out at Pizza Hut, if we're lucky.'

'Were my mother's or Dad's Claddagh rings in with the things the solicitor sent? I haven't seen them in ages.'

'No, I have no idea where those are. But Dad's pen's in the envelope.'

Philippa gives Addy another quick air-kiss then picks her way around the other patients, carefully avoiding the nausea buckets. She raises her hand and wiggles her fingers without looking back.

Addy unties the string on the manila envelope and shakes out her father's fat black Montblanc fountain pen with the silver nib. She flips open the faded red cover of the top album and flicks through the stiff cardboard pages. Parisian landmarks, the Coliseum in Rome, a red-sailed dhow bobbing on the water in front of the Hong Kong skyline, the evening sun silhouetting the pyramids. Images displayed like butterflies between cellophane and sticky-backed cardboard pages.

A white envelope slips out of the album, its flap dog-eared and torn. She reaches into it. More Polaroids tumble from the folds of a sheet of thin blue airmail paper, its two sides covered in her father's blue-inked scribble.

She opens the letter:

3rd March, 1984
Zitoune, Morocco

*My darling Addy,*

*I'm sorry it's taken me so long to write. You know how crazy things can be when I'm over in Nigeria. I loved your letter about your initiation week at Concordia, but please tell me that was a purple wig and that you didn't dye your lovely titian hair. Just like your mother's.*

*Well, I'm not in Nigeria any more. Things are still unsettled here with the politics and all that, and with the glut of oil on the market right now, they terminated my contract early. No need to have a petroleum geologist searching for oil when they have more of it than they can sell!*

*The job down in Peru doesn't start till May, so I've headed up to North Africa for a bit before going there. It's dinosaur land up here, so I thought I'd do a little independent oil prospecting. Remember what I used to tell you when you were little? Where there were dinosaurs, there's probably oil. I might try to stop by Montréal to see you when I get back before flying back to Nanaimo. Is The Old Dublin still there? They do a cracking pint of Guinness.*

*Addy, my darling, I've been doing a lot of thinking up here in the mountains. It's a beautiful place – you must come here one day. I know how much you love the Rockies. There's something about mountains, isn't there? Solid and reassuring. A good place to come when life wears you down.*

11

*I know it hasn't been easy for you since your mother died. You know there was no option but the boarding school, what with me having to travel so much for work. You made a good fist of it, though. Honour student. I never told you how proud you made me. I'm sorry for that. I'm sorry for a lot of things . . . I hope you know how much I love you and your sister.*

*There's something I need to tell you. I'm not sure how you'll feel about it. I've met someone here. Up here in a tiny village in the Moroccan mountains. You know they talk of thunderbolts? It was like that. I can't explain it. Maybe you'll feel it yourself one day. I hope you do.*

*She's a lovely young woman from the village. She writes poetry. She has such spirit. She's only twenty-three, Addy – nineteen years younger. I only hope*

Addy peers into the envelope. Nothing. Where was the rest of the letter? What did her father hope? Who was this woman?

She looks at the Polaroids fanned out across her lap. The colours faded – the red turning into orange, the purple into pale blue, the green into yellow. The images slowly disappearing into memory. The splayed imprint of the footprint of a large bird in red clay. Something that looks like prehistoric cave carvings. An old man on a bicycle in an ancient clay-walled alleyway. A circular stone opening in a seaside wall. The shadows of a couple silhouetted on a sandy boardwalk – their loose clothing billowing about them, caught by a gust of wind. A woman's slender brown hands holding an intricately carved wooden box inlaid with mother of pearl veneers.

Addy holds the photo up and squints at the fading image. The ring on the woman's left ring finger. Golden hands clasping a crowned sapphire heart. A Claddagh ring. Her mother's wedding ring. Hazel's ring.

One by one, she turns the photographs over. Her father's handwriting. The blue ink from his fountain pen. *Dinosaur footprints,*

*Zitoune, December 1983 – with H and . . .* Addy squints. She can't make out the other initial. *Cave art, near Zitoune, February 1984 – with H; Alley in the Marrakech medina, March 1984 – with H; On the fortifications, Essaouira, April 1984 – with H; Le Corniche boardwalk, Casablanca, May 1984 – with H.*

With H? Who's H? Is she the woman in the letter?

Addy shifts in the chair and a final Polaroid slides out of the envelope into her lap. Its corners crushed and bent, the gloss cracking. Her father. In his forties, still fit and handsome, standing in front of a fairy-tale waterfalls. He has an arm around a woman. She's young, with long black hair falling onto her shoulders. Her skin is a warm brown, her eyes the colour of dark chocolate.

They're both smiling. Her father has never looked so happy. But it isn't his smile that draws her gaze. It's the round bump straining the fabric of the purple kaftan. Addy turns the photo over. The blue ink. The familiar impatient t's and g's. *Zitoune waterfalls, Morocco, August 1984 – with Hanane.*

# Chapter Two

'Higher, Hanane. You can do it.'

Hanane glances down at the laughing boys, her fine black eyebrows raised in doubt. 'You think so? It looks a lot higher when you're up here.'

'Look, I'll show you.' Omar grabs a low branch of the olive tree, swinging his lithe body up onto the bough. He jiggles a branch, raining fat black olives over his older brother, Momo, and their friends, Driss and Yassine Lahcen.

'Stop! Stop, Omar!' Momo yells. 'They hurt!'

'Don't whine, Momo,' Hanane says. 'Get the basket and fill it up. We don't want them to go to waste. They'll make good oil this year.'

Omar reaches down through the branches. 'Take my hand, Hanane. I'll help you.'

Hanane peers up through the grey-green canopy of the olive leaves. 'How did you get up there so quickly, Omar? You're like one of the monkeys by the waterfalls.'

'I'm the best climber in Zitoune, you have to know it.'

'I'm not as small as you. It's harder for me to squeeze through the branches.'

'Is it true you will be married soon?' Momo's best friend, ten-year-old Driss Lahcen, shouts up to her.

'Who told you that?'

'I heard your brother talking in the café. He said your father made a deal with your uncle in Ait Bougmez for you to marry your cousin, Mehdi, after Ramadan, and Ramadan finished already.'

Hanane grimaces and shakes her head, her long black braid swinging across the back of her blue djellaba. She'd never marry fat, ugly Mehdi, no matter what her father and Mohammed said.

She had a plan. She needed to convince her father to send her to university in Beni Mellal to study as a teacher. The new school rising up on the hill would need teachers. She was lucky that her poor mother had demanded that she learn to read and write at the village school, even though it had meant sitting behind a curtain so as not to distract the boys.

It had been wonderful, learning the magic of transcribing her thoughts into words that she'd scribble with her mother's kohl stick onto the scraps of paper she'd collect from the alleyways and hoard in her cupboard, rolled up in the folds of a hijab. Behind the dirty flowered curtain in the schoolroom, she'd discovered a talent that was hers and hers alone. Poetry. Short, sweet aches of life. The poems sprung from her like water flowing from the fountain of the garden of Paradise.

Then her mother had died. The baby hadn't managed more than two days of breath before he'd joined her. Her father had pulled Hanane out of school. A home needed a woman to cook the tagine and wash the clothes, he'd said. Someone needed to feed and care for him and her older brother, Mohammed. Even though she was only twelve. When her father had married the dull girl Hind the following year, nothing changed. Her education was over. But Hanane would escape her duties in the house whenever she could to range around the valleys and fields, helping the *shawafa* find the plants for her medicines and potions. In the mountains, she was free.

15

She was twenty-three now and the world was changing. Even here in the mountains. She'd often pause from washing the clothes in the river to watch a group of giggling white-smocked girls heading up the hill to the old school, their slates and chalk clutched against their chests. And the tourists were coming in from Marrakech more and more often to see the waterfalls. She'd even seen a lady on a motorcycle not three weeks ago! But since her twenty-third birthday in June, all her father and her brother, Mohammed, could talk about was her marriage.

'I'll never marry Mehdi. Mohammed only says it because his stupid wife, Bouchra, wants her brother here.'

'Oh, c'mon, Hanane,' seven-year-old Yassine Lahcen protests. 'We want to go to dance at a wedding.' Yassine pokes his brother on the arm. 'Look, Driss.' He waggles his shoulders and wiggles his hips like he'd seen the women do at Mohammed's wedding in the summer.

Driss shoves his brother's shoulder. 'What are you, a girl? Stop it. Don't be stupid.'

'What's wrong with being a girl, Driss?' Hanane calls down from the tree. 'You wouldn't be here without your mother. You must be respectful.'

An oily black olive smacks Driss on his forehead. He peers up into the branches just as Omar launches another one at him, hitting him square on the nose.

Omar bursts into giggles. 'It's raining. It's pouring. Driss Lahcen is snoring.'

A deep chuckle wafts over from the river path. A tall, black-haired European man in beige trousers and a navy jumper rolled under his chin stands on the compacted earth, holding an odd black object.

'May I take a picture?' he asks in accented French.

'Hey, mister,' Omar shouts from his perch. 'What's that thing?'

'It's a camera. But it's a special camera. It can make the pictures here, right in front of your eyes.'

'Serious?'

'Definitely serious.'

'Let him take our picture, Hanane,' Omar shouts down through the branches. 'I want to see it come out of the magic box.'

Hanane sweeps her eyes over the tall man. He's much older than her brother, Mohammed, but there's still a youthfulness about him, despite the lines that sweep out from his eyes when he smiles. His skin is very white and even from this distance, his eyes reflect the sharp blue of the November sky. His short, straight black hair shines blue where it's caught by sunlight. He carries himself with assurance, she thinks, like a man who's comfortable with his place in the world. What can he think of her, up here in the tree with a boy? What would her father think if he saw her talking to a foreigner?

'I don't think so, Omar. It's not proper.'

Omar breaks into a wide smile. 'She says it's fine, mister.'

'Omar!' Hanane hisses. 'You're a bad boy.'

'For sure, I'm a bad boy. Even Jedda says it and she loves me a lot.'

'I don't believe that at all. Your grandmother thinks you're the prince of Zitoune.'

'Wait there,' the man shouts up to them. 'I'll take a picture of you two first, just as you are.'

Hanane bites her lip. Omar kicks her shoulder with his foot.

'Your brother stinks of cumin.'

She giggles despite herself.

'Perfect.'

The man presses a button. A whirring sound and a square of shiny grey-and-white card slides out of the camera's mouth. The boys cluster around as the man waves it in the air.

Momo wrinkles his nose. 'It's smelly.'

Yassine pinches his nose with his fingers. 'Like donkey piss.'

Driss squints at the grey paper. 'Nothing's happening.'

The man laughs. 'You won't see it until I peel back this piece

17

of paper. We have to count one minute. Then you'll see a picture appear' – he waves his hands like a magician – 'like magic.'

Omar scampers down the tree. 'C'mon, Hanane. Come see the magic picture.'

Hanane peers through the leaves at the cluster of black heads huddled over the shiny square of card. She'd have to swear the boys to secrecy. Her honey cookies should do the trick.

'Who wants to peel back the plastic to see the picture?'

Omar shoots his arm into the air. 'Me! Me, mister!'

The man laughs and hands over the card. 'There,' he says, indicating a loose corner of the grey plastic film. 'Pull there.'

The boys huddle closer as Omar peels back the film.

'It's there!' Momo shouts. 'It's you and Omar in the tree. Hanane, come see.'

Hanane grabs a branch and shimmies down through the leaves. The man takes the photograph from Omar and holds it in front of Hanane. She's there, laughing in the tree with Omar, in black-and-white. Like magic.

'Take it. Please. So you'll always remember your day up in that olive tree.'

Hanane shakes her head. 'You are kind, but I couldn't.'

Bouchra would be sure to find it, no matter how well she hid it. Only yesterday, Hanane had found her rifling through her scarves. Luckily, she'd hidden her poems in Jedda's potion shed. If her lazy sister-in-law found the poems or a photo like this, Bouchra would frighten the devil Shaytan Iblis with her curses. Because, of course, Bouchra would betray her secrets, now that she considered herself the mistress of the Demsiri household. Bouchra would do anything to topple Hanane from her place as favourite.

'Well, then, I'll keep it. As a memento of a happy day.' The man tucks the glossy photograph in his back pocket and turns to the boys. 'Now, how about a picture of all of you boys there by the river?'

Hanane watches the boys jostle for the best place, which is taken, naturally, by Omar.

'I'm Gus Percival,' he says to her as he squints into the view-finder. 'I'm a geologist. I'm staying in Zitoune for a few months doing some research in the area.' He waves at the boys to squeeze more closely together. 'Say cheese.'

Hanane watches the shiny square of paper spew out of the camera's mouth. The man waves it in the air to dry, out of reach of the excited boys.

'Can I ask your name?'

Hanane hesitates. Why would he want to know her name? He had no place in her world, nor she in his. But why, then, did she suddenly feel like the earth had tilted and everything she'd known, everything she'd dreamed, had shifted to an unknowable place?

Omar jumps up and grabs the photograph from Gus's hand. He peels back the grey film as the others fight to see. 'Hanane! Come see!'

'Hanane,' Gus repeats. 'It's lovely to meet you.'

# Chapter Three

**Marrakech, Morocco – March 2009**

The reedy whine of the snake charmers' flutes flutters through the baseline of African drums and the water sellers' bells as Addy weaves through the crowds in Jemaa el Fna Square. Women with veiled faces sit on stools, bowls of green mud and syringes balanced on their laps. They grab at Addy as she walks past and point to photo albums showing hands and feet covered in intricate henna patterns. A band of boy acrobats in ragged red trousers jumps and tumbles in the square. Addy snaps a string of photos as they leap from one tableau to another. A small boy grins a gap-toothed smile and thrusts a dirty wool cap at her. She digs into her pocket and grabs a handful of change, tossing it into the cap.

'*Shukran*,' the boy shouts, then he turns and runs along the line of tourists jangling the coins in his cap.

Addy wanders into the shaded alleyways of the souks, clicking photos of anything that catches her eye: a green gecko sitting on lettuce in a bamboo cage, antelope horns hanging from an apothecary's shop front, two men eating snails from steaming bowls by a snail seller's three-wheeled stand. Overhead, loosely woven bamboo obscures the blue sky, and shards of sunlight slice through the dust and incense that clouds the air.

Addy jostles against short, stout women in citrus-coloured hooded djellabas and hijab headscarves. Some of the women are veiled, but many of the younger women are bare-headed, with long, glossy black ponytails trailing down into the discarded hoods of their djellabas. There are girls in low-rise skinny jeans, tight, long-sleeved T-shirts with CHANNEL and GUCHI outlined in diamante, their eyes hidden behind fake designer sunglasses studded with more diamante. They totter arm-in-arm down the alleyways in high-heeled sandals, ignoring the catcalls of the boys who buzz through the crowds on their motorbikes. 'How are you, baby? Come here, darling! I love you!'

Addy stops in front of a stall selling tote bags and straw bowls. She points to a wide-brimmed hat hanging by a loop from a nail in the wall.

'How much for the hat?'

'You like the hat?' The shop seller's lips curl back, exposing large yellow teeth. 'No problem, *mashi mushkil*.' He grabs the hat and presents it to Addy like a crown.

She sticks her finger through the loop and swings the hat back and forth.

'I've never seen a hat with a loop before.'

'It's for hanging. It's very clever design.'

'How much?'

'Two hundred dirhams.'

Addy makes a mental calculation. Around eighteen pounds. 'Okay.'

The shop seller leers at her and Addy sees the brown rot eating through the yellow enamel.

'It might be you would like a bag, madame? It's very beautiful quality. The best in Marrakech.'

'No, just the hat. Thanks.' She hands him two crumpled dirham notes.

The shop seller eyes her as he slips the money into the pocket of his beige djellaba. He holds up a fat finger. 'One minute, madame.

Please, you wait. I am sure you will like a special bag. It's from Fes. Very, very nice quality. Louis Vuitton.'

When he disappears behind the curtain, Addy puts on the hat and dodges out of the shop. She's halfway down the alley towards Jemaa el Fna when she hears his shouts.

'Come back, madame! I make you very good deal. A very beautiful bag. The best quality original fake in Marrakech!'

The sun is blazing hot when Addy steps into the square. She skirts along the perimeter in the shade of the restaurant canopies, picking her way around the café tables crowded with tourists sipping tepid Cokes and local men smoking Marlboros with tiny glasses of thick black coffee on the shaded terrace of the Café de France.

She heads down an alley towards the Koutoubia mosque, stopping short in front of a display case of cream-stuffed French pastries crawling with black flies, shaded from the sun by a faded red-and-white striped canopy. A sandwich board plastered with excursion photographs leans crookedly on the cracked paving in front of the pastry shop: desert camel trekkers silhouetted on the crests of towering dunes, blue fishing boats carpeting a seaside harbour, fairy-tale waterfalls coursing down red clay cliffs. Under the waterfalls a handwritten scrawl in blue marker fuzzy at the edges where the ink has leached into the flimsy card:

COME TO VISIT THE MOST BEAUTIFUL WATERFALLS OF NORTH AFRIQUE. ITS MAGIQUE IS AMAZING! THE CASCADES DE ZITOUNE WILL BE A WONDERFUL MEMORY FOR YOU. COME INSIDE TO BOOK A TOUR VISIT. ONLY 3 HOURS FROM MARRAKECH TO PARADISE.

Zitoune. Where her father had met Hanane. Where Hanane and her child may still be. She'd been wondering how she'd get there. Addy ducks under the frayed canopy into the pastry shop.

That night, Addy wakes up with an image in her mind's eye. The

22

waxing moon casts a muted light over the hotel room furniture, the shapes like hulking animals lurking in the shadows. She shuts her eyes and the image pulses against her eyelids. The figure wears a gown and turban of vivid blue. Addy lies in bed, the blueness staying with her until she falls back to sleep.

# Chapter Four

**The Road to Zitoune, Morocco – March 2009**

The tour bus rattles across the plains of Marrakech. A wall of towering snow-capped mountains thrusts skywards at the edge of the olive groves spreading out over the plains like a green sea to the right of the road. The March sky is achingly blue. Addy unzips her camera bag. She takes out her camera and the 24–105 mm zoom lens, changes the lens and screws on the polarising filter and lens hood. Leaning out of the window, she braces her elbows against the window frame.

As the bus bounces along the potholed asphalt, she snaps pictures of the squat olive trees, cactus sprouting orange prickly pears, and green fields dotted with blood-red field poppies. Towns of pink earth buildings materialise from the land, lively with mongrel dogs chasing chickens, women riding donkeys and men with prune-like faces shooing flocks of sheep.

The sun is warm on her face and her naked arms. She settles back into her seat. The faded blue vinyl is ripped at the seams and burns her hand when she touches it. She fans her face with her straw hat. Philippa's voice rattles around her head: *Are you mad, Addy? You're probably suffering from post-traumatic stress or something. A woman alone in the Moroccan mountains for three months? You can't be serious.*

Philippa had obviously missed the envelope of Polaroids. Missed the photo of Gus and Hanane and the letter. She'd have said something, definitely. Gloated. Anything to show up their father as a feckless, irresponsible wanderer, leaving abandoned women and children in his selfish wake. That wasn't the father Addy knew. The doting father she'd adored. But who was this Hanane? Why was she wearing her mother, Hazel's, Claddagh ring? Why had their father never said anything about Hanane and the baby after he'd come back from Morocco? Surely he wouldn't have just abandoned them. But he'd done it once before, with Essie and Philippa, hadn't he?

Maybe she and Philippa had a Moroccan brother or sister living in Morocco. A twenty-three-year-old now. Surely someone in Zitoune would know where Hanane and her child were now. Once she'd found out what had happened to them, she'd let Philippa know. That would be soon enough.

She leans her head against the vinyl seat, the bumps and sways of the bus lulling her into a dozy torpor. Nerves flutter in the pit of her stomach. Just three months. Three months to see what she can find out about Gus and the pregnant Moroccan woman in the photograph. Three months to work on the travel book. Three months to change her life.

The tour bus arrives at a junction in front of a one-storey building constructed of concrete blocks. A donkey stands tethered to a petrol pump with red paint faded by the sun. Above a window a Coca-Cola sign in looping Arabic script hangs precariously from a rusty hook. Someone's nailed a hand-painted sign of waterfalls to a post, an arrow pointing towards mountains in the distance. The driver grinds the gears and steers the bus towards the mountains.

A half-hour later, the bus pulls into a dirt square surrounded

25

by a jumble of buildings in various stages of construction. A group of men sits on the hill overlooking the square. The younger men wear designer jeans and hold cell phones close to their ears. The faces of the older men are deeply creased, like old leather shoes. Some suck on cigarette stubs. They wear dusty flannel trousers under brown hooded djellabas. Many of them have bright blue turbans wrapped around their heads. They're like hungry eagles eyeing their prey.

One of the younger men separates from the group and jogs down the hill. He moves lightly like a deer, his feet finding an easy path down the rocky hillside. He wears a bright blue gown embroidered with yellow symbols over his jeans. The long tail of his blue turban flaps behind him as he lopes down the hill.

'*Sbah lkhir*,' he calls to the driver.

The driver laughs at something he says and offers him a cigarette from a crumpled Marlboro packet. The young man shakes his head and slaps the driver on the back. The driver shrugs and holds the Marlboro packet up to his lips then pulls out a cigarette with his teeth. He grabs a green plastic lighter from his dashboard, clicking under the end of the cigarette until it glows. Sucking in his cheeks, he blows out the smoke with an 'Ahhh.'

The young man turns to face the passengers. He's tall and slim and his blue gown floats around his body. His face is angular, his jaw strong, and his amber eyes are almond-shaped and deep-set. His lips are full and when he smiles a dimple shadows his right cheek.

'*Sbah lkhir.* Good morning. *Allô, bonjour, comment ça va*?' He flashes a white smile. 'I am Omar. I am your tour guide, *votre guide touristique.*' He thumps his chest with the flat of his hand and gestures around him. 'You are welcome to my paradise and to the place of the most beautiful waterfalls in Morocco, the Cascades de Zitoune. In English, the Waterfalls of the Olive.'

He claps his hands together and flashes another white-toothed smile. 'So, you are all happy? You are ready for the big adventure of your life?'

Addy waves at him.

'Yes, *allô*?'

The blood rises in her cheeks as she feels the eyes of the other tourists on her.

'I'm sorry. I'm not here for the tour. I just caught a lift on the tour bus because it was the easiest way here. I need to find the house I'm renting.'

'I'm so, so sorry for that.' His accent is heavy, the English syllables embellished with Arabic rolls of the tongue. 'You'll miss the best tour with the best tour guide in Morocco. But, anyway, what is the address? Is it Dar Fatima? The Hôtel de France? I can take you.'

'No, it's a house near the river. I can manage. I don't want to delay your tour.'

Omar waggles his finger at her. '*Mashi mushkil*. I know the house. It's the place of Mohammed Demsiri. Where's your luggage? Your husband is coming soon?'

'No. Just me. My bags are at the back. I don't have much.'

'No problem. I'll make a good arrangement for you.'

'I, but . . . I don't want to be any trouble.'

Omar says something to the driver, who tosses his cigarette out of the window and starts the ignition. The door's still open and Omar hangs half in and half out, his feet wedged against the opening. As the tour bus cuts across the square towards a small rusty bridge, he calls out to acquaintances in a guttural language. Addy sucks in her breath as the bridge's loose boards clatter beneath the bus's tyres.

The tour bus turns right down a narrow lane and stops in front of a squat mud house. A large inverted triangle is centred on the blue metal door and two tiny windows protected by black metal grilles have been cut into the orange pisé wall. Omar jumps out of the bus and bangs on the blue door. A woman's voice calls out from behind the door.

'*Chkoun*?'

'Omar.'

The door opens. A young woman in pink flannelette pyjamas and a lime green hijab stands on the threshold. She wears purple Crocs and carries a wooden spoon dripping with batter. She has the same full lips and high cheekbones as Omar in her dark-skinned face. Omar gestures at the bus, his guttural words flying at her like bullets. The girl waves her spoon at Omar, flinging batter over his blue gown as she volleys back a shrill response.

Omar catches Addy's eye. 'One minute, one minute.' He grabs the girl by the arm and they disappear behind the door.

A few minutes later he emerges and beckons to Addy.

'Come.'

'This isn't the house on the Internet.'

'Don't worry. It's the house of my family. We'll put the luggage here and you can come on the tour. I'll bring you to your house later.'

'But . . .'

He presses his hand onto his chest. 'I am Omar. Everybody knows me here. It's no problem. Don't worry.'

Philippa's voice echoes in her head: *Whatever you do, Addy, don't trust those Moroccan men. They're only after one thing. A British passport.*

Omar shrugs. 'Okay, so no problem. You don't trust me, I can see it. It's not a requirement for you to come to my house. We go to the waterfalls.'

'No, it's fine. I'm coming.'

'About bloody time, too,' a girl with a Geordie accent grumbles from the back of the bus. 'We could've crossed the bloody Sahara by camel by now.'

Omar stands in a dirt-floored courtyard with the girl and two older women. A woman who looks about fifty-five stands ramrod straight and wears a red gypsy headscarf, an orange blouse buttoned to her chin, and a red-and-white striped apron over layers of skirts and flannelette pyjamas. Silver coins hang from her pierced ears and the inner lids of her amber eyes are ringed with kohl.

Beside her, an old woman in a flowered flannel housecoat and red bandana leans heavily on a knotty wooden stick. A thick silver ring marked with crosses and X's slides around one of her gnarled fingers. Her left eye is closed and the right eye that peers out from her wrinkled face is a translucent blue. She has a blue arrow tattooed on her chin.

'It's my mum, my sister and my grandmother,' Omar says, waving at the women.

Addy sets down her camera bag and her overnight bag. A clothesline has been strung across the yard and fresh washing hangs on the line dripping onto the dirt floor. A couple of scrawny chickens scratch in the red dirt. Addy extends her hand to his mother.

'*Bonjour.*'

The woman takes hold of Addy's hand in both of hers then smiles and nods. Her eyes sweep over Addy's naked arms. She says something to Omar, who chuckles.

A small boy barges in through the door dragging Addy's suitcase and tripod bag and deposits them next to her other luggage. Omar retrieves a coin from the pocket of his blue robe and flips it to the boy, who catches it, shouting '*Shukran*' as he runs out of the door. The metal door bangs against its loose hinges.

The old woman waves her stick at the door and shuffles off through an archway, mumbling. Omar's mother and sister pick up Addy's luggage and follow the old woman into the next room.

'Where are they going?'

'Don't worry. They put them in a safe place so the chickens and donkey don't break them.'

'Oh. Thank you.'

'No problem. *Mashi mushkil.*'

'*Mashy mushkey.*'

'It's a good accent. It's Darija. Arabic of Morocco.'

'It sounds different here from what I heard in Marrakech.'

'Here we speak Tamazight mostly. It's Amazigh language.'

'Amazigh?'

'Yes. We say Amazigh for one person and Imazighen for many people. Everybody else says Berber, but we don't like it so well, even though we say it for tourists because it's more easy. The Romans called us that because they say we were like barbarians. It's because we fight them well. We are the first people of North Africa. We're free people. It's what Imazighen means. We're not Arab in the mountains.'

'Oh. I didn't know that.'

'So, I'm a good teacher, isn't it? My sister speaks Darija and some French from her school, but my mum and grandmother speak Tamazight only.'

'And your father?'

'My father, he's died.'

'I'm sorry. I didn't mean . . .'

Omar shrugs. 'Don't mind. It's life.' Omar pinches the fabric of his blue gown between his fingers. 'It's the special blue colour of the Imazighen. It used to be that the Tuareg Berbers in the Sahara crushed indigo powder into white clothes to make them blue to be safe from the djinn. But when it was very hot the blue colour make their faces blue as well. People called them the blue men of the desert.'

Omar drapes the loose end of his blue turban across his face, covering his nose and mouth. 'It's a tagelmust. It's for the desert, but the tourists love it so we wear it everywhere now. For us, it's the man who covers his face, not the ladies.' He folds his arms across his chest and spreads his feet apart. 'I'm handsome, isn't it?'

'I'm sure you break the hearts of all the women tourists.'

Omar tugs at the cloth covering his face. 'I never go with the tourist ladies. It's many ladies in Zitoune who want to marry me, but I say no. My mum don't like it. She want many grandchildren.'

'I'm sorry. I didn't mean to offend . . .'

Omar tucks the tail of the tagelmust into his turban. '*Mashi mushkil*.'

A black-and-white cat brushes against her legs and Addy reaches down to brush its tail.

'What a pretty cat.'

Omar shifts on his feet. 'It's the cat of my grandmother. It's very, very old.'

'Really? It doesn't look old.'

'She had it a long time anyway. It always follows her. It's very curious all the time.'

Omar clears his throat. 'It must be that I know your name.'

She stands up quickly and thrusts out her hand. 'Addy.'

A wet pant leg wraps around her wrist like a damp leaf. She tries to shake it loose but the clothesline collapses, throwing the damp laundry into heaps on the dusty ground. The cat shoots across the courtyard and out through a crack in a thick wooden door.

Addy stares at the dust turning to red mud on the clothes. She stoops to pick up the dirty laundry.

'I'm so sorry. I've messed up your mother's laundry.'

Omar lifts the wet bundle out of Addy's hands. 'No mind, Adi.' The vowels of her name curl and roll off his tongue, the accent on the last syllable. Omar stacks the wet laundry on top of a low wooden table. 'It's a boy's name in Morocco. You have short hair like a boy anyway.'

Addy runs her fingers over her cropped hair. The softness still surprises her. Hair like a baby's. A side effect of the Red Devil.

Omar wipes his muddy hands on his gown. 'So, Adi of England. *Yalla*. We go.'

31

# Chapter Five

**Zitoune, Morocco – March 2009**

The tour group trails behind Omar as he leads them on a path through an olive grove beside the river. Stopping, Omar points out donkeys saddled with bright-coloured blankets, eating the fresh spring grass in the dappled shade.

'These are Berber four-by-fours. They fill up on the gasoline when the drivers go to the market. The donkeys eat the marijuana there. You can see?'

Addy squints at the donkeys. 'That's not marijuana.'

Omar slaps his leg and laughs. 'You know marijuana, Adi?'

The tourists laugh and the colour rises in Addy's face. 'I didn't mean it like that. Everyone knows what marijuana looks like.' She searches the faces of the other tourists for affirmation. Surely she wasn't the only one who'd gone to university in the Eighties.

'*Mashi mushkil.* It's so nice to know if a lady like marijuana.'

'I didn't say that.'

'Don't be mad. I'm joking with you.'

'Fine.' Addy looks over at Omar and frowns. Was he chatting her up? He was handsome, there was no denying that. But, so what? She was here to work and to find Hanane and the baby. The last thing she needed was to get involved with a cocky Moroccan ten years younger than herself.

Omar presses a hand against his heart. 'Now the lady of England is angry at me, I can tell it well. My heart is crushed like an egg for the Berber omelette. I must apologise.'

He wades out into the green meadow grass and picks a red poppy. He makes his way back to the path and holds out the flower to Addy.

Addy's irritation dissipates. A sweet gesture. She reaches for the flower and Omar closes his hand around hers. She meets his gaze. A waft of memory. She looks away in confusion. His hand slides from hers. When she looks back, he's on the path, the tourists clustered around him.

Around a bend in the river they come across several local women washing clothes in the clear water. Jeans and T-shirts in the colours of European football teams hang to dry over pink flowering oleander bushes. The women laugh and chatter, their skirts and aprons tucked into the waistbands of their flannelette pyjama bottoms, which are rolled up over their knees. Their hair is hidden by colourful bandanas. Many of them have blue arrow-like tattoos on their chins like Omar's grandmother.

'This is the manner the ladies wash the clothes in the village,' Omar explains as the group stops to take photos.

Addy rests her camera on top of a large boulder and peers into the viewfinder. What do the women think of us, stealing their souls with our cameras? She presses the shutter then loops the strap around her neck, letting the camera flop against her chest as she replaces the lens cap.

She looks over at Omar, a smile tugging at the corner of her mouth. 'So, where do the men wash their clothes?'

Omar laughs. 'I'm very clean, even if I don't wash my own clothes.' He raises his arms and approaches her. 'You can smell me.'

Addy stumbles away, holding her nose. 'Men should share the housework. It's only fair.'

'That's a big pity for your husband,' Omar teases. 'It's a job for ladies to wash the clothes. At least I hope you cook well.'

'Afraid not. I hate cooking. But I'm great at desserts. I have a sweet tooth.'

'That's good at least. Moroccans love sugar. Our blood is made of honey.'

The dimple appears on Omar's right cheek. Addy's heart thumps. She looks down at her sandals. The dry earth coats her toes in a fine red dust.

The sun dances on the river, shining silver on the swirling ripples. Addy falls back behind some newlyweds from France. A couple of Geordie girls from Newcastle flutter around Omar as he teases them with stories of djinn and the evil eye.

She looks away at the river, at the water glittering like diamonds. Ridiculous to be feeling like a teenager at her age. She needs to focus on her purpose. She sucks in a deep breath of the mountain air and exhales slowly, letting the warm air brush over her lips. Better. The yoga classes Philippa had forced her into were paying off at last.

Her thoughts wander to her father and Hanane. Whether they'd walked along this path on their way to the waterfalls. Why had her father never said anything to her about visiting Morocco? He'd obviously intended to, or he'd never have written her that letter. And where were the missing pages? What really happened to Hanane?

He was always travelling for his work. There had been times when she and her mother didn't see him for months. She still had the postcards he'd sent her from all over the world. Mexico. Peru. Nigeria. Russia. Kuwait. After her mother had died, Addy had plastered her bulletin board in her room at St Margaret's in Victoria with them. But none from Morocco.

She eyes Omar, who's busy pointing out turtles sunning on a rock in the river. He was definitely too old to be her half-brother. Around thirty, she'd guess. He would've been a child when her father was in Zitoune. Probably too young to remember him. But what about Hanane? Would he remember her? She'd ask him, when she had a chance. Show him the old Polaroid. It was as good a place to start as any.

Addy's mind settles as she listens to Omar's voice resonating in the warm morning air. Further along the path, he points out beehive-shaped clay structures in which, he explains, the village women take steam baths. He pokes a stick with his foot and it metamorphoses into a thin green grass snake, prompting squeals from the two Geordie girls. Every now and then, Omar catches Addy's gaze as he spins his multilingual patter about carob trees, petrified tree roots, or the wiry, grey-furred macaque monkeys that live in the caves and crevices of the cliffs.

The French newlyweds, Sylvain and Antoinette, ask to be photographed next to a donkey. Omar suggests that Antoinette climb up onto the animal as Sylvain holds the lead. Omar unwinds his tagelmust and wraps it around Sylvain's head. He pulls off his blue gown, revealing well-worn Levis and a white T-shirt, and offers it to Antoinette. It's like a tent around her tiny body.

The tourists shout out instructions to the pair as Omar snaps the photos. *Ouistiti! Mirar al pajarito! Käsekuchen! Say cheese!* Addy hovers at the edge of the group, watching Omar. He's lean and muscular and the white of his T-shirt glows against his brown skin. His hair is a close-cropped cap of tight black curls. He moves like a swimmer, lithe and graceful and unselfconscious.

They continue through a dense olive grove, following a narrow path in a gradual descent through the trees. The morning is filled with the noisy peace of the countryside – a dog's bark, a donkey's bray, the underlying buzz of cicadas. The group breaks out of the shade into a meadow where the sky opens above, blue and cloudless.

Addy takes off her new straw hat. She closes her eyes and breathes in the clear air, letting the heat penetrate her skin. The weight of all the worry and anxiety of the previous months slowly falls away until she's light and new again.

*

Tessa and Nicky, the two Geordie girls, buzz around Omar like chubby bees. They wear tight halter tops, cropped shorts and flip-flops. On the bank of a wide hill stream, Omar stands by to help as the group steps over the rocks to the other side. When he offers his hand to Tessa and then to Nicky, Addy sees him eye the English girls' angel wing tattoos, which stretch across the tanned skin of their lower backs.

Addy's the last one to cross the stream. Her breath catches when his fingers close around hers. On the other side of the stream, Omar places his hands on her waist to steady her. His breath is warm on her neck. She rests her hands on his for an instant, then steps forwards onto the path.

An hour into the hike, the group reaches a lookout platform facing the waterfalls.

Omar sweeps his hand towards the view. 'This is my Paradise.'

The tourists crowd towards the flimsy bamboo railing, hurrying to pull out their cameras. Foaming water crashes over a red earth cliff, forming pools and mini-waterfalls as the water thunders into a churning pool at the base. A rainbow arches across the pool, its colours hazy in the river mist. The waterfalls in the Polaroid. Her father and Hanane had stood here, on this very spot, smiling for the photo that August day in 1984.

There's a modest café at the lookout and Addy buys herself a warm bottle of Coca-Cola from a slender, sharp-faced Moroccan about Omar's age at a bar cobbled together from produce crates. The Moroccan makes a show of wiping the Coke bottle clean with the tail of his tie-dyed turban and his fingers linger on her palm when he hands her the Coke.

When Addy returns to the lookout, Omar's talking to the Geordie girls.

'I studied at university,' Omar's saying. 'English literature. Chakespeare. "To be or not to be, that is the question."' He thumps his chest with the flat of his hand. 'I'm a graduate of the university in Beni Mellal. Nobody else in Zitoune is graduated from university.'

Addy leans against a bamboo post and sips the tepid soft drink. 'English literature? I studied that, too. Did you study Milton? Donne? Marlowe? The Romantics?'

'I know Chakespeare.'

Nicky rolls her blue-lined eyes. 'You've got to be flipping kidding me. I'm on bloody holiday in Morocco and you're talking about Shakespeare? I think I'm gonna gag.' She points a long pink fingernail at the Coke bottle. 'Where'd you get the Coke?'

'Over there.'

'C'mon, Tessa. Let's get a Coke. I'm gasping.'

Omar nods at the turbaned barman. 'It's my friend, Yassine. He sells the best Coca-Cola in Zitoune, even if it's not so cold. It's better like that. Not so many calories.'

Nicky grabs Tessa's arm. 'Oo-er. He's a bit of all right. C'mon, Tess, I'm getting thirstier by the minute.'

Tessa, a sun-streaked blonde with a generous cleavage and pink gloss lipstick, squints at Yassine. He gives her a slow, appreciative smile.

'Oh, all right. I can't be doing with Shakespeare, either. I'm on my hols.'

The girls saunter over to the bar, their flip-flops slapping on the compacted earth. Yassine flashes them a white-toothed smile as he sets out two bottles of Coca-Cola on the worktop.

Omar nods. 'Yassine will make them happy. He likes English girls. He likes to practise his English. More tea, Vicar? See you later, alligator.'

'In a while, crocodile.'

'In a while, crocodile.' Omar grins. 'I like it.'

Addy sets her empty Coke bottle down on the ground. She lifts up her camera and focuses the lens on the rainbow. '*Paradise Lost.*'

'What?'

'*Paradise Lost.* Anyone who studied English literature would've heard of *Paradise Lost*. It's a classic. *Le Morte d'Arthur*? Maybe something more modern. George Orwell? Virginia Woolf?'

'I studied at university. It's the truth.'

'If you say so.'

'You don't believe me.'

'Never mind. It's not important.'

Addy glances over at Omar. His hands are on the bamboo railing and he's staring out at the waterfalls. Why had she been so rude? If he wants to chat up girls with lies, what business is it of hers? It wasn't like her to be so mean. That was Philippa's domain.

'I'm sorry. I was rude. Of course you went to university.'

'No problem.'

She rests her hands on the railing and looks out at the waterfalls, willing her heart to calm its bouncing inside her chest. 'I had an unusual dream last night.'

'Yes?'

'I dreamt about someone wearing a blue gown and turban. I couldn't see his face. Then I saw you today and you were wearing exactly the same thing.'

Addy looks over at Omar, who's staring at her.

'What? What is it?'

'It was Allah who send you this message.'

She shakes her head. 'It was just a dream.'

'No. Allah sent me to you in your dream. It's our fate to meet today.'

A couple of rafts constructed of bamboo poles and blue plastic oil drums bob on the water at the base of the waterfalls. Scavenged wooden chairs are festooned with garish fabrics and plastic flowers.

Omar points to the rafts. 'Everybody, we must take the boats to the other side. These are the *Titanics* of Morocco. But don't worry, it might be they will not sink today, *inshallah*.'

A fine mist hangs in the air, settling on Addy's skin like dew.

Omar directs the group onto the two rafts, grabbing hands and elbows to steady the tourists as they step onto the lurching rafts. Addy settles down on a damp chair beside Sylvain and Antoinette. A middle-aged German couple in safari outfits and laden down with binoculars and cameras shift onto the chairs at the rear.

Omar jumps onto the other raft with the Geordie girls and a retired Spanish couple. Addy feels a stab of disappointment.

'What are you doing over there, when the lady is here?' Sylvain calls over to Omar.

The blue gown whips around Omar in the breeze. 'Because I can see her better from here.'

Halfway up the hill, Omar settles everyone at rusty circular tables on a restaurant patio overlooking the waterfalls. A flimsy bamboo latticework fence is the only barrier between the patio and a vertical drop to the churning pool far below.

Addy sits at a small table beside the fence. A smiling boy looking about nineteen or twenty jogs down the stone steps to the patio, four large bottles of water tucked under his arms as he carries two in his hands. A blotch of white skin covers his left cheek and his brown hands are mottled with dots of white.

'Amine, *ici*,' Omar shouts to the boy, pointing to the tables occupied by his group.

Omar moves between the tables taking orders for lamb tagine and chicken brochettes, translating into Tamazight for Amine. The boy nods, his shiny black hair flopping into his large brown eyes. Omar follows Amine into the restaurant and returns with large plastic bottles of Coca-Cola and plastic baskets of flat discs of bread. He sets a bottle of Coke and a basket of bread on Addy's table.

'Everything's okay, Adi?'

'Fine. Thank you.'

'It's okay for me to sit with you to eat my lunch?'

'Sure. Fine.'

Omar's knees brush against hers as he sits in the empty chair.

He tears off a chunk of bread and rolls it into marble-sized balls with his fingertips.

'I'm so sorry for disturbing you.'

'It's fine. I'm fine.'

He tears off another piece of bread and begins the rolling motion again. He squints at her in the sharp sunlight, his light brown eyes glowing almost amber.

'You have to know I never eat my lunch with tourists.'

A cat rubs itself against Addy's legs, purring. The thunder of the waterfalls, a fine mist on her skin. A table littered with dough marbles.

# *Chapter Six*

## Zitoune, Morocco – November 1983

From his perch on an aspen branch, Omar watches the Irishman knock in the final tent peg with a rock. The man – Gus he'd said his name was – has chosen a good location. No one comes up here to the source of the waterfalls with the Roman bridge. No olive trees up here. And tourists never find the path. They only want to see the waterfalls then go back to Marrakech for their supper.

This Gus isn't like the other tourists. Omar has spied on him at the weekly market, bargaining for mutton and vegetables in Arabic. Like the Arabic he's learning in school, not like Darija. It's probably why no one understands Gus well. Sometimes Gus tries to speak Arabic to the Amazigh traders from Oushane and the villages even further in the mountains, which is crazy. Everyone knows they speak only Tamazight.

Yesterday, Gus bought a small round clay brazier and a tagine pot from the market. Old Abdullah charged him too much: fifty dirhams. And the man paid! Omar will try this when he sells the ripe olives to the tourists. '*Fresh olives from Morocco. Fifty dirhams!*' He'll make a big profit. He'll give his brother, Momo, and his friends, Driss and Yassine, olives to sell, as well. Pay them one

41

dirham each. He'll be a rich boy soon, especially since he steals the olives. Almost one hundred per cent profit. Maths is the only subject he likes at school. Maths and French, because he needs to talk to the tourists. He rubs the angry red welt on his arm. His grandmother was right to punish him with the hot bread poker for missing his classes. If he was to be rich one day, he couldn't be lazy. One day he won't have to sleep by the donkey, and he'll build his mother a fine big house, better even than the house of the policeman. And they'll all have new clothes from the shops in Azaghar, not the old clothes his mother brought back from helping the ladies with the babies in the mountains. One day for sure he'll be a rich man.

Hunching over the brazier, Gus takes a silver lighter out of his shirt pocket and lights the coals he's stacked inside. Too many. Jedda would punish Omar if he used so many coals.

Omar's eyes follow a flash of silver from the man's shirt pocket to his fingers. Gus flicks the silver lighter. A thin blue flame waves in the air. Gus leans over the brazier with the flame until a coal catches light. He flips back the lighter's lid. Back into his pocket. Silver. Gus must be rich.

Gus throws a handful of sticks onto the coals and sets the grille on top of the brazier. He sits back onto a low wooden stool. A pan of water is on the ground by his feet. He reaches into a canvas rucksack and pulls out a potato. His other hand in his trouser pocket. A red pocket knife. The knife scraping against the potato skin. Shavings falling onto the earth. Fat chunks of white potato plopping into the water. Gus doesn't know how to make tagine well.

Omar shimmies down the skinny aspen, its yellow autumn leaves falling around him like confetti.

'Mister Gus! Stop!'

'Looks like I've got a spy. Omar, isn't it?'

'Yes. Everybody knows me here.'

Omar lopes over to Gus, his Real Madrid football shirt loose

42

on his slender body. His toes poke out from the torn canvas of his running shoes under the rolled-up cuffs of his jeans.

'That's not how you cut vegetables for tagine. They will never cook like that.'

'A spy and a professional chef. You're a very talented boy.'

Omar sticks out his hand. 'Give me the knife.'

The corners of the man's eyes crinkle as he smiles. He hands Omar the pocket knife.

'So, Mister Boss. Show me how it's done.'

Omar picks a potato out of the sack and squats next to the pot of water. After scraping off the skin, he cuts the potato into four long white slices.

'Like this,' he says. 'Like fat fingers. Then the heat will cook them well.'

He pulls out a long carrot and rasps the blade against the skin, the dirty orange shreds spiralling onto the ground. He chops off the leafy top and the tip, then slices the carrot into two vertically. Then he scoops out the green core and cuts the carrot into thin strips.

'Like that.' He drops the slivers into the pot. 'Very good.'

Gus holds out his palm. 'Let me try.'

Omar hands back the knife. '*Mashi mushkil.*'

'No problem. That bit of Darija I've learned.'

Omar rests his elbows on his thighs as he watches Gus scrape the skin off a carrot.

'You sound different than the French tourists from Marrakech.'

'I'm Irish, but I live in a very faraway place called Canada. A very beautiful place by the sea. But really I'm a nomad. I travel the world to search for oil in rocks. That's why I'm here. There were a lot of dinosaurs in Morocco. Wherever there were dinosaurs, there's usually oil.'

'I know where there are some footprints of dinosaurs. Not so far from here.'

'Really? Will you show me?'

Omar shrugs. 'For fifty dirhams.'

'Twenty dirhams.'

Omar's eyebrows shoot up: twenty dirhams? He would've shown the man for free. He screws up his small angular face.

'Thirty dirhams.'

Gus raises an eyebrow and holds out his right hand. 'Highway robbery – thirty dirhams. Deal.'

Omar puts his small brown hand into the man's large, square-fingered hand and they shake.

'It might be that you will need a guide here, Mister Gus. I know all the good places to visit around Zitoune. I know a place of dinosaur feet and a cave with many old drawings. We can make a good negotiation.'

'You'll make me a poor man, for sure, Omar. What about if I teach you English so you can talk to any English tourists who visit the waterfalls, not just the French? You can corner the tourist market. No one here speaks English.'

Omar squints at the glowing coals as he mulls over the offer. Dirhams now would be good. But then once the man leaves, the money stops. But, if he learns English, even when Gus leaves, he can still earn money. Lots of money. Omar holds out his hand.

'Deal.'

# *Chapter Seven*

## Zitoune, Morocco – March 2009

A flat-roofed house of orange sandstone rocks sits on a hill thick with cacti. Blue shutters frame the square windows and a basement level hugs the hillside, jutting out to provide the base for a veranda shaded with a twisted grapevine. An olive tree with a gnarled trunk as thick as Addy's waist leans over the house. A donkey is tethered in its shade. Scrawny black chickens scratch around the donkey's hooves.

Omar sets down Addy's luggage on the gravel path. 'You like it?'

'It's perfect.'

'It's okay. It's a bit small. I'm making a big house.'

Addy shades her eyes from the stabbing rays of the late afternoon sun with her hand. 'For your family?'

'One day, *inshallah*. Or maybe it will be a guest house for tourists. I must to be rich one day.'

Addy shifts her camera bag to her left shoulder. 'Let's wait on the veranda for Mohammed.'

On the veranda, she sets down her camera bag on a long wooden table and leans on the stone railing. Below the house the river winds its way towards the waterfalls through budding oleander bushes and shivering ash trees. Across the river the sandstone cliffs of the Middle Atlas Mountains ripple around the valley, while in the distance the snowy peaks of the High Atlas Mountains stand resolute against the fading blue of the sky. Addy sighs.

Omar leans against the railing. 'You don't like it?'

'No, I love it. This is just what the doctor ordered.'

'Your doctor told you to come here?'

Addy laughs. 'It's just an expression. It means it's perfect.'

'Just what the doctor ordered. I like it.' Omar nods his head towards the blue door. 'Why do we wait to go inside?'

'I texted Mr Demsiri to tell him I've arrived. He needs to bring me the key.'

Omar strolls over to a flowerpot spilling with red geraniums. He tilts the pot over and holds up a key.

'You knew where the key was?'

'Everybody knows. *Mashi mushkil*. Don't worry. It's very safe in Zitoune. You don't need to lock the door. Nobody will bother you.' The dimple in his cheek. 'Except me.'

'Omar . . .'

A crunch of footsteps on gravel.

'*Allô*, madame! You find the house okay?'

A tall, bald middle-aged man climbs up the path, his brown djellaba straining at his sturdy belly. An impressive hooked nose lends him the regal appearance of a Roman emperor.

Omar gestures to the older man. 'Adi, honey, this is Mohammed Demsiri. He owns many places in Zitoune. He's a rich man.'

Addy raises an eyebrow at Omar. Honey? She extends her hand to the older man. 'It's a pleasure to meet you. The house looks lovely. It's such a beautiful setting.'

Mohammed smiles, two bright gold teeth where his canines should be. Ignoring Addy's extended hand, he pats his broad chest and nods. A thick silver watch encircles his wrist and several chunky silver rings decorate his fingers.

'It's a pleasure for me to welcome you to Morocco, madame. I remember you well.'

46

'You remember me?'

Mohammed slaps Omar on the back. 'I was at the restaurant today when you ate the lunch with Omar. He came into the restaurant to tell me he met a beautiful lady with hair like fire. I looked outside and I saw you. I told Omar he choosed well, Adi, honey.'

Omar chokes. '*Laa*. Her name is Adi. It's only me who calls her honey. It's like *habibati*.'

Mohammed's face freezes into a look of horror. 'I'm so, so sorry, madame. Please excuse me.'

'Don't worry. *Mashy mushkey*. Just call me Addy.'

Mohammed gestures towards the bright blue wooden door studded with large black nail heads. 'Please to come into the house. You will like it very much. It's the most beautiful guest house in Zitoune.'

'Until I build my guest house.'

Mohammed chuckles. 'You can see already Omar will be a rich man one day, *inshallah*. He's a hard worker. I must be careful. He will make me to look like a poor man.'

'You'll never be a poor man, Mohammed. Amine is a lucky boy.'

Omar picks up Addy's suitcase and slings the black nylon tripod bag and the brown leather overnight bag over his shoulder. The wine bottles clink and Addy winces.

'Who's Amine?'

'It's my nephew.' Mohammed opens the blue door, waving them to enter. 'He work in my restaurant. He serve you the lunch today.'

'Oh, yes. He seemed very nice, although Omar ran him off his feet.'

Mohammed furrows his forehead and asks Omar something in Tamazight. Omar shrugs.

'Excuse me, madame. Amine still have his feet.'

Addy laughs as she swings the camera bag over her shoulder. 'I mean Omar kept him busy. Ran him off his feet is just an expression.'

47

Mohammed nods. 'I run Amine off his feet every day. It's good to learn English well.'

Addy stands on the veranda and waves at the two men as they trek down the gravel path towards the village. Golden light from the waning sun falls across the sides of the mountains. Somewhere in the village a dog barks. A clatter of metal against metal. Sharp feedback from a microphone slices through the stillness. '*Allahu Akbar. Allahu Akbar.*' The amplified voice of the village's muezzin echoes around the valley as he recites the call to prayer: God is great. Addy listens until the last words dissipate on the cooling air.

The night is drawing in fast. The sun has turned fat and orange, and streaks of red splay across the darkening sky. She wanders back into the house. The large whitewashed living room is furnished with low, round wooden tables. Banquettes strewn with colourful striped cushions line two of the walls and pierced tin lanterns hang from the beamed ceiling. A thick white wool rug marked with crossed black diamonds covers the polished grey concrete floor.

She enters the larger of the two cool white bedrooms. The solid wooden bed is draped in a blue-and-green striped bedcover and a filmy white mosquito net bunches on the floor around the bed. Addy opens her overnight bag and pulls out a plastic duty-free bag. She unwraps the two bottles of white wine. Good French Chablis. Luckily screw top.

In a kitchen cupboard Addy finds a water glass and pours out a generous serving. She kicks off her sandals and crosses the cool concrete leading out to the veranda. She feels like a butterfly shrugging off its chrysalis. Free of London. Free of Philippa. Free of Nigel. Free of cancer. The scar on her left breast throbs and she touches the coin-sized divot in her flesh.

She leans against a stone pillar and gazes out over the branches of the olive trees towards the mountains. What's she going to do about Omar? She'd be an idiot to get involved with him. She was probably just one of a slew of women he's charmed over the years. Yes, it would be diverting. Fun. But she had too much to do and only three months to do it in. A fling isn't what she's come here for. No, she has to nip that in the bud. She takes a sip of wine and watches the sun set.

# Chapter Eight

**Zitoune, Morocco – April 2009**

'Philippa?'

'Addy. Wait. I'm reading my online Tarot cards.'

Addy tucks her phone under her chin. She props her bare feet on the wooden table, careful not to knock off the stack of research notes.

'How's the job going for that banker couple in Fulham, Pips?'

'Don't get me bloody started. They've gone and bought sofas from the Ugly Sofa Company. They're covered with that leatherette rubbish that takes your skin off when you sit on it. Burgundy. When was burgundy ever fashionable? I'll tell you when. Never. Bloody humungous things. What in the name of Nicky Haslam am I supposed to do with those?'

'Maybe call it tongue–in–cheek chic.'

'Oh, ha ha. That'd be my career down the loo. I swear this interior design rubbish isn't getting any easier. Damn. The Tower card. That's not good. Probably something to do with the Russians. How is everything, anyway? You're still alive at least.'

Addy lets the cell phone slip from under her chin into her hand. 'Still alive. The Internet's finally working. Well, mostly working. I've had to get a dongle thingy. The water supply's a bit iffy, so

I've been washing with bottled water for the past two days. There's nothing on TV except reruns of *Desperate Housewives* in Arabic and Turkish soap operas, so that's not a distraction. I've managed to stock up on some food from the local market and I've still got a bottle of wine from duty-free. So, aside from desperately needing a shower, I'm fine.'

'Good. Good.'

Addy sifts through the stack of research notes and slides out the Polaroid of Gus and Hanane that she's tucked into his unfinished letter. She examines Gus's face.

'Pippa, do you remember when Dad spent those two years working for the oil company down in Nigeria?'

'Hmm?'

'Are you listening?'

'What? Nigeria? Yes, yes. Sorry, I'm just trying to remember what the Three of Swords means. I'd just married Alessandro, more fool me. Dad stopped by London on his way back to Canada to wish us well. Too little too late if you ask me.'

'What was he like when you saw him in London? Did he seem happy?'

'How am I supposed to remember that? I can barely remember my phone number.' Philippa sighs heavily into the phone. 'What's all this about?'

'Nothing. He was away so much when I was growing up. Just trying to fill in the dots.'

'Well, he wasn't all that keen on Alessandro, I can tell you. Maybe I should've taken the hint. They argued a lot. Dad was very touchy. I remember that. Our father fancied himself as some kind of bloody adventurer. He loved to say he had gypsy blood. I honestly don't know why he ever married your mother. She was such a little homebody.'

Addy grimaces. 'You know what they say. Opposites attract.'

Her pretty red-haired mother, Hazel, packing a suitcase for Addy's peripatetic father. One of Addy's strongest memories of her mother. The big, old Victorian house on the Vancouver Island shore that was never enough for him. Hazel and Addy were never enough for him, even though Addy had tried hard to be Daddy's girl when he was home. Digging in the spring bulbs with him in the autumn, sitting with him watching for the black triangles of the orcas' dorsal fins skimming along the surface of the Strait through the telescope he'd set up on the veranda. He'd promise that he'd stay. But then the suitcase would come out and he'd be gone again. Another postcard to add to her collection.

Addy swings her legs off the table and slides her feet into her new turquoise leather babouches.

'I found some old photos Dad took in Morocco in the stuff you gave me. He must have spent some time here after Nigeria. Lots of pictures of donkeys, monkeys, mosques, palm trees, camels, that kind of thing. I'm using them as inspiration for the travel book. Following in Dad's footsteps. It's a nice hook, don't you think?'

'You live in the clouds. You're going to end up broke again. You're just like your father.'

'Your father, too.'

'Ha! The closest I had to a father was Grandfather's valet.'

Addy stares at her father's smiling face in the Polaroid. At least she'd had a doting mother until she was thirteen, and a loving, if often absent, father. Philippa had had a huge stately home to rattle around in, but only Essie's elderly father and a handful of servants for company when she wasn't away at boarding school. A runaway father and a drug-addled mother. It explained a few things.

'Didn't he write you? Call you?'

'It's not the same thing, Addy.'

Addy folds the blue letter around the Polaroid and slides it under the pile of papers.

'Anyway, I've finished the book outline and plotted out the places I need to photograph based on Dad's photos. Marrakech, a fishing village called Essaouira, Casablanca, the desert.'

'Desert? Which desert?'

'The Sahara.'

'Is that where the Sahara desert is?'

Addy rolls her eyes. The line goes silent.

'What card did you just turn over?'

'The Ten of Swords. It's a dead body full of swords. I'll have to look it up. I bought a Tarot book.'

'I don't think Tarot cards are meant to be literal.'

The sound of shuffling cards.

'Can't you get the book done any faster than three months, Addy? I need you to photograph a penthouse I've just finished in Mayfair for some Chinese clients. Never met them. Did it all through their PA. A million pounds on the interiors and they're only going to use it for a week at Christmas. Apparently, it's an investment.'

Addy swats at a fly. 'The visa lasts for three months and I need the time to do this book. And . . .'

'And what?'

Addy sighs. 'Oh, Pippa. I met someone. I don't know what to think. He's a Berber mountain guide. Well, Amazigh, actually. He's very nice. A bit younger than me.'

'Oh, good grief. Define younger.'

'Thirty-ish. Nothing's happened. It's just . . . . I don't know.'

'My sister, the cougar.'

Addy watches a black-and-white cat slink across the gravel path as it eyes a rooster strutting under the olive tree with a harem of chickens.

'Don't worry. I've been avoiding him. I've still got Nigel to deal with. But then sometimes I think maybe a fling would do me a world of good. I mean, what's the harm, Pips? It's not like it'd ever be a long-term relationship.'

'You don't want to know what's inside my mind. It's a dustbin in there.' The cat pounces. The rooster and chickens scrabble, flapping away in a cloud of dust and ear-splitting cackles. 'What's that racket?'

'A cat chasing some chickens. His name's Omar.'

'The cat?'

'No. The Berber guide.'

'Have you slept with him?'

'Pippa! I just got here.'

'Why not just be on your own for a while? You're always looking for a man to rescue you.'

'I'm not!'

'Really? When was the last time you were single?'

'I was single in Canada.'

'Twenty years ago. Don't you think it's time for you to stand on your own two feet instead of going after inaccessible men?'

'I am standing on my own two feet! I'm in Morocco, aren't I?'

'Running away, more like.' Philippa huffs into the phone. 'What's a Berber, anyway?'

Addy sighs and shifts the phone to her right ear. 'I've been doing some research online for my travel book.' She shuffles through her papers and pulls out a piece of paper covered in scribbled notes. 'Berbers, or Imazighen as they call themselves – Amazigh singular – are the indigenous population of North Africa. The Arabs converted them to Islam in the eighth century. Before that they practised everything from paganism to Christianity and Judaism.'

'The Fool. Bloody hell. I want the Lovers, not the Fool. That one's probably meant for you.'

'You're not listening.' Addy sips her coffee. It's gone stone-cold. She sets down the mug and peers out over the railings.

'It's all very interesting, Addy. Good research for your book.'

A donkey emerges from the olive grove ridden by a bare-footed boy. Amine. The boy with vitiligo from the restaurant. He smiles and waves at her as he passes by. She waves back.

'What do you think I should do, Pippa? About the man, I mean.'

'You can't seriously be considering a relationship with a Moroccan goatherd. It's not so bad being on your own. Look at me. Divorced twenty years and I couldn't be happier. Free as a bird. I can tango every night till dawn if I want to. If only the knees would hold up.'

'C'mon. You're always talking about wanting to find a man.' Addy picks up the mug and pads over the cool stones into the house. 'You're glued to that house in Chelsea. The world's a bigger place than Redcliffe Road. You should travel more.' She dumps the cold coffee in the kitchen sink and turns on the tap to rinse the cup. The pipes groan. 'Bugger.'

'Bugger? There's nothing wrong with Redcliffe Road. It's a very good address.'

'No water.'

'Exactly. How can you live like that? You want my advice? Get on the first plane back to London and sort out your life. As for men, well, I've given up on the whole bloody lot of them. Everybody my age wants a twenty-year-old bimbette or someone to nurse them through their dotage. Once you hit forty you're done for, Addy. I may as well have "Danger, Radioactive" tattooed on my forehead. Thank God I've got a career.'

'What about the tango guys?' Addy heads across the living room's cool concrete floor back to the veranda.

'A bunch of mummy's boys and sexual deviants. But at least I get to touch a man, otherwise it's just me and the neighbour's cat. The Wheel of Fortune. That's more like it.'

Addy flops into the chair. 'That can go up or down.'

'Let's say it's on the way up, shall we? Seriously, this Omar person probably makes eyes at all the girls. Though you're way past the girl phase.'

'I don't think he's like that.'

'He's a mountain guide. In Morocco. Of course he's like that.'

'He's a university graduate.'

'Really?'

'In English literature.'

'Uh huh.'

'That's what he said.'

'And you believed him.'

'Well . . .'

'You're naive. That's part of your problem. You trust people. Everyone's out for themselves. It's a Me! Me! Me! world.'

Addy massages her forehead with her fingertips. 'What do you mean "part of my problem"?'

'You have terrible taste in men.'

An image of her ex-fiancé, Nigel, plants itself in Addy's head. Floppy brown hair, 'trust me' hazel eyes, the teasing grin. Despite how much he'd hurt her, she couldn't help but feel some lingering affection towards him. They'd had some fun together, when Nigel wasn't off somewhere climbing the ladder to a legal career. They'd play hooky to catch a mid-week movie matinee at the Clapham Picture House, or check out a band at the Brixton Dome. All that petered out as Nigel got busier with work. But then she'd been busy with her photography studio too. It had just all gone wrong at the end. Badly wrong.

'Nigel wasn't so bad. He was under a lot of pressure at work. He was trying to get taken on as a partner at the law firm. My cancer was hard on him. It couldn't have been easy holding my bald head over the toilet while I puked my guts out.'

'My heart bleeds. Did I ever tell you he used to come crying on my shoulder when you were sick? I was completely taken in. I was the one who pulled strings to get him into that law firm in the first place. More fool me. He's a bastard for fooling around when your hair fell out.'

Finding the bill from The Ivy was a shock. Dinner for two. But it wasn't as bad as finding the hotel invoice. Both dated the night she was in hospital having the blood transfusion. Nigel should've been more careful. Shoving the receipts in an envelope on their shared desk was stupid. Cancer did strange things to people. There was a lot of collateral damage.

'I guess.'

'I don't mean to upset you. It's just that when I think of Nigel, I want to poke his eyes out with a burning poker. I hate being taken for a fool.'

'Never mind about Nigel. That's over. *Mashy mushkey*.'

'Mashy *what*?'

'It means no problem.'

'So, now you're speaking Moroccan.'

'Darija, actually.'

The rooster rends the air with an ear-splitting crow. Addy watches him strut across the path. He stops and stares at her with a cold black eye. Thrusting out his red feathered chest, he bellows out another piercing crow.

'Good God, what a racket. The Devil card. Addy, that one's definitely for you.'

# Chapter Nine

**Zitoune, Morocco – April 2009**

'It's working?'

Omar's mother, Aicha, flicks through the TV remote but the images on the large flat-screen TV wobble and fizz like the European soft drinks Omar brings them from Azaghar for the Eid al-Adha celebration dinner.

Aicha walks through the archway from the living room and yells up the steps to the roof. '*Laa*! Not yet!'

Fatima pops her head around the kitchen door. 'Maybe it's not a good television. It's not new like the one Yassine bought for his wife.'

'Yassine never bought it for Khadija, one hundred per cent.' Omar's head appears in the patch of blue sky over the open courtyard. 'He only buys stuff for himself, you have to know about it. Anyway, this is a good television. It's a bit new. You'll be able to watch your Turkish shows better.' Omar's head disappears from view. '*Yamma*, try now!' he yells. 'I fixed the satellite with the clothesline.'

Aicha hands the remote to Fatima. 'You do it, Fatima. It's too complicated for me.' She heads up the rough grey concrete steps to the roof of the extension Omar's building. Stepping over a stack of wood, Aicha grabs a rusty iron strut to steady herself. Omar is by the satellite dish, tightening her clothesline around the white disc to correct its tilt.

Fatima's voice floats up to the roof. 'It's working! Don't move it! Just like that!'

Omar steps back from the satellite dish and slaps the dust off his hands. 'Good. I'll buy you another clothesline, *Yamma*. Don't worry.'

'*Mashi mushkil*.' Aicha steps over the discarded paint cans and bends down to collect the workers' dirty tagine pot. Finally, she has Omar on his own. It's time to discuss the situation.

'Zaina's mother was here yesterday.'

Omar's eyebrow twitches. 'Oh, yes? She's well? Everyone's well?'

Aicha props the tagine pot on her hip as she picks dead leaves off her pots of pelargoniums. 'Everyone's well. But, you know, Zaina is getting older. Her parents are worried about her.'

Omar begins stacking concrete blocks into a neat pile. 'No reason to worry about her. She's a clever girl.'

'Omar. You know what I'm talking about. You're not so young. You must think about marriage. Zaina is waiting for you. You promised . . .'

'*Yamma*, I didn't promise anything. You promised her parents I'd marry her. Full stop.'

'I don't understand what the problem is. She cooks well. She cleans her parents' house well. She's young and healthy and very pretty. She'll be a good mother.'

'I'm sure you're right.'

'So, why are you waiting? They'll marry Zaina to someone else soon.'

'If Allah wills.'

'Omar, I'm only thinking of you and your happiness. All you do is work. Your life is passing you by. Don't you want to have a fine son?'

'I think you want to have a fine grandson.'

Aicha twists her mouth into a pout. 'What's wrong with that? Yes, I want many grandchildren. We must think about Fatima as well. She must be married soon, even though she says no to everybody.'

'Fatima can do as she likes. She's a free Amazigh woman like the Queen Dihya of history. I won't put my sister in a prison to make her marry someone she doesn't want, like what happened to Uncle Rachid's daughter. Fatima must be happy when she gets married. That's my responsibility to her.'

'Fatima thinks only of romance like she sees on the television. She has to be practical. It's not easy to find her a husband because of her black skin, even if she's your sister. It's easy to find a good wife for you because you're a hard worker. If you don't want to marry Zaina, tell me. Everybody wants their daughter to marry you.'

Omar stacks the last concrete block onto the pile and sits down on it with a sigh. He rubs at the crease between his eyes.

'I don't like to talk about this situation. Anyway, maybe I'll marry a foreign lady. It's possible.'

Aicha bolts upright, dropping dried pelargonium leaves over the concrete.

'You shouldn't say things like that. You're Amazigh. You must have an Amazigh wife.'

'Uncle Rachid doesn't have an Amazigh wife.'

'He has an Arab wife, and this has caused many problems for him in his life.'

'*Yamma*, I'm Amazigh, so I'm a free man. I can marry who I like. Anyway, I like a foreign lady. You met her.'

The beautiful woman with the red hair like a boy. Aicha shakes her head.

'This is not a good situation, Omar. You'll have problems with a foreign lady. Will she live in Zitoune? I don't think so. She'll want to be with her own people. She'll make you live far away.'

Omar chews on his lip. His eye catches a movement and he

looks up to see a falcon fluttering high in the blue sky, eyeing the green fields for prey. He couldn't explain it. Why his heart jumped in his chest whenever he saw her. How her face haunted his mind. It wasn't just Addy's dream of seeing him the night before they met, though that was incredible. The moment he saw her in the bus, her face, red and sweaty from the ride, under the farmer's hat, it was like they were magnets being drawn together. Like they knew each other already. Like all the days he'd lived had been steps to the moment they finally met.

'I'll have a big problem, then.' He looks at his mother, at her still handsome face lined with worry. 'She has captured my liver.'

# Chapter Ten

## Zitoune, Morocco – April 2009

Omar shouts through a window grille into his mother's house. *'Yamma!* Fatima! *Jedda!'*

The blue metal door creaks open and Fatima steps out into the alley. Addy waves at her shyly from across the lane. Fatima pushes past Omar and runs up to Addy and kisses her on both cheeks.

*'Bonjour. Marhaba à la maison de Fatima,'* she says, welcoming Addy to her home. She grabs Addy's hand and pulls her towards the door. *'Viens avec moi pour le thé.'*

Omar shakes his head. 'Now my sister takes you away from me, Adi honey. It will be so hard for me to get you from her.'

Omar's cell phone rings out the first notes of 'Hotel California'. He wrinkles his nose at the screen and rejects the call. He slips the phone back into his pocket.

'Was that the plumber, Omar? Shouldn't you tell him you're on your way to my house?'

'He knows I'm coming. It's urgent to fix the problem with your water.'

Fatima tugs at Addy's hand and pulls her into the house.

Omar follows his sister and Addy into the narrow room that serves as both the living room and Fatima's and Jedda's bedroom.

A low wooden table is set with a chocolate cake and plates of home-made cookies. Aicha greets Addy with several '*Marhaba*'s as she pours a stream of fragrant mint tea into tiny gold-rimmed glasses.

Fatima pats a place on the banquette next to her grandmother, Jedda, who grumbles and points to the opposite banquette with her cane. When Addy has settled sufficiently far enough away from Jedda, Fatima sits beside her and gives her a hug.

'Stay with me, not with Omar,' Fatima says to Addy in French. 'You can be my sister.'

Omar picks up a handful of cookies and turns to leave. 'Now I'm really jealous.'

Addy licks the sugary chocolate icing off her bottom lip, leans back against the flowered cushions and pats her stomach. '*Shukran. Le gateau c'est très bon.*'

Aicha smiles widely. She points to the chocolate cake sitting on a blue-and-white Chinese plate in the centre of the low round table. '*Eesh caaka.*'

Addy shakes her head. '*Laa, shukran.*' Another piece of cake and she'd explode.

The Polaroid presses against her thigh. Aicha and Jedda would surely recognise Hanane. Zitoune was a small village. The type of village where everyone knew everyone else's business. She reaches into her jeans pocket and pulls out the Polaroid, wrapped in her father's blue letter. Leaning over the table, she hands the photo to Aicha.

'*Baba Adi,*' she says, pointing to Gus. My father.

Aicha squints at the photo, fine wrinkles fanning out from her deep-set amber eyes. Jedda taps Aicha's arm impatiently with her stick. Aicha hands the old woman the Polaroid.

'It's my father in the picture,' Addy says in French to Fatima. 'He came to Zitoune many years ago. I'm trying to find the woman in the picture. I think she was from Zitoune. Can you ask your mother and your grandmother Jedda if they recognise her?'

63

Fatima translates for Addy. Aicha takes the photo from Jedda and frowns at it before handing it to Fatima, her coin earrings dangling against her cheeks as she shakes her head.

Fatima runs her fingers along the Polaroid's frayed edges. 'Your father is very handsome. You have the same nose and blue eyes.'

'They don't recognise her?'

Fatima shakes her head as she hands the photo back to Addy. 'No. My mum and grandmother are the medicine women of the village. They know everybody in the mountains here. If she was from Zitoune, they would know her.'

Addy brushes cookie crumbs off the plastic tablecloth into her hand. She picks up her empty tea glass. Aicha nods and smiles, her coin earrings bobbing against her neck. Jedda sits on the banquette like a wizened oracle, eyeing Addy's every move.

Addy follows Fatima out into the courtyard and through a green door into a tiny windowless kitchen. The room is a random mix of wooden cupboards and tiles painted with seashells and sailboats. An enormous ceramic sink propped up on cement blocks takes up most of one wall. Across from it a four-ring hob sits on top of a low cupboard next to a battered black oven connected to a dented green gas canister. Utensils and ropes of drying tripe hang from a wire hooked across the room.

'*Ssshhh*,' Fatima hisses, flapping a tea towel at the rangy black-and-white cat who's poking its head into a bread basket. The cat slinks out, a crust of bread in its mouth. '*Moush*,' she says, pointing at the cat.

Addy makes a circle around the room with her hand.

Fatima smiles. '*Cuisine. Comme français.*'

'*En anglais*, kitchen.'

'*Smicksmin*.' Fatima shakes her head. '*Très difficile.*'

Omar pokes his head into the kitchen. 'Come, Adi honey, we go.'

'You missed some delicious chocolate cake.'

He thrusts his hand into the room. It's full of cake. 'I don't miss

64

'nothing.' He takes a bite and wipes the crumbs from his chin with the back of his hand.

'Did the plumber show up? Is the water fixed? I haven't been able to get a hold of Mohammed. He hasn't been answering his phone.'

'I know, I know. Mohammed is very busy. It might be he is in Marrakech. He goes there a lot for business. The plumber went to Azaghar. He'll be back later.'

Addy frowns. 'The water's still not fixed? What took you so long?'

'I did a tour by the waterfalls. I earned five hundred dirhams, so I'm happy for that. I want to buy a refrigerator for Fatima, but it's very, very expensive.'

Omar beckons at Addy with a crumb-covered finger. 'Come, let's go for a walk by the waterfalls. Say goodbye to my grandmother. If you kiss her on her head, it shows her good respect. She'll love you for that.'

'I don't think she wants me anywhere near her.'

'She does, she does. You'll see.'

Addy kisses Fatima on her cheeks and follows Omar into the living room. She edges around the low table past Aicha and bends over Jedda, kissing her on the top of her red polka-dot bandana. Jedda waves Addy away with her stick. Aicha grabs Addy's hands and smiles. 'Thank you for the tea and the cake and cookies of deliciousness,' Addy says to her in rusty French. 'I appreciate your hospitality of kindness. It would be my honour to invite you at my house for tea.'

Aicha smiles broadly and Addy realises with a shock that her teeth are false. Omar says something to his mother, who nods vigorously, setting her earrings swinging.

'What did you say?'

'I say you love chicken brochettes. We'll come later for dinner.'

'Oh, no, Omar. I don't want to impose on your family. I've just eaten my weight in cake.'

65

'It's no imposition, Adi. She don't like for you to eat by your-self. It makes her feel sad. It's not normal for people to be alone in Morocco.'

Addy looks at Jedda. The old woman's one good eye bores into her like she's trying to excavate Addy's soul. 'Except for your grandmother.'

Omar shrugs. 'My grandmother don't like tourists. Don't mind for it.' He takes hold of Addy's elbow and steers her across the courtyard to the front door. 'Anyway, you are not a tourist to me. You are like an Amazigh lady. Even my mum says it.'

'She did?'

'Maybe she didn't say it, but I know she think it.' He opens the metal door. 'She love your red hair and blue eyes for her grandchildren.'

'Omar, honestly, I—'

Omar laughs. 'Don't mind, Adi. Don't believe everything I say. Oh, and Adi? My mum, she don't speak French. It's lucky because you don't speak it so well.'

The daylight is fading when Omar and Addy reach a terrace paved with stones overlooking the waterfalls. A young Moroccan couple sits on the stone wall holding hands. The man speaks quietly and the woman leans her head in to listen. He plays with her fingers.

Omar and Addy sit on the wall. The last of the day's sun throws a beam of light across the waterfalls, setting off sparks like fireflies on the water.

'It's a romantic place here, Adi. Sometimes couples come here to be private.'

'Are they single?'

'No. Everybody marries young here. But maybe there are children and parents and grandparents in the house. It's the Moroccan manner. It's difficult to be private.'

Addy feels a pang of sadness. As a child she'd wished on a star every night, hoping for a brother or sister to play with in the big house by the sea.

'It must be nice to have a big family.'

Omar takes hold of her hand and plays with her fingers. 'You have brothers and sisters, darling?'

'A half-sister.'

Omar draws his black eyebrows together. 'What's that?'

Lights are coming on in the restaurants below, forming pools of yellow around the waterfalls.

'Her name's Philippa. She had a different mother. My father married twice.' Addy presses her lips together into an apologetic smile. 'We don't get on very well. We're very different.'

Omar nods. 'It's possible for a man in Morocco to marry four wives. It's good to have many children. Then your heritage continues even when you go to Paradise.'

'Oh, my father didn't have two wives at the same time! He divorced his first wife and then married my mother. We don't marry more than one person at a time. In fact, it's illegal.'

Omar drops Addy's hand and rests his arm around her shoulders. 'I know it, honey. It might be that it's better like that, anyway. It's hard to have many wives. It's very expensive.' He rolls out the 'r' in very for added emphasis. 'Each wife must have a house. Often, the ladies don't like each other. Anyway, now it doesn't happen so often. Only if the first wife doesn't have babies, then you marry a second wife. But the first wife is the boss.'

'Why don't you just adopt or get fertility treatment?'

'You must know your blood is the same in your children for your heritage, so nobody adopts here. It's very hard to have fertility treatment – you must be very rich for that. Nobody in the mountains can do that. Anyway, they think you're crazy to do it since it's easy to marry a second wife.'

'I see.' Addy's head is spinning. Why does she care if Omar gets married? Has two wives – three wives – four . . . And kids. Lots of kids. If they got involved, it could only ever be a holiday romance.

'You know, Adi, some men come to ask me for Fatima to be their second wife. Fatima tells me "No." She says no to everybody. It's a big problem for me, but I don't make her do nothing she doesn't want. It's for her to decide, even if my mum wants her to marry quick to have babies. She must go where her heart tells her to go.' He looks at Addy out of the corner of his eye. 'Me too. My mum wants me to marry quick to have babies.'

'Oh.' It's like she's been wading out into the sea and suddenly steps off a sandbar.

Omar squeezes her shoulder. 'Don't mind. I'm making a joke with you. I don't mind for ladies. I look only for one lady.' He kisses Addy on the top of her head. 'So, maybe you have a boyfriend in England?'

'I wouldn't be sitting here with you if I had a boyfriend.'

'Maybe you had a boyfriend before?'

Addy remembers the last time she'd seen Nigel, in the kitchen of their flat the night before she'd flown out to Morocco, when he'd made her so angry she'd thought she might hit him. So angry that she'd stormed out and walked around the park for an hour to calm down. Alone in a London park after midnight. She must have been crazy.

'Once I did. But it's over now.'

'I'm jealous.'

What was the harm in a holiday flirtation? Maybe it was just what she needed. Nothing serious. Short and sweet and then back to London. She wasn't looking for a man to rescue her. What was Philippa talking about?

'There's no reason to be jealous, Omar. You must have had girlfriends before.'

'There's no boyfriend–girlfriend situation in Morocco, Adi. It's not a possibility. We must wait to be married to be together.'

'What about the tourist girls?'

'I don't like that situation, even though it's true it happens sometimes. My friend Yassine has a wife and two children and a

68

Dutch lady in Holland who visits him. She bought him a car. She bought a refrigerator for his wife. It's where I get the idea for the refrigerator for Fatima. But, you have to know, it's not my cup of tea. I feel bad for Yassine's wife, Khadija.'

*Cash cow.* Addy could hear Philippa's voice in her head. *He's playing nice just to get you into bed.* What if Omar knew that she was teetering on the brink of bankruptcy? Would he be so keen on her then? He couldn't be that good an actor. Or could he?

Below their perch on the stone wall, the lights of Mohammed's restaurant switch on. Amine is setting out large bottles of water on the tables. A macaque monkey the size of a large cat leaps out of the branches of an olive tree onto a table. Amine shoos it away with a tea towel.

'What about me? I'm a tourist.'

'You're not a tourist, Adi. You are the honey of my life. When you came to Zitoune my world was opened.' He waves his hand out towards the waterfalls in a sweeping gesture. 'It's you I've been waiting for.'

'Omar . . .' Addy's head spins with confusion. 'I . . . I'm not Muslim.'

'*Mashi mushkil.* I can marry a Muslim lady, or a Christian lady or a Jewish lady. No problem for that because we are all people of the book. We all have Moses and Ibrahim and Adam. But Muslim ladies can only marry Muslim men.'

'That doesn't seem fair.'

Omar shrugs. 'It's like that.' Omar reaches for Addy's hand and slides his fingers through hers. 'Adi, when you told me about your dream, I knew for sure you are the lady I wait for. I made a prayer to Allah today. It's the first time in a long time I did it.'

'What did you pray for?'

'I prayed to Allah to thank Him for making me for you. And for sending you to me.'

Addy gazes at the haloes of light below. It's like a door is opening, but does she dare step over the threshold?

69

'Omar, you asked me about my family. My mother died when I was young. My father died last fall.'

'I'm so, so sorry for that, Adi.'

She concentrates on the waterfalls, avoiding his gaze. 'I grew up in Canada. When I graduated from university I moved to London. My father travelled a lot for work, so there wasn't any reason to stay in Canada. I thought I'd have more opportunities in London as a photographer. Lots of magazine work, you know? That's when I finally met my half-sister, Philippa. I was looking forward to meeting her, but . . .' Addy remembers Philippa's frosty welcome, her absolute disinterest in her Canadian half-sister.

'She was married to a rich Italian banker then, but she's divorced now. I live on my own. Philippa and I aren't . . . close.' Better that Omar doesn't know she still shares a flat with Nigel. Another problem to deal with when she gets back to London.

'But she's your sister. You must be close.'

Addy grunts. 'Let's just say that I don't aspire to her way of life and this has caused us some conflict.' She smiles at Omar ruefully. 'I'm a constant disappointment to her.'

Omar shuts his eyes tight. When he looks at her again, his eyes are glazed with tears.

'Me too. My father died. I'm so, so sorry for that, *habibati*. It's a hard fate to be alone. It never happens like that in Morocco. We have many relatives here. We can visit all of Morocco and you will see I have family everywhere. The doors of my family are open to you.'

Addy rests her hand on her thigh. She feels the glossy card of the Polaroid through the soft denim.

'Omar, how old are you?'

'What do you mean?'

'How old are you? When were you born?'

'I have thirty-three years. Anyway, don't mind for age, Adi. It doesn't matter for a man and lady to be the same age.'

'That's not what I meant.' Addy reaches into her pocket and

slides out the photo wrapped in her father's letter. 'Do you remember an Irishman who came here around 1984? He had a Moroccan wife. I think she was his wife. I think she might have been from Zitoune. I don't know for sure.' She hands Omar the photo. 'I have a picture of them.'

A deep crease forms between Omar's black eyebrows as he examines the Polaroid. 'It's a long time ago. I was a small boy.' He looks out at the waterfalls and shakes his head. 'I don't remember them. Why you ask about it?'

'You don't recognise the woman in the picture?'

Omar rubs his thumb across the fading image of Addy's father and Hanane. He flips it over.

'"*Zitoune waterfalls, Morocco, August 1984 – with Hanane*".' He hands the Polaroid back to Addy. 'No, I don't know her.'

She stares down at the faces of her father and Hanane smiling at the unseen photographer in front of the Zitoune waterfalls, then she carefully wraps the blue letter around it and slips the picture back into her pocket.

Back at Aicha's house, the aroma of grilled chicken, garlic and ginger wafts through the courtyard. Women's voices float over the spiced air from the kitchen. The afternoon's tea is pressing on Addy's bladder.

'Toilet?'

Omar points to a door flaking with red paint. 'You might need some tissue.'

Addy pulls a pack of tissues out her jeans pocket and waves it at Omar.

The reek of bleach assaults her nose when she opens the door. It does little to mask the underlying odour of sweat, urine and faeces. A string brushes her cheek. When she tugs at it a light bulb flickers on. The room is no bigger than a phone booth. The tiler has made an attempt at a pattern on the white-tiled walls with tiles printed with pink stars, but halfway up the pink stars have been replaced by tiger stripes. A tap sticks out of the wall at knee height with a blue plastic bucket underneath. A large white ceramic square with a hole in the centre is set into the concrete floor. Ridges shaped like feet flank the hole.

Peeling down her jeans and underwear, Addy steps tentatively onto the ridged feet. As she squats, her cheek slaps up against the pink stars. She wobbles around to face the door, propping herself up with one hand on the door and one on a tiled wall. She teeters over the hole and sprays her loafers with wee.

A knock on the door. 'Honey, are you okay?'

'One minute. Where do I wash my hands?'

'Put water in the bucket and pour it down the toilet.'

When she opens the door, Omar's leaning against the courtyard wall waiting for her. He examines her loafers.

'You made your shoes wet.'

Addy peers down at the dark splotches on the tan leather.

'I know. It's hard for me to squat. I kept falling over. I tried to clean them with some water.'

Omar shouts for his sister. 'Fatima!'

Fatima emerges from the kitchen, wiping her hands on an apron printed with apples and oranges. She's followed by a pretty girl in purple velour pyjamas and a pink hijab with matching pink babouches. Omar says something to Fatima. The girls look at Addy's shoes and break into giggles. Fatima disappears behind a blue wooden door beside the kitchen. The other girl says something to Omar and he laughs. Fatima returns with her purple plastic Crocs.

'Give her your shoes, honey. She'll clean them for you.'

'She doesn't have to do that.'

He takes the Crocs from Fatima and pushes them into Addy's hands. 'She's happy to do it.'

'If you're sure . . .'

'It's fine. *Mashi mushkil*.'

Gripping Omar's arm to steady herself, Addy changes her shoes. Omar picks up her discarded loafers and shoves them into the hands of Fatima's friend. Fatima bursts into another fit of giggles. The girl drops the loafers like they're infectious and storms out of the courtyard, slamming the metal door behind her.

Addy stoops down to pick up the offensive shoes. 'Who was that?'

'Zaina,' Omar says as he takes the shoes from Addy and hands them to Fatima. 'She's a friend of Fatima.'

Addy watches Fatima disappear into the kitchen with her loafers. 'I don't think Zaina likes me.'

'She don't like foreign ladies. It's normal.'

'What do you mean by that?'

'Amazigh ladies don't like foreign ladies because they go with Amazigh men. They're jealous.'

Fatima rests her chin on Addy's shoulder and wraps her arms around her waist. 'Come, sister,' she says in French. 'It's the time of supper. I make delicious brochettes of chicken for my sister, Adi.'

'You go eat, honey.' Omar turns and heads towards the front door.

'Where are you going? Aren't you eating?'

'Later. I'll go to find the plumber. Enjoy.'

Fatima reaches for Addy's hand and leads her into the living room. Aicha smiles her white smile and pats a place for Addy beside her on the flowery banquette. The low table is laid out with stacks of glistening chicken brochettes, a salad of chopped tomatoes, onions and olives dressed with olive oil, and fragrant discs of warm bread dusted with semolina.

Aicha grabs a disc of bread out of the blue plastic basket and tears off a large chunk. She offers it to Addy. '*Eesh*, Adi. *Marhaba.*'

'*Shukran.*'

Addy tears off another piece and bites into its warm yeastiness. As she chews, she looks around the narrow whitewashed room. A poster of a girl praying at Mecca is tacked over the banquette on the opposite wall. Beside it a framed photograph, garlanded with pink and yellow plastic flowers, shows a sharp-suited King

Mohammed VI. At the far end of the room, a large flat-screen television hangs on the wall, the dark screen filmy with pink dust.

Fatima picks up the remote. The television screen springs to life. She flips through the channels until she comes to a Turkish soap opera. Addy wonders where Jedda is. The black-and-white cat slinks into the room and settles on the mat by Addy's feet.

They're silent as they climb the steps to Addy's veranda. She's conscious of his warmth behind her, the gentle pressure of his hand on her waist when she stumbles on the final step. She walks over to the railing and gazes out at the night-cloaked mountains. The air is cool and stars cluster like glass chips in the black sky. A low buzz of cicadas underpins the silence.

Omar joins her and looks out at the inky outline of the High Atlas Mountains in the far distance.

'It's dark tonight, honey. No moon.'

'Yes. But you can see the stars really well.'

'The plumber called me when I was at Mohammed's restaurant watching the football. He said he fixed your water. It might be I should check it for you.'

'No, it's okay. I'm sure it'll be fine.'

'Adi . . .'

It happens before she knows she's done it. Her lips on his neck. Softness. A pulse. His moan. A kiss. His body warm against hers. Her arms around his neck.

'Adi . . .'

No. She can't. She mustn't. It's too complicated. Her life's already a mess. She drops her arms and steps back from his embrace. She presses her fingers against her burning lips.

'I'm so sorry, Omar. I shouldn't have done that. Please forget I've done that.'

He reaches out to her. 'Adi, what happened? Don't worry.'

She hurries to the blue door and into the house. Her heart's in her throat, pounding, pounding. *Oh, my God. What was I thinking?*

# *Chapter Eleven*

**Zitoune, Morocco – December 1983**

Hanane skids through a slick of thick blood-red mud.

She laughs. 'Omar, the surprise had better be worth it. I'm getting splattered with mud.'

The boy waves his hand in the air on the path in front of her. '*Mashi mushkil*. It's not so far now.'

Hanane stops to catch her breath. Wisps of her thick black hair escape the purple scarf draped loosely over her head. The sky is a canopy of blue over the damp red earth. Nothing but rocks and mud. A few leafless bushes. The river, about ten metres below, courses roughly on its path through the canyon walls.

'If I'd known we'd be walking to Oushane, I'd never have come.'

Omar turns around, smiling broadly as he opens his arms wide. 'So, why would I have told you, then?' He flicks his eyes over her shoulder.

Hanane glances back but sees nothing but the narrow goat path they've just descended.

'What is it, Omar?'

'Nothing.' Breaking into a jog, he waves at her to follow him. 'Not far now, Hanane. *Yalla.*'

'I'm not running, Omar.' She steps gingerly along the muddy plateau. 'I'll break my leg.'

'Stop.' Omar shoots his right palm into the air like the traffic police she's seen in Azaghar. 'Stop. There, just there. Where you are.'

'What? Why?'

He points at the muddy path in front of her. 'Look down.'

Pressed into the mud is a huge, three-toed footprint.

'What is it?'

'Dinosaur.' Omar curls his hands under his armpits, staggering around the ground like a cross between a monkey and a wounded chicken. He lets out a howl.

Hanane looks around nervously. 'Be quiet. There might be another one.'

Omar bursts out laughing, slapping the knees of his dirty jeans. 'Don't be stupid, Hanane. The dinosaurs are all dead now. I learned about it in school.' He points to the ground ahead of him. '*Yalla*, there are more. Lots of them. Big and little. A whole family.'

'Seriously?'

'Yes, seriously.'

Hanane spins around. The Irishman with the black hair jogs down the final metre of the goat path, the big black camera on its strap slapping against his chest.

'Be carefu—'

Too late. His foot slips and the man's booted feet fly out from under him, sending him sprawling on his back into the red mud.

Hanane giggles then, remembering her manners, composes her face into a frown of concern. 'Are you all right?' she asks in French.

Gus sits up, holding up palms coated in thick red goo. 'Fine. I've only hurt my pride.' He holds out a hand to Omar. 'Here, boss. Give us a hand.'

Omar picks his way across the mud to the Irishman. Holding out a skinny hand, he yanks Gus to his knees.

'Thanks, boss.' Gus winks at Omar as he gets to his feet. 'I can take it from here.'

76

'Mister Gus, show her the other footprints, over there.' Omar points to the ground a few metres away.

Hanane raises an arched black eyebrow at Omar. 'So, this is your surprise.'

Omar's right cheek dimples. 'The dinosaur footprints were the surprise.' He points at Gus. 'He's just extra. He promised me not to tell you.'

'Boss,' Gus says as he adjusts the camera strap around his neck, 'did anyone ever tell you that you talk too much?'

Hanane shifts on her feet, sinking deeper into the mud. 'I really have to get back. I need to feed the chickens.'

'You never feed the chickens, Hanane. Mohammed's wife does that.'

Hanane glares at Omar. 'Well, today I need to feed the chickens.'

'I'm sure the chickens can wait half an hour,' Gus says. 'Since we're here, why don't we have a look? Think about it. A whole herd of dinosaurs walking over this very ground millions of years ago.' He tromps through the mud in the direction Omar had pointed. He hunkers down to look at something in the ground. 'Hanane, come and look. They really are amazing. You must come and see.'

He beckons Omar over and points out some detail to the boy. He has so much enthusiasm, Hanane thinks. So much energy. He seems so much younger than the older men of the village. All of them have somehow shrunk from their prime, like dates left to dry in the sun. But this Irishman still looks at the world with the eyes of a curious boy. Still bears himself like a man in the prime of his life. Still glows with the vitality of a man half his age. But with an assurance missing in the village boys she's grown up with.

The two black-haired heads lean together as they inspect the marks in the ground. Man and boy. The Irishman looks over at her. His blue eyes are the colour of the sky. He smiles at her, lines carving themselves into the fine skin around his eyes.

'Come, Hanane. Come and have a look. It's marvellous. Obviously some large theropods. I've seen something similar in the Kem Kem Beds by the Algerian border.'

Marvellous. Such a beautiful word. A word of treasures beyond imagination. She takes a step forwards, knowing, as she does, that she's walking into her future.

# Chapter Twelve

**Zitoune, Morocco – April 2009**

A knock on Addy's front door.

'Come in,' she calls as she tinkers with a close-up of a grey-furred macaque on her laptop.

The blue wooden door squeaks open and Omar sticks his blue-turbaned head around the door, smiling broadly. 'Good morning. It's okay for me to come in?'

Addy glances over at him then turns back quickly to the laptop. 'Yes, okay. Fine. I'm editing the pictures I took of the monkeys the other day. I've got some good images of the shop sellers, too. I've made a start on the text.'

Omar leans over her shoulder, his breath warm on her neck as she manipulates the mouse to add a richer grey tone to the monkey's fur.

'It's clever what you do.' He brushes his fingers along Addy's neck.

She shifts away from his fingers and rubs at her neck where he's touched her. 'Just lots of practice.'

Omar drops his hand. From the corner of her eye, Addy watches him wander over to the kitchen. He turns on the tap over the sink. The pipes groan and ping. A fan of water sprays out across his gown, turning the bright blue a deep navy. Omar flaps the wet fabric in the air.

'The plumber didn't fix it well.'

'I thought it would be fine. The shower's a nightmare, too. The water's cold and it stopped just when I put the shampoo in my hair. I used up all my bottled water rinsing it out.'

He flops into a wooden chair. 'It's a rubbish situation. Did you tell Mohammed?'

'He said he'll get it fixed "next tomorrow".'

Omar grunts. 'I'll arrange it for you. Don't worry. I'll take you to the public shower later so you can have a hot shower. Or you can have a hammam with my sister and my mother.'

Addy looks up from her laptop. 'A hammam?'

'It's like a room for steam. I showed it to you when I made the tour the first time. The buildings like the beehive behind the houses.'

'Oh. Like a sauna.'

Omar shrugs. 'It might be.'

'Maybe I'll try it another time. A proper hot shower would be great.'

She stares at the blinking cursor on her laptop screen, her concentration dissolving like sugar in hot tea. She'll be back in London at the end of June. There's no point getting involved with Omar. Tempting, but . . . it would be stupid. Someone would end up getting hurt, and she was damned if it was going to be her.

She was getting nowhere in her search for Hanane here in Zitoune. With every squint through her camera lens, she'd been searching for a hint of a mature Hanane, or a glimpse of her father's features in the faces of the young men swimming under the bridge, or in a passing young woman's shy smile. Hanane's child would be twenty-three now. Not a child, even though all Addy could picture was a baby swaddled in white blankets.

No one she's shown the Polaroid to recognises her father and Hanane. If was as though Hanane had never existed. What happened to her? Where's her child now? Maybe Hanane wasn't from Zitoune or one of the nearby villages, after all. But then why did her father's photos '*with H*' start in Zitoune?

Omar picks up a pencil and drums it on the table. 'You would like to come to the waterfalls today, Adi? A driver called me from Marrakech. He has twenty tourists on his bus. It's good business for me.'

Addy looks over at Omar and chews her lip. She'd like to take some more photos around the waterfalls. What harm could it be? She'd be with a group of tourists. Safety in numbers.

'Adi, you don't have to worry for me. If you don't like me, I can accept it, even though it hurts my heart.'

She nods. 'Okay. I'll bring my camera and the tripod.'

Omar drops the pencil onto the table and stands, tipping the chair over in his haste. 'Sorry. Sorry.' He rights the chair and slides it under the table. 'Come to the bridge in half an hour. You can test me to see if I'm a good tour guide or not.' He turns to Addy, his hand on the door handle. 'Fatima don't let me eat the crêpes she made this morning. She say they are for you, full stop.' He shakes his head. 'It's difficult to be the man in my house since you came to Zitoune. Soon I will be starving.'

'Poor you. She brought me the crêpes for breakfast. They were delicious.'

'Never mind, Adi. I took some already this morning from the kitchen. Even if she say no, I take them anyway. Nobody can say no to me.'

'Oh, really?'

'It's true.'

'Maybe one day I'll say no to you.'

Omar steps out onto the veranda. 'It's impossible.'

'Why's it so impossible?'

The dimple appears in his cheek. 'Because I'm so charming.'

Addy smiles as she reaches for her camera and loops the strap around her neck. '*Que sera sera.*'

'What you said?'

'What will be, will be. It's Latin.'

Omar nods. 'It's like fate. Even so, you'll never say no to me. I'm sure about it.'

Half an hour later, Addy's on the old iron bridge, stepping carefully over the loose wooden boards. Resting the tripod against an iron girder, she leans her elbows on the rusting railing and watches the river sliding past, underneath her feet. She can see through the clear water to the pebbles and stones on the sandy bottom. It's still early, and the village boys haven't yet congregated on the riverbanks to dive and swim in the cool water. Only boys, never girls. The girls are in their homes, Addy guesses, helping with the cooking and cleaning. Being dutiful while the boys have all the fun.

Addy gazes up the hill towards the mosque's thick minaret. A sheep's carcass hangs from a hook in front of the butcher's stall next door to the new concrete tower. The butcher leans against a bamboo post holding up an awning constructed from an old Méditel hoarding advertising cell phones. He swats at the flies buzzing around the carcass with a goat tail.

Leaning her chin in her hand on the rusted iron railing, Addy watches three women carry baskets of laundry down a path to the river. They stop at a flat rock, set down their baskets, and tuck the hems of their skirts and aprons into their pyjama bottoms. They roll their pyjamas over their knees and lay out T-shirts on the rock. A tall, slender, black-skinned woman showers the shirts with a snowy sprinkling of laundry detergent. When the T-shirts are sufficiently soap-laden, the women wade out into the river and dunk the shirts into the water. They scrub and pummel the cloth until Addy feels her own knuckles burn.

Fatima and her friend, Zaina, emerge, chatting and laughing, from the shadows of the olive trees, carrying brightly coloured plastic baskets spilling over with clothes. Addy waves at them, calling out Fatima's name. Fatima smiles and waves back. Zaina stares up at Addy, the humour erasing from her pretty face.

Addy leans back against the rail and inhales the fresh spring air with a deep breath. So Zaina doesn't like her. So what? But the others – Aicha, Jedda, Fatima, Omar . . . Why do the people here touch her in a way no one in London touches her? Certainly not Philippa, who loves to play the role of her disapproving and long-suffering older sister. She loves Philippa, of course. She's her sister. She just doesn't like her very much most of the time.

And Nigel? Addy tries to dredge up the memory of her ex-fiancé, but his face is like a puzzle whose pieces she can't quite fit together. Nigel got close. She'd let her guard down because he could make her laugh with his dry humour. Then he'd left her heart as torn and bloodied as the raccoon she'd once seen caught in a hunter's trap in the Québec woods. Another selfish man. Wrapped up in his career. What did Philippa say? Always falling for inaccessible men. Selfish and inaccessible. Just like her father.

'Adi!' Omar waves at her from the road leading down from the car park.

She watches him stride down the dusty road, trailed by a crowd of sunburnt tourists in floppy sun hats and baseball caps, cameras bumping on their chests. Despite herself, her heart flutters.

Omar points out the donkeys tethered to the olive trees, saying something she can't hear. The tourists laugh. In his turban, Omar towers over them. As he approaches, she follows the line of his neck to the point where it meets his angular jaw. The soft spot just under his jaw where she'd kissed him last night, in the moonlight on her veranda. She remembers his quiet moan, and her cheeks flush. But that was before she came to her senses. Retreating back into her shell, like a turtle hiding from the world.

'Everybody, this is a tourist lady who'll join us for the tour.'

Addy waves at the group. A few middle-aged European couples and a clique of Spanish students. The girls flick their eyes over her. She's of no interest to the boys. Omar collects her tripod and

83

tucks it under his arm. He heads through the olive grove to the river path. Addy follows at the rear of the group, just like the first time.

Omar stops on the riverbank by the women washing clothes. The tourists congregate around him and snap photos of the toiling women.

'This is the manner we do wash the clothes in the village.'

'So, it's only the women who are clean, then?'

Omar snaps his head around and stares at Addy. The dimple appears in his cheek. A Scottish man asks him a question, but Omar doesn't answer. The man repeats his question. Omar shakes his head as if to wake up.

'I'm sorry. I been sleeping.'

The group trails Omar through the twisting trunks of the olive trees, past the lookout by Yassine's café. Rather than heading to the bottom of the waterfalls where the rafts bob in the pool, Omar veers right onto a different path. He stops in front of a red mud wall of petrified tree roots. He stumbles over his words, forgetting his English.

The path leads to a pool of clear water fed by mini-waterfalls. Addy peers down the river towards sun-baked canyon walls in the distance and sees half a dozen pools, feeding lazily into each other, veiled by pink oleander bushes and branches of the old olive trees on the riverbanks. The freshness of the early morning has succumbed to a dry heat and sweat trickles down her neck. She fans herself with her hat.

Omar leans her tripod against the grey trunk of an olive tree and leaps onto a rock in the pool.

'Everybody, it's very, very hot even if it's not summer yet. So, you can swim if you would like. We will stay here thirty minutes. It's very safe, no problem. The water is very clean. Enjoy.'

The older tourists roll up their trousers and Bermuda shorts and wade cautiously into the water. The Spanish students strip off their clothes in a burst of Latin enthusiasm, revealing surfing shorts and bikinis. They clamber across the rocks to the mini-waterfalls and leap into the pool, screaming as they slam into the cold water. The girls are tanned and slim in their bikinis. Addy runs her hand along the waist of her jeans, conscious of her white skin and the roundness of her belly, hips and breasts under her clothes.

Omar laughs and shouts at the Spanish boys as he unwinds his tagelmust. He jumps back to the riverbank and loops the blue cloth around Addy's waist.

'So, I capture you, Adi.' He leans over and plants a quick kiss on her lips.

A Spanish boy shouts out a catcall. Omar answers him in Spanish, putting off the boy's timing, and he belly-flops into the pool. The boy's friends erupt into peals of glee.

'What did he say?'

'He say I am a robber of the ladies. I tell him I am the robber of one lady only.' Omar laughs. 'I tell him he have to make a good dive because all the Spanish ladies watch him. So, he is nervous and he made a bad dive.'

The students' carefree spirits are infectious and Addy ignores the alarm going off in her head.

'What are you going to do now that you've trapped me? Carry me off?'

'It's so, so hot, darling. There's no way for me to carry you.'

'Maybe you'd like one of the Spanish girls instead. They've been eyeing you.'

'I don't mind for Spanish ladies.' Omar drapes the tagelmust around them like a blanket and slides his hand under Addy's T-shirt, cupping her right breast. He runs his fingers over the lace of her bra and expels a whisper of breath. 'Come with me, Adi.'

For a moment they stare at each other. Addy drapes the blue cloth around her shoulders.

'Where are we going?'

'To be alone, darling. We can swim.'

'I didn't bring a swimsuit.'

'*Mashi mushkil.* You can wear your underwear. It'll dry quick in the sun. No one will see. It's a private place.'

He leads Addy along the riverbank until they reach a flat rock jutting into a quiet pool. It's hidden from view of the others by a screen of oleander bushes. He pulls off his blue gown and white T-shirt. His faded Levis cling to his hips. His naked chest is lean like a swimmer's, tanned to the colour of milky coffee.

Addy lifts the camera strap from around her neck and sets the camera down on a rock, covering it with her straw hat. She begins to undo her belt, but Omar brushes her hands away.

'It is for me to do it.'

He unfastens the belt and discards it on the riverbank. Slowly, he peels off her jeans, running his hands over her body as her skin is revealed to the sun. She stops him as he is about to lift her T-shirt over her head.

'I think I'll keep this on, if you don't mind.' She ties the T-shirt into a knot under her bra.

He smiles, his teeth gleaming against his brown skin. 'As you like, Adi. Anyway, it's better to imagine. It's more spicy.'

Omar shrugs out of his jeans and sandals until he wears only red jockey shorts, which cling to the contours of his body. He climbs over rocks to the top of the cascade feeding the pool. He looks over at Addy to see that she's watching, then he executes a perfect dive into the centre of the pool.

Addy scans the surface of the pool, waiting for his head to surface.

'Omar?' She searches for a sign – bubbles on the pool's mirror-like surface, the gleam of skin under the water. 'Omar?'

His hands grab her ankles. He surfaces, spouting water.

'You been worried, weren't you, darling? I watched you underneath the water.'

Addy splashes his face with water. 'I was worried about how I was going to get the tourists back to the village if you drowned.'

'That's not nice.' He pulls at her ankles and she loses her balance, splashing into the pool. She surfaces next to him, spewing water and blinking.

'Bastard! I've got contact lenses.'

'What you say?'

She slaps the water, spraying Omar's face. 'Bastard.'

'It's rude, Adi.' He dives underneath.

Addy treads water, scanning the surface for where he'll reappear. The tight wool of his head brushes between her legs. He slides up the front of her body, running his lips over her naked belly as he rises to the surface.

He bursts through the water, gasping. 'I forgot to breathe, darling. I wanted to stay to kiss you under the water and I lost my air.'

Addy reaches her arms around his neck and folds her legs around his body. He leans his head back, closing his eyes as she kisses her way across his neck. His hand cups her head and he kisses her. She's hungry, ravenous, wanting to taste him, to devour him, until there's no Addy and no Omar. Only their essences, together, in a pool of water under the hot Moroccan sun.

'*Alli estan!*'

A gigantic splash. And another.

Addy pushes away from Omar. The Spanish students have found them.

Omar slaps the water. '*Habss*. It's a place for us to be private. Not to have people here.'

Addy swims to a rock by the riverbank and heaves herself out of the water. Her heart's racing. She wipes the dripping water from her eyes. She'd almost made a huge mistake.

Omar swims over to her, but she's already pulling on her jeans.

'Fuckers,' Omar says, gesturing rudely at the laughing students. 'I'm so sorry, darling. I wanted to make a special day for you. I knew you would love it here.'

'It's okay.' She unties the knot in her T-shirt and twists it to wring out the water.

He hoists himself up onto the rock. 'Wait, darling.'

She shoves on her straw hat and reaches for her camera. 'I should be getting back. I have a lot of work to do.'

She turns away, unable to meet his eyes. Is she a coward, or just being sensible? She knows what Philippa would say. *You're making a fool out of yourself, Adela. He just wants to shag you. And get you to pay for things. You'd be stupid to think anything else.*

She's damaged goods. How could she let him see her breast? No one has seen it outside the hospital. Not Philippa. Not Nigel. No, it's better to stop this right now, before it was too late.

# Chapter Thirteen

## Zitoune, Morocco – April 2009

Omar and Addy stand outside a whitewashed building beside the mosque. A hand-painted sign reading *Douches Publiques* hangs over the door. On the left, men sit on a covered terrace drinking orange juice and watching European football in French on a large plasma-screen television.

'Wait here, honey.'

Addy hovers in the shadows and tries to make herself inconspicuous. She lifts her T-shirt away from her soaking bra. A few of the men glance at her, but when the television commentator's voice rises in anticipation of a goal, they quickly turn back to the screen. A collective moan when the player overshoots the goal.

A couple of men rush out of the showers – one is still drying his hair with a towel; the other clutches his wet shower bag against his red shirt, a damp circle spreading across his chest like a wound. Omar stands in the doorway and beckons Addy to enter.

'Are you sure it's okay?'

'*Mashi mushkil*, Adi. You must have a hot shower. Your clothes are wet a long time. I insist for it.'

'Well, yes, but . . .'

'Don't mind. It's clear. I made an arrangement for the plumber to come again next tomorrow to fix your water. I insist to him to make it well or he will be in troubles with me. He has gone to a wedding in Azaghar today.'

Addy shifts the plastic bag of toiletries and the towel that Omar's retrieved from his mother's house from one hand to the other.

'Will my camera equipment be okay?'

'I put it in my room. Nobody will go there. It's forbidden.'

'Did you tell them we were coming here?'

'Nobody was home. It's fine, Adi. Don't worry. I come here all the time. It's normal. It's not many places to have a shower in Zitoune. Everyone use the hammam.'

She looks down at the pink plastic shopping bag. 'Okay then.'

Inside, six shower cubicles line up against one wall, yellow plastic shower curtains hanging on rails in front of each. A row of shelves sits under a mirror opposite them.

'Did you chase those men out of the shower?' Addy's voice echoes off the white tiles and wet cement floor.

Omar leans against a metal trough and folds his arms across his chest. 'I tell them a European lady needs to have a shower. They were frightened of that. They ran away.'

'You'll make sure nobody comes in while I'm showering?'

'For sure, honey. I'm a bodyguard for you. I'll wait outside by the door. If anybody comes I'll give them troubles. *Mashi mushkil.*'

Addy tugs aside a yellow curtain. The tiled walls are dripping and tepid water trickles out of the shower head. She takes the shampoo bottle and soap out of the plastic bag and sets them down on the concrete floor inside the cubicle, then she hangs the towel on a hook by the trough.

Once she's in the cubicle, she peels off her wet clothes and shrugs off her leather sandals. Her feet are covered with pale pink dust, which turns blood-red when she steps onto the wet concrete floor. She squints down at her left breast. It looks like a small, sharp-toothed creature has bitten into it. She prods at the pink scar with her fingertips. No lump.

Bundling up her clothes and sandals, Addy peers around the curtain into the empty room. She shivers as the damp air slides around her body. She makes a lunge for the shelves, but the curtain catches her foot and she lands with a thud on the wet floor.

The door opens a crack. 'Honey? What happened?'

'Don't come in! I'm fine.'

Addy clutches the curtain around her body and shuffles over to the shelves. She dumps her bundle onto a shelf and hobbles back to another shower cubicle. She drops the torn curtain onto the floor and steps into the shower. She turns on the water. Pins of hot water penetrate her skin like acupuncture needles. The tension in her shoulders melts away.

A brown hand holding a shampoo bottle thrusts through the side of the curtain. She gasps and shields her body with her hands.

'Adi, don't mind. It's me. You left the shampoo in the other shower.'

Addy grabs the bottle. 'I almost had a heart attack. Who's at the door?'

Omar's left hand offering the bar of soap appears around the other side of the shower curtain.

'It might be you need the soap, too.'

She takes the soap and holds the white bar and the shampoo bottle against her breasts like weapons.

'Thanks. Now go.'

'I'm a good servant, isn't it?'

'Very good, thanks. Go back to the door before someone comes in.'

'Maybe you need to have help to wash your back?'

'No! Go away.'

'Okay, no problem. Anyway, I'm a bit smelly, too. I'll have a shower next to you.'

'What? What about the door? What if someone comes in?'

The sound of the metal belt buckle clinking against the rivets in his pockets.

'*Mashi mushkil*. I paid a boy to wait outside, honey.'

The metal curtain rings slide against the rusty metal pole in the next cubicle, water splashing as Omar turns on the water. His hand reaches around the partition between the two cubicles. 'Can I have the shampoo, darling?'

'Stop calling me darling.'

Addy hands him the bottle. She stands under the coursing water, her brain whirling with confusion. She hears Omar moving around under the water on the other side of the partition. The sooner she gets out of here the better. She reaches her hand around the partition.

'Could I have the shampoo, please?'

Omar slides his fingers into Addy's and he steps through the curtain into her cubicle. He folds his arms around her and kisses her. His body's like wet brown stone.

'You are my darling,' Omar whispers against her ear. 'You are the water for my desert. I've been thirsty, Adi. I've been waiting for you for a long time.'

Addy feels her arms slide around his body. But as he pushes her against the shower's tiles, worry jabs at her like a mosquito. She can't. She mustn't. Her life is too complicated. She's too old for him. She lives in another country. He's Muslim. He wants children. What will he think about her scar? Maybe she's just an easy tourist lay. Addy, what are you thinking?

'Omar. Stop.' She pushes him away. The cold tiles press against her back. 'This is crazy. We could be arrested.'

Confusion clouds his fine, angular features.

She stumbles out of the cubicle and picks up the torn shower curtain. She drapes it around her body like a shield.

Omar steps out of the shower, the water dripping off his naked body.

'Adi. Darling. I'm so, so sorry.'

She holds up her hand like a traffic cop. 'Don't come near me.' A flare of anger. How could he have put them in such a dangerous situation? How could she have been so stupid? They could be arrested.

Omar grabs the towel off the hook and wraps it around his waist.

'I'm so, so sorry, darling. You have to know I respect you well, Adi.' He presses his hand against his wet chest, his amber eyes imploring. 'You are the wife of my soul.'

Addy turns her back on him. 'Go. Just go.'

She hears him pull on his clothes. The door slams as he leaves. Her body shakes. She can barely breathe. She sinks down onto the floor, the yellow curtain billowing out around her, and cries.

# Chapter Fourteen

**Zitoune, Morocco – April 2009**

The muggy air sits on Addy's chest like a fat, wet cat. The damp sheets hang off the bed in an avalanche of crumbled white cotton. A spasm grips her stomach. She leans over the side of the bed and heaves into the plastic wastebasket. Flopping back against the pillows, she throws her arm across her forehead, but the spasms start again. She needs the toilet.

Stumbling out of bed, she crawls like a baby across the thick wool rug and the cool concrete floor to the bathroom. She lifts herself onto the toilet just in time. When it's over, she lies on the floor and surrenders to its welcoming coolness.

*She's swimming in a green sea. The sea dissolves into a photograph of a face swathed in blue cloth. A man in a blue turban. The man's features waver and float until they suddenly align. She cries out and reaches for him, but she's drowning. He looks at her and shakes his head. 'I'm sorry,' her father says. Then he's gone.*

*She flails in the stormy sea. Philippa appears holding a Tarot card with a picture of a crumbling tower. A lightning bolt strikes the tower, and a man and a woman fall out of its windows towards jagged rocks below. The couple turn to look at Addy as they fall. She feels herself scream, but the sound locks inside her throat. It's Omar and herself.*

*There are voices, muffled by the rising storm. Someone lifts her up and lays her on a bed of red roses. Something cool touches her face. Like the soft, cool rain of Vancouver Island. A woman's voice is singing. Then Addy's swimming up through layers of a rainbow. A rooster crows somewhere far away.*

Someone has opened the shutters. Bright sunlight reflects off the whitewashed walls. Addy squints at the room and her heart jumps. Omar's grandmother is sitting on the foot of the bed, resting her head and hands on her stick as she stares at Addy with her one good eye.

There are sounds of movement in the kitchen. Addy opens her mouth to call out, but her throat is dry and nothing emerges except a cough. Fatima's hijab-covered head peeks around the bedroom door.

'Adi? *Bonjour. Sbah lkhir. Tu vas bien?*'

Addy's stomach rumbles and she throws her hand across her mouth. Fatima runs across the room and holds up the wastebasket. Addy retches up what little remains in her stomach.

'Poor Adi. Someone give you the bad eye.'

Addy wipes her mouth and flops back into the pillows. 'I think it was the water from the shower. I should be more careful.'

Jedda shuffles across the floor, her stick stabbing the concrete like a hobbled donkey. She pokes Addy's shoulder with her bony finger, her silver ring digging into Addy's skin, mumbling something in Tamazight.

'What did she say, Fatima?'

Fatima dips a cloth into a bowl of water on the nightstand and dabs at Addy's forehead.

'She say it's the bad eye. It's many people who are jealous in Zitoune. All the ladies are jealous that Omar looks only at you.

You look like the Queen of Morocco. For sure it's the bad eye. But my mother have a very good medicine for that. In one day you will feel better. Jedda insist for it.'

Addy grunts. She's been sick like this before. Usually a takeaway curry. It'll probably be over in twenty-four hours. She reaches over to Jedda and gently squeezes the old woman's gnarled hand. The crosses and X's on Jedda's ring make an indentation into Addy's palm.

'*Shukran*, Jedda. *Shukran*, Fatima.'

Fatima leans over and kisses Addy on the cheek. 'You are my sister, Adi. It is my pleasure.'

Where's Omar?

Aicha sits on the foot of Addy's bed holding a white chalky lump. She raises Addy's right hand and circles it with the white lump three times. Then she repeats the process with Addy's left hand. Finally, she leans over and circles Addy's head three times. When she's done, she beams at Addy with her bright, false-toothed smile. She pats Addy's shoulder and leaves the room.

Addy looks at Fatima. '*C'est tout?*' That's it?

'You will see. You will feel better tomorrow.' Fatima tucks the sheet snugly around Addy. 'I will come in the morning with the breakfast.'

'No, no breakfast.'

'You will see. You will be hungry tomorrow.' She kisses Addy on both cheeks and places her hand over her heart. 'Adi is like the baby of Fatima.'

'You'll be a good mother one day.'

'*Inshallah.*' If God is willing.

When Fatima arrives the following morning, Addy's already up and sitting on the veranda. A light breeze wafts through the leaves of the grapevine and she lifts her face to the cool air.

'*Sbah lkhir*, Adi,' Fatima calls as she climbs up the path. In her orange djellaba and purple hijab, she's a jolt of colour on the muted landscape. 'Allô, Fatima.'

Fatima mounts the steps, a basket covered with a red-and-white checked cloth hooked over her arm. She kisses Addy's cheeks and unloads plates and a feast of flat square crêpes, discs of warm bread, a jar of runny honey, marmalade, olive oil and shiny black olives.

'Fatima. It's so much food.'

'Eesh, Adi, eesh. I will make some tea.'

The scent of the warm bread is heady. Addy's stomach rumbles. She tears off a piece and drizzles it with honey.

'It's so good to see you are better.'

She spins around in her chair. Omar leans against the old olive tree by the path, the blue tagelmust wrapped around his head into a turban.

'It's okay if I come? I must talk to you serious, Adi.'

Addy chews the bread as she eyes him. 'Fine.'

He mounts the steps and sits on a chair at the far end of the table. His amber eyes bore into her. Dark circles shade the skin under his eyes.

'I'm so, so sorry, habibati. I made a big mistake.' He sighs and rubs his eyes.

Anger and confusion churn up Addy's blood like the fizz in a glass of cola. 'Get me in the shower and fuck me. That's what you do with tourists here, isn't it?'

'No, it's not like that for me. I swear it.' Omar leans his elbows on the table and buries his head in his hands. 'My family is so, so angry with me to take you to the showers. They think I made you have the bad eye. They said you should have a hammam to be private. I should protect you well.'

Addy sets down the crêpe and wipes her fingers on the checked cloth. She holds tight to her anger. Knowing that her anger is the only thing that protects her from falling into an unknowable future with Omar.

'I don't need a protector. I can take care of myself.'

Footsteps approach from the house. Fatima emerges on the veranda carrying a plastic tray laden with an ornate silver teapot and tea glasses.

Omar mumbles a greeting to his sister. He looks back at Addy. 'It's okay for me to have some breakfast with you? I didn't eat for one day. I suffered with you.'

Addy glares at him as Fatima picks up the teapot and pours the steaming mint tea in a perfect arc into a small glass. She tips the tea back into the teapot and repeats the procedure twice more before filling the glasses with fragrant tea.

'The mint is good for the stomach,' Omar says. 'I told Fatima to pick it fresh from the valley for you.'

Fatima hands Omar a plate with a crêpe. He spreads a pancake with marmalade, folds it into a sandwich and wolfs it down.

Addy eyes him across the table. 'You're hungry.'

'Yes. If you couldn't eat, I couldn't eat as well.'

Addy tears off a piece of crêpe and spreads it with a thin layer of marmalade. The tart orange melts into the doughy crêpe in her mouth.

'You like it, Adi?'

Addy swallows and wipes her lips with her fingers. 'Delicious. I've never put marmalade on pancakes before. I'm a maple syrup girl.'

'It's called *msemen*. Moroccan crêpe. Fatima makes the best in Zitoune.'

She wipes a dab of marmalade off her chin. '*C'est très délicieux*, Fatima.'

'*Marhaba*, Adi.' Fatima loads another *msemen* onto Addy's plate. '*Eesh msemen. Eesh.*'

'Fatima loves you a lot, you have to know about it. You made a big impression on my family. Even my grandmother is angry at me for you being sick. She insisted to come here yesterday to stay with you. She said you are a good lady.'

98

'Your family has been very kind. It's you I'm not so sure about.'

'My grandmother agrees with you. She said I'm a bad man. She said if I was smaller, she would punish me.'

Omar reaches across the table for her hand, but Addy slides her hands into her lap.

'You can be sure about me, darling. I would never hurt you. I would die one thousand times if you are hurt.'

He picks at his *msemen* and chews without enthusiasm.

The last embers of Addy's anger sputter out. 'It wasn't all your fault, Omar. I shouldn't have gone into those showers. I knew it wasn't a good idea.'

'No, Adi. It's not your fault at all. It's my responsibility.' Omar presses his right hand against his heart. 'I apologise a million per cent.'

Addy sips the sweet tea and sets down the glass. Parameters. That's what they need. She's not ready to get involved with anyone. Not with her damaged body. How could anyone possibly want her now?

'Apology accepted, but I have work to do here. I'm going back to London in two months. I have some travelling to do. I have to go to Essaouira, Casablanca, the desert. I'll soon be out of your hair and we can both get on with our lives.'

A shadow crosses Omar's face. 'As you like, darling.'

'Please, no more darlings or honeys, okay? My name's Addy. Look, why don't you help me work out my travel itinerary around Morocco? You told me you've done that before for other tourists. You can help me find a driver. I'll pay you. It'll be a professional arrangement.'

Omar sips the hot tea and rubs at a drip on his chin with the end of his tagelmust.

'I know Morocco well. I can do it. I can go with you to be your bodyguard.'

'I didn't say that. I said help me. There's one more thing . . .'

'What's that, dar . . . Adi?'

'What happened with that white stuff your mother used on me yesterday?'

Omar pops an oily black olive into his mouth and spits the stone out over the railing. 'She put it in water.'

'And?'

'If it fizzed everywhere then it means she took away the bad eye. If it didn't fizz then you don't have the bad eye and you must go to the doctor.'

'So, what happened?'

Omar asks Fatima something in Tamazight. She waves her hands in circles and exhales her breath like a deflated balloon. '*Poussshhh.*'

Omar reaches for another *msemen*. 'Very bad eye.'

# Chapter Fifteen

**Zitoune, Morocco – January 1984**

Hanane pulls the brown wool djellaba tightly around her body and rubs at the rough fabric shielding her arms from the cold winter air. Under her feet the earth is hard and uneven, frozen into ghost prints of mules and donkeys. The night is black and silent, the canopy of olive leaves lit silver by the moonlight. Only the puff of her breath breaks through the still air, hanging like a cloud before it dissipates like a lost thought into the night.

She steps forwards gingerly, hugging the shadowy fringes of the path as she moves past the gnarled trunks of the old olive trees, alert to footsteps or the clop of hooves on the frozen earth. She's deep in the olive grove now, far away from the querying glances, the hushed whispers, the hastily turned heads of the villagers. The trees have eyes in Zitoune and secrets are the villagers' kief.

The squat outline of the olive oil hut materialises in a clearing ahead. The new metal door, blue in the daylight but black as the night tonight, is shut tight against the clay walls. Hanane looks up at the small, high windows covered with curved grilles. A sliver of yellow light escapes around the edge of a piece of fabric hung over the window inside.

She runs her tongue over her dry lips and breathes in the cold January air. It's not too late to turn back. Back to her father's mud-walled house, back to her warm bed on the living room banquette, back to the safety of the familiar. But her father's house offers no refuge from the certainty of her fate if she doesn't knock on the blue metal door. Her bridegroom has already been chosen. Her father had announced her engagement to her last night – not the dreaded Mehdi from Ait Bougmez, who'd suddenly chosen a local girl – only fourteen! – but a distant cousin from Tafraout. She hasn't even seen a photo.

She knocks on the door, the sound hollow and tinny. The latch turns. She steps back into the shadows as the door swings open. Gus stands in the doorway, his solid, masculine form a silhouette against the warm light.

'You came.'

'Yes.'

A man steps out of the shadows of the olive grove. He sucks on the stub of his cigarette, the red tip glowing in the black night. The woman hovers under the hut's windows. Waiting. The door opens. The Irishman stands in the yellow light. The woman enters. The door closes.

The man tosses the smoking stub onto the frozen red earth. He crushes it with the toe of his black boot and heads down the path.

Another shape emerges from the gloom. A tall, sturdy man with a heavy staff of freshly stripped wood moves out into the moonlight. He watches the other man follow the path into the village. There's no mistaking the man's identity. The new young policeman.

He must tell Jedda.

# Chapter Sixteen

**The Road to Essaouira, Morocco – May 2009**

Staccato beeps and the blaring wails of an Amazigh singer infiltrate Addy's house. She waves at the rusty black Renault through the open window.

'*Yalla*, Adi,' Omar shouts out from the car. 'Hurry. We'll be late for the concert.'

She shuts the window and slings her leather overnight bag over her shoulder. After locking the blue door, she slides the key under the flower pot and hurries down to the car.

Omar stands by the car's open boot, a yellow-and-black Boston Bruins baseball cap shading his eyes from the bright May sun. As he stacks her bag on top of a pile of tattered backpacks, Addy looks through the dirty car window to a view of broad male shoulders. *What in God's name, Adela?* Just as well she hasn't told Philippa that she's off on a road trip around Morocco with a car full of strange men. But Omar's been on his best behaviour since the shower incident. Like a brother. And he knows Morocco like the back of his hand. It makes sense for him to be her guide. It's much better than trying to travel around Morocco alone.

She follows Omar around to the front of the car. Yassine reaches out through the driver's window and grips Addy's hand.

'My sister, you are welcome. I'm happy to be the driver for you. I am at your disposition.'

A turban in colours of red, yellow and green sits on his head like a balled-up flag. His sharp face splits into a leering grin and he brushes his thumb against her palm. Omar barks at him in Tamazight. Yassine shrugs and releases her hand. He turns to fiddle at the radio's volume control.

Addy frowns at Omar.

'It will be fine, Adi. Yassine is a good driver. I'll watch him well so he don't disturb you.'

The back door behind Yassine swings open. The smiling boy with the white-skinned cheek from Mohammed's restaurant presses his hand onto his chest and touches his lips with his mottled fingers. '*Sbah lkhir*. I Amine.'

'I'm Addy. I recognise you from your uncle's restaurant. You speak English?'

He makes an O with his thumb and finger. 'Leetle English.'

Addy peers past Amine and waves at her landlord, Mohammed, who's busy rolling a cigarette. The loose tobacco showers his djellaba with brown flakes.

'Hello, Mohammed. I didn't know you were joining us. Have you been away?'

'Yes, I do much business in Marrakech. You are enjoying the house? You like it well?'

'Oh, yes. There was an issue with the plumbing, but Omar's sorted it out. The house is lovely. It's *zwina*.'

Mohammed laughs. 'You hear that, Omar? My house is beautiful. It's very good Arabic. Come, madame, sit beside Amine. It's plenty of room.'

Amine scrunches up next to Mohammed and Addy slides into the back seat. She reaches for the seat belt but finds only a frayed end.

'I don't seem to have a seat belt.'

Yassine eyes Addy in the rear-view mirror. 'It's better to be free. It's Moroccan manner.'

Omar swings into the front passenger seat and loops his arm around the headrest. 'Everybody's happy?' He slaps his chest with the flat of his hand. 'I am Omar. I am your tour guide. Today we go to the beautiful place of Essaouira by the ocean *d'Atlantique* for the big festival of Gnaoua music. Essaouira is very famous because Jimi Hendrix lived there a long time ago.'

'Omar used to have hair like Jimi Hendrix,' Yassine says as he reverses the car down the lane, narrowly missing the donkey tied to the olive tree.

Omar rifles through the stack of bootleg CDs in photocopied sleeves littering the dashboard. 'Not Jimi Hendrix. Like Bob Marley.' He ejects the Amazigh singer and slips in a CD. 'Hotel California' jangles into the car.

'Dreadlocks? Really?'

'Yes, it was in my eyes like a sheep. Now I'm a man and I'm serious.'

'You pray five times every day?' Mohammed asks.

'My mother and my sister pray for me. I will be a good Muslim one day when I'm older. I will grow a long beard like my uncle's brother-in-law, Farouk.'

'I didn't know you had an uncle.'

Omar digs a pair of aviator sunglasses out of the glove compartment and puts them on. 'I have many relatives everywhere in Morocco, Adi. It's normal. Farouk is the brother of my aunt who's the wife of my uncle Rachid. His wife died when she had a baby, so he lives close to my uncle's family in Casa.'

Addy's ears prick up. 'What happened to the baby?'

'He lives with Farouk. He has a sister as well. Malika. They are small children. It's a pity. Farouk looks for a new wife.'

'Oh.' Small children. Not Hanane's child. It's like Hanane and her baby have disappeared into thin air. 'Where's Casa?'

105

'Casablanca,' Mohammed says. 'We say Casa. It's more easier.'

Casablanca. Humphrey Bogart in a white dinner jacket nursing a Scotch while Dooley Wilson plays the piano. Ingrid Bergman being luminous.

'Casa is not so far from Essaouira,' Omar says. 'It's fine for you to drive there, Yassine? Or we can take the bus.'

Yassine catches Addy's eyes in the rear-view mirror. '*Marhaba*. It's my pleasure to drive Adi to the moon if she like.'

Omar mutters under his breath and adjusts the rear-view mirror until his eyes meet Addy's. 'That's better.'

'Yassine needs to see the road behind him, Omar.'

'It doesn't matter what is behind, Adi. Life is only forward, isn't it?'

On the outskirts of Marrakech, Yassine pulls into the car park of a hulking aluminium-panelled megastore. Addy's head throbs from the onslaught of Yassine's CDs and the hair-raising journey: most of the drive in fifth gear on a narrow potholed road at 180 kilometres an hour. A miracle they haven't ended up splats on the road to Marrakech.

She presses her fingers to her temples. The veins throb under her fingertips. 'What are we doing here? I thought we were going to stop for lunch somewhere.'

'Soon,' Omar says as he climbs out of the car. 'We need to buy some stuff for Essaouira.'

Addy's T-shirt sticks to her back. Dust grits her contact lenses and she rubs her eyes as she watches Mohammed, Yassine and Amine disappear through the sliding doors of the store. Drops of sweat trickle down her cheek and she fans her face with her straw hat.

'I don't need anything in the store. I'll just wait in the car.'

'Are you sure, Adi? It's cooler inside.'

'I'm sure.' A few minutes to herself. In the quiet. On her own. That's what she wants.

'As you like.'

Omar heads towards the store, leaving Addy sitting alone in the back of the black Renault, the sweat trickling down her cheeks.

Mohammed emerges from the store, his brown djellaba flapping around him in the warm breeze. Addy leans against a petrol pump in the shade of the service station canopy, fanning her face with her hat.

'Madame, you will come inside? It's very cooler there. We buy some Coca-Cola.'

Addy wipes a trickle of sweat from her hot cheek. She nods. Sometimes she could be too stubborn for her own good.

'I need to use the loo, anyway.'

She follows Mohammed across the melting asphalt towards the sliding doors.

'Mohammed? Have you lived in Zitoune all your life?'

'Yes, my family comes from Zitoune for many years.'

The doors slide open and an icy blast of air blows into their faces. Addy follows Mohammed down a wide aisle stacked with French groceries and household goods.

'Do you remember a woman named Hanane and an Irishman from around 1984? I'm trying to track her down.'

'This would be something to remember, for sure. Why do you look for this lady?'

'It's a long story. But I think they may have been married. Or, if not married, I think they had a child.'

'If this lady had a baby and she wasn't married, this would be very bad for her.'

'I know. I'm trying to figure out what happened.'

'This is a strange story to hear. How do you know this story?'

'The Irishman was my father.'

Mohammed shakes his head. 'I don't know these people. I'm sorry for that.'

They find Omar, Yassine and Amine in the liquor section stacking cans of beer and bottles of cheap whisky into a shopping trolley.

'Alcohol? We stopped for alcohol?'

'It's very hard for Moroccans to buy alcohol,' Yassine says as he stacks six-packs of Heineken into the trolley. 'It's only a few places to buy it.'

'I thought you weren't supposed to drink alcohol.'

Yassine shrugs. '*Mashi mushkil.*'

'Right, well, in for a penny, in for a pound.' Addy walks past Omar and grabs two cheap bottles of Moroccan white wine from the shelf.

Omar touches her shoulder and leads her to the next aisle. 'Adi, it's better if you don't drink alcohol. They'll think you're not a good lady. I'm so sorry for that. It's the way it is here.'

'Wait a minute. I like wine. I drink it all the time in London. I don't see why I need to stop just because you're worried about what the others will think of me.'

'I'm so, so sorry, Adi. I'm just thinking for your reputation.'

'Oh, please.' She moves past him and places the bottles into the trolley. 'I need to find the ladies'. I'll meet you outside.'

'Wait.' Omar takes hold of her elbow. 'Can you come to the *caisse*?'

'Why?'

Omar looks over at Yassine, who's in the gin section checking prices on the largest bottles.

'Yassine, you go to the *caisse* with the alcohol. We'll come soon.'

'Okay, my friend.' Yassine adds two bottles of cheap gin to the trolley. '*Allons-y*, Amine, *pousses.*'

Amine pushes the trolley out of the liquor section as Yassine and Mohammed steer it around the carefully stacked displays.

'Omar, don't worry about the money for the wine. My wallet's in my bag. I'll pay you later. I'm not a freeloader.'

'Don't worry for that.' He digs into his back pocket and hands Addy a wad of dirham notes from his wallet.

She stares at the stack of dirty bills in her hand. 'What's this for?'

'It's for the alcohol. It's not only my money. It's from Yassine and Mohammed also.'

'What am *I* supposed to do with it?'

'I'm so, so sorry, Adi. A foreigner must buy it.' Omar sighs. 'If it was just you and me, we wouldn't be in this situation. Mohammed and Yassine insist for the alcohol. You'll have good honour with them.'

'Good honour if I buy it, but not if I drink it.'

'Amazigh ladies don't drink alcohol.'

'I'm not an Amazigh lady.'

'You're a good lady, anyway. I know it well. I want them to know it well also. You can drink it when we're private if you like.'

'And if I say no?'

'You can say no if you like. It's not such a good situation for you, I can feel it well.' Omar regards Addy, then he reaches for the wad of dirhams in her hand. 'Never mind. I'm so, so sorry. I apologise one million per cent. I put you in a bad situation.'

Addy clutches at the money and stuffs it into her pocket.

'No, it's fine. This isn't my country and I don't make the rules. As long as you can find me cold Coca-Cola, I won't drink wine in front of the others and I'll buy the alcohol. Just this once.'

Omar nods. 'You're a hard lady sometimes, Adi, but your heart is soft.' He brushes a drop of sweat off her red cheek. 'I will find you the coldest Coca-Cola in Morocco, even if I have to go across the desert to *Algérie* for it.'

109

# *Chapter Seventeen*

### The Road to Essaouira, Morocco – May 2009

Addy follows Omar from the roadside café back to Yassine's car, leaving the remains of a lunch of lamb and prune tagine congealing in the tagine pot on the table behind them. Yassine lights a rolled cigarette. The pungent scent of marijuana wafts towards her. She grabs at Omar's arm.

'Is he smoking a spliff?'

'Spliff?' Omar asks, chewing on a toothpick.

'You know, marijuana?'

He spits the toothpick into the dust. 'Oh yes, kief.'

'But, Omar, he's driving.'

'He always drives and smokes kief. He's used to it.'

'Omar! It's dangerous! And illegal.'

'Adi, many peoples smoke kief in Morocco. I know somebody in the mountains near Chefchaouen who has a big farm to grow it.'

'It's legal to grow marijuana here?'

'Not really, but what can we do? In the Rif Mountains it's very dry. Not even the olive trees grow there well. Only the kief will grow, so many peoples grow it. It must be like that to survive. Sometimes the police ask for money. People come from Europe to buy it if you can make it into hashish. My friend, he does that and makes a lot of money, not like the simple kief farmers. His son goes to university in Tangier to be a politician.'

'You've got a friend who's a drug dealer?'

'Don't worry. I meet him in Zitoune. I was his tour guide with his family. He's a normal man.'

Mohammed joins them and hands Omar a can of Heineken.

'*Shukran bezzef*, Mohammed.'

'*Marhaba.*'

Mohammed meanders over to the car where Yassine's sharing the spliff with Amine and doles them out cans of beer. The lamb tagine churns in Addy's stomach.

'Omar, Yassine's drinking alcohol. He can't drive. What if the police stop us?'

'Adi, don't worry.' Omar pulls the ring off his beer can and tosses it on the ground.

Addy stoops over and picks it up, handing it back to him.

'Morocco would be beautiful without all the rubbish lying around.'

Omar twirls the ring around his finger. 'I apologise. It's true what you say.' He pockets the ring and lifts his arm to take a swig.

'You're not going to drink that, are you?'

'Why not? It's so hotter here. I'm thirsty.'

'You need to drive us to Essaouira. Everybody else is drunk or stoned or both. Look at them.'

Mohammed's sprawled across the back seat sucking long draughts from the spliff. Yassine fiddles with the CD volume as he swigs from Amine's beer while Amine giggles in the driver's seat. Bob Marley's 'One Love' blasts out of the speakers.

Omar sighs. 'Okay, Adi. I can drive for your honour.' He strides over to Mohammed and kicks the sole of the older man's shoe. 'Mohammed, have some more beer.'

Mohammed leans on his elbows, the spliff hanging like a long white tooth from his lips.

'*Shukran bezzef*, Omar. You are my friend. My brother.'

Omar opens Yassine's door. 'Amine. Yassine. Sit in the back with Mohammed. I will drive to Essaouira. Adi will be my copilot.'

'You drive?' Yassine says as he peers at Omar blearily.

Omar presses his hand against his chest. 'Please, Yassine. It's for the honour of Adi.'

Yassine's mouth forms into a leering grin as he squints at Addy. 'For this reason I would give you all the cars in Morocco.'

He and Amine stumble out of the car and stagger into the back seat, sandwiching Mohammed between them. Addy slides into the passenger seat and turns down the volume.

Omar turns the key in the ignition. 'It's too loud for you?'

'I want "One Love" to give me some love, not destroy my hearing.'

Omar grinds the gears. The car hops forwards and lurches to a stop. Addy stares over at him.

'You do know how to drive, don't you?'

'I'm so, so sorry. I never had the opportunity to learn it. Not many peoples have cars in Zitoune.'

Addy rubs her throbbing forehead. 'Shove over, Omar. Let's see if I remember how to drive a manual car.'

The car resonates with the snores of Omar's friends. Omar sits next to Addy, his hand over hers on the gear lever. He follows her movements as she shifts gears. She catches him looking at her in the rear-view mirror.

A yawn in the back of the car. Omar moves his hand back to his lap and looks out of the window. The concrete block walls of half-finished buildings grow larger on the horizon as Addy drives towards them. A mass of children in white smocks emerges from one of the buildings. The children move off in different directions, their leather schoolbags flapping against their hips.

A car flashes them as she drives through the town.

'*Habss.*' Omar reaches over his seat and shakes Yassine's shoulder. 'It's police ahead. Yassine, Mohammed, wake up. Amine. Wake up.'

A tinny clang and crush of beer cans as they struggle out of their doped sleep. Omar points to a half-finished concrete building with a rusty fuel pump sprouting from the dirt in front.

'Adi, go there behind the station of gas. Do it quick.'

She swings the car across the road and down a bumpy track beside the petrol station. Pulling up on a patch of waste ground, she turns off the engine. Tattered plastic bags stick to the branches of a dead tree, and plastic water bottles and Coca-Cola cans glint amongst the dust and chunks of discarded concrete. The men fling open the car doors, kicking beer cans out into the rubble. Yassine kneels on the back seat and flicks kief roaches out of the car door.

A row of metal spikes is lined up on the asphalt like the teeth of a prehistoric dinosaur. A police car stands on either side of the road. A couple of white-gloved police officers in navy uniforms stand in the middle of the road, white gun holsters sitting on their hips.

A heavyset police officer with a thick black moustache waves the black Renault over to the roadside. Addy's stomach spasms as she parks the car. Omar squeezes her hand on the gear stick. The black plastic knob is slick with her sweat.

The police officer removes a pad and pen from his pocket. Addy watches him in the mirror as he circles the car, peering inside as he passes the windows. He approaches Addy's window and gestures for her to get out. She steps out into the dust and hears Omar's door open. Omar hurries around the car and holds out his hand, greeting him politely. The police officer ignores him and addresses Addy in Arabic.

She shakes her head. 'English.'

He repeats himself, slapping the palm of his gloved hand with the notepad.

'I'm sorry. I don't understand.'

'Your licence of driving,' Omar says. 'Show it to him.'

'It's in the boot, Omar. In my bag.' With the alcohol.

He inclines his head almost imperceptibly. 'No problem, darling. I'll get it.'

He says something to the police officer and heads towards the boot. The police officer follows. Yassine swings open his door and jumps out of the car, waving three identity cards. He retrieves the registration documents and his driver's licence from the glove compartment as he keeps up a stream of Arabic. The police officer scans the documents and beckons him over to the police car.

Omar thrusts Addy's leather overnight bag at her. 'Here, honey.'

She roots around her clothes until she find her wallet. She hands her driver's licence to Omar.

'Give him some money, Adi.'

'What?'

'I'm sorry. It's the Moroccan manner. Give him some money. One hundred dirhams.'

Addy's heart's beating so hard she's sure that even in his car the policeman can hear it. 'That's bribery.'

Omar lifts a one hundred dirham note out of her wallet. 'If he asks you, say you don't know about the money.' He folds the bill between his fingers. 'Give me your passport.'

Addy unzips a compartment in her bag and retrieves her passport.

'It's not so safe there. In Essaouira there are many thiefs.'

Omar strides over to the police car. A thin policeman with a concave chest and a sour expression joins them. He flicks his eyes back to Addy as he scans the documents. She rubs her arms nervously and gets back in the car.

'Water?' Mohammed offers Addy a large bottle of water.

She drinks thirstily and hands him back the bottle.

'It's no problem for the police, Madame Adi.' Mohammed points the water bottle at the police car. 'It happen all the time like that in Morocco. Many peoples go to the festival. The police look for terrorists.'

'Terrorists?'

'Yes, it's many peoples at the festival so the police are careful for that.'

'The festival is a terrorist target?'

114

He swigs from the bottle and passes it to Amine. 'No problem, Madame Adi. If it's fate, it's fate.'

'Fate?' Omar slides into the passenger seat and drops the documents into Addy's lap. 'What's fate?'

'Mohammed's saying that if we get blown up by a bomb in Essaouira, it's our fate.'

'*Mashi mushkil*, honey. Then we can go to Paradise together.'

'Maybe we shouldn't go to Essaouira if it's dangerous. We can go back to Marrakech or go straight on to Casablanca.'

'No, no, it's not dangerous, excuse me.' Mohammed leans over the driver's seat. 'Many police are there. So, no problem.'

Amine nods vigorously. 'No problem. Gnaoua music very good.'

Omar squeezes Addy's hand. 'Don't worry. I'm your bodyguard. Nobody can touch you.'

Yassine emerges from the police car. He walks towards the Renault, his arm around the police officer. They're laughing. Yassine shakes the man's hand and slides into the back seat. The police officer waves for Addy to move on.

She quickly turns the key in the ignition. The gear stick slips in her sweaty palm and the car stalls. The sour-faced policeman steps in front of the car and holds up his white-gloved hand.

'*Attendez. Pas assez vite. Ouvrez le coffre.*'

'What's he saying? What's *le coffre*?'

'*Merde*. He wants to see in back of the car.' Omar jumps out of the car. '*Mashi mushkil, mashi mushkil.*'

Addy switches off the ignition and watches in the rear-view mirror as Omar opens the boot. The car's boot rises, obscuring them from view. Addy catches Yassine's gaze in the mirror. His face is like a mask, stiff with panic.

Omar appears at her window. 'Adi, you can come out, please?'

She licks her lips; dry as chalk. She follows Omar to the rear and looks into the boot. Beer cans, bottles of liquor and the two bottles of wine, wedged between the knapsacks and her bag.

\*

Addy looks at the policeman. 'It's mine. *C'est pour moi.*'

The policeman sweeps his hand over the boot's contents. '*Toutes sont pour vous?*' Is this all for you?

'*Oui.*'

The police officer huffs. '*C'est impossible.*'

She meets his unblinking gaze and juts out her chin. '*Je suis anglaise.*'

The policeman's eyes narrow and his lips curl into a sneer. He waves dismissively at Addy. '*Bon. Va-t-en.*'

# Chapter Eighteen

**Essaouira, Morocco – May 2009**

The whitewashed buildings of Essaouira shimmer in the heat. The doors and windows are painted bright blue. Wooden fishing boats the same vivid blue fill the harbour as densely as stepping stones in a garden. Squealing gulls glide overhead, eyeing their chance to steal a fish head or broken crab leg from the fishermen offloading their hauls.

Addy shields her eyes from the sun's glare as she looks out of the car window. 'Why's everything painted blue?'

'So the djinn can't come to make problems. The djinn don't like the blue colour. It's why Imazighen like the blue colour a lot. It's nice that you have the blue eyes, honey. It makes you lucky. The djinn don't like you well.'

'What are djinn?'

'They're like spirits. They can change their shape. They can be an animal or a person. They can be good or bad. Sometimes they can go inside somebody. You can see the djinni in the eyes. This is not a good thing when it happens. Some people have their own djinni they can control.'

'Like your grandmother,' Amine pipes up from the back seat. 'Everybody say she have a djinni.'

117

'It's true,' Omar says, 'but she don't call it often. Anyway, it's better not to disturb the djinn.'

Addy parks in a car park in the crenellated shadow of ancient stone fortifications. She shoves her camera and a couple of lenses into her leather overnight bag and slings it over her shoulder, rubbing her growling stomach as they head towards the blue-and-white open-fronted restaurants beside the harbour.

A mustachioed fish vendor in a white lab coat splattered with blood greets them effusively. He waves his hands in front of his display of glistening fish and sea creatures on an iced wooden table. Next to the display, fat slabs of fish grill over hot coals, the charring skins sizzling as the chef drizzles them with lemon juice and thick yellow olive oil. Addy captures images of the seafood and the vendors on her camera. She wanders over to the table Yassine and Amine have found and sits on the white plastic chair beside Amine. She focuses her lens on Omar and Mohammed as they haggle over the price of dinner with the fish vendor.

'Excuse me, Adi,' Amine says. 'I go for toilet.'

'*Mashy mushkey*, Amine.'

Addy sets down her bag by her feet and fusses with the zipper as she tries to avoid eye contact with Yassine. When she can't avoid it any longer, she sits up and fiddles with a turquoise and silver bracelet she'd bought in the Zitoune souk as she watches the gulls fight for discarded fish heads.

Yassine reaches across the table and taps the bracelet. 'I like this colour for you, Adi. It goes well with your eyes.'

Addy glances over to Omar, who's deep in conversation with Mohammed and the grill chef. Yassine follows her gaze.

'Omar is a good man. He's like my brother.' Yassine presses Addy's hand against the table with his palm.

Addy tugs her hand free and glares at Yassine. 'It seems everyone is everyone's brother in Morocco.'

'For us it's like real brothers. I drink the milk with Omar from his mother when I was a baby because my mother was died from me being born. So, we are tied like brothers of the blood.' He sits back and sweeps his eyes over her. 'You are very beautiful, Turquoise.'

'Don't call me that.'

The corners of Yassine's mouth turn up. The smile doesn't reach his eyes.

Omar arrives back at the table holding hands with an older man. He swings their hands up and kisses a ring on the man's finger.

'Adi, it's my uncle Rachid. He's the brother of my father. I told you about him before. He lives in Casa. He is a teacher of English for children.'

Addy presses her right hand against her chest and smiles. 'I'm very happy to meet you. Omar's told me about you.'

The same high cheekbones and amber eyes as his nephew, but shorter and stockier, and there are twists of grey in his close-cropped curly black hair. Grey flannel trousers and highly polished black shoes peek out from underneath Rachid's beige cotton djellaba, and a brown knapsack hangs over his shoulder.

Rachid touches his chest and his lips with his fingers. 'I am very happy to meet you, madame. Omar has been telling me all about you. I understand you're travelling around Morocco to take photographs for a book you are writing. How impressive. You must come to visit the Chouhad family of Casa. My daughters would be very excited to meet you. Maybe after Essaouira.'

'That would be lovely. We're planning to head to Casa in a few days anyway. Omar? What do you think?'

Omar grabs two white plastic chairs and hands one to Rachid. 'Inshallah. If it's our fate, then we will go. Sit beside Adi, Uncle, and we can talk altogether while we eat.' He sets his chair beside Yassine and glances at Addy and back to Yassine. His eyes narrow. 'Everything's all right?'

Yassine squirms in his chair. 'It's good. Adi, she is a nice lady. She is like the special flower in the desert.'

119

Omar leans towards Yassine until their noses almost touch. 'You be careful for Adi.'

Yassine laughs and stretches his arm across Omar's shoulders. 'I am your brother of the milk, Omar. I respect you well.'

Omar pushes Yassine's arm off his shoulders. 'Even if you are my brother, I will fight you like a lion if you disturb Adi.'

Mohammed sets down a large platter of grilled seafood on the blue-and-white checked oilcloth covering the wooden table.

'Everybody's okay?'

He shoves a plastic chair between Omar and Yassine and sits down. Amine appears with a plate of lemons and two large plastic bottles of Coca-Cola. A boy arrives with a stack of mismatched plates and glasses.

They dig into the mound of steaming seafood. Addy sucks her fingers for every drop of the unctuous grease and lemon. Omar calls over to the restaurant owner and soon two more plates of grilled fish and seafood appear. She's never tasted food this good.

After the meal, they head towards the long stretch of beach that fans out in an arc in front of the town. A huge stage constructed of metal scaffolding is set up in the main square. Technicians mill around, fiddling with sound equipment. The whines and screams of feedback slice through the air. Vendors wander through the growing crowd selling knitted caps with fake dreadlocks to clusters of squabbling boys.

Addy kneels and takes her camera and her wide-angle lens out of her big leather bag. She changes the lens and focuses her camera on the white buildings glowing golden in the late afternoon sunlight.

Feedback screams from the speakers. The Rolling Stones' 'Start Me Up' blasts out over the square. Addy thrusts her bag into Omar's hands. She reaches out her arms and twirls around the square. The fresh breeze caresses her face and the salty air fills her lungs.

Omar laughs. 'You're crazy, Adi,' he shouts.

She can't stop smiling. In this moment she's free and everything is as it should be.

They lose Yassine and Mohammed to a cheap bar by the water-front.

'As you like,' Omar says to them when they try to persuade the others to join them. 'It's not a nice place for Addy. We'll go to the souk to see some atmosphere. We'll come back in one hour and we can go for a walk on the beach and look for a place to sleep.'

The lanes of the souk are filled with backpackers and foreigners jostling among the crowds of Moroccans. At a crossroads of two lanes, Omar stops at a kefta stall. The owner's busy frying sweet-smelling onions on a grill. Omar signals for four sticks of the lamb meatballs as bodies push and jostle around Addy.

Omar divvies out the kefta to Rachid and Amine and thrusts one into Addy's hands.

'No, Omar. I'm full. I can't eat another bite.'

'You can. Enjoy, it's good. You're skinny yet.'

She licks at the garlicky grease trickling through her fingers and takes a bite of the succulent meat. Before long, there's nothing left but the stick.

Addy follows Omar and Rachid through the crowds, Amine bringing up the rear like a bodyguard. They pass by stalls laden with wooden trinkets carved from fragrant Moroccan thuja cedar wood, stands full of argan oil soaps and body creams, and stacks of colourful babouches and jewellery. She watches Omar as he laughs with his uncle. As he teases Amine. He's been on his best behaviour since the shower incident. Like a solicitous brother. Be careful what you wish for, she thinks. You might just get it. Why is it that now that she's killed any chance of a holiday romance, all she can think of is the feel of his lips on hers, his hand on her breast at the waterfalls, his moan as she kissed him on the veranda?

She dabs scented argan oil onto her wrist and waves it under Omar's nose. He smiles, but nothing more. She drapes a turquoise scarf embroidered with Amazigh symbols around her shoulders.

'*Bishhal*?' he calls over to the shop seller.

'*Miyat* dirhams.'

Omar frowns and holds up three fingers with one hand and makes an O with the other. '*Laa. Tlateen* dirhams.'

The negotiations gallop on across the heads of the shoppers, the shop seller refusing to budge. Omar reluctantly hands over a fifty dirham note.

Addy runs her fingers over the intricate embroidery. 'Thank you. It's lovely. It's like the one Hanane's wearing in the photo with my father. Maybe they bought hers here, too. I know they came to Essaouira.'

Omar holds the end of the scarf up to Addy's eyes. 'It makes your eyes the colour of the sea in the days of summer.' He kisses the scarf and lets it drop. 'The guy made a hard negotiation. If you like something it's better to tell me after we pass. Then I can go back after and pay Berber prices. If the seller sees you he will charge European prices.'

'Fifty dirhams is cheap.'

'If I was by myself I would pay ten dirhams. No reason to waste money, Adi. We're not in Europe here.'

African drums, flutes and tambourines spread on the pavement in a jumbled display outside a music shop. Grabbing a drum, Omar sits down on the pavement and wraps his legs around the clay casing.

'Can you give me your scarf, Adi?'

He hands her his baseball cap and wraps the scarf around his head into a turban. He starts a slow, steady beat on the drum.

'Amine, *Yalla*.' He gestures at a drum with his head.

Amine picks up a drum and perches beside Omar on the kerb. He starts drumming out a counter rhythm. His black nylon dread-locks bounce around his head as he pounds at the animal skin.

Addy places her leather bag between her feet, resting Omar's hat on it. She changes her lens again and focuses her camera on the two drummers, trying different angles, apertures and shutter speeds. The drumming quickens, the beat urgent. Her blood thrums to the beat. She watches Omar through the lens, stealing images of his hands, his eyes, his mouth.

'It's good?' Rachid asks as he claps on the offbeat.

Addy blushes as she lets the camera fall against her chest. 'I had no idea Omar played the African drums.'

'It's normal. Many Imazighen play the drums. It's in our blood.'

Omar begins to sing a song from one of Yassine's CDs: '*Sudani, wehey ay, Sudani, wehey ay.*'

Amine joins in. A woman in the crowd holds a hand up to her mouth and ululates. The shrill warble floats on the air like birdsong. A couple of small boys spin and dance, giggling as they catch the eyes of the foreign tourists. Addy joins in the clapping.

'You are enjoying Morocco?' Rachid asks as they clap out their different rhythms.

'Very much. Omar's a wonderful help.'

'Omar likes you very much.'

Addy glances at Rachid. 'Does he?'

'Your name is always on his lips. Adi. Adi. Adi. Perhaps you will marry him.'

'I . . . I . . .' Addy loses the beat.

'You have a big welcome in our family. But let me say one thing.' Rachid makes a gesture as if he's letting something small drop out of his fingers. 'When a pebble drops into a pond, the smooth water is disturbed. The waves grow larger and larger until the pond is no longer still. If you and Omar were to marry,' he places his hand on his chest, '*marhaba*, you are welcome in our family. But you must know you will be changed. Morocco is charming, but life here is not easy. Tourists don't see the real situation.'

*The chemo room and the looping tubes of the Red Devil. No one ever sees the real situation.*

'Life can be difficult anywhere.'

'It's true. But, Madame Adi, it is not only you who will change. You would be the pebble in the pond of Zitoune. Omar will change. His family will change. In some way, everyone you meet will change. Sometimes change is good.' Rachid shrugs. 'Sometimes change is not good. Many people find change difficult. Especially in Morocco. We are a very traditional country here.'

Addy regards Rachid's worried face. The African sun and the struggles of life have left their mark on him. Lines fan out from the corners of his golden-brown eyes and an indentation is etched in his forehead from years of squinting at the blinding sun.

'Are you saying I shouldn't encourage a relationship with Omar? Because you needn't worry—'

Rachid holds up a hand. 'No, no. Do not mistake me.' He touches his hand to his chest. 'I only ask that you understand that what you do with Omar affects us all.'

The song finishes. The crowd claps and whistles. Amine takes Omar's baseball cap from Addy and moves through the audience, soliciting for tips.

Omar sets the drum aside and stands, waving his arms like a conductor. '*Merci, tout le monde*. Thank you, everybody. If you like Berber music, come to the beautiful Cascades de Zitoune and ask for me, Omar. I will make you a good tour. *Si hablo español, français, Deutsch, italiano, English, Tamazight, Al-Arabiyah*.' He counts off the languages he speaks on his fingers. 'So, I will see you soon? Welcome to Morocco.'

Rachid's warning is like a splash of the icy Pacific water Addy had swum in as a child. She shivers involuntarily. Maybe Hanane's family hadn't approved of her father. He wasn't Moroccan. He wasn't a Muslim. He couldn't possibly have been the husband they would've wanted for her. Did they marry? Could they marry? Omar had told her that Muslim women are forbidden from marrying non-Muslim men. Was the baby illegitimate?

The water drop smashes through the pond's surface. Her father

124

couldn't have done that to Hanane and their baby. Or could he? He'd abandoned Essie and Philippa, but Essie's wealthy family were there to help. It would've been a catastrophe for Hanane. And for the baby. What kind of man was her father?

Omar hugs Addy, lifting her off the ground. 'So, you like Berber music?'

Addy pushes against his chest. 'Omar, put me down.'

He sets her down. 'What happened?'

'You're just my guide.'

'You've been talking to my uncle, isn't it?'

Rachid places his hand on Omar's shoulder. 'Adi is a good lady. I can see that well. You must treat her with respect.'

'Adi, you have to know with all my heart I respect you well. I say it in front of my uncle to be clear.'

Addy stares at Omar. She's the pebble. Just like her father.

# Chapter Nineteen

**Essaouira, Morocco – May 2009**

'There! There it is.'

Addy points to the round window framed with key stones in the tower's thick stone wall.

Omar takes Addy's hand and they climb the stone steps up to the fortified wall with Rachid and Amine close on their heels. They head up to the fortified tower. Waves crash on rocks below, turning the grey Atlantic water into a stew of swirling foam. They stop on the rampart. An old man, as grey and wizened as an old heron, breaks off bits of bread and tosses them over the water. The screaming gulls dive and fight each other for the scraps.

Addy looks down to the wall protecting the harbour from the crashing Atlantic waves. 'These fortifications don't look very Moroccan.'

'No, that's right,' Rachid says. 'It's Portuguese. From many years ago when Essaouira was called Mogador. It was a place for trading and for the Barbary corsairs.'

'Barbary corsairs?'

'Pirates. Very skilled. The navies of Europe avoided them as much as possible. They took many slaves from the coasts of Europe. It's said they even sailed across the Atlantic to Newfoundland to raid the coasts for slaves and concubines. The sultan and the administrators loved the ladies with white skin and red or yellow hair. It's one of the reasons you see fair, blue-eyed Berbers in the mountains sometimes.'

Omar hugs Addy against his side. 'I'm your Barbary corsair, Adi.' He brushes Addy's fringe from her eyes. 'You should grow your hair longer a bit. It would look lovely.'

She pulls away and steps towards the window, running her fingers through her short hair. 'I like it short.' If only he knew.

'*Mashi mushkil*. I'm sorry if I say something wrong.' He points at the round window. 'It's a nice view there, *habibati*. It's lovely for your book.'

The same view exactly as in her father's photo. Just missing his and Hanane's clasped hands. Addy kneels on the stone and focuses her lens, capturing the diving gulls and the view of the town through the window, while Rachid contemplates the horizon, and Omar and Amine straddle a European cannon, teasing the gulls as they pretend to toss sandwich crumbs into the sea.

They leave Amine trailing after the technicians by the stage and head down stone steps dusted with sand to the beach. Addy hands Rachid her leather bag as she leans on Omar to remove her sandals. Her feet sink into the warm sand.

He grabs Rachid's hand and holds it aloft. 'You see, Adi? In Morocco, it's normal for men to hold hands. Even to hug each other and to kiss each other. But it's *haram* to do this with ladies unless you are private with your wife.'

'What do you mean, *haram*?'

'It means it's sinful,' Rachid says as he slips the strap of Addy's bag over his shoulder.

Omar slides his fingers through hers. Addy extricates her fingers from his grip.

'This is not a problem for me for you to hold hands,' Rachid says. '*Marhaba*.'

'You know I don't mind for peoples, Adi.' Omar grasps her hand. 'If I want to hold the hand of my wife, then I will.'

Addy chokes and tugs her hand free. 'Your wife?'

'You are like my wife in my heart, even yet.'

Rachid pats his nephew on the back. 'When you have your wedding you can have your celebration in my house in Casa. My wife and daughters will be very happy for that.'

'Wait a minute . . .'

Omar tuts. 'No, no, Uncle. The wedding will be in my house that I will build in Zitoune, one hundred per cent.'

'Hold on, hold on.' Addy stops short, her feet sinking into the sand. 'Omar, you'd have to ask me first.'

Omar winks at his uncle and they both laugh. 'Adi, in Morocco it doesn't matter to ask the lady. I must ask your father. If he says yes, then we go. If he says no, then no problem. I find another lady.'

'My father's in Paradise already.'

Rachid presses his hand against his heart. 'I'm so sorry for your father. Maybe you have a brother?'

'No. No brother.'

'An uncle?'

'No. I have an older half-sister, though. She'd be happy to sign me over.'

Rachid shakes his head sadly. 'This is a problem. There is nobody to ask.'

'I guess you'd just have to ask me, then, Omar.'

Omar scratches this forehead. 'This is not the Moroccan tradition, Adi. So, since you have no man to protect you, I will carry you away with me to be my wife, like a Barbary corsair.' He picks her up and throws her over his shoulder like a sack.

Addy slaps him on the back with her sandals. 'Put me down. I'm heavy.'

'Not so heavy. It's easy for me.' He anchors her over his shoulder with one arm across the back of her knees.

128

'Omar, we're attracting attention.'

'*Mashi mushkil*. If they say something, I will say you're my wife and you make me troubles.' He turns to Rachid. 'So, Uncle, your family is well? My aunt is well? My cousins are well?'

Addy pounds the back of Omar's green denim jacket. 'Omar! This is embarrassing.'

Omar releases his grip and Addy slips down the front of his body until her feet touch the sand.

'Thank you.'

'*Mashi mushkil*.' He leans over and rubs his back, groaning exaggeratedly. 'Anyway, I don't want to marry you any more.'

'Oh, really? Why's that?'

'You are heavy like potatoes.'

'What?!'

Rachid says something to Omar in Tamazight and Omar rubs his chin, nodding.

'What did he say?'

'My uncle made me a good offer to be your husband, Adi. You can be his second wife. You can live with my aunt and my cousins. They will teach you well how to cook and to clean to be a good wife.'

Addy presses her hand against her heart and smiles her most winning smile at Rachid. 'Thank you, Rachid. You are most kind. I will consider your proposal and let you know.'

Rachid bows his head and touches his hand to his chest. '*Marhaba*, Madame Adi. I await your answer with anticipation.'

Omar drops his arm across Addy's shoulders and pulls her against him. 'Okay, okay. I don't like this joke any more. I'm jealous.'

Addy pokes Omar's arm. 'You said I was as heavy as potatoes.'

'I'm joking with you, darl . . . Adi. You are skinny yet. You must eat well to be fatter like the Amazigh dancers. It's good to be healthy. Even if you are heavy like an elephant I don't mind. Then if I lift you, you will crush me and I will die and go to Paradise happy.'

Omar slips his fingers between hers and they continue their walk along the beach, the sun turning the waves to molten gold as the first fingers of orange streak across the sky.

Had Gus and Hanane walked along this beach, hand in hand, ignoring the curious stares of onlookers? Had they seen the town's lights slowly flutter on as the day faded into night? Seen the way the sea turned gold in the waning sunlight? They'd been here. On this beach. She could feel it. If only she could find someone who remembered them.

# Chapter Twenty

Yassine and Mohammed have their arms around two women. Amine trails behind them, dreadlocks from his new cap bouncing around his face like tassels. The women are young. They wear tight skinny jeans and sleeveless T-shirts with D & G and Chanel spelled out across their breasts in gold sequins. Their high-heeled sandals leave peg marks in the sand like the tracks of a wounded animal. Their long black hair lashes through the wind, tangling around their designer sunglasses and sticking to their glossy red lips.

'Hello, my brother,' Yassine says to Omar. 'We find some nice ladies of Essaouira. It's Layla and Nabila. They are sisters.'

Omar greets the women in Arabic. Addy offers her hand and one of the girls gives it a limp shake.

'Hello, my name's Addy,' she says in French. 'Do you speak English?'

'*Un peu*. Leetle English. I am Layla.' She gestures to the other girl. 'My sister, Nabila. I have twenty-three years. Nabila have twenty-one years.'

'Your English is very good.' Addy extends her hand to Nabila, who releases her grip on Mohammed's arm to shake the tips of Addy's fingers. She has long nail extensions painted magenta.

131

'Okay, we go.' Omar grabs Addy's hand and strides ahead.

'What's the matter?'

'I don't like those ladies.'

'Why not?'

'They're Arab ladies. Not Amazigh ladies.'

Mohammed catches up to them, puffing with the effort.

'Omar, wait!'

He's abandoned Layla to his nephew. Amine is trying to keep Layla from toppling over without touching her, waving his hands around her body as she teeters through the sand.

'It's good, it's good,' Mohammed says as Rachid joins them. 'We can have a place at the apartment of the girls. It's very cheaper. It's hard to find a place in Essaouira. Many peoples come for the festival.'

Omar shakes his head, the crease running between his eyebrows. 'I don't like it.'

Mohammed rests his arm on Omar's shoulders, his fake Rolex and heavy silver rings glinting in the fading light. 'My friend, my friend. It will be fine. It is good we found a place to sleep. No necessity to worry.'

Omar shoves Mohammed's arm off his shoulders. 'No way. No possibility of that.' He heads off towards the stone steps to the promenade, pulling Addy behind him.

'It's true,' Rachid says as he catches up to Omar. 'I have been looking for a room since I arrived this morning for my interview at the school, but no success.'

'It's no problem, Uncle. We'll find another place.'

Addy glances over at Omar as he hurries her along the promenade towards the car. The lines of his angular face are sharp with tension.

'What is it, Omar? What's the matter?'

'I don't like you to be with those ladies.'

'Just because they're Arab and not Amazigh?'

'It's no problem they are Arab.'

132

'Then what?'

Omar stops short. 'They're whores.'

Omar orders Addy a *nus nus* coffee and a mille-feuille from the bow-tied waiter at a café table on the square by the harbour. They strike up a conversation in Arabic and the waiter scribbles something down on the back of the receipt. Omar slips the paper into his back pocket and hoists his knapsack over his shoulder.

'Enjoy your pastry, Adi. Rachid and I will go to see some rooms.'

'What about Amine?'

'He stayed with his uncle. It's his choice. Rachid and I will come back soon.'

Addy roots through the clothes in her leather overnight bag for her diary. Her finger catches on a jagged slice in the leather.

She lurches to her feet and tears the clothes out of the bag, tossing them onto the black metal chair. No wallet. No passport. She finds her cell phone inside a shoe. Dead. Her laptop is there, too. Her heart pounds as she scans the square for Omar and Rachid. The waiter approaches from the café carrying a tray with a small glass of coffee and the pastry. He sets the items onto the mosaic-topped table and hands Addy the bill. He eyes the pile of clothes on the chair as he hovers beside her.

'*Pas de monnaie.*' Addy points in the direction Omar has disappeared. '*Il a le monnaie.*' Heat spreads across her face. 'I don't have money. He has the money.'

The waiter shrugs and walks back into the café.

She flops into a chair and tries to let the cries of the gulls and street vendors numb her escalating panic. What has she done? What if this has all been a huge set-up? Didn't Philippa warn her about trusting Moroccan men? And those two girls. Maybe they were in on it, too. Naive. You're so naive, Addy. Think. Think.

Her hands shake as she tears open a sugar sachet. The brown

133

crystals drop like pebbles through the milky foam. Breathe, Addy. Breathe, drink the coffee, find the police.

Hands cover Addy's eyes. She screams and jolts out of the chair.

'Adi, what happened?'

'Jesus Christ, Omar. Don't ever do that. You scared the life out of me.'

'Darling! Don't swear. It's not nice.'

'Sorry. You surprised me.' She collapses into the chair. 'And stop ordering me around. Say "Please don't swear." It's politer.'

'Sorry. Jesus is a prophet of Islam as well. We call him Isa. I feel bad if you swear his name like that.'

'Sorry. You sound like my mother.' Addy holds up her leather bag. 'Someone slashed my bag. My wallet and passport are gone.'

Omar runs his finger along the slash in the brown leather. He frowns. 'Yes, it's a knife that did this, for sure. Did you lose anything else? Your phone? Your camera is fine?'

'My camera's here. It's just the wallet and passport. It must have happened when we were in the souk. I remember getting pushed around when you were buying the kefta.'

'So, no problem.'

'What do you mean by that?'

Omar sets down the leather bag. He unbuttons a pocket on the leg of his jeans and places Addy's wallet and passport on the table.

'You gave them to me when the police stopped us. I said Essaouira has many thiefs.'

'Thank God.'

Addy picks up the passport and flips to the photo page. Her unsmiling face peers back. Her hair's long and curly. Pre-Red Devil.

'It's your passport, yes? You don't want to check your money is there? Maybe you think I'm a thief, as well. I can see it.'

'I'm sorry. For a minute I thought . . .' She shakes her head and hands him back her passport. 'Sorry. Here, you better keep it until I get a new bag.'

'*Mashi mushkil.*' He slides the passport back into his pocket. A vein in his temple throbs. He opens Addy's wallet and counts out twenty dirhams in change. Addy grunts and he glances at her. 'Your money is my money. My money is your money, Adi. Same same.'

'Right.'

Addy chews the mille-feuille as Omar piles her clothes back into the leather bag. How much does she really know about Omar? In Zitoune he sometimes disappears for days. And the phone calls. So many phone calls. Who are the callers? He said he had a friend who was a drug dealer. And Yassine is hardly a pillar of virtue. Should she get her passport back? But, it would be rude to ask now, after she's just given it to him. She'll get it tonight. She pushes the plate with the pastry away and looks at Omar. What has she got herself into?

'Where's your uncle?'

'We found a flat in the souk. It's a recommendation of the waiter. Rachid is having tea with the owner lady. She insist for it. I am your guardian angel, Adi. You have to know it.'

'You know about guardian angels?'

'For sure.' He holds up his hand and counts off his fingers. 'Jibrail, Mikail, Israafiyl – a lots of angels.'

'Gabriel, Michael, Raphael. Same angels. We're not so different, really.'

'Not really. But a bit.' He tucks Addy's leather bag securely under his arm. 'Are you fine, Adi? I will walk slow for you.'

'What do you mean?'

'I looked at your passport. You have forty years. It's close to be the age of my mother.'

'That would've made her seven when she had you.'

Omar laughs. 'Forty, fifty, sixty. I don't know for age. It's no problem for me, *habibati*. I don't mind you are older. We are lucky to be on the earth together. I could have been born one hundred years ago. Then we don't meet each other. This would be the tragedy of our lives.'

\*

135

That evening, they meet up with the others in front of the stage in the square. Omar wears his blue tagelmust and embroidered blue gown, and he grips Addy's hand as he parts the crowd like a blue-sailed ship cutting through the waves of Moroccans and tourists.

Yassine's yellow, red and green turban bobs amongst the crowd in front of the stage. He wears a blue gown like Omar's and Nabila is tucked under his arm like a bright red package. Layla leans against Mohammed, smoking a thin cigarette as she pulls strands of wayward hair out of her lip gloss with her lacquered nails. Addy spies Amine perching on the stage scaffolding like a bird, his fake dreadlocks bouncing to some inner rhythm.

Yassine pulls Omar to him in an embrace. 'Hello, my brother. What happened for you? Why you didn't come with us to the house of the ladies?'

'I found another flat with Adi and Rachid.'

Yassine shrugs. '*Mashi mushkil.*' His eyes dart down to Omar's hand, and his eyebrow twitches when he sees Omar's and Addy's entwined fingers. 'You spent a good time in Essaouira, Turquoise? Omar was a good guide?'

Addy glances at Omar, but he's chatting with Mohammed and hasn't heard the nickname.

'Yes, thank you. I took a lot of photos for my book. Rachid told us all about the Barbary corsairs.'

'Ah, the pirates of Morocco,' Mohammed says. 'They were the kings of the ocean.'

Addy nods at Amine. 'Amine already has the pirate dreadlocks. He could be a Barbary corsair.'

'My nephew? He is only a boy and he has the skin of a leopard. The corsairs must be brave and handsome. Like Omar.' Mohammed taps his broad chest. A gold tooth glints as he smiles. 'Or me.'

Omar waves his hand impatiently. 'I don't mind for corsairs and sultans and harems. It's all in the dust now.'

'You are not a man of history and romantic stories, Omar?' Rachid asks.

'History is finished. It's only today that is important. But I am romantic in my own manner.'

Yassine leans towards Addy, garlic and beer wafting from his hot breath. 'It is easy to be romantic with Adi because she is so beautiful.'

Omar pushes Yassine's shoulder, knocking him off balance. '*Allah i naal dine omok*,' Omar swears.

Nabila teeters on her heels and unleashes a stream of irritated Arabic.

'Be careful, my brother,' Yassine says as he regains his footing. 'If you curse my mother, you curse your mother. We are brothers of the milk.'

'Be fine, Omar,' Rachid warns, resting his hand on Omar's shoulder.

'I'll be fine, Uncle. But you' – he points his finger at Yassine – 'you must be careful like a rabbit from the eagle. You are my friend from a long time, Yassine, but I will fight with you if you disturb me, Yassine, one hundred per cent.'

A band of Senegalese musicians beat out a trance-like rhythm on African drums and cymbals. The lead singer sings out and the other singers respond in low, repetitive tones, moving and swaying to the hypnotic rhythm. Another group of musicians ambles onto the stage. Black-skinned Tuareg Berbers from Mali, dressed in blue gowns and turbans. The music becomes a thunder of drumming. The crowd's infected by the drug of the beat. Addy's feet and hands join the percussion. The music dampens down the friction between Omar and Yassine. In the square on a warm spring night, they all become the beat, and the beat becomes the world, and the world is a fishing village on the Atlantic coast in Morocco.

# Chapter Twenty-One

**Zitoune, Morocco – January 1984**

Gus holds the small tin teapot high in the air, watching in deep concentration as the tea streams into the small tea glass on the low wooden table. The remains of a chicken tagine sit in a tagine pot with a stack of dirty plates under the hulking wooden frame of the olive press.

'You've been practising,' Hanane says in French.

Lifting the spout, he hovers the teapot over a second glass, aiming carefully. 'You have no idea how much tea I've wasted learning to do this.' He sets down the teapot and reaches for a glass, offering it to Hanane.

She sips at the steaming liquid. 'Very good. Sweet. You made it the Moroccan way.'

'It tastes better that way.'

She sets down the glass and moves to rise from the striped donkey-blanket cushions he's strewn over a cactus silk rug on the beaten earth floor.

Gus rests his hand on her arm. 'Where are you going?'

'To wash the plates and the tagine.'

'I'll do it later, Hanane. You're my guest. What kind of host would I be if I made you do the washing-up? Besides, there's no

138

water here. You'd have to wash them in the river and it's cold out there. And the middle of the night.'

Hanane sits back on the cushion. 'I almost didn't come.'

A gentle squeeze on her arm, or did she imagine it? His hand drops to his knee.

'Then I'd have had to eat all this myself. I'm a very good cook.'

Hanane smiles. 'You're okay for a man.'

Gus pulls a face of exaggerated disappointment. 'Just okay? I think that's called damning with faint praise.'

Hanane draws her eyebrows together. 'I'm sorry. I didn't mean to offend you.'

'Don't worry. I'm just delighted you ate it.' Gus stares at his tea glass, jiggling it until the fronds of mint swirl like a cyclone in the pale yellow brew. He looks over at her, his eyes as blue as the sky in the lantern light. 'I'm delighted that you came, Hanane.'

How can she tell him that her heart was about to burst with the joy of being here with him? 'I had to.'

'You're my first guest, you know.'

'I'm honoured.'

'Not counting Omar.'

Hanane laughs. 'Omar goes everywhere. He's become your shadow.'

'He's a clever boy. I'm teaching him English. I just gave him my book of Shakespeare. My grandmother gave it to me when I was a boy. It felt right to pass it on.'

'It's very kind of you to teach him.'

'It's a fair exchange of services.'

Gus reaches for a paper bag sitting on the cactus silk rug. He pulls out a fat red-skinned pomegranate.

'A pomegranate? Where did you get that? The season is finished.'

'Omar has sources. He won't tell me. I teach him English and he brings me fruit and nuts.'

'He'll be a good businessman one day.'

'One day? He's already a good businessman. He takes my shoes when I'm sleeping, polishes them up and then insists I pay him before he returns them. He says he's holding them as collateral until I pay. I taught him that word. I think I've created a monster.'

Hanane chuckles, pulling the end of her headscarf across her lips. Omar's always been like this. How else would she get her hands on the lipstick and mascara she loved? Cosmetics in return for her doing his Arabic literature homework. A fair trade.

'I like to hear you laugh.'

'You say funny things. You make my heart light.'

He smiles, the lines around his blue eyes deepening. 'I make your heart light?'

'When I'm with you, I feel like my feet are floating above the ground. Like I'm a bird.'

'And if you were a bird, where would you fly?'

Hanane fixes her eyes on his. 'I would fly to my future.'

A flash in the blue, like the sun flickering through cloud.

'Where's your future, Hanane?'

'That depends on you.'

# *Chapter Twenty-Two*

**Essaouira, Morocco – May 2009**

As Omar slides the key in the lock, the door to the flat is yanked open. A man in his late twenties stands at the foot of the stairs, barring their way. He jabs his finger in Addy's direction and yells at Omar in Arabic. Omar and Rachid attempt to placate him, and he finally moves aside to let them enter. At the top of the stairs, Addy looks back. The man is a black silhouette against the yellow light emanating from a street lamp. She can feel his eyes burning into her back as she follows Omar and Rachid into a bedroom.

'He's the son of the lady who rented us the flat,' Omar says. 'He doesn't like that a foreigner lady is with a Moroccan guy. I could go in jail for that.'

'Jail? Why? You're sleeping in the other room with your uncle.'

'I know. But he didn't believe that. I told you before, Adi. In Morocco, people must be married to be together.'

Rachid rubs his neck and emits a tired groan. 'It's true. It's illegal for Moroccans and foreigners to be a couple if they are not married. If the police think you and Omar are together, you could be deported and Omar can be put in prison for several months.'

'But I saw a lot of mixed couples at the concert tonight.'

Omar nods. 'Yes, it's true. Even so, we must be careful. Some

141

people have bad eyes for foreigners and Moroccans together. They like to make trouble, even if it's not their business.'

Addy sits on the striped cover of the large bed. 'What should we do?'

'Don't worry, Madame Adi,' Rachid says. 'We told him I am a driver and Omar is a tour guide and you are a journalist who is writing about Morocco for a newspaper in England. He was satisfied with that. For the moment, anyway.'

'It's a good story, isn't it? My uncle is clever.'

Addy rubs her temples. 'He won't bother us any more?'

'Don't worry. My body will be sleeping in the room of my uncle, even if my heart is sleeping in the room of Adi.'

*The sun glints off the waves of the English Channel beyond the white sprawl of Brighton in the distance. Addy strolls across the rolling green hills of the South Downs near the South Coast of England. The air trills with birdsong. It's springtime and her heart pings with joy. Her doctor's called. The lump is benign. There's nothing to worry about. She doesn't have cancer.*

*She and Nigel are marrying in the summer. She's found a tiny shop near the Brighton seafront where she'll set up her photo studio. From somewhere far away in the valleys, carried over the fresh spring air, the soft baas of sheep float up to her as she stands on the crest of the Ditchling Beacon. Nearby, someone cuts wood – chopping and hammering. The sound is muted, as if the axe is covered in moss.*

Addy opens her eyes. Someone's knocking on her door, but softly, as though they don't want anyone else to hear. Addy slides out from under the sheet and tiptoes over to the door.

'Hello?'

'It's Omar.'

Addy's heart skips in her chest. She unlocks the door. He stands in the hallway, his figure a palette of soft greys in the moonlight.

'Omar.'

He enters the room and locks the door. Reaching for Addy's hands, he holds them down by her sides as he walks her backwards until her thighs knock against the bed. He rubs his nose against her neck, tracing a path with his lips.

'I had to come. You are in my blood, Adi. You are behind my eyes.'

Addy closes her eyes. Her blood is honey. 'I'm glad.'

He kisses her. His tongue is soft and insistent in her mouth. Wrapping his arms around her waist, he presses her down onto the bed. Addy traces her fingers along his neck, over his shoulders, down to the curve of his back. He lets out a sound, almost imperceptible, like a gust of air through an open window.

He switches on the table lamp. 'I must see you, darling.'

The blue of his tagelmust and gown glow violet in the fluorescence. He lies on the bed beside her and leans his cheek in his hand, his elbow pressed into the pillow. His cheekbones and jaw are even sharper from this angle, throwing his deep-set eyes into shadow. Addy follows his gaze and sees that the sleeveless T-shirt she's been sleeping in has shifted, exposing her left breast. He touches the scar, tracing its outline with his fingertip.

'What happened, darling?'

Addy swallows and closes her eyes. How can she tell him about the cancer? She opens her mouth but the word locks in her throat.

'It's a wound of life.'

Omar leans over her and kisses the scar. She brushes her cheek against his. He smells of soap and musk and sweat. The bed creaks and he's on top of her. He spreads his arms and legs over hers until they're mirrors of one another.

'You fit me well, Adi.' He rolls his fingers through hers and holds her arms out to her sides. 'Allah made me for you.'

He kisses her and her mouth opens to his probing tongue. He whispers words in Tamazight as he presses soft kisses on her neck, along the round curve of her shoulder. She kisses him deeply and he moves against her, finding the place. She opens

143

up to him and takes him in. A flush of fire over her neck and her breasts, the waves washing over her, spreading out from her belly to her breasts, her shoulders; circles of eroticism, her body contracting. A death of pleasure.

'If I die today, *habibati*, I'll die happy.'

Omar reaches across their entwined bodies and raises Addy's hand to his lips. He opens her palm and presses the gentle plumpness of her Mound of Venus against his mouth.

Addy smiles. 'I'm happy for that, my darling.'

'In Arabic you say *habibi*. It means my love. For a lady it's *habibati*. So you are *habibati* for me.'

Addy rolls over and kisses Omar's neck just under his ear.

He sucks in his breath. 'It makes me crazy when you kiss me there. It's a special place for me.'

'I need to find all your special places, *habibi*.'

Addy traces her fingers along Omar's jawline to his throat, resting for a moment in the dip between his collarbones, then moving down his chest, detouring around his brown nipples, down along his smooth chest to his belly. She rests her hand there, tracing circles on his smooth brown skin with her fingers.

Someone pounds on the bedroom door.

Addy drops her hand. 'Who could that be?'

'*Habss*.' Omar throws off the sheet and pulls on his jeans. He grabs his blue gown from the terrazzo floor and drops it over his head. 'Go to the toilet and put on your clothes, darling,' he whispers. 'Be quick, *habibati*.'

Addy jumps out of the bed, grabbing her jeans and her kaftan top out of her leather bag as she hurries across the room to the bathroom. When she emerges, Omar and Rachid are waiting for her. Rachid has Addy's leather overnight bag in his hands, the slash repaired with electrical tape.

'Where are we going, Omar? It's the middle of the night.'

'The police station.'

'The police station? Why?'

'The son of the owner is upset,' Rachid says. 'He insists we go to the police station.'

The colour drains from Addy's face.

'Don't worry, *habibati*. It will be well. But we must be clever. You remember what we told the guy before?'

'That I'm a journalist?'

'Yes. It's okay for you?'

Her heart jumps around like a loose spring. 'Yes.'

'It will be well, Adi,' Rachid says. 'You have a camera. You have a laptop. If we must say a lie, it's better to say one that is like the truth.'

# Chapter Twenty-Three

**Essaouira, Morocco – May 2009**

The landlady's son, Abdul, keeps up an assault in Arabic on Omar and Rachid as he drives a battered green Dacia through Essaouira's dark streets. On the outskirts of the town he stops the car in front of a square grey building. An illuminated sign hangs over the door. Underneath the Arabic script, a word flickers blue in the black night: Police.

Omar turns around to Addy from the front passenger seat. 'It's okay?'

She smiles weakly, her stomach a knot of nerves.

They follow Abdul up the steps into the police station. A policeman with a broad, acne-pitted face sits behind an old wooden desk. He looks up as they file into the small room. Abdul launches into Arabic, flapping his arms like an agitated bird. The policeman scans the group, his eyes narrowing every now and again after some specific accusation.

He rises, his chair scraping against the concrete floor, and gestures to them to wait. He walks down a hallway and stops in front of a door. A muffled voice answers his knock. He opens the door and disappears inside the room.

Addy shivers. The night has turned cold. She blows on her hands. Her warm breath coats her hands with damp.

The door opens and the policeman emerges. He waves at them to enter.

A senior police officer leans back in a dark brown leather chair behind a black lacquered desk. He's in full uniform and the brass buttons on his jacket shine like small suns. His black hair is slick with gel, gleaming blue where the electric light catches the neat ridges from a recent combing. His eyes shift across the group and rest on Addy.

'*Wach katklam Al-Arabiyah?*'

'I'm sorry. I don't understand,' Addy says in a shaky English accent.

The police officer grunts. '*Est-ce que vous parlez le français?*'

Omar answers quickly. '*Non, elle parle seulement l'anglais.*'

Addy listens intently as Omar explains that she's an English journalist and that he's her tour guide. He reaches into his back pocket and takes out his wallet, extracting a laminated card, which he hands over to the police officer.

The man's eyes flick from the card to Omar's face and back. '*Vous êtes un guide touristique professionel?*'

'*Oui.*'

'*Laa, laa!*' Abdul protests, jabbing his finger at Omar.

Addy musters up her best rendition of Philippa's clipped English accent and launches herself into her role.

'I don't know what he's saying, but I don't understand what the problem is.' She surprises herself with the patronising officiousness of her tone. 'I'm a freelance journalist writing an article on Morocco for the *Sunday Times*, at the invitation of your king, I might add, who is working closely with the UK government on tourism initiatives in Morocco.' She points to Omar. 'This man is my tour guide and the other gentleman is our driver. I was having a discussion with Mr Chouhad about our itinerary for tomorrow when we were very rudely interrupted by this gentleman.' She gestures to Abdul. 'I have to say I very much resent any implication of impropriety between Mr Chouhad and myself. I wish to make a call to the

British Embassy in Rabat to lodge an official complaint, which I have no doubt will cause some severe issues at the very highest levels of the Moroccan government once the story is published in the *Times*.'

The police officer stares at her, his eyes a flat black without light or depth. Addy holds his gaze, even as she feels the colour rise in her cheeks.

'*Ma fhemtch*.'

'He don't understand English, Adi.'

'Tell him what I said.'

Omar translates Addy's objections into Arabic. When he's finished, the police officer snaps his fingers at Addy.

'*Passeport*.'

'*Naam, naam*,' Omar answers as he unbuttons the pocket on the leg of his jeans and places it on the desk.

The police officer shifts his flat black gaze back to Omar and slaps his hands over the passport. He slides it across the green leather blotter, and flips through the pages until he finds Addy's photo. He stares over at her, his eyes narrowing into slits, then he tosses the passport back on the desk.

'*Syr fhalek*.'

Abdul starts to speak. The police officer slams his hand down on the desk.

'*Syr fhalek*!'

Omar scoops up Addy's passport. '*Shukran bezzef*.' He pushes Addy and Rachid towards the door. 'He say we go.'

The tail lights of Abdul's car trace zigzags in the black night as he tears away from them down the dirt road. Addy slumps against Omar.

'I've never even had a parking ticket before and I've managed not just one but two run-ins with police in one day, Omar. This has got to stop.'

'It will, it will, *habibati*.'

'*Inshallah*,' Rachid says.

148

'Maybe someone gave me the bad eye.'

Omar watches the retreating vehicle. 'It might be.'

'Do you really think he believed our story?'

Omar shrugs. 'Maybe he doesn't want troubles. He wants to have an easy life.' He drops his arm over Addy's shoulders and gives her a squeeze. 'You did well, *habibati*. You're a clever lady. I'm so proud for that.'

'It's true,' Rachid says. 'You were not frightened.'

'Don't you believe it. I had visions of *Midnight Express* running through my head.' She shifts her leather bag to her other shoulder. 'What are we going to do now? We can't go back to the flat.'

A rooster's crow saws through the air, joined by the tinny sound of a megaphone. A muezzin calls out the dawn prayer, his voice floating across the sleeping town.

'The sun will come soon. We'll walk and we'll find plenty of taxis. I'm sure about it.'

'You're a man of boundless optimism, Omar.'

They head towards the harbour lights blinking in the distance. Addy stops to shake a stone out of her sandal, leaning on Omar for support.

'You know,' she says as she refastens her sandal, 'it occurred to me when we were in the police station that Rachid is supposed to be our driver but we don't have a car.'

Rachid looks over his shoulder at the flickering blue 'Police' sign. 'This is a good point. Maybe we should be quick before he thinks about it.'

'Rachid doesn't need a car,' Omar says. 'He's a driver in the Moroccan manner.'

'Don't tell me. He drives a donkey.'

'No, *habibati*. The donkey is for Berbers in the country. Rachid is from the city.'

'So what do Berbers from the city drive?'

'The best way, *habibati*. It's only today that's important. We don't know for the future.'

# Chapter Twenty-Four

### The Road to Casablanca, Morocco – May 2009

The bus is packed with Moroccan families travelling up the coast to El Jadida and Casablanca. Men in grey flannel trousers and beige cotton djellabas sit next to women in djellabas of vivid hues of pink, orange, turquoise and mauve, filling the bus with colour like desert flowers. Children sit squashed between the thighs of their parents. Babies nurse at their mothers' breasts. At lunchtime, food is extracted from plastic bags and wicker baskets – cold chicken legs, discs of bread, olives dripping in oil, hunks of cold mutton with a film of congealed white fat glistening on its flesh. Food is thrust on Addy, Omar and Rachid – no fellow traveller permitted to go hungry.

Through the dust-streaked window, the glass-green waves of the Atlantic Ocean flatten out to a line on the horizon. Addy manages to make out the tiny black silhouette of a boat sitting on the line, a man-made dot on the canvas of green sea and blue sky. A tanker, possibly. Heading south towards Agadir or beyond.

Omar's thigh is warm through his jeans, bumping against hers as the bus jolts along the paved road. His arm rests on her shoulder. The pads of his fingertips press against the thin cotton of her turquoise kaftan top.

Rachid sits across the aisle, engaging Omar in an animated conversation in Tamazight, their voices blending with the hum of languages inside the bus. Tamazight, Arabic, a few words of French. The words run over Addy like water, until the sounds meld into the landscape of red-brown earth, rocks, scrub brush and sea that passes like a movie by her window.

Did her father travel on the bus up the coast with Hanane when they'd visited Casablanca back in the spring of 1984? Why had they left Zitoune? Maybe Hanane was shunned for her relationship with a European. Had they married? Why did Gus never say anything to her or Philippa about all of this? Perhaps he never sent her the letter. Maybe he didn't even finish writing it. And then there was the fact that no one recognised Hanane. It didn't make sense. Unless they were all hiding something . . . but that would mean Omar was lying to her, too.

Addy traces her name – *Adi* with an 'i' – on the dirty window. No longer Gus and Hazel Percival's bookworm daughter, Adela Patricia; or Nigel's stressed-out fiancée, Della; or Philippa's bohemian sister, Adela. Who is this Adi Percival? What does she want? If she hadn't found the Polaroids, would she have come to Morocco at all? It's like she's a pawn being pushed across a chessboard by an invisible hand. Addy sighs. She had to stop listening to Philippa and her Tarot stuff. Coming to Morocco had been an impulsive decision. Like every decision she'd ever made. Her father's photographs had just given her an itinerary, nothing more.

Her phone vibrates in her jeans pocket – nine missed calls: a text message from the hospital reminding her of her follow-up appointment in July, three text messages from Philippa: *Still alive? Busy, busy, busy here. Russian job a nightmare as you can imagine. Love Pxx. Nothing on news about kidnap in Morocco. Assume you're still alive? Text me. Px.*
*Am I altogether an orphan? Am booking ticket to come out if you don't text me back. This, I assure you, is not an experience either you, or I, will relish. P.*

Addy smiles. Philippa's the only person she knows who uses commas in her texts.

Another message pings into her phone.

Nigel. *We need to talk.*

Addy switches off her phone. She'll answer Philippa later. Nigel . . . she's just going to ignore.

An expanse of smooth beige sand stretches out on the other side of her window. Not a soul. The landscape bordering the beach is scrubby with hunchbacked cypresses and argan trees with tiny grey-green leaves and flesh-piercing thorns. She lays her hand on Omar's leg and gives it a squeeze.

'It's fine, *habibati*?'

'Yes.'

'*Inti lkoubida diali.*'

'What's that mean?'

'You have captured my liver.'

Addy laughs. 'I've captured your liver?'

'Yes, darling. I'm serious. For Imazighen, the liver is the place of emotion, not the heart.' He presses his hand against the right side of his chest 'My love lives in here.'

'It doesn't seem as romantic as the heart.'

'Even so.'

Addy gazes out of the window to the horizon. Somewhere on the other side sits sprawling, raw-boned Canada. Her lost land. England had never been a good fit. Too small. Too claustrophobic. She'd always felt broad-shouldered and ungainly in London's unforgiving, historic greyness. Morocco was another sprawling, raw-boned country. Somewhere she could fit. Maybe her father is guiding her home.

# Chapter Twenty-Five

**Casablanca, Morocco – May 2009**

Just after five o'clock, the traffic through Casablanca has turned the roads into slow-moving rivers of cars, trucks, vans, motorbikes, bicycles and the occasional donkey cart. Pedestrians weave through the congestion, waving their hands like traffic cops to stop the cars as they negotiate pathways through the chaos.

The bus pulls into the bus station tucked behind the grey concrete hulk of the Sheraton Hotel. Addy steps off the bus onto the pavement and stretches, shaking out the stiffness in her legs. Tall whitewashed buildings adorned with crumbling Art Deco nymphs and charioteers line the street. Drying clothes hang from open shutters and balconies with wrought-iron railings rusting to dust in the salty air.

Omar dodges into the traffic and hails a red *petit taxi*. He directs it over to the roadside near the bus station, and dashes back across the street to join Addy and Rachid.

'That was crazy, Omar. I thought you'd get run over any minute.'

He picks up his knapsack and Addy's leather bag, and heads towards the taxi. 'It's Moroccan manner. If I die, it's my fate.'

'I don't see any point in tempting fate. You looked like a juicy morsel out there in the traffic.'

Rachid slides into the passenger seat with his knapsack. Omar tries to open the dented boot, but it's stuck shut. Omar and Addy squash into the back of the taxi with their bags.

The driver swings the taxi out into the traffic without checking his mirror and almost up-ends three girls on a motorbike. He throws his hand up as their motorbike swerves back into the stream of cars.

'*Bint lkhab.*'

'What did he say?'

'He doesn't like ladies driving.'

Rachid directs the driver in Arabic, and they eventually make it out of the city centre, past the concrete tourist hotels and the clay fortifications surrounding the medina, and onto a highway along the seafront. The Hassan II Mosque thrusts its towering minaret into the blue sky like an ocean liner moored on the coast.

'Wow.'

Rachid waves his hand towards the mosque. 'It's magnificent, isn't it? It is the largest mosque in Morocco. The minaret is two hundred and ten metres high, the highest in the world. It was built by King Hassan II, the father of our current king, Mohammed VI.'

'It's stunning.'

'It was built over seven years by ten thousand artisans and thirty-five thousand workers. They finished it in 1993. You see it is built over the ocean? Inside you can see the ocean under the glass floor in the hall.'

Omar stares out of his window at the mosque. 'It is a great mosque to the glory of King Hassan II.'

Rachid spins around. 'Omar! This is not good to speak this way. You must show respect.'

Omar grunts. 'I was a boy when the police came to my mother for money for the mosque. You were gone to Casa already, Uncle. My father was died and my mother she earn money only from her medicine and from the milk and butter of our cow. Even so, she had to pay money anyway. It's the same for everybody in Morocco. We had to pay even if we were poor. We couldn't have a sheep for Eid for three years. So King Hassan II had a big honour and the Moroccans suffered for it.'

Omar flips his hand towards the mosque. 'The police gave my mother a certificate. It's nice, isn't it? A certificate for five hundred dirhams. We didn't eat meat for many months. But, anyway, we had a nice certificate. I help my grandmother burn it. I remember it well.'

'Omar, the honour is for Allah, not for King Hassan II. You must apologise.'

'Fine, I apologise to Allah. But I don't apologise to King Hassan II for making my family suffer.'

The taxi follows the coast road past French advertising hoardings touting exclusive luxury condominiums for a million dirhams. Shiny Ferraris and Maseratis line the road in front of Italian and French restaurants in sharp-edged, architect-designed buildings. A huge cinema complex advertising a Bollywood film dubbed into Arabic looms up ahead. The taxi loops around the cinema, past cheap tourist hotels and fast-food restaurants. To their right, a boardwalk stretches as straight as an arrow along the beach to the horizon.

The taxi turns left up a hill away from the coast. Neatly trimmed date palms border the road, and terracotta-tiled roofs of sprawling houses rise up behind stone walls draped with pink and orange bougainvillea. The driver takes a sharp right turn and stops the car abruptly in a patch of gravel. A water tap protrudes from the ground like a periscope. Sprawling below on the side of a hill is a sea of shacks constructed of concrete blocks and discarded wood, their corrugated iron roofs glinting in the burning sun.

Rachid gestures towards a narrow lane, but the driver refuses to go any further. Omar extracts a few crumpled dirhams from

Addy's wallet and shoves them into the driver's hand. They stumble out of the car with their luggage. Addy follows Omar and Rachid down the lane towards the shantytown. The wheels of the taxi spin on the gravel as it speeds off.

# Chapter Twenty-Six

**Casablanca, Morocco – May 2009**

Rachid pulls aside the flowered curtain hanging over the doorway of one of the shacks.

'*Allô?*'

'*Baba!*'

A couple of pretty teenage girls in flannelette pyjamas and babouches run down the hallway to Rachid and wrap him in exuberant hugs. The older girl wears a pink hijab headscarf carefully pinned to cover her hair, but the younger girl's loose black curls dance wildly around her plump face as she babbles to her father in Arabic.

An older woman in a white hijab and a black djellaba emerges from the kitchen. Her sturdy face is a web of fine lines, and smudges the colour of bruises underline her dark eyes. She smiles at Addy. A porcelain gleam of false teeth. As she waddles down the hallway, the black cloth of her djellaba strains against the swell of her pregnant belly.

The girl with the wild hair hugs Addy and kisses her wetly on her cheeks.

'Hello, I'm Habiba,' she says in French. 'It's a lovely name, isn't it? What's your name?'

'Addy.'

'She's a Canadian lady,' Omar says in French. 'She's my girlfriend.'

Addy turns to Omar. 'Are you sure it's okay to say that?'

'Darling, I'm happy to tell everybody you're my girlfriend. They will love you because I love you.'

The older woman places a hand on her large bosom. '*Adi marhaba. Ana* Nadia. *Tata* Omar.' Welcome, Adi. I'm Nadia. Omar's aunt.

Nadia takes Addy's hand and leads her into a small living room. The concrete block walls have been rendered with plaster and whitewashed. Woven plastic mats in colourful zigzag patterns are spread out over the beaten earth floor. A single light bulb hangs from a wire attached to the corrugated metal ceiling with packing tape. Banquettes covered in a bright fabric of blue and red roses sit against two of the walls. Against another, a large flat-screen television sits on a shelf made of blue plastic crates. Someone's turned the sound off, but on the TV screen the heavily made-up face of an Arabic singer mouths her soundless love lament while semi-naked belly dancers gyrate in the background.

Omar's aunt pats a banquette. '*Atay*?'

'Tea? *Shukran*.' Addy sets down her bag and sits on the banquette.

The girl wearing the hijab points to Addy's leather bag and smiles shyly.

'I Salima. I take?' She points to a blue door at the far end of the room.

'Thank you, Salima. *Shukran bezzef*.'

She picks up the bag and laughs. 'It heavy.'

'I'm sorry. It has my laptop in it. You can leave it here if you like.'

The girl shakes her head. '*Mashi mushkil. Plaisir.*'

Salima disappears into the room behind the blue door. Addy looks around for Omar and Rachid but they've disappeared. Habiba jumps onto the banquette and kicks off her babouches, tucking her feet underneath her like a swami.

'I speak leetle English. I better than Salima. I practise, yes?'

'You speak very well, Habiba. That's a pretty name.'

'It is the name of love.'

'You're lucky to have a name like that.'

She twists a curly strand of hair around her finger as she inspects Addy with her dark eyes. 'I have eighteen years. You have how many years?'

'A few more than you.'

'You are beautiful.' She touches Addy's hair. '*Zwina*.'

'Thank you. Your hair is beautiful too, Habiba.'

Her round face lights up. 'I love you.'

Addy laughs. 'Thank you, Habiba.'

Habiba jumps up and grabs Addy's hand, pulling her off the banquette.

'Come to the room of Habiba and Salima.' She slips her feet into her babouches and tugs at Addy's hand. 'Come with me, Adi. You are the best friend of my life.'

Behind the blue door the small room has a narrow banquette against one wall, a large wooden cupboard and a dressing table. A piece of broken mirror sits on top of the dressing table, propped against the wall. Clear plastic is tacked over a small square window and another bare light bulb hangs from the ceiling. Salima is bent over brushing her black hair, which hangs to the floor, obscuring her face like a silk curtain. She stands quickly and her hair fans into the air in a graceful arc before settling into a mass of shiny black strands on her shoulders and back.

Habiba grabs the brush from her sister and starts to sing an Arabic pop song into it. Salima twists her hair into a tight bun and fixes it into place with a couple of hairgrips while Habiba belly dances around her. She picks up her pink hijab from the banquette then wraps it tightly over her head and around her neck, securing it into place with a single straight pin. Addy catches Salima's brown-eyed gaze and looks away quickly, aware that she's been staring.

159

'You like?' Salima pats her hijab.

'It's very pretty.'

Habiba drops the brush onto the banquette and swings open the wardrobe door. She pulls out a length of turquoise cloth and holds the cloth up to Addy.

'You like hijab?'

'You want to put the hijab on me?'

Salima smiles. Her large, almond-shaped eyes are the colour of milk chocolate, framed by a fan of thick black lashes.

'Omar will like.'

Addy fingers the piece of turquoise cloth. 'Okay, why not?'

The two girls wind the cloth over her short hair, around her ears and neck. Salima retrieves a pin from the dressing table drawer and fastens the end of the cloth into place on top of Addy's head. She stands back and smiles. Habiba grabs the mirror and holds it up. She flicks the fingers of her right hand at Addy's face.

'*Zwina*. Beautiful.'

'We show Omar.'

Addy stares into the mirror. Her face is so round, her nose so prominent.

'I don't know. Maybe not.'

Salima nods encouragingly. 'Yes, he will like.'

Addy glances from Salima to Habiba. Their delight at their handiwork overrides her reticence.

'All right.'

Rachid and Omar are watching a football match on the TV. Omar looks up at Addy and blinks. Rachid's face breaks into a wide smile.

'You are like a Muslim lady.'

Omar clears his throat. 'Adi, you are so, so beautiful. I never imagined you like that.'

Nadia enters the room carrying a tray of tea glasses and cookies. '*Aiyh*! Adi *zwina*.' She sets the tray down on a low table and makes her way across the living room floor to Addy, swaying like a ship

160

sailing through waves. Her pregnant belly squashes against Addy when she hugs her. The baby kicks.

'I must take a picture, darling,' Omar says. 'Where is your camera?'

'In my bag.'

'*Mashi mushkil*. I put it in another room. When I come back I'll take a photo of everybody. It's a good memory for you, and for me as well. It makes my heart go like an earthquake.'

When Omar returns with the camera, Addy wraps her arms around the two sisters – Salima in her pink hijab on one side and Habiba with her wild hair on the other. What would Philippa say if she could see her now?

# Chapter Twenty-Seven

**Casablanca, Morocco – May 2009**

They're sitting on the banquettes eating from two platters heaped with lamb and prune tagine when a man strides into the room with two children – a boy of about five and a girl of about eight. He's middle-aged, sturdily built, with a round belly pressing against his floor-length white tunic. He wears a white prayer cap, and a full beard streaked with grey obscures the lower part of his face. When he sees Addy his eyes widen and he spins around, pulling the boy with him through an open door into a room opposite the kitchen. Omar and Rachid exchange a glance. They rise and follow the man into the other room. Nadia picks up a platter of meat and several discs of bread and hurries after them as quickly as her heavy belly permits.

'Malika, come here, sit,' Habiba calls to the stranded girl.

The girl gives Habiba and Salima a kiss on both cheeks and settles down beside Addy. She wears a white hijab and a white school smock over her black trousers.

Addy extends her hand. 'Hello, I'm Addy. I'm a friend of Omar's. Do you speak English?'

The girl nods shyly and touches the tips of Addy's fingers with her hand before folding her arms tightly against her body. The girl's eyes are beautiful – clear green with a ring the colour of sunflowers around the irises.

'She is my cousin,' Habiba says. 'She learn English in her school. She speak French also. She is clever, but her father only want her to speak Arabic. He say he will take her away from school soon. He say it's for girls to be wives and mothers in the house only. He say it only makes problems for mans when girls are educated.'

Malika's cheeks flush pink and she buries her head against Habiba's shoulder.

'Was that her father?'

'Yes, he my uncle Farouk. He is the brother of my mother. His wife, she died one year ago. She had a baby but it didn't go well. The baby, it died as well.'

An image of the pregnant Hanane flashes into Addy's mind. Is that what happened to Hanane? Did she die in childbirth? Was that why her father had never sent the letter?

'I'm so sorry to hear that. It's hard for the children to have no mother.'

Habiba shrugs. 'It was her fate.'

Addy's struck by this fatalistic acceptance of misfortune. By the idea that fate controls the lives of everyone, like a capricious puppeteer who pulls or cuts strings at will.

'Does your uncle live nearby?'

Habiba plucks a prune from the platter and pops it into her mouth. She spits the stone into her hand and drops it onto the table.

'Yes. He come here many times for eating. My mother wash his clothes and the clothes of the children. He never talks to me or Salima. I don't like him.'

'Habiba, you must be polite,' Salima admonishes as she scoops the date stone into her palm.

Habiba makes a face at her sister. 'He come here all the time. He never work. He only prays. He take money from our father. He make troubles for our mother and father.'

The door to the other room opens and Nadia enters the living room, carrying the empty platter. 'Salima, *atay*,' she says as she heads into the kitchen. Salima wipes her hand on a piece of torn towel and rises from the banquette to follow her mother.

The door opens again and Omar emerges. He flops down onto a banquette and leans over to grab a disc of bread from the table. Tearing off a piece, he dunks it into the oniony grease and plops it into his mouth.

'So?' Addy says.

'Yes?'

'Habiba says he's Nadia's brother.'

'Yes. He doesn't like that I'm with a foreigner lady. He told me to take you to a hotel, but I told him no. I told you are with me full stop. If he doesn't like it, it's his problem. So he'll go. Only he'll first eat my uncle's food to be fatter.'

'Habiba says he's very religious. That he prays all the time.'

'It's good to pray. My mother, my sister, my aunt, they pray all the time. Even in the night, which is so hard. They pray for the goodness of the world. They pray for everyone to be happy. They're good Muslims. But Farouk is fundamentalist. He's very, very strict. He doesn't like Europe or America. He doesn't like my uncle because he's Amazigh and he speaks English. He doesn't like me, too, because I don't pray often.

'He made his wife who died wear a niqab to cover all of herself, even her hands and her face. It's not so normal to do that in Morocco. I knew her when she was young. Her name was Radwa. She was a normal girl like Salima and Fatima. Then after she was married she stayed in her house all the time by herself with her children. It's a pity for her. At least she's in Paradise now so she's free. He don't like you for sure because you are a European lady. But I don't mind for him.' Omar shrugs. 'So no problem.'

Nadia hands Addy a lit candle to take into the toilet. When Addy closes the toilet door, she moves the circle of yellow light around the dense blackness. The room smells of urine. She holds the candle over the centre of the floor. Instead of a flat white Turkish toilet, there's a hole in the earth.

Someone knocks on the door.

'Who is it?'

'Omar.'

Addy opens the door. He's carrying a bucket of water.

'You might need some water, *habibati*. It's from the well in the car park.'

'Thanks. They don't have running water?'

'No.'

'They have to go up to that tap every time they want water?'

'Yes, but it's not so far.'

Addy imagines Nadia carrying heavy buckets of water down the lane. 'It's hard.'

'Yes. It's fate.'

'Fate doesn't play fair, does it?'

Addy sets the bucket down on the earth floor and closes the door.

The flickering light from the candle throws ghostly shadows against the walls of Rachid and Nadia's room when Addy enters. Omar lies under a thick flowered blanket on one of the two banquettes.

'Where are your aunt and uncle sleeping?'

'They sleep in the room of my cousins. My cousins sleep in the room of the TV. It's fine.'

Addy slips off her sandals and tiptoes across the straw mat to a vacant banquette. Her toe catches the corner of the mat and she stumbles.

'Shit.'

Omar chuckles. The wooden base of his banquette groans as he shifts and leans up on his arm. 'You can turn the light on, darling. The candle is just for the toilet.'

Addy sits down on the banquette and blows out the candle. 'I don't want to waste their electricity.'

'Okay, it's a good reason.'

She slips under the blanket in her clothes and pulls it up to her chin to shield herself from the chilly night air. 'It's kind of your aunt and uncle to let us use their room.'

'It's true it's not normal, *habibati*. But they insist for it. You are like my wife in their eyes since I bring you into my family.'

A rustling, and Omar is on top of her, the blanket the only barrier between them.

'It's not a possibility for me to sleep away from you, Adi.' He pins the blanket around her with his hands and kisses her. 'You're in my blood. You can eat me, I don't mind. You can kill me, I will be happy for it. I'll be a slave for you. You're my fate and I'm yours.'

Addy breathes in his scent, of soap and musk. 'Come under the blanket with me, *habibi*. We must be quiet.'

# Chapter Twenty-Eight

**Casablanca, Morocco – May 2009**

'No, *merci*. I'm full, *shukran*.'

Nadia ignores Addy's plea and dishes another *msemen* onto her plate, drizzling it with honey.

Addy watches the honey slide into the crevices of the pancake. 'You'll make me fat.'

'It's better to be fat,' Habiba says, chewing on her *msemen*. 'Fat is better for the belly dancing and for making the babies. Mans like it better.'

'Habiba!' Salima glares at her sister, oblivious to a dribble of honey running down her chin.

'Habiba, you must be polite,' Rachid reprimands. 'This is not good conversation.'

Omar pockets his cell phone and reaches for a *msemen*. 'Habiba's a crazy girl.'

Addy sits back against the cushions and licks the honey from her fingers. 'Did you finish your phone calls?'

'Yes. I must organise guides for the tourists in Zitoune. Many drivers call me from Marrakech to be the guide. They don't like me to be in Casa. I do good animation for the tourists so the tourists pay me well. So then I pay the drivers a good commission.' He shrugs. 'The money is flying away from me like a bird.'

Addy looks at Omar and frowns. 'I'm sorry. I promised to pay you for guiding me around Morocco. I don't want you to be out of pocket for helping me.'

'Don't mind, darling. Money comes and money goes, and money will come again. It's a vacation for me. It's so nice for me to visit the family of my uncle in Casa, anyway.'

Rachid pats Omar's arm. '*Marhaba*. So, we will go to visit the mosque today? I am sure you will love to take photos for your book, Madame Adi. My wife wishes to come as well. She has never seen it inside. It will be nice for her.'

Omar rises off the banquette and stretches. 'I'll go to the big road to get a taxi.' He looks at Salima and Habiba. 'But it's not so big for everybody.'

Rachid blows at the steam coming from his glass of tea. 'Salima and Habiba must make some food for a wedding of a neighbour tonight. They will stay here.'

Nadia hands Addy a piece of torn towel and Addy rubs off the sticky honey. 'I'll get my camera.'

Instead of walking up the hill to the water spout, Omar heads deeper into the shantytown. Addy follows him through the twisting alleyways, ducking under lines of laundry flapping in the ocean breeze. Every few steps, she stops to capture an image on her camera. Door curtains twitch as they walk by. They collect a wake of children, who run up to Addy crying out '*Stylos! Stylos!*'

'*Laa.*' Omar shoos them away.

'Why are they asking for pens?'

'They want to sell them to buy candy. But if they sell pens they don't go to school. It's better for them to be in school.'

They continue down the alleyway. The children whisper and giggle behind them.

'Omar, isn't your uncle a teacher?'

'Yes.'

'Couldn't he . . .' The words blunder out of her mouth. 'Couldn't he live somewhere better?'

Omar stops short. 'You don't like the house of my uncle? It's a problem for you to be here?'

'No, no. I'm honoured that your uncle has invited me into his house. It's just that . . . I would've thought he could live somewhere else other than . . .' She gestures at the shabby buildings. Her face burns. The words are coming out all wrong. 'They're building new flats all over Casablanca. I've seen the signboards.'

Omar spins around and walks on ahead in silence.

'I'm sorry, *habibi*. It's none of my business.'

'You think my uncle can buy a flat for a million dirhams? Are you crazy, Adi? They're not for Moroccans those flats. They're for Europeans.'

'I'm sorry. I didn't know . . .'

'It's complicated in Morocco, darling. Tourists don't understand the situation well. My uncle, he's Amazigh. His wife, she's Arab. He went away from the family of my father when he was young to find a job in Casa and to be educated and to send some money to my mother after my father died. My aunt met him in Casa and she respected him. So they married. But her family didn't like that she married an Amazigh man. Only Farouk speaks to her because she feeds him, so she loves him for that. My uncle gave her family all his money to marry her, but they didn't make a wedding, even though it was their responsibility. So he borrowed money from some not so good people to make a wedding for her honour. He pays them yet.'

'What about his teaching?'

'My uncle went for work to teach many times. He went to Essaouira for a job when we saw him there. But always they hire an Arab teacher. What can he do? He must earn money for his family, so he does parking for cars by the cheap hotels. He has many daughters, so he must save money for them to be

169

married. Already he has two daughters who are married in Italy and France with Moroccans. And he has a baby soon again. It's a hard situation.'

'I'm sorry. I didn't realise.'

'No problem, *habibati*.'

Omar takes her hand and they walk down the lane, the children giggling behind them.

Omar's right. She knows nothing about Morocco. In London she's in debt to the banks and credit card companies like everyone else. Even so, she'll jump into a money-gouging black cab if she's running late for a meeting. And she never goes without her grande skinny latte in the morning. Get an urge to travel to Morocco? Just bung the plane ticket on the credit card and hop on the plane.

Is she just the ultimate tourist, dipping a manicured toe into this charming world of donkeys, and outdoor hammams, and roosters as alarm clocks before running back to her comfortable, vacuous life? Could she live this way every day? Would she be as cheerful as Habiba, as happy as Fatima, as dignified as Rachid, or as industrious as Omar?

She looks inside herself and is ashamed.

The *petit taxi* pulls up beside the water tap. Omar says something to the driver in Arabic and the man grunts and turns off the ignition. He pulls a pack of Camel cigarettes out of his checked shirt pocket and sits back in his seat for a smoke.

Rachid and Nadia are waiting for them in the living room, dressed in freshly pressed djellabas. Despite the unseasonable spring heat, Nadia's twisted a white wool pashmina around her head as a hijab.

Salima and Habiba join them to stroll up the lane to the taxi. Salima loops her arm through Addy's.

'You come to the wedding later, Adi? It is the party of henna for the ladies.'

'Yes, come to dance with Habiba.' Habiba jiggles her hips like a belly dancer.

'But I haven't been invited.'

'I invite you.' Salima smiles at Addy.

How pretty she is, her face as delicate as a bird's, Addy thinks. 'Then I'd love to come to the henna party tonight. Will you come too, Omar?'

'It's not for men to go. The men will have a celebration separate.'

'Really?'

'Yes, it happens like that. But the wedding will be for three days, so another day the men and ladies will be all together. Tonight it's just for the ladies. You will love it, darling. It will be a big experience for you.'

A monumental colonnade of graceful Arabic arches stretches out either side of the mosque's giant minaret-like wings. Addy stops to take photos of Omar and his uncle and aunt in front of an enormous wall fountain embellished with millions of coloured mosaics.

Rachid runs his hands over the glazed tiles. 'It is *zellige*. It is very beautiful, isn't it? To make *zellige* is an ancient art of Morocco. The men who make them are called *malems* and they learn the art from childhood. The tiles are terracotta, which is painted and enamelled. It takes a long time to do it.'

Addy rubs her finger against a tiny, diamond-shaped, green-glazed tile. 'It's impossible to find anything like this in London. Everyone's in a rush. There's no time for this kind of craftsmanship.'

'It's a pity. We honour ourselves and we honour Allah when we take care in whatever it is we do.' Rachid gazes up to the top of the minaret. 'Do you not feel Allah in this place?'

Inside the mosque they remove their shoes. Omar hands Addy his tagelmust to drape over her hair and they wait in the foyer to join a tour group for a tour of the mosque's interior.

Omar squints as he focuses on the intricate ceiling decoration. 'It's the first time I wait to come inside the mosque. I can go as I like because I'm Muslim. It's special for you to come inside a mosque, Adi. In many mosques it's *haram* to go inside if you are not Muslim.'

A group of French tourists congregates near the entrance doors and Omar steers Addy and Rachid towards them.

'We'll follow the tour because we must do it for you to see the mosque. But my uncle can be your tour guide. He knows everything about the mosque.'

They follow the group into the enormous prayer hall and break off into a satellite group of four. Gleaming white marble arches carved with plasterwork as delicate as icing frame them like figures on a wedding cake. Murano glass chandeliers hang from the ceiling like the earrings of a giantess.

'It's wonderful.'

Rachid looks up at the chandeliers. 'Whenever I am here, Madame Adi, I feel like a flea on an elephant.'

Addy drags her eyes away from the ceiling. 'Where's the glass floor where you can see the sea underneath?'

'Ah, this is a problem.' Rachid gestures to the front of the hall where velvet ropes cordon off an area of the floor. 'It is over there. But it is only for the king and his family to kneel on it. Our eyes cannot see it.'

Omar grunts. 'It should be for all Muslims to pray over the water.'

Rachid glances over at Omar and frowns.

'Why is the mosque built out over the ocean, Rachid?'

'King Hassan II wished it so. He said it was because Allah's throne is on the water. But there have been problems with the salt in the foundations. It went through the concrete and the steel rusted. They made many corrections for this since the mosque was built.'

Further into the prayer hall, Addy points to an impressive wooden balcony projecting from the mezzanine flanking the hall to the right, with a latticework of decorative carvings.

'What's that for?'

'It's for the ladies. They must be separate from the men. It's for their privacy and their modesty.'

'The men get the whole prayer hall and the women only get a balcony?'

'Not so many ladies come to the mosque to pray,' Omar says. 'The ladies like to pray in their house, like my aunt. It's more private. But when they come, there is a place for them.'

Rachid looks up at the ceiling. 'Do you see the ceiling? It can open in five minutes so that we can worship under the stars and be closer to Allah. All because King Hassan II wished it so.'

Outside the mosque, they wander through the courtyard and under the arches towards a public garden nearby. Omar spreads out his tagelmust on the grass like a blanket and they sit on it, watching the gulls swoop over the ocean waves. There's a vendor selling bags of roasted nuts nearby and Omar strolls over to him. Addy takes a picture of Rachid and Nadia, smiling like newlyweds, the sea and the mosque in the background. She shows them the image on the camera.

'Nadia *zwina*.'

Nadia shakes her head. '*Laa, laa*. Adi *zwina*.'

Addy scrolls through the photos. Nadia and Rachid smile and exclaim as the images flip by. She stops at the image of herself in the turquoise hijab with Habiba and Salima. Omar leans over, smelling of salted almonds.

'Maybe you can be a Muslim lady one day, Adi.'

Rachid translates this for Nadia, who smiles a toothy porcelain smile. '*Inshallah*.'

Addy sets down the camera on the blue tagelmust. 'Don't hold your breath. I'm a Welsh–Irish Catholic girl from Canada. Well, I was. I haven't been inside a church since . . . well, for a long time.'

Omar squats down and doles out paper bags of warm almonds. 'It doesn't matter, darling. Anyway, it's permitted for a Muslim man to marry a Christian lady. So, no problem. Then we can have many children.'

'Children?'

'Yes. It's natural. I want to have many children to leave my heritage in the world even when I die.' He leans over Addy and whispers, 'Our children will be beautiful, Adi. They will have hair of fire and eyes like the sea.'

Omar picks up the camera and flicks through the photos, stopping to show a picture of Fatima to his uncle and aunt.

'Fatima?' Nadia raises her hand in the air to indicate Fatima has grown.

They chat in Arabic as Omar scrolls through the photos. Their words wash over Addy like the ocean waves splashing against the foundations of the great mosque.

Her stomach lurches. She hands her bag of almonds to Omar. *She's in a car that's going too fast and she has no seat belt to keep her safe when it crashes.*

# Chapter Twenty-Nine

**Casablanca, Morocco – May 2009**

That evening, the girls dress Addy up in a silky purple kaftan, embellished with silver embroidery around the high collar and flowing sleeves. Salima loans her a pair of silver leather babouches and Habiba finishes off the costume with a heavy silver leather belt studded with colourful glass gems. They dress themselves in kaftans as well, Habiba in bright orange embroidered with gold thread, and Salima in blue with delicate white embroidery, their hair loose around their shoulders.

They're excited about the henna party and Addy tries to match their enthusiasm, but a weight has settled over her, pressing down on her mood like a stone. Children? How can Omar be talking about children? Everything's moving too fast. How can she tell him she's had cancer? That her eggs are dead. She'd had a choice. Let the doctors pump her full of oestrogen that fed her breast cancer so they could harvest the eggs, or let her eggs wither and die from the Red Devil. Nigel hadn't wanted children. Nor had she. Was she going to commit suicide or murder? She'd murdered her eggs.

And now, what now?

\*

They walk through the dark alleyways, laden down with plastic bags of cakes and cookies, guided by the sound of women's voices singing and ululating on the still evening air. There's no moon and Addy stumbles several times on the uneven earth. They pass a hole-in-the-wall shop lit by a string of Christmas lights. A group of men cluster around a dusty analogue television watching football. One of them says something in Arabic as they pass by. Habiba makes a rude gesture with her finger.

'What did he say?' Addy asks.

'*Mashi mushkil*, Adi. He crazy man.'

The singing emanates from a long whitewashed building with a row of small windows high up along the front façade. A wooden door hangs loosely on its hinges. Yellow light escapes around the gaps where the doorframe meets the concrete block walls.

Salima knocks on the door and Addy follows the sisters into the large room. Women in djellabas, kaftans, aprons and pyjamas sit, as colourful as a flower garden, on carpets and mats spread out over the dirt floor. A group of wizened women, their hair covered in bandanas, sit cross-legged on cushions in a corner, singing loudly as they pound on large tambourines.

On a platform at the front of the room, a girl of about Habiba's age sits on a chair draped with red-and-gold satin. She's dressed in a green velvet gown embroidered with gold thread, and her hands and feet are tattooed in an elaborate design of flowers and curlicues in bright red henna. Her eyes are rimmed with black kohl like an Egyptian goddess and her black hair is piled on top of her head, a silver crown holding it in place. Her face is flushed. A woman standing next to her leans over from time to time to dab with a tissue at the droplets of sweat trailing down her cheeks.

They hand their bags of food to a woman standing in the doorway of the adjoining kitchen, which is filled with chatting and laughing women making tea and setting out platters of food. Habiba and Salima each take one of Addy's hands. They pick their way over the seated women until they reach the bride on her patchwork throne. The cousins greet the bride, kissing her on her cheeks. Addy does the same. The young bride smiles at her and says *Marhaba*.

They squeeze into a space on the floor near the singers and sit down. The women's eyes bore into her.

'Are you sure it's okay for me to be here?'

Habiba squeezes her hand. 'Yes, you are with me. Everybody know Habiba.'

She jumps up and begins a wild belly dance, swooping her curly black hair around her head in swishing loops. The women laugh and clap.

Habiba grabs Addy's hand and pulls her to her feet.

'No, Habiba.'

'Yes, Adi. Come, dance with Habiba. I teach you to dance like Arab lady.' She thrusts her hips in a wide circle and jolts her pelvis forwards with a jerk.

Salima pushes Addy towards her sister. 'You go, Adi. You will do well.'

Addy senses every eye on her. 'Omar was right, Habiba. You're crazy.'

Habiba giggles and takes Addy's hands in hers. 'You follow what I do.' Habiba's heels rise and fall as her hips swing in a graceful figure of eight. She releases Addy's hands and claps to the music's rhythm. 'Like that.'

Addy mimics Habiba's movements as best she can. Salima joins them and dances a more graceful version of Habiba's wild gyrations. One of the old women ululates and the shrill warble sits on the air like a challenge. Another woman joins in and the singers' song grows louder. A couple of younger women rise and dance, swinging their loose hair to the beat of the tambourines. The women clap and stamp their feet. Addy shuts her eyes and dances.

A woman whose djellaba strains against her rolls of fat sits beside Addy, pressing cookies and sweets on her. She smiles toothlessly

177

whenever Addy takes one and Addy tells her she's *zwina*. She grabs Addy in a bear hug and crushes her against her bosom until Salima comes to Addy's rescue.

'It will be your turn next, Salima,' Habiba says.

Addy raises a questioning eyebrow. 'Salima's turn?'

'Yes, I will marry a Moroccan man in France. He's the brother of my sister's husband there. They live in Paris. I must go with my father to Rabat soon to get the visa.'

'Rabat?'

'It's where all the countries have offices for visas,' Habiba says. 'One day, I will marry a man of England so I can visit you, Adi.'

One of the singers calls over to Habiba in shrill Arabic.

'Omar! Adi!' Habiba shouts back.

The singer slices through the noise of the women's conversations with a sharp ululation. She claps out a rhythm. 'Omar Adi! Omar Adi!' The other singers take up the song, beating their tambourines, and soon the whole room is singing the names.

'What's going on?'

'It's a song for the marriage of Omar and Adi,' Salima explains.

Habiba pats her stomach. 'They are singing for you to have many babies.'

Salima strokes Addy's hair. 'You are Arabic lady now, and Amazigh, too. Like me and my sister. *Nus nus*.'

The front door rattles with thudding knocks. Men yell outside in the alley. The singing and music waver and stop. The flimsy door slams open and men tumble inside, their faces contorted with rage. The men they'd passed earlier are there. One of them points at Addy and yells in Arabic.

Addy feels the blood drain from her face. 'Oh, my God.'

Habiba leaps to her feet and screams at the man. The woman sitting beside Addy struggles to her feet and joins in, shrieking in Tamazight. The bride pulls herself up out of her chair, the sleeves of her gown smearing the wet henna on her hands, and joins in with high-pitched remonstrations.

Soon, the room is full of women's voices, like a hundred train whistles going off at once. The men push towards Addy, but the women block their path with their bodies. She's like a helpless, vulnerable child and they're all her mothers. The women scream and throw their arms about as the men crowd at the doorway, angry but impotent. Finally, the men leave, slamming the door behind them.

Addy and the two sisters leave the wedding party, surrounded by a guard of twenty women. Halfway back to the house, she sees Omar running down the alleyway to meet them. He grabs Addy's hands and holds them against his chest. The line between his eyes is carved deep with worry.

'You are okay?'

'We had some trouble.'

'I know, darling. I heard about it.' He scans Addy from head to foot. 'You're fine? Nobody hurt you?'

'I'm fine. Just a bit shaken.'

'You go in the house with Habiba and Salima. I'll be back soon.'

'Where are you going?'

The vein in Omar's temple jumps against his skin. 'Don't worry, darling.'

'Be careful.'

'Be sure about it. Nobody can touch me.'

His moonlit silhouette disappears down the alleyway. Addy stands in the lane until she can no longer hear the crunch of his footsteps on the gravel.

When Omar and Addy are alone in Rachid and Nadia's bedroom later that night, he hugs Addy tight against him.

'You are fine, *habibati*?'

'Yes, I'm fine. We were having a wonderful time. And then these men came.'

He rubs Addy's back with his palm. 'I know about it. I don't like it at all. I talked to them to be calm. I said you are my wife, so they accepted it. But we must be careful. Some men here don't

179

like foreigners at all. Some of the men who bomb the trains in Madrid lived here. Maybe al-Qaeda is here.'

'Al-Qaeda's here?'

'Maybe.'

Addy's breath is coming so fast that she can barely get her words out. 'Don't you think I'm a pretty obvious target for kidnapping?'

Omar rubs his forehead. 'I didn't think about it, Adi. I took you to my family. It's normal for me to come here.'

Addy pushes him away and staggers over to a banquette. 'What do we do now?'

Omar sits down beside her. The banquette's wooden frame groans. 'Tomorrow, we go early. We'll go back to Zitoune. There is a bus that goes there from Casa.'

'I was hoping to go to Rabat to visit the Canadian Embassy to see if they have any records of my father and Hanane, and I wanted to take some pictures on the boardwalk here for my book.'

'Another time for Rabat, *habibati*. I'm so sorry for that situation. I'll make the taxi go to the boardwalk in the morning for you to take pictures before we leave. It's better to be safe in Zitoune.'

'We'll be safe tonight?'

Omar takes Addy's clenched hands into his and holds them against his heart. 'Adi, I'll kill all of them before they can take you, you must be sure about it.' He kisses her hands and rises from the banquette. 'You can sleep well.'

'Where are you going?'

'Darling, I don't sleep tonight. I'm the guard for you. Don't worry at all. I can kill, it's no problem for me. I can do it. Nobody can touch you. So you'll be fine.'

It's early, about six o'clock. A taxi is waiting by the water tap. Addy hugs Nadia and kisses her cheeks as she stands in the doorway.

Nadia hands Addy a plastic bag full of bread and oranges. '*Beslama*, Adi.' She grabs Addy's shoulders in her sturdy grip and kisses her cheeks.

'*Beslama*, Nadia. *Shukran bezzef.*'

Rachid and Omar head up the lane to the taxi. Habiba and Salima walk either side of Addy, their arms entwined. Door curtains twitch and as they pass each doorway, a woman emerges. In the alleyways, silent men stare as they make their way up the lane. The women cluster in front of their doorways like an honour guard of rustic angels, ensuring Addy's safe passage out of their world.

# Chapter Thirty

**Zitoune, Morocco – May 2009**

Aicha takes one look at Addy's damp, bloodless face and wraps her arms around her.

'Oushane?'

Addy nods weakly. They have just come through the mountains in a decrepit Mercedes taxi on the one-lane dirt road from the mountain village of Oushane, having been dropped off there by the Casablanca bus.

Aicha waves her hand at Omar and scolds him in shrill Tamazight. Fatima appears from the kitchen, wiping her hands on her apron. She grins broadly when she sees Addy.

'Are you okay, Adi?' she asks in French. 'The road from Oushane is terrible. I'm sick all the time on the bus from Beni Mellal. It's very bad for Omar to take you that way.'

Omar throws up his hands. 'Womens. I make a safe trip from Casa and you are not satisfied. I'm going to see some football at the café. Eat the brochettes of chicken my mum made for you, *habibati*. Enjoy. I'll come later.'

When Omar hasn't returned after Addy's sat through three histrionic Turkish soap operas with Aicha, Fatima and Jedda, Aicha insists that Addy sleep in her bedroom to recover from the bus ride. Addy's so tired that her body sinks into the mattress like an anchor. Her mind spins like a top. She wonders how safe she really is. How she can tell Omar she's infertile. There again, that hardly matters now. It's not like they're getting married. They barely know each other. Her mind turns to where she's left her father's Polaroids and why no one in Zitoune recognises Hanane, what happened to her, and her baby. What's she going to do about Nigel? What on earth is she doing with her life?

Something drags her from the depths of sleep. She sits up and leans into the darkness, but all she hears is the soft pelt of rain against the plastic tarpaulin Aicha's strung up to cover the courtyard. She punches a pillow back into shape and settles under the blanket.

The tinny sound of someone knocking on metal filters through the rain.

'Adi? Where is she? I lose my key. One minute, maybe I find it. Adi? Open the door. Darling? Oh no, my key is gone in the water. *Habss.*'

Addy pulls one of Aicha's djellabas over her head and stumbles out into the courtyard. She tiptoes across the damp earth, feeling her way against a clay wall. When she hauls open the metal door, Omar stands there dripping water. He steadies himself against the door jamb and leans forwards, kissing her sloppily on the lips.

Addy reels back from the smell. 'You reek of whisky.'

'You have to know I never drink alcohol, only Coca-Cola.' He stumbles into the courtyard. 'Oops, it's a bad step there. I must fix it.'

'You're drunk.'

'No problem, *habibati.*' He drapes a wet arm over Addy's shoulders. 'The policeman have some whisky, so he invited me and some others to drink it with him. I must do it to be well with him.' He slumps against a wall and pulls Addy into a hug. 'What happened to you, darling? I looked for you at your house.'

Addy peels his wet arm from her shoulders. 'Your mother insisted I stay here. She didn't want me walking there in the dark.'

'It's a good decision. There are many bad men at night. I'm a bad man for you, darling. You must be careful of me.'

'Let's get you into the room. You don't want your mother to see you like this.'

'My mother can see me like this, no problem. I can walk fine, darling. I have control of myself.' He straightens his shoulders and takes a deep breath. Then he strides straight across the courtyard to his bedroom door. Addy shuts the metal door and runs across the courtyard.

'I'm sleeping in your mother's room, Omar.'

'If I am here, you sleep with me, *habibati*. Nobody can say anything about it.'

Addy hesitates, her hand on the door handle to Aicha's bedroom. What will his family think of her sleeping in Omar's room? Rachid and Nadia had seemed to be fine with it, but what would Aicha and Omar's grandmother think?

Behind his bedroom door, Omar retches.

The rooster wakes Addy early the next morning. Omar lies beside her, fully clothed in his jeans and his damp green denim jacket, his arm slung over the white sheet across her breasts. His face is turned away and her eyes follow the curve of his ear to the black wiry curls of his hair. The room is dark, but a halo of bright sunlight glows around the edges of the shuttered window, outlining his sleeping body.

As her eyes adjust to the dim light, shapes emerge – a guitar propped in a corner, a large wooden wardrobe missing a door, a desk of planks and concrete blocks, an Art Deco dresser with a cracked mirror, an analogue TV protruding from the wall on a bracket, a set of African drums.

She leans over Omar and studies his face. She kisses the hill of his cheek and slides out from under the sheet. Dressing quickly, she slips out of the room and tiptoes across the courtyard. The chickens are awake and scratching around the earth for titbits. The rooster glares at her and emits an ear-splitting crow as she hurries past.

Inside Aicha's bedroom, Addy rummages through her leather bag for her toothbrush, a comb, a pocket mirror and a lipstick. She skirts around the rooster and the chickens and heads to the tap by the kitchen door. She brushes her teeth and splashes her face with cold water. Twisting the lid off the lipstick, she examines her reflection in the pocket mirror. The purple smudges under her eyes from the Red Devil are gone and her complexion's the colour of milky coffee. Her eyes are almost turquoise in the Moroccan light. She twists the lipstick back into its tube and puts it into her pocket.

Addy sits beside Fatima on a log in front of the bread oven in the stable yard, doing her best to help her to bake the day's bread. Omar squats down beside Addy and scratches his bare head.

'It smells good. I'm very hungry.'

'Good morning.' Addy points to the bread. '*Agroume*. Fatima's teaching me Tamazight.'

Fatima giggles and prods a hot disc of bread out of the home-made clay oven with a poker and a wooden paddle. She adds it to a stack of bread in the straw basket by her feet. After scooping a raw circle of flattened dough onto the paddle, she slides it into the oven.

'I'm so sorry for last night, Adi.'

'Don't worry about it.'

'No, I'm sorry for it. I did a mistake.'

'You know, it's possible to drink and not get drunk if you only drink a little bit.'

'In Morocco, it's not possible.' Omar rises and stretches, letting out a loud yawn. 'We don't have alcohol often, so it's easy to get drunk. I even don't like alcohol, *habibati*. It tastes rubbish to me.

185

But it's nice to be with my friends, to feel good altogether. Then everybody is sick after. It's normal.'

Addy follows him through a heavy wooden door into the courtyard. 'You're not supposed to drink to get sick.'

'I'm only sick on the earth. Everybody else is sick in the car of the police. Even the police. He needs to clean it well. It's smelly.'

'You were out driving in the police car last night? When you were all drunk?'

Omar shrugs. 'It's fine. He's been the police of Zitoune since he was very young. He drives well. We went only to Oushane to see some friends.'

'You went back to Oushane? On that mountain road? With a drunken driver? Are you crazy? You all could have been killed.'

Omar drags the low wooden table and two stools out of the kitchen into the centre of the courtyard.

'Don't worry, darling. We know the road even if our eyes are closed. It wasn't our fate to have an accident last night.'

'I'll take you for a walk to the gorge today,' Omar says to Addy as they walk to her rented house. 'Today must be a special day for you since I did rubbish last night. The paths are for goats only, so tourists never go there.'

'That sounds great. I'll bring my camera.'

While Omar's in the bathroom, Addy roots through the chest of drawers. What has she done with the envelope of her father's Polaroids and his unfinished letter? She's been so absent-minded lately. Too much on her mind. She knocks *Let's Go Morocco* off the chest of drawers and the envelope plops onto a black zigzag on the thick white rug. Addy stoops to pick it up. She doesn't remember putting it inside the travel book. But, then, maybe she did.

She wraps the blue letter around the photo of Gus and Hanane and tucks it into her jeans pocket, hiding the envelope with the other Polaroids in the drawer underneath her underwear.

186

Omar emerges from the bathroom, his face dripping with water and his blue tagelmust wound around his head into a turban. He rifles through the wooden wardrobe and pulls out a long piece of white cloth.

Addy looks at Omar. 'A tagelmust?'

'Yes, darling. I know that Mohammed has tagelmusts here for tourists. You might lose your hat in the wind. You will be like the Amazigh Queen Dihya.'

'There was an Amazigh queen?'

'Yes, a long time ago in history.' He twists the fabric around Addy's head. 'Maybe one hundred years. Or one thousand.' He shrugs. 'Dihya was a Jewish lady, or maybe Christian. But for sure, she was an Amazigh lady. Anyway, she fight the Arabs for many years. They called her the Kahina. It means the Lady Who Sees the Future. They were frightened of her. They came to Africa to make everybody Arab and Muslim. Dihya made a big Amazigh army. She said the Imazighen are proud and we must be free. After many years of wars the Arabs became stronger and they won. So the Imazighen became Muslim then, so at least that's good. But we never became Arab.' He stands back and assesses his handiwork.

'A strong woman.'

Omar catches Addy's gaze in the mirror. 'For sure. It's why I choose you, darling. You are a strong lady like Dihya. You are the queen of me.'

Addy shifts her eyes away from his gaze. 'It's nice to be back in Zitoune. It almost feels like home.'

'It is your home.'

'Not really.'

'What you mean, *habibati*?'

'Nothing.'

Addy walks over to the mirror and stares at her reflection, patting the white turban. She drapes the long, loose tail of fabric across her shoulders. 'What happened to the Kahina?'

'She was captured. Then nobody knows. Some people say her djinni took her away to be safe.'

'Her djinni?'

'Yes. You must control djinn well or they can make big troubles.'

'You really believe in that?'

'For sure. Everybody believe in djinn.' Omar shrugs. 'Or maybe she poisoned herself.'

'Like Cleopatra.'

Omar tucks the end of his tagelmust into his turban. 'The Queen of Egypt. I know about her.'

'From school?'

'From Chakespeare.' He turns around and smiles. 'You are so beautiful, *habibati*. You are pure like a white flower close to my heart.' He comes over to her and cups her face with his hands. He brushes her lips softly with his.

Addy closes her eyes. The familiar warmth spreads across her belly and she leans into him.

Omar drops his hands and heads towards the door. 'So, we go?'

'Now?'

A smile plays on his lips. 'It's a long walk, *habibati*. We must keep our energy.'

# Chapter Thirty-One

**Zitoune, Morocco – February 1984**

Gus looks over his shoulder. 'Are you okay, Hanane?'

Hanane stumbles through the crevice and into the cave. She blinks to adjust her eyes to the morning sun streaming into the cave's dark recesses.

'I'm fine.'

She brushes the fine pink dust of the sandstone mountainside off her pink djellaba.

Gus takes her hand and leads her over to the far wall, where an ancient hunt gallops across the stone.

'Look, Omar showed me this place. I don't think there's a place he doesn't know in these mountains. I'm amazed he has time for school.'

'Omar is a very bad boy about school, not like his brother. Momo is such a good student. He told me he wants to be a teacher one day, like me.' Hanane traces her fingers over the delicate carvings, along the graceful curves of horned antelopes running from slender hunters with spears and bows and arrows. 'It's lovely. Whoever did this drew well.'

'I didn't know you were a teacher, Hanane.'

'I'm not. Not yet. But it's my dream to be a teacher. I practise on the boys. I help them with their homework. Maybe one day I'll be a real teacher.'

Hanane looks at Gus as he examines the carvings. She shouldn't be here with him, alone. It's only a slight comfort to know Omar and Yassine are down by the river keeping lookout for them. If she and Gus were seen alone together . . . no, she couldn't think about that. They're far away from the village. No one comes here. She didn't even know this cave existed. Even when she'd had the run of the fields and mountains when she was a girl, she'd never discovered it. And the fields where she searched for the plants for Jedda's medicines and potions were on the other side of the village, in the valleys around the river's source.

She taps the odd cuneiform letters running under the drawings like a lazy river. 'It's Tifinagh. Our language. I wish I could read it. I only recognise a few letters.'

Gus peers at the X's, zigzags and triangles, squinting as he takes a closer look. 'This is Tamazight?'

'Yes, I think so. There are several Amazigh dialects, but Tifinagh is the alphabet of all of them. Tamazight is the one we speak in the Middle Atlas Mountains.'

'It's amazing the language has managed to survive.'

'It's because the Imazighen are mountain and desert people. We were nomads for a long time. Many are nomads yet. We were away from the influences of the cities and the Arabic culture.'

Hanane watches Gus as he takes a picture of the drawings with his strange camera. A man of curiosity. Always wondering, looking, reading, sketching, taking pictures. Wanting to know all he can about the world around him. To absorb all that life has to offer into his very soul.

She wanders over to a large rock by the cave's mouth and sits down, the view of the valley, lush with spring green, below her.

'I've brought some more poems for you,' she says. 'I wrote them in English to practise.' She reaches through the side slit in her djellaba for the sheet of folded paper in her apron pocket.

He turns to her and smiles. His eyes the colour of the blue wild irises she seeks out for Jedda in the spring. The special flower that hides in the shade, like a shy girl, hesitant to reveal its beauty.

'That's wonderful, Hanane. I love your poems. I've got something for you, too. Wait one minute.'

He disappears into the wall crevice, leaving Hanane on her own. Maybe she made a mistake to bring these poems. Poems of love. Poems from her heart to his. What will he think of her boldness?

He staggers out of the crevice, a string bag laden with wrapped packages in his hand. He walks across to the rock and sits beside her, then pulls out a package wrapped in a tea towel. He unwraps it to reveal discs of fresh bread. He hands her another package wrapped in wax paper. Cold chicken legs.

'I got Omar to bring us a picnic.'

'I didn't see him carrying this on our way here.'

'No, he was out here earlier this morning. He hid it on a ledge in the wall and covered it up with stones. He's very resourceful.'

They spread out the picnic on the tea towels over the rock and share out the food. Bread sprinkled with semolina, fat black olives, plump chicken legs, hard-boiled eggs, and oranges as big as Gus's hand.

'Read me your poems,' Gus says as he chews on the bread.

'I've written short ones. The words flew into my mind and out of my fingers.'

'You have my undivided attention.'

She reaches through the side slit in her djellaba for the sheet of folded paper in her apron pocket. The sheet quivers in her hand. She takes a breath and reads:

> *Sky-riding swift*
> *Make your feathers a pen*
> *And write my love in the sky.*

*My heart is a harp*
*Silent until your fingers*
*Strum its silent song.*

*Settled by your side*
*We are like cats*
*In warm sun*
*Content in silence.*

She folds the paper and slides it back into her apron pocket. Silence. She folds her hands in her lap. The heat rises in her cheeks. She's made a terrible mistake.

Gus reaches over and rests his hand on hers. 'They're lovely, Hanane.'

She looks over at him. He swallows hard and stands. He walks over to the cave's mouth and rests a hand on the sandstone wall as he surveys the valley.

'Hanane, I love you. I don't know how or why it's happened.' He shakes his head and looks over at her. 'I shouldn't have let it happen. It can't happen, my love. I'm a Catholic. You're Muslim. One of us would have to convert, and I don't see that happening. My faith is the one constant I've had in my life. I'm so sorry. I should never have let it get this far.'

A heaviness descends over her liver, over her heart, as if her body's turning into the stone of these mountains. She blinks at the tears that threaten to weep from her eyes.

'I understand. It's all right. I understand.'

# Chapter Thirty-Two

**Zitoune, Morocco – May 2009**

Just past Yassine's café, Omar veers left down a narrow path through the olive grove. They meet a broad-shouldered farmer in coarse brown wool clothes leading a donkey towards Zitoune, the panniers fat with mounds of mint and thyme. He looks familiar – she's sure she's seen him in the village, or possibly in the olive groves. The farmer carries a thick, freshly-peeled wooden staff, which he jabs into the earth to steady his footing as Addy clings to an olive tree to let them pass. But Omar's as nimble as a goat, jumping out of their way as he greets the man in Tamazight. As the farmer disappears through the trees, Omar reaches behind and takes hold of Addy's hand.

'I miss to feel you, darling.'

'You're not shy about holding my hand?'

'Of course not. Your hand is my hand.'

'My last boyfriend didn't like to do it. It embarrassed him.'

Omar squeezes Addy's hand. 'I don't like to hear about your boyfriend. I'm jealous.'

'It's ancient history. Like Cleopatra.'

Omar looks over his shoulder. 'What happened?'

'He went with another lady. I didn't like it, so I finished with him.'

193

'In Morocco, it's not so strange for a man to go with another lady. I can have four wives.'

'Not with me you can't.'

Omar laughs. 'Darling, I know it. Anyway, I don't have energy for another lady. So, no problem.'

Addy drops hold of his hand and stops in the middle of the path. 'Omar. I . . . I . . .'

'What is it, *habibati*?'

She brushes her fringe out of her eyes. 'Why haven't you married? All your friends are married. I'm sure there are many Amazigh girls who'd love to marry you.'

The line between Omar's eyes deepens. 'Be sure about it, Adi. Since I was eighteen, many people came to my mother to arrange a marriage for me with their daughters. From all over Morocco, even.' He waves his hand in the air for emphasis. 'But I don't want it. Since I got older, the fathers come to me direct. They come from Beni Mellal, from Azaghar, even from Casa. In the mountains everybody knows about me.'

'I'm sorry, I didn't mean . . .'

Omar shrugs off Addy's tripod bag and leans it against the thick trunk of an olive tree.

'I work hard, Adi. I'm proud of myself. I made a good position for myself in Zitoune. Everybody wants me to be their son, but I say no.'

'Why?'

He scrutinises Addy and shakes his head. 'I don't want a lady who is quiet. I don't want a lady who is calm. I want a lady who challenges me well. So, I waited. Then I met you and I knew in my heart you are the lady I wait for.'

'I'm older than you.'

Omar slams his hand against the tree trunk. 'Adi, I don't mind for age. I told you that before.' His eyes narrow. 'Maybe it's a problem for you that I'm younger. That I'm not a professional man. That I'm an Amazigh man. You think I want a passport for England, isn't it?'

Addy hesitates. 'No. That's not true.'

Maybe she should walk away now. Let Omar live his life. Go back to England. Forget about the whole Hanane business and the travel book. Hanane and the baby are probably dead. The Fool. Philippa's Tarot card was right. She's just a fool to think this trip to Morocco was a good idea. She's all wrong here. Blast Rachid with his bloody pebble-in-the-pond business.

'I'm sorry, Omar. I've messed things up for you.' She peers through a screen of olive leaves at the shining river below. 'I'm not a naive young girl. I've had relationships, but I've never felt anything like this before. When I wake up in the morning, you're the one I want to see. You're in my mind. You're in my blood. But I don't know how we can make it work.' Tears sting her eyes and Addy wipes at them with her fingers. 'We're just too different.'

She has to tell him everything. About the cancer. About her infertility. This is no holiday romance. It's bigger than that. This is her life. She rubs the back of her hand against her wet eyes.

'Omar, I . . .'

Then his arms are around her. 'Never mind, Adi. You are the lady of my life. You have to know about it.'

Addy closes her eyes. The tears are rivers down her burning cheeks. Another time. She'll tell him another time.

The twin cliffs of the gorge tower above the river, like a giant has ripped the earth in two. The sky is as blue as Omar's tagelmust, throwing the red clay cliffs into sharp relief. Pigeons dive in and out of crevices, then burst out into a grey cloud that circles above the river until it dissolves back into the cliffs.

Omar points above. 'Falcon.'

The brown wings are silhouetted against the blue sky, the wing tips splayed like fingers. Addy captures images in her camera as the bird glides slowly down between the cliffs. Catching a thermal, it circles up to the top of the cliffs again in a lazy dance with the air.

'He'll be patient, Adi. One of the pigeons will be his lunch today.'

The bird folds its wings close to its body. It drops out of the sky like a stone. The pigeons burst out of the cliff, masking the sky with their grey cloud bodies. There's a screech and feathers falling, then the falcon's on the ledge pulling at the body of a pigeon with his hooked beak.

Addy's stomach rumbles.

Omar laughs. 'He makes you hungry, darling?'

'I'm actually starving. We should've brought some lunch.'

'We'll eat, don't worry about it. I made a good arrangement. We'll go to a cave. You see it over there?'

Addy follows his finger to a hole halfway up the cliff on the opposite side of the river.

'Up there? Are you kidding? How do we get up there?'

'I know a way. *Mashi mushkil.*'

Addy shades her eyes with her hand and squints at the cave. 'Heights make me nervous.'

'You will be fine, *habibati*. I'l keep you safe, I'm your guardian. You'll love it. I guarantee.'

Addy sucks in her breath and releases a long exhale. 'I'll do my best. No promises.'

Omar leads Addy over river stones to the opposite bank. She fights her natural cowardice as she leaps from stone to stone, the quick-flowing water splashing at her feet. On the far bank they follow a goat path up the cliff to a plateau. There's a crevice in the cliff, hidden from view from below. Omar takes Addy's hand and they squeeze into it, walking sideways. The cliff is so close to Addy's face that her nose itches from the dust.

'Are you sure this is safe?'

'Very safe. I been here many times.'

Omar pulls Addy through an opening in the rock. She blinks as her eyes adjust to the contrast of the black cave and the bright light streaming in from the cave's mouth.

The cave walls are alive with carvings. The same carvings as in her father's Polaroid. Crude grey gashes resembling horses, and drawings wrought by someone with some skill – the lines graceful, animals caught on the run, figures poised with spears behind them, curving lines of ancient writing framing the figures.

Dropping Omar's hand, she wanders over to a wall and traces along the outlines with her fingertip. Her father had been here, too. In February 1984. With Hanane.

'This is incredible.'

'They are very old. Like prehistoric.' Omar comes up behind her and lays his hand on hers, following her movements as she traces the curves of the fleeing animals. 'Antelopes. No antelopes here now.' He points to an animal with a spiky collar framing its face. 'A lion.'

'There were lions here?'

'Yes. Someone kill one near Oushane maybe fifty years ago. It's the last one.'

'Poor lions.' She runs her fingers over the odd angular letters – X's and triangles, zigzags and lines. 'They were trying to say something.'

'It's Tifinagh. Amazigh language. It's very, very old. Even me, I don't know how to read it. We only speak it. They don't teach Amazigh language in school, only Arabic and French. I'm so sorry for that situation, but the king he said he will change it. I hope so.'

'Can Jedda read it?'

'Jedda and my mother can't read or write, full stop. It's like that in the mountains for the older ladies.'

Addy turns around and finds Omar staring at her, an odd expression on his face. He releases her hand and walks over to the sunlit mouth of the cave. Reaching into his jeans pocket, he retrieves his cell phone.

'You're calling someone?'

'Yassine.'

'I thought you didn't like Yassine.'

197

Omar shrugs. 'He's like my brother. I grew up with him all my life. Only I will kill him if he touches you.'

Addy leans against the cool stone, watching him as he speaks to Yassine in a mix of Darija and Tamazight. Phone to his ear, he stands at the cave mouth, surveying the red sandstone cliffs and scrubby trees below like a king taking stock of his kingdom.

He pockets his phone. 'Yassine ask if you are well. I said you are the light of my forest making the darkness of the night pass.'

Addy crosses her arms. 'You shouldn't tease him. It'll come back to haunt you.'

'No problem, darling. I don't mind for ghosts.' He ambles over to Addy and untwists her arms, threading his fingers through hers. 'I teased Yassine since we are children. I was a clever boy. I had to teach Yassine to be clever as well. It's not natural for him.' A dimple forms in his cheek.

'How were you a clever boy?'

His eyebrows draw together. He leads her over to a large grey rock near the mouth of the cave, its edges polished by the wind and rain. They sit on the rock and Omar gazes out over the valley, his profile like a bust carved from the mountain stone.

'I must be clever, darling. My father died when I was a boy. It was an illness of the kidneys. Even my grandmother couldn't help him. She asked her djinni to help, but it didn't work. My family was very poor. I slept next to the donkey.'

'I'm so sorry, Omar.'

'So, I need to earn money so my family can live in a better way. In the night I would steal figs from a big tree which belong to a neighbour. Then in the day I sold the figs to the tourists. I did it for the almonds and the olives as well. I earned money and I made the other boys steal for me, like Yassine. I paid them one dirham each time and I keep the rest. So my family had better food. I followed the tour guides to learn English and Spanish. I was a good student.'

'Didn't you go to school?'

'Sometimes. I learned French and Arabic and mathematics. But sometimes I was a bad boy. I didn't go. So my grandmother punished me. She took a stick and put it in the fire and she burned me on my arm. I still have a mark here.' He pushes up the sleeve of his jacket and exposes the thin, smooth scar that Addy had assumed was from some teenage fight or a misstep on a mountain path.

Addy rubs her finger along the scar. 'That's an awful thing for her to do.'

'She had to. After my father died I was a wild boy. I didn't listen to my mother. I know my grandmother loves me a lot. I give her big respect.'

Addy eyes him as he stares out over the valley. His experience is so far removed from hers that it's like a work of fiction. Philippa wouldn't believe a word of it. *He's just after a British passport, Addy. It's all a sob story to get you tangled up with him.*

'Habibi?'

'Adi?'

'Did you really graduate from university in English literature?'

'You don't believe me?'

'The first day I met you, you said to me and the English girls at Yassine's café that you'd graduated from university.'

'Darling, it's for my honour I said I graduated. Sometimes it's better to say a smaller lie. It makes the path more smooth. I studied English literature for two years in Azaghar. When I was a boy I met a tourist who taught me English well. He lived in Zitoune for the summer. He liked me so I was the guide for him. I took him to the source of the waterfalls and here to the gorge. He loved it. He had a book and he taught me about Chakespeare and Julius Caesar. Good stories. I decided to go to the university in Azaghar to study English literature to become a teacher to make a better life for my family.'

'Why didn't you finish?'

'My family was proud of me but it was hard for them. I saved my money well to pay for the food of my family. I worked at the university even though I'm studying. I was in charge of an apartment with six students. I was military with them like the police, to make them study, to pray, not to drink alcohol. But it was hard for me. So one day after two years I walked over the mountains from Azaghar to Zitoune. I slept in the mountains. It was very cold. But I came home to make my family well. I built them a good house, with a kitchen and a toilet.

'After that I studied for one year to be a professional guide with the government. I can go in the mountains, I can go in the desert. It's true I didn't graduate the university.' He shrugs. 'It's a pity. But what can I do? It's my fate.'

'Do you like being a guide?'

'It's fine. It pays me well, but even so I think next year I will rent some land by the river to make a small restaurant for the summer. I can do guiding in the day and the restaurant in the night. I will do tagine and brochettes and Coca-Cola. My mum and my sister can cook it.' He jiggles Addy's shoulder with his. 'I have to earn more money so I can build a nice house for us.'

Addy's heart skips a beat. 'A house? For us?'

'I have the land already. I bought it when I was twenty-five years. I'm making a guest house for tourists. I'll make the best room at the top of the house for us so you can see the mountains. I have a plan to make tours to the desert and the mountains. One day, I want to build a big kasbah hotel, *inshallah*. With a swimming pool. Anyway, it's a nice dream.'

He smiles at Addy, the dimple marking his cheek. 'I talk a lot today, *habibati*. I never told anybody all this before. Nobody knows me like you do.'

Addy leans her head on his shoulder and he hugs her against his side. They sit in silence, watching the clouds slide across the hot blue sky. Philippa's voice fades to nothing.

When Addy rises, Omar takes her by the shoulders and turns

200

her to face the wide mouth of the cave. The sun bleaches out the cliff wall on the other side of the gorge. He lifts the tail of her white tagelmust and draws it across her eyes, tucking the end into the folds of fabric covering her head.

She reaches up and touches the white cloth. 'What are you doing?'

Omar whispers into her ear. 'You trust me, *habibati*?'

A quiver in her stomach. 'Yes.'

'Stay like this, darling. Don't look for me.'

She hears him move away and she shivers, even though the cave is warm from the hot sun. Then his fingers are at her mouth and she tastes the firm, waxy skin of a grape. The ripe pulp explodes in her mouth. She spits out the seed and swallows the sweet fruit. Omar feeds her another. The juice runs down the side of her mouth and she feels his tongue lick it away.

He walks away, his footsteps like sandpaper on the fine dust of the cave's floor. Addy stands there – for a minute, then five minutes, the time elastic. Should she do something? Move? The billowing fabric of his tagelmust settles around her body. He's behind her and he draws her against his body with the fabric. His lips soft on her neck, tasting her earlobe, tracing a path to her shoulder. He pulls the fabric tight and she's wrapped against him like a package.

'*Hemlaghkem, hemlaghkem*,' he whispers as he maps her pliant body. 'I love you, Adi. I say it in my own language, so I mean it for true.'

Is she Adi? Addy? Della? Adela? Does it matter? She's the warm cave air, the dry red dust, the drifting clouds. She's the falcon gliding on a thermal up into the hot blue sky . . .

Omar unwinds the white cloth over Addy's eyes. He points to the picnic he's spread out on his blue tagelmust on the cave floor. 'I know I made you even more hungry, *habibati*.'

Grapes and bread, olives, oranges and cold mutton. Even a bottle of white wine. He lifts up the bottle, giving it a shake.

'You recognise it, darling? You bought it in Marrakech. You forgot about it. I bring it from Essaouira. Yassine bring everything to the cave for me this morning. I called him to find where he hid the food so the animals didn't eat it.'

They sit in the mouth of the cave and let their legs dangle over the edge of the cliff as they eat the lunch. Below, the view over the mountain valley spreads out like an exotic quilt. Except for the birds gliding across the blue sky, and the occasional shiver of a scraggy bush as some unseen animal skims by, they have the world to themselves.

Addy slips the Polaroid out of her pocket and unwraps it from the blue letter. Gus and Hanane leaning towards each other as they smile at the photographer.

'Are you sure you don't recognise them?'

Omar takes the photo from her. He shakes his head. 'I told you before, I don't know them. How you get this picture, Adi?'

Addy taps her father's smiling face. 'He's my father. Gus Percival.'

'Serious?'

'Yes, he was here in Zitoune for several months twenty-five years ago. Is there anyone in Zitoune who might remember them? I've shown it to your mother and Mohammed and your grandmother. I've even shown it to the policeman. He gives me the creeps. I don't like him.'

'You showed them the picture?' The crease appears between his eyes. 'Nobody recognised them?'

'No. No one.'

He taps the blue letter. 'What's this?'

'Nothing. A letter my father sent me from Morocco, but I don't have all of it. It just makes me feel like he's with me.'

Omar hands the Polaroid back to Addy. 'Many tourists come to Zitoune. Anyway, it's a long time ago. It's history now. Like Cleopatra.'

# Chapter Thirty-Three

### Azaghar, Morocco – May 2009

Yassine leaps out of his car. His tie-dyed tagelmust and voluminous blue gown swamp his slight frame. He sweeps his hand towards the dusty black Renault as he calls up to her on the veranda.

'My chariot is open to you, Turquoise.'

Addy rolls her eyes as she puts on her straw hat. She slings her camera around her neck and heads down the gravel path. When she reaches the car, Yassine grabs her hand and traps it between his palms.

'Since Omar is my brother, you are my sister.'

Omar reaches across the driver's seat and prises Yassine's fingers off Addy's.

'I am happy for that, Yassine. But if you touch her again, you'll be in troubles.'

A shadow passes across Yassine's face before he sets his mouth into a toothy smile. '*Mashi mushkil*, my brother. I only admire my beautiful sister. You are very lucky, my friend.'

'Maybe I'm lucky.'

Addy snaps her head around to Omar, surprised by his tone. 'Is there something wrong?'

'*Mashi mushkil*. Close the door, Adi. We must hurry to pick up my mother and Fatima.'

She wrenches the door closed as Omar sifts through a stack of CDs. 'Don't forget, we need to stop at the city hall in Azaghar.'

'I know. Even so, you'll find nothing, I'm sure about it.'

What was wrong? Was it the photo? Had he remembered something that had upset him?

Fatima and Aicha crowd into the back of the car with a net bag stuffed with towels, combs and a bottle of shampoo, squashing Addy between them like jam between bread.

Outside Zitoune, Yassine pushes the engine of the Renault like a Formula One driver. He careers around the curves, shifting gears wildly, and presses the accelerator to the floor on the straight stretches of road. A straw-hatted farmer on a donkey emerges from behind a cluster of bushes onto the road ahead. Yassine swerves the car, throwing Addy against Aicha and then against Fatima. Aicha clutches her hand to her mouth, her eyes glazed with panic.

'Yassine! Stop the car! Omar's mother's going to be sick.'

Omar waves his hand without turning around. 'No problem, darling. She'll be fine. She's always like that in a car.'

Droplets of sweat glisten on Aicha's top lip and Addy thrusts her straw hat at her. Fatima presses the end of her hijab against her mouth and gags.

'Now! Stop now!'

Yassine slams on the brakes, jerking the car to a stop on the side of the road in a cloud of red dust. Aicha and Fatima stumble out of the car and lean over a ditch, heaving and retching. Addy climbs out to help. Her straw hat lies in the dust, full of Aicha's breakfast.

A car door slams shut with a bang. Omar strides over to his mother, clutching a large bottle of water. Aicha rinses out her mouth and splashes water onto her face. She hands the water bottle to Fatima, who drinks thirstily. They dry their faces with the ends of their hijabs.

'I'm sorry for your hat, Adi.'

Addy shields her eyes with her hand. 'I'm going to need a hat today. Otherwise, I'll turn as red as a tomato.'

Omar picks up the hat by the loop on the brim and slaps it against a rock. He takes the water bottle from Fatima. Holding the hat away from him like a soiled nappy, he splashes it with water until the straw is clean and hands it to her.

'There. It's clean. Now we go.'

'You have no records of a woman named Hanane from Zitoune marrying a foreigner in 1984? You're sure?'

The clerk looks up from the Polaroid and hands it back at Addy, his fleshy face dull with disinterest. '*Non*, madame.'

'I told you it was impossible, Adi. It's a long time ago. You should forget about it.'

'I know, Omar. I thought it was worth a try. I don't know what else to do.'

'It's better to go forward than to go backward.'

'But I might have a half-brother or a half-sister in Morocco somewhere. If Hanane had had a child, I'd be its sister.'

Omar raises his eyebrows. 'It's true?'

'Yes, we'd have the same father.'

Omar shakes his head. 'It's a crazy situation. Anyway, fate doesn't want you to know about it. The door is closed.'

'Why doesn't anyone in Zitoune remember her? She was very beautiful. Everyone knows everybody in your village. You were young, so I know why you wouldn't remember her, but Mohammed? Your mother? Jedda? The policeman? They're old enough to remember.'

'Maybe the lady was from another village.'

Addy sighs as she wraps the Polaroid in her father's letter. 'You're probably right. It looks like I've hit a dead end.'

Yassine swings the car onto a large square of waste ground surrounded by the backs of shop buildings. To the right, a

205

windowless orange clay building abuts a stony hill. Women and girls dressed in colourful djellabas, hijabs and babouches pass through a tall green metal door.

'It's the hammam,' Omar says. 'Today is the day for ladies only.'

Another cluster of chatting and giggling women exits the building.

'How long will we be here?'

'A while. I don't know for time.'

'A couple of hours?'

Omar sighs. 'Maybe. I don't know. I'll come when you're finished.'

'But how will you know when?'

'Don't worry, Adi. I'll know. I'll go with Yassine and we'll come later.' He gestures to her camera. 'You must give me your camera. It's forbidden to take pictures in the hammam.'

She lifts the strap over her head and hands the camera to Omar. 'Be careful with it.'

'What do you mean? I'm not a rubbish guy. I can take pictures well. I learned from the tourists since I was a boy. You have to know, your camera is safe.'

A sturdy woman in a lime green djellaba pays an old woman, as brown and wrinkled as a prune, who sits behind a wooden table. Three small children, a boy and two girls, wrap their arms around the woman's green bulk. The old woman groans, clutching her back as she levers herself up from her stool. She shuffles over to a shelf stacked with washing mitts and small packages wrapped in wax paper, and hands one of each to the woman in green. The woman thanks her and waddles over to a long bench, the children clinging to her all the way.

Aicha steps forwards, handing her net bag to Fatima. She chats with the old woman as she retrieves a small leather pouch rattling with coins out of a slit in the side of her djellaba. Addy offers her money, but Aicha wags her finger at her.

'*Laa*, Adi.' She puts her hand on her breast. '*Yamma* Adi.' I am the mother of Adi.

The old woman supplies Aicha with washing mitts and three small waxed paper packets. The palms of her hands are dyed red with henna.

Addy peels open the packet. A sticky brown goo clings to the waxy paper. She holds it up to her nose and sniffs.

Fatima makes a scrubbing motion over her arm. '*Savon*.'

'Soap?'

Fatima nods. 'Soup.'

Aicha pulls the towels out of her net bag and stuffs them into one of the cubbyholes lining the walls. She fills the bag with the mitts and packets of soap, then steps out of her babouches and Addy follows suit, kicking off her sandals. Addy eyes Fatima and Aicha to see how much clothing to remove. Her jeans are around her knees when she hears the chatter of female voices. Three young women appear around a corner, naked except for the bikini underwear clinging to their slim brown bodies. Their long, wet hair spiders across their shoulders and breasts.

Their chatter stops abruptly. Addy recognises Fatima's friend Zaina, who sweeps her eyes over Addy's pale body. Holding Zaina's gaze, Addy steps out of her jeans and reaches behind her back to undo her bra. Zaina flicks her eyes over Addy's breasts. The scar on her left breast is still red and angry, but Addy resists the urge to cover it with her hand.

Zaina says something to Fatima; Addy catches Omar's name. Fatima snaps back at Zaina in Tamazight. Addy shoves her clothes into a cubbyhole. When she's done, Aicha loops her arm through one of Addy's. Fatima slings the net bag over her shoulder and does the same. Then they stroll, arm in arm, past the girls and into the hammam.

Nothing that Omar's said prepares Addy for what she sees when they pass through the wooden door into the bath house. Crumbling Corinthian stone columns flank walls hewn out of the stony hill. Fingers of light filter through the steam from circular holes in the high domed ceiling. Intricate mosaics of smiling dolphins, curling waves and bare-breasted sea nymphs cavort across the floor. A muscular stone Neptune with a broken trident poses on a pedestal at the centre of the vast room.

The space is alive with women – washing, chatting, pouring buckets of water over their hair and bodies. The water plasters the wet fabric of their underwear translucently against their bodies. Naked children run squealing over the mosaic sea world.

Addy slips across the wet floor, struggling to keep her balance as Fatima pulls her over to a small wooden stool. Aicha drags over two more stools and hands Addy a packet of soap and a mitt, while Fatima fetches a plastic bucket of steaming water from a water spout beneath Neptune. Aicha demonstrates how to rub the sticky brown goo into the mitt, wet it in the water bucket and rub it over her body.

The soap seeps into Addy's pores like glue. As she scrubs with the coarse mitt, pellets of black dirt roll off her skin. Aicha rubs at Addy's back until Addy's convinced several layers of skin are peeling off with the dirt.

Fatima gestures for Addy to get up and she stands, self-conscious of her short red hair plastered over her forehead, her reddened skin and her exposed nipples. She clutches her arms in front of her breasts, glad of the black bikini underwear that protects her from full exposure. Fatima pours the bucket of hot water over her like a shower.

Dripping with water, Addy shuffles behind Aicha and Fatima through an archway into a smaller domed room. The mosaic floor is dry and warm, and women lie stretched out on it like starfish. Ancient leather-skinned women, their breasts hanging loose like empty sacks, pummel the women's bodies.

Aicha calls over one of the women. Addy lies down on the warm tiles and rests her head on her arms as the woman pounds and kneads the tensions of the past year out of her flesh. The warmth of the heated floor seeps into her skin, until she's floating in a warm green sea, the waves circling and kneading her body.

A crash of freezing water. Addy jolts upright, coughing and sputtering. Above her, Fatima holds an empty bucket, giggling. Aicha stands next to her, a hand up to her mouth, her eyes wide with alarm.

Addy staggers to her feet. The chatter of the women in the spa trickles to a stop. Fatima's giggles fade away, swallowed up by the silence. Addy extracts the bucket from Fatima's hands and strides across the floor to the cold water tap. She fills the bucket to the brim and carries it over to Aicha, gesturing at Fatima with her chin. Aicha's worried face breaks into a wide grin. She grabs the side of the bucket and they swing it between them, deluging Fatima with icy water. The room erupts into peals of high-pitched laughter.

'*Marhaba*, Fatima.'

Laughing, Fatima wrings the water out of her long black hair. She flings her hair over her shoulders and grabs Addy, kissing her on her cheeks.

'Adi *watnasse* Fatima.' You are my sister.

'I'm glad for that,' Omar says when Addy tells him about the experience in the hammam. 'I made you a good experience so you can carry it with you all your life.'

She rolls over on her bed to face him. 'I saw Fatima's friend Zaina there. She always looks at me like she's sizing me up. I don't think she likes me.'

'Don't worry about her.'

Addy picks at a loose thread on the sheet. 'Has she been a friend of Fatima's for a long time?'

Omar looks up at the ceiling and frowns. Addy follows his gaze. A large black spider hangs from a web in the corner.

'For sure. They been to school together. Her family lives close to our house. Zaina comes all the time to see Fatima. It's normal.'

'So, she's the same age as Fatima?'

'Yes. Maybe twenty-five years.'

'Twenty-five? And she's not married yet?'

Omar reaches over to the bedside table and picks up his cell phone. He starts running through his messages.

'It might be she will marry soon.'

'She's very pretty. I'll bet she makes a good tagine, too.'

Omar sets down his phone and rolls over on his side. He leans on his elbow. 'For sure. She cooks well. She helps Fatima to make the bread sometimes. Don't mind for Zaina.'

'She'll make someone a good wife someday.'

'If it's her fate, it's her fate. No reason to be jealous.'

'I'm not jealous.' Addy leans over and kisses him. 'You're mine and I'm yours.'

'You're sure, Adi?'

'Yes. What do you mean?'

Omar rolls off the bed and pads across the floor. He picks up Addy's camera from the top of the chest of drawers. Flopping down on the bed, he scrolls through the images and stops at a photo of Nigel and Addy, arms around each other, smiling in front of a Christmas tree in their flat. Her heart sinks.

Omar taps the screen and Nigel's face grows until only his hazel eyes are visible. 'He's your boyfriend?'

She bites into her lip. 'Not any more.'

Omar flips through the photos. More of her and Nigel with Philippa at his birthday dinner the past October. She places her hand over the screen and prises the camera out of his hands.

'None of this matters, Omar. It's over.'

'You're sure?'

'Yes, I'm sure.'

'A hundred per cent?'

'A hundred per cent.'

He reaches his arms around Addy and pulls her against his chest. 'It's a hard situation, *habibati*. You go back to England soon and you'll forget about me. You're in my blood, Adi. If you leave me, I'll throw myself in the waterfalls. It's not a possibility for me to live without you. Full stop.'

So this is why he's been acting so strangely today. He's jealous of Nigel. He's afraid she'll abandon him as soon as she's back in London. Addy rests her cheek against his chest. Everything'll be okay. They'll find a way. She shuts her eyes and listens to Omar's heartbeat. A vision floats into her mind.

Zaina.

# Chapter Thirty-Four

**Zitoune, Morocco – May 2009**

Addy's cell phone buzzes and spins on the table. Philippa. She should've phoned her back.

'Hi, Pippa. Sorry I haven't called. I've been really busy with the book.'

'Finally. I was about to ring Interpol. Why don't you answer any of your bloody messages?'

'Sorry. I was going to call you today. Honestly.'

Philippa snorts. 'How busy can you be? What's there? A desert and some mountains. It's hardly a hotspot on the jet-setter's guide to the high life.'

Addy swings her bare feet onto the wooden table and leans back in her chair. 'Well, there's the sex, of course.'

Philippa chokes and coughs. 'Good God, Addy. I'll have to remember not to call you when I've got a gin in my hand. It's all over my new Stella McCartney. Don't tell me you're shagging the goatherd?'

Addy unwinds the white tagelmust from around her neck and flaps at a fly. She wasn't going to let Philippa get the better of her this time.

'You know how they say sex is good for the skin? Well, they're right, Pippa. My cheeks are as soft as a baby's bottom.'

Philippa sucks in her breath, the 'sss' of the saliva sloshing against her teeth. 'Addy, are you mad? Do you have any idea what you're getting yourself into? The next thing you know he'll be asking you for money. Mark my words.'

'He's not like that. He works really hard, he's smart and funny, and good-looking. You should see him when he wears his turban. So, well done me.'

'Oh, rub it in, why don't you? You know I haven't had a date since shoulder pads were in fashion.'

Despite herself, Addy laughs. 'Sorry, Pippa. About getting annoyed. Not about the shoulder pads.'

'Fine. Apology accepted.' The line goes silent.

'Pip? Are you there?'

'Addy, I hope you're sitting down.'

'Why?'

'Nigel's been in touch.'

The stones on the path crunch and Addy peers over the railing. Omar is strolling up the hill to the house, a straw hat swinging from his fingertips.

Addy lowers her voice, covering her mouth with her free hand. 'He's been texting me. I haven't answered.'

'He dropped by my house and cried on my shoulder for an hour last week. He feels awful about what happened. He said he was suffering from post-traumatic stress or some such rot. I actually started to feel sorry for the wanker.'

Nigel's handsome face, flattened into a mask of panic after the doctor had given Addy the diagnosis, floats into Addy's mind. She squashes the image like a bug. The steps up to the veranda creak.

'That's all water under the bridge, Pippa. Listen, I have to go.'

'There's something else.'

213

Omar tosses the straw hat to Addy like a frisbee. She points to the phone and mouths 'Philippa'.

Pressing a finger against his lips, he tiptoes across the stone slabs. He grabs the phone and presses the speakerphone button.

'I . . . I really should get back to the book, Pip.' Addy eyes Omar nervously. 'Still lots to do and time's running out.'

'Oh, all right. So, I don't need to call Interpol then?' Philippa's clipped vowels echo around the terrace. 'You haven't been kidnapped and sold as a sex slave?'

Omar backs away from Addy, holding the phone to his ear. '*Allô? Allô?*'

Addy swings her legs off the table and grapples for the phone. 'Hello? Addy? Who's this?'

'It's Omar.'

'Would you kindly put my sister back on the phone, please?'

'No, it's not possible.' Omar winks at Addy.

Addy's eyes widen and she shakes her head at Omar.

'Why isn't it possible?' Philippa's words shoot down the phone connection like bullets.

'It's not a good situation to discuss.'

Addy lunges for the phone, but Omar sidesteps her.

'Give me the phone, Omar.'

'Addy? Are you okay?'

'She's okay. Don't worry. *Mashi mushkil.*'

'Give me the flipping phone, Omar. This isn't funny.'

'Mashy what? What do you mean it's not a good situation? Put Addy back on the phone this minute. Addy? Can you hear me?'

He holds the phone up out of Addy's reach. 'I think Adi will stay in Morocco.'

'Oh, for fuck's sake. Put Addy back on the bloody phone right now, you idiot.'

The corners of Omar's mouth twitch. 'No, I'm sorry for that.

214

It's impossible. She'll stay in Morocco. So, goodbye.' Omar ends the call and drops the phone into Addy's hand.

She stares at the phone. He has no idea what he's just done. Philippa'll never forgive him.

'Omar! Why did you do that?' Pressing Philippa's number, Addy holds the phone up to her ear as she shoots daggers at him with her eyes.

Omar slaps his hands on his legs and bursts into laughter. 'Don't worry, darling. It's a big joke.'

'That wasn't funny.'

'Omar?' Philippa's voice has risen several decibels.

'It's Addy. Don't worry, Pippa. I'm fine. I'm so sorry.' Addy glares at Omar. 'Omar was being a total idiot. He thought he was being funny.'

'Are you sure you're okay? You can talk freely?'

'I'm fine. Everything's fine.' She glares at Omar who is doubled over in laughter. 'Except I'm probably going to kill him after I hang up.'

Philippa expels a long breath. A faint clink of ice against glass and a loud swallow.

'You're turning me into an alcoholic. Maybe we should have sorted out a safe word. Like umbrella.'

'Okay, umbrella. I'm okay, really. Don't worry.'

The ice clinks. 'Tell your bloody boyfriend he's a total ass.'

Addy shoots Omar another ugly look. He's wiping tears from his cheeks with the end of his tagelmust.

'I already did.'

'Will you get the bloody hell out of there as soon as you can? My nerves can't take much more of this.'

'I'll be home before you know it.'

'Fine. Just please answer my messages or I *will* call Interpol. You're the only family I have. Don't go leaving me an orphan.'

'Don't go getting mushy on me, Pips. I prefer you when you're stroppy. I promise I'll call.'

'Good.'

'Oh, was there something else you wanted to tell me?'

'Never mind. It can wait.'

'I'm really sorry about this.'

'You're forgiven. This time. Just remember where your home is. It's not in the middle of bloody nowhere with a fucking idiot. And I hope he heard that.'

# Chapter Thirty-Five

**Zitoune, Morocco – May 2009**

*Her reflection stares back at her in the hospital cubicle mirror. Her beige linen trousers puddle over her tan loafers, too long, but she hasn't had the time to get them hemmed. Blue veins spread over her breasts like vines. A white plaster hides the puncture wound left by the needle biopsy. She leans into the mirror and pokes at the plaster. The lump underneath is hard and throbs from the puncture. An odd pressure encircles her neck. She puts her hand on her throat. Lumps erupt through her fingers. She digs at the lumps with her fingernails until her fingers run red with blood.*

'Adi! *Habibati*! You been dreaming.'

She opens her eyes. Omar's face hovers over her. She gasps and reaches for her neck. The lumps are still there. She sits bolt upright. A rope of turquoise stones falls into her lap.

Omar picks up the necklace and fastens it around Addy's neck. He sits back on the bed and smiles.

'It's so nice on you, honey. You're like an angel of Zitoune. I know you love this colour.'

Addy runs her fingertips over the stones, as large as Medjool dates. She brushes a stone against her teeth – slightly rough, like a large blue-green pearl. 'It's beautiful.'

'I looked for turquoise for you, darling. I heard Yassine call you Turquoise in Essaouira. I don't like it at all. I find the most beautiful necklace of turquoise for you in Azaghar when you were in the hammam. Now, if anybody calls you Turquoise, you will think of me.'

After Omar leaves to meet a tour bus from Marrakech, Addy stops by Aicha's house to return a cooking pot. Jedda sits on a stool in the courtyard, the black-and-white cat snoozing at her feet, slitting open peapods with her fingernail and popping the bright green peas into a large pot.

Addy drags over a stool and perches on it, setting the cooking pot on the ground by her feet. She picks up a handful of the peapods and dumps them into her lap. She runs her fingernail along the ridge of the peapod, but it snaps in two. Omar's grandmother Jedda flashes her a toothless smile. She demonstrates her technique as she chatters to Addy in Tamazight. Addy slides her fingernail along another peapod and flicks the peas around the courtyard to the squawking delight of the chickens.

Fatima emerges from the kitchen with a basket laden with vegetables. '*Bonjour*, Adi.' She sets down the basket and kisses Addy's cheeks.

Squatting beside her grandmother, Fatima takes a paring knife out of her apron pocket. She selects an onion from the basket and prises at the papery skin with the knife. Tears trickle down her cheeks.

'*Oh, la la. Labass?*' She brushes away the tears with the back of her hand.

Addy points to the onions. '*Labass?* Onions?'

'*Oui. Awnyonz.*' She reaches into the basket and holds up a carrot. '*Zroudiya.*'

'*Zroudiya.* Carrot.'

Jedda grabs a potato and pretends to bite it.

'*Batata*,' Fatima says.

'*Batata.* Potato.'

Fatima and Jedda grin at Addy.

'*Awnyonz, krut, badado,*' Fatima repeats as she points to the vegetables, like she's revising for an exam.

Someone pounds on the metal front door. The tinny sound reverberates around the courtyard.

'*Chkoun?*'

'Zaina.'

Fatima drops her knife and the half-peeled onion into the pot and crosses the courtyard to the door. Zaina enters carrying a basket of laundry. When she sees Addy, her eyes narrow for an instant before she recovers herself.

Reeling out the familiar greeting, Zaina kisses Fatima on her cheeks and Jedda on the top of her head. Addy extends her right hand.

'*Sbah lkhir,* Zaina.'

Zaina touches Addy's hand with the tip of her fingers as if she's contagious. Fatima tugs on Zaina's arm and the girls disappear into the kitchen. Addy picks up Fatima's knife and a potato. She rasps the knife along the brown skin. Glancing up, she sees Jedda staring at her with her clear blue eye.

Jedda picks up her stick and jabs it at the kitchen.

Addy nods. 'Zaina.'

Fatima and Addy break out of the shade of the olive grove near a shallow bend in the river, safely away from the churning current. A woman's voice calls from the path behind them. A tall, slender woman carrying a plastic basket of laundry joins them by the river. Her skin's as black as liquorice and tendrils of pure white hair escape from her red headscarf.

'Lamia! *Sbah lkhir!*' Fatima greets her, kissing the woman several times. She turns to Addy. 'Lamia lives in the mountains. She likes to be private. She never marry. She knows my grandmother a long time.'

'*Sbah lkhir,*' Addy says as she smiles at the woman. She looks around for Zaina but she's striding ahead towards the women washing laundry in the river.

Fatima calls out to Zaina. She turns around and glares at Addy, huffing as she shifts her laundry basket over to her other hip.

Addy sets down the pink plastic basket full of Omar's dirty laundry that Fatima has given her and rubs at the red dents in her fingers. Half a dozen women stand knee-deep in the cold water, chattering in Tamazight as they scatter washing powder over clothes like snow. Others beat and twist the clothes in the water to force out the dirt. The women shout greetings when they see Fatima and Lamia. Fatima puts her arm around Addy and calls out Addy's name.

The women wave and shout. '*Marhaba*, Adi.'

They join Zaina on the riverbank and set down their laundry baskets. Fatima, Lamia and Zaina roll up their pyjama legs then discard their socks and shoes. Addy pulls off her sandals and sits on a rock to roll up her jeans over her knees as the others grab clothes out of their baskets and head out into the water. Fatima beckons to Addy, pointing to a bag of washing powder she's left on the riverbank.

'*Prendre le Teede.*'

Addy collects the plastic bag of Tide detergent and an armful of Omar's laundry then wades out into the water. She shivers as the cold water creeps up past her knees. The river current pulls at her ankles and she wavers on the slippery stones as she tries to stay upright.

They settle a short distance from the other women, where the water is relatively calm. Addy sprinkles the washing powder over the dirty clothes and hands the detergent to Fatima. As Addy rubs the white granules into the fabric, the hard grains scrape against her knuckles like sandpaper. She sucks on a knuckle, coughing and spitting as the residue of the washing powder coats her tongue.

'*Laa*, Adi.' Fatima laughs as Addy rubs the end of her kaftan top against her tongue.

Lamia wades over to join them. She moves with such youthful grace that it's only when she's close that Addy sees the deep lines around her eyes.

Fatima taps the skin on her cheek. 'I am dark like Lamia. The mans like ladies to be pale. Only poor mans ask to marry me. I don't want to marry a poor man.'

A crash of water. A scream rips through the air. Addy, Fatima and Lamia spin around and see the current sucking Zaina out towards the river, her washing drifting around her like water lilies. She screams as she flails in the current.

The women rush towards her and reach out to her, but the current pulls her away from them faster than they can get to her. Addy takes a deep breath and dives into the churning river. The current wraps around her body, tugging her into the middle of the river. She gasps and chokes as she's swept along. The water pushes her against a submerged rock. Addy clings to it like a lifebuoy. She sees Zaina being pulled along the river towards the waterfalls. She hears Fatima scream. She doesn't see the branch that hits her. And then, nothing.

221

# Chapter Thirty-Six

**Zitoune, Morocco – May 2009**

'Adi?'

Addy chokes and coughs, water spewing from her mouth. Someone pulls her to a sitting position and slaps her back. She gasps and opens her eyes.

'You are fine?' A familiar face with worried brown eyes hovers over her.

Addy wipes her mouth and gulps in air. 'Amine?'

'Adi!' Fatima throws her arms around her and covers her face with kisses.

'I'm okay. *Je suis bien.*' An ache spreads across the back of her head. She sucks in her breath when her fingers touch the soft lump.

'A tree, it hit you,' Amine says.

She scans the faces crowding over her. 'Where's Zaina?'

'*Mashi mushkil,*' Amine says. 'She went on a rock and we take her out of the water. She's okay. They take her to the house of her family.'

'Good.' Addy wipes droplets of water from her eyelashes. 'What happened?'

Amine squats down beside her. His clothes are dripping wet

222

and he shivers. 'Omar tell me when he go for guiding to watch you to make sure you are fine. When you go to the river to make the washing, I follow you.'

'You're soaking.'

'I go in the water for you. *Mashi mushkil.*'

'Amine, you could've been killed.'

Amine's teeth chatter. 'It's fine. I swim many times in the river.'

'It happened so fast. It seemed safe where we were, but when Zaina fell, I—'

Fatima wails to Amine in Tamazight and points frantically at the river.

'What is it, Amine?'

'She say Zaina fall in the water because she is jealous for you. She make a theatre.'

'No one would do something like that.'

'It might be.'

Amine and Fatima pull Addy to her feet. Her clothes stick to her body and her teeth click against each other. Lamia, her skirt and pyjamas sodden, emerges from the crowd with a blanket and wraps it around Addy's shoulders. She rubs Addy's arms and pats her on the back like a baby.

'Lamia's almost as wet as you,' Addy says to Amine.

'She help me get you out. She's very strong.'

'You must be freezing, Amine. You're as wet as I am.'

'*Mashi mushkil.*' He flashes Addy a bright smile through his shivers.

Fatima and Lamia wrap their arms around Addy's waist. They hug her close and follow Amine along the riverbank back to the house. The crowd slides around them, murmuring and patting Amine on the back.

No one mentions Zaina.

'Adi? Where are you?' The front door rattles against the clay wall.

'In here.'

Omar rushes into the living room, the deep crease of worry between his eyes. Addy is perched on the banquette in Aicha's living room drinking tea, wrapped like a Buddha in layers of blankets. Jedda sits next to her, mumbling as she stamps her walking stick on the ground. On the opposite banquette, in Omar's Chelsea T-shirt and a pair of Omar's jeans, Amine sits munching on one of Fatima's home-baked cookies.

'What happened, *habibati*? When I went to the café of Yassine, he told me you fell in the river. I left the tourists and I ran here like a wild animal.'

'I went to help Fatima and Zaina with the washing. Zaina fell and I tried to help her but I got into trouble in the current.'

Omar draws his eyebrows together. 'Fatima!'

'Don't blame Fatima. It's not her fault.'

Fatima and Lamia enter carrying trays of tea, cookies and bread, with bowls of honey and olive oil.

'*Naam*?'

Omar rips into Fatima in angry Tamazight.

'No, Omar.' Amine wipes cookie crumbs off his chin. 'It's true what Adi say. Zaina fall into the water and Adi try to rescue her but a tree hit Adi on the head.'

'You are supposed to watch her. *Allah i naal dine omok*. You been sleeping.'

Addy shakes her head. 'If it wasn't for Amine, I'd have drowned. I owe him my life.'

Lamia glances over to Jedda. Addy catches the exchange. Is there a nod? A blink? No, she must have imagined it. Lamia taps on Omar's arm and whispers to him urgently.

Omar looks at Addy. 'She says Zaina pretended to be in trouble in the water so you would drown.'

'That would've been a crazy thing for her to do. It's too dangerous.'

'It's not so dangerous for her. She knows the river well. She knows where there's a big rock to be safe.'

224

'Why would she hate me enough to want me to drown?'

Jedda whacks her stick on the floor and mumbles angrily.

Omar's eyes narrow. 'Jedda says Zaina has a bad djinni in her. She has a big jealousy for you. She says Zaina wants you to be died so I will marry her. She says Zaina put the bad eye on you.'

Jedda nudges Omar's arm with her stick and says something. Addy glances at the old woman. Her clear blue eye is staring at Addy, sharp and intense.

'What did she say?'

'She says she put a bad eye on Zaina as big as the waterfalls. Zaina will be in troubles now. My grandmother has a big magic.'

# Chapter Thirty-Seven

**Zitoune, Morocco – May 2009**

A knock on the metal door of Aicha's house and it squeaks open. Fatima is midway through pouring a graceful spout of mint tea into tea glasses. Amine crosses the threshold, his smile bright and wide in his mottled face. His jeans and T-shirt are spotlessly clean and he wears glowing white Adidas trainers.

Addy waves him over. 'Hello, Amine. Come, have some tea.'

Fatima collects the empty Chinese plate from the table and disappears into the kitchen. Aicha rises from her stool and points to the heavy wooden door leading to the stable yard.

'*Ighiyoule.*'

Addy looks at Amine. '*Ighiyoule?*'

'Donkey.'

Aicha grins, her porcelain teeth gleaming as she heads towards the door. 'Dunky. Dunky.'

Fatima enters the courtyard with a tea glass and the Chinese plate stacked with *msemen*. She sits down beside Amine on her mother's vacated stool and fills the tea glass with steaming mint tea.

Addy rolls up a pancake and drizzles it with honey. 'Have you seen Omar?'

Amine peels a pancake from the top of the stack. 'He go to the waterfalls with the tourists.'

'The tour bus was early again today?'

'It might be.'

'And you're here to keep an eye on me, I suppose.'

Amine spreads honey over another *msemen*. 'I have to. It's for your safety.'

For her safety? Seriously? She'd play along with this charade for now, but on her own terms.

Addy smiles at Amine. 'Well then. I think I'll go for a walk along the river today. Omar said the source of the waterfalls is a few kilometres south towards the mountains. I'll bring my camera and take some photos.'

Amine looks at Addy in panic. 'It might be it's better to stay in the house to make the cooking with Fatima.'

'No. I think a walk is exactly what I'd like to do today. Fatima, would you like to walk by the river with me?'

Fatima's eyes widen. '*Une promenade*?'

'Omar didn't say—'

Fatima scoops the tea glasses onto her tray. '*Yalla*, Adi. *Eesh*, Amine. *Eesh*.'

Amine grabs at the plate of pancakes. 'I will be in troubles with Omar.'

'Don't worry. I'll tell Omar I was stubborn and wouldn't take no for an answer. He'll sympathise with you completely.'

Addy strolls along a deeply rutted lane with Fatima and Amine, who carries Addy's tripod bag over his arm like a golf caddy. Addy links her arm with Fatima's, who's changed from her household pyjamas into a blue hijab and a pink djellaba that skims her purple Crocs.

After half an hour, they break from the dark shade of the olive grove into a field knee-high with green grain. They stroll along the narrow path, past shivering ash trees and pink flowering oleander bushes. On a hill overlooking the river, someone's dug foundations for a building.

Did her father ever stroll along this path with Hanane? Did they walk to the source one day, all those years ago? The air's full of ghosts and Addy looks down at the dusty path, imagining that she sees footprints: a man's and a woman's. But she blinks and they're gone.

They come upon a mud-walled shed, the wooden door studded with nails. Addy points at it.

'What's that for?'

'It's for the harvest of olives,' Amine says. 'The donkey, he go inside and they tie him to a press for the olives. He walk around like this.'

Amine circles them, braying like a donkey as Addy unzips the bag and sets up the tripod and camera. Fatima giggles and buries her face against Addy's shoulder.

'The olives go flat and the oil comes out.'

Addy presses the shutter and peers at the image on the screen. She checks the histogram, adjusts the exposure and takes another shot.

'When's the olive harvest? I'd love to photograph that.'

'The time of winter. *Novembre*. My English is not so good.'

'Your English is very good.'

'I practise with many tourists in the restaurant of my uncle. I want to be a guide like Omar so I can be richer. Then I can make a good family.'

Addy adjusts the tripod and focuses the lens on Amine's face. He's made an effort to comb down his straight black hair with gel, but a cowlick sprouts from his crown.

'I'm sure you'll make a great guide one day, Amine. When we get to the source, why don't you practise on me? You can tell me all about it. I'll give you a pass or a fail, just like a teacher.'

Addy sees Amine's eyes shift towards Fatima, who's staring

228

down at her Crocs, the corners of her mouth lifted into a smile. Addy clicks the shutter.

An hour later they reach a wide clearing at the base of the mountain foothills. Tufts of bright green grass sprout from red sandstone crevices in the hills. Rocks line a pool of water so clear Addy can make out the markings on the stones below. Pink and white oleanders bloom along the banks. At the far end of the pool by the base of the hills, the arches of an ancient stone aqueduct stand in water, orphaned from the banks on either side. The sun is high in the sky and the sunlight sparkles off the ripples of the pool.

'It's beautiful. *Zwina*.'

Fatima's round face breaks into a beaming smile. '*Zwina*.'

'Where does the river start? From the mountains?'

'No, it's here.' Amine points to the pool. 'The water for the waterfalls come up from the ground underneath.'

Addy scans the glass-like surface. 'It's hard to believe this little pool will turn into the waterfalls just a few kilometres away.'

'Yes, but the tourists they don't come here often.' Amine sets down Addy's tripod and rests his hands on his hips as he gazes at the aqueduct. 'It's so far for them to walk. Imazighen people don't mind about the source. There's no olives here. So it stays quiet like this.'

Addy sits on a large rock and gestures to Fatima to stand in front of the pool. As she focuses the camera on Fatima's face, Amine shouts out in Tamazight. Fatima blushes and giggles as Addy clicks a run of images. Fatima laughing by the pool, her face transformed into beauty by Amine's words.

'Go next to her, Amine. I'll take a picture of both of you.'

Amine pushes a stone into the water with the tip of his Adidas trainer. 'It might be Omar will be angry for me to be with Fatima.'

'Don't worry about Omar. These pictures are for my memories. I want to remember this lovely day here with the two of you.'

Amine stands awkwardly beside Fatima. He examines the

229

ground as if it holds the answer to some ancient dilemma. Fatima leans over and whispers. Amine grins and looks up as Addy clicks the shutter.

They hurry over to Addy and lean over the image on the camera screen.

'You go with Fatima, Adi,' Amine says. 'I will take a picture for your memories.'

They spend the next few minutes taking photos: Addy and Fatima; Addy and Amine – a little crooked and out of focus; and one of them all as Addy clicks the photo with her extension cable.

'I want to take some pictures of the aqueduct. Make sure Fatima doesn't fall into the water.'

She looks back at Fatima and Amine, sitting together on the big rock. Their laughter floats like feathers on the fresh mountain air.

On the walk back to Zitoune, Addy dawdles behind, photographing sheep on the hillsides, donkeys saddled in colourful blankets tethered to olive trees, red poppies springing out of the meadow grass, and nimble Imazighen boys playing with hoops and sticks by the river. Amine and Fatima stroll on ahead, their heads bent together in conversation, their footsteps slow on the dusty path.

# Chapter Thirty-Eight

**Zitoune, Morocco – May 2009**

The rooster's ear-splitting crows jar Addy out of a deep sleep. Her face is squashed into her pillow. She reaches over to Omar's side, but her fingers find only an indentation in the mattress. The mosque's megaphone squeals to life. The muezzin sings out the dawn call to prayer, the rippling sounds blaring through the open window. She reaches for Omar's pillow and folds it over her head.

She's sinking into sleep, when a car's horn rattles her awake. *Beep beep beep. Beep beep beep. BEEEPPP. Beep beep beep. Beep beep beep. BEEEPPP.* She tosses the pillow onto the rug and untangles herself from the sheets and mosquito net. Pulling her kaftan over her head, she pads through the house and out to the veranda.

'*Allô*, Turquoise.' Yassine leans out of his car window and waves, smoke from a cigarette threading through the air.

'Yassine? Where's Omar?'

Yassine smiles a slow, heavy-lidded smile. 'He ask me to pick you up.'

A cool breeze wraps around Addy's body, sending goose bumps up her arms. She rubs her naked arms.

'Pick me up? Why?'

Yassine's eyes flick over her wrinkled kaftan. 'It might be there is a problem with his grandmother.'

'Jedda? She's ill?'

'It might be. She's so older. Maybe she will die.'

'What do you mean she might die? Do we need to get her to a hospital? Where's Omar? Is he with her?'

'Darling, darling, don't worry.' Yassine exhales a trail of smoke. 'Maybe the grandmother of Omar is okay. He just say for me to pick you up.'

'Is Jedda okay? Maybe I should call Omar.'

'As you like, Turquoise, but she is okay. I'm sure about it.' He presses his hand against his chest. 'I am your servant.'

'Don't call me that.'

'No problem, darling. I call you Turquoise only when we are alone. It can be the secret of you and me.'

'I don't need any secrets with you. Be careful, Yassine.'

Yassine touches his hand to his lips. 'I am always careful, Turquoise. I am more clever than Omar thinks.'

Omar waves from the concrete terrace in front of the police station. He and the stocky, middle-aged policeman with a thick grey moustache sit in white plastic garden chairs either side of a white plastic table drinking Coke. The policeman throws a cigarette stub onto the concrete and stubs it out with his black boot.

Yassine beeps the horn and steers the car sharply into the dirt car park. Omar leaps down the steps and jogs over.

'Omar, is Jedda okay?'

'Yes, of course. *Mashi mushkil.*'

Omar leans into Yassine's window and speaks to him in Tamazight. Addy glances up at the terrace and catches the policeman staring at her. He stands, swigs the dregs of Coke from the can and steps back into the building.

Yassine hands Omar the keys and climbs over the gear stick into the passenger seat as Omar slides into the driver's seat.

Addy frowns. 'What are you doing?'

'I made a surprise for you, darling. Yassine teach me to drive. It's the reason I been going out early in the morning.'

Yassine loops his hand over Omar's headrest. 'He drives well, Turq . . . Adi. I'm a good teacher.'

'Really?'

Omar's eyes meet hers in the mirror. 'Yes, for sure, darling.'

'Jedda's not sick?'

'No. She's okay.'

'Hmmph.' Addy sits back in the seat and fans her face with the end of the white tagelmust she's draped around her neck. 'Don't run anybody over.'

'Darling, if I run over somebody, it's his fate.'

Omar grinds the gears, slowing down to avoid a group of boys on donkeys outside the busy market square. Flimsy stalls covered with torn scraps of advertising banners cluster around a dusty patch of earth behind the permanent butchers' and grocers' stalls.

'Look. It's Fatima and Zaina.'

'What? Where?'

Addy points towards the girls. 'Over by the popcorn stall. They look like they're arguing.'

The car jerks violently to a stop. He thrusts open the car door and steps out into the gravel road.

'Omar! We're in the middle of the road.'

'*Taboune omok.*'

Yassine laughs, sending fine strands of tobacco from the cigarette he's rolling over the dashboard.

'Okay, okay.' Omar climbs into the car and slams the door. 'We go, but I must speak to her later. She knows she doesn't go to the market except if my mum or I'm with her.'

'What do you m—'

'Adi. It's not England here. You don't understand the situation well.'

Addy slumps against the seat. She certainly didn't understand the situation at all. She'd do everything she could to get Fatima out of the house as often as possible. If she was going to be involved with Omar, he'd have to change his attitude.

The car judders forwards. Omar leans on the horn. Fatima and Zaina glance at the car. Omar waggles his finger at Fatima as he steers past the market.

Addy catches Zaina's eye. Omar's words echo in Addy's mind. *It's not England here. You don't understand the situation well.* Then it dawns on her. In Zaina's eyes she's not a tourist, or a traveller. To Zaina she's much worse. She's an intruder.

The car bumps over the track she'd walked with Amine and Fatima the day before. At the river, Omar steers the car left up a hill and parks it amid mounds of gravel and sand. Weeds grow from the sand and bites have been taken out of the gravel where someone's helped themselves to the crushed stone. The excavated ground is rimmed in knee-high concrete walls with rusty iron supports protruding from the four corners. Moss spreads over the concrete blocks like a carpet.

Adjusting her tagelmust, Addy follows Omar out of the car. Grabbing an iron support, he leaps up onto the low wall and surveys the foundations.

'You like it?'

'What is it?'

'It will be a guest house for tourists. From the roof you will see the river and the mountains all around. I built it on the hill so if the river floods it's no problem.'

The Renault's engine revs and Yassine beeps the horn. He waves through the window as he reverses the car down the hill.

'I'm glad he's gone,' Addy says.

'Why?'

'He makes me nervous.'

Omar frowns. 'He made you trouble in the car?'

'No, no. It was fine. Never mind.' Addy hears the false note in her voice, like she's pranged the wrong key on a piano. She slips her hand into Omar's. 'Show me the guest house.'

Omar gives her a lingering kiss. 'I wanted to kiss you ever since the police station, darling, but it's not possible to do it with everybody watching.'

'*Mashi mushkil, habibi*.'

'You are like the flower in my desert, *habibati*. I am the rain for you.'

'You do have a way with words.'

'It's easy for me, darling. You are the beautiful white flower in the garden of my heart.'

'Okay, okay. You're the camel in my desert.'

'That's not so romantic.'

'I'm not a poet like you.'

'A lady teach me well.'

'A lady?'

Omar hesitates. 'When I was a boy there was a lady in the village. She wrote poems well. She read them to me many times. The words made my heart buzz. Anyway, never mind for that.' He pulls Addy up onto the concrete wall. 'Come look where the house of Adi will be.'

'The house of Adi?'

'Why not? *Dar Adi*. It sounds nice.'

They jump down onto the rubble-strewn earth. As they walk around the perimeter, Omar kicks at Coke cans and beer bottles.

'I feel bad that I didn't build anything yet.'

'What's stopping you?'

'It's very expensive. I must pay an architect to make the plans so I can have a licence to build it. All the time it's papers, papers and dirhams, dirhams.'

'How much does an architect cost?'

'A lot. Like seven hundred euros. Maybe one thousand.' They sit on the concrete block wall. 'Maybe I can come to live with you in England and earn well there. Then I can spend the money in Morocco to build a good house for us and make a good business.'

'Come to live with me in England?' Philippa's warnings ricochet around Addy's head like a bullet. *He's probably just after a passport. Just wait till he asks you for money. He will, you know. They all do.*

Omar shrugs. 'Why not?'

'The weather's terrible and London's crowded with people. I don't think you'd like it.'

'If you're there, I would love it, *Adi*, one hundred per cent.'

'A thousand euros is a lot of money.'

'I know, darling. It's why I stopped building it.'

Addy chews her lip. Omar worked so hard. It was sad to see his dream crumbling and rusting in the olive grove. She didn't have much, but maybe she could loan him something. She'd sell her old Peugeot when she got home. She didn't really need a car in London. It wasn't like Omar'd asked her for the money.

'What if I give you some money towards the architect? I could possibly manage about five hundred pounds.' It made sense. He could build the guest house and she'd have a place to stay with him when she visited. No need for him to come to England.

'You don't have to do that. It must be I do it for myself, even if it take a long time.'

'I want to do it.'

The furrow between Omar's eyes deepens. 'It's a big imposition on you.'

'No, I want to do it. Then we'd have a private place to stay when I visit. It's perfect.'

Omar presses his fingers against his eyes. When he looks at her, his eyes are wet.

'Thank you, Adi. Nobody ever did something like that for me before in all my life. It's always me who take care of everybody.'

She puts her arms around his shoulders and kisses his wet cheeks. 'I'm glad to do it, *habibi*.'

Philippa must never know.

# Chapter Thirty-Nine

**Zitoune, Morocco – May 2009**

Addy follows Omar through a flimsy brown-painted door into the stable yard behind Aicha's house. A movement near the stables catches her eye. A glimpse of a red headscarf? The wooden door in the clay wall of the stable bounces on its hinges and Jedda's black-and-white cat slips into the stable.

'Was that Lamia?'

Omar shakes his head. 'Lamia? She live in the mountains.'

'I thought I saw her go in that door with Jedda's cat.'

'Nobody goes in there except my grandmother. She have a big key. Her medicines are in there. Even my mother is not permitted to go without the permission of my grandmother.' Omar pushes open the heavy wooden door into the house.

'*Allô*? Omar?' Omar's Uncle Rachid pops his head around the door to the living room.

'Uncle Rachid? What are you doing here?'

Rachid emerges, smiling broadly. He's wearing a crumpled grey suit and pointed yellow babouches. Omar hugs his uncle, kissing him several times on his cheeks.

'Why didn't you tell me you were coming here, Uncle? Did Fatima take care of you well? You had tea?'

'Yes, yes. Tea and cake and everything. You are well, Madame Adi? Your family is well?' He gestures towards the living room. 'Come, we are making a nice celebration.'

'Which celebration? You came with my aunt and the baby?'

'No, no. Nadia is at home with our little daughter.'

They follow Rachid into the living room. Farouk sits opposite Aicha in a long white tunic over yellow babouches and a white prayer cap. On the dirt floor next to his feet sits a large bamboo birdcage. A small bright green budgerigar sits on a perch.

The round wooden table is covered with a floral plastic table-cloth, and glasses of steaming mint tea are laid out with plates of cookies, cake, dates, bread, bowls of thick amber honey and fat black olives. Farouk munches on a cookie, his beard catching the crumbs like a net. When he sees Addy, he drops the half-eaten cookie on the table and barks at Rachid in Arabic.

Jedda shuffles into the room, the black-and-white cat slinking in behind her, and stops short in front of Farouk. She stamps her stick on the plastic mat and gestures to him as she remonstrates shrilly.

'What's going on?'

'Farouk doesn't want you to come in the room. My grandmother is unhappy for it.'

Jedda settles beside Aicha and reaches for a glass of tea. She glares at Farouk with her good blue eye. Rachid speaks to Omar in Arabic. Farouk tugs at the sleeve of Omar's denim jacket and fills the air with his objections as he jabs his finger at Addy.

Omar takes Addy's arm and steers her towards the door. 'Adi, we go out.'

'What's going on?' Addy asks when they're in the courtyard. 'Where's Fatima?'

'She's in the room of my mother.'

'Is Lamia with her?'

'No, Lamia's not here. I told you before.'

'What's Farouk doing here?'

He presses his fingers against his temple. 'Farouk wants to marry Fatima.'

'What?'

'Nadia saw the photo you took of Fatima when we were at the Hassan II Mosque in Casa and she told Farouk about her. He needs a wife for his children. He brought Fatima a bird for a present. For sure my uncle paid for it. Farouk wants to have the wedding quick.'

Addy rakes through her memories of that day. Sitting on the grass near the mosque. Flicking through the camera images. Nadia raising her hand in the air to indicate how much Fatima has grown. Her camera. Her pictures. What *has* she done?

'What does Fatima say about this?'

'She doesn't want to marry him.'

'You said she's said no before. So it's fine, isn't it?'

'It's a big problem this time, because Farouk is the brother of my aunt. It hurts the honour of my uncle Rachid if Fatima doesn't marry Farouk.'

A vision of Fatima shrouded in a black niqab flashes into Addy's mind. 'What are you going to do?'

He presses the palms of his hands against his eyes. 'I don't know. It might be good if you go back to your house. I must talk to Farouk.'

Addy knocks on Aicha's bedroom door. 'Fatima? *C'est* Adi.'

The bed creaks. The shuffle of babouches against the concrete floor. The door opens and Fatima stands there in flowered flannelette pyjamas, her face puffy and wet, strands of hair plastered to her cheeks. Fatima opens her arms to Addy and bursts into tears. Addy shuts the door and when the crying settles into soft chokes, she leads Fatima over to the bed.

'Talk to me, Fatima.'

The words tumble out of Fatima in a jumble of French and Tamazight. How Rachid and Farouk had arrived in the morning. How Farouk has asked Aicha for permission to marry her. How

Aicha's thrilled to have Fatima marry into the extended family and is already planning the wedding. How they're just waiting for Omar's permission to make it all official.

'Do you want to marry Farouk?'

Fatima shakes her head and bursts into choking sobs. Addy holds the weeping girl against her.

'Don't worry. I'll tell Omar how you feel. He won't force you to marry Farouk.'

Fatima sniffles. Addy tugs a packet of tissues out of her pocket and hands it to Fatima. Fatima dabs at her eyes.

'*Merci*, Adi. *Shukran bezzef.*'

Addy moves to leave, but Fatima pulls her back onto the bed. '*Attends*, Adi.'

She walks over to a tall wooden door-less cupboard and slides out a photo album from underneath a pile of neatly folded rugs. She sits on the bed and flips open the orange vinyl cover. Along with school photos, the book is stuffed with report cards, postcards and doodles. Fatima picks up a fading Polaroid. A much younger Aicha sits with a tiny baby in her arms, a boy on either side of her.

Addy takes the Polaroid from Fatima and turns it over. Her father's handwriting. The blue fountain pen. *Aicha Chouhad with her children, Zitoune, December 1983.*

'Where did you get this photo?'

'My mother. It's very old.'

'Yes. I can see that.' The reds fading to orange. The greens to yellow. Her father's photo. She holds up three fingers.

'*Oui.*' Fatima taps a finger on the faces. 'Momo, Omar, Fatima.'

'Momo?'

'Yes. Our brother. He die when he is ten years old.'

A brother? 'Was he sick?'

Fatima shakes her head. 'It was a flood. Momo was with the brother of Yassine. They drown.'

Fatima turns over the pages. Photos of Fatima, Aicha, Jedda

241

and Omar. Even one of Fatima swimming in the river. Labelled in neat Arabic script. All from Addy's Nikon camera.

She carefully flips the page over. A red rose. Pressed flat by the weight of the rugs in the wardrobe. She picks it up and waves it under her nose.

'*Romancia*.'

'*Romancia*?'

Fatima tucks her head against Addy's shoulder. 'Amine.' She takes her cell phone out of the pocket of her pyjamas and scrolls through the messages. '*Kanbghik,* he loves me.' She presses the phone against her chest.

'I'll speak to Omar. You won't have to marry Farouk.'

Fatima throws her arms around Addy and kisses her on her cheeks.

'You are my beautiful sister. I love you.'

Addy lies on Omar's bed and watches the spider wrap silk around a large fly that's flown into its web. Omar's still in the living room with Farouk and the others. Sliding off the bed, she pads about the room. She opens the bedside drawer and stares into the startled black eyes of two mice munching through a bag of almonds. She slams the drawer shut, her heart hammering in her chest.

Edging away from the bedside table, she wanders over to the makeshift desk littered with crumpled receipts, loose change and discarded sunglasses. A stack of books and magazines leans precariously near the edge of the desk. She straightens the pile. A book catches her eye and she pulls it out. *The Collected Works of William Shakespeare*.

Addy lies down on the bed with the book. The red leather cover is stained with a ring from a tea glass and the spine is broken. She carefully opens the front cover. *To my darling Augustus from Nanny Percival, Christmas 1945.*

# Chapter Forty

**Zitoune, Morocco – May 2009**

Omar falls onto Addy's bed in her rented house. 'Why didn't you come for supper, darling? My mum is upset for that.'

Yawning, Addy shakes herself awake and shifts onto her side. 'How could I after what happened with Fatima? I made myself an omelette here.'

He rubs the throbbing vein in his temple. 'I must talk to Fatima tomorrow.'

'I spoke to her.'

'You spoke to her? When?'

'After we arrived. I knocked on her door to see if she was all right. She was in tears. She wants to marry Amine, not Farouk.'

'Amine?' Omar's eyes cloud over. 'It's forbidden. She knows this well.'

Addy leans up onto her elbow. 'Forbidden? Why?'

Omar reaches for Addy's arm and pulls her against his chest. 'Amine's father didn't marry his mother. He has no papers. Since he has no papers, he doesn't exist in Morocco, so he can't go to school or to the doctor. Fatima knows it. If they marry and have children, the children don't exist as well.' He glowers at the spider web. 'I don't know when she talked to him.'

Addy squirms against Omar's chest. 'Maybe they met up at the market. We saw her there with Zaina this morning, remember?'

'Zaina. *Habss*. She makes a big problem.'

Addy sits up against the pillows and smooths out the wrinkles in her T-shirt. She wraps her arms around her knees. 'Can't you speak to Rachid? Explain to him that Fatima doesn't want to marry Farouk. Rachid's a reasonable man. Surely, he'll understand.'

'Everybody thinks Fatima is just shy to marry Farouk. My mum wants Jedda to make a medicine to make Fatima love him.'

'A love potion? Your grandmother does stuff like that?'

'My grandmother does all that kind of stuff. Medicine for people to be healthy, to have babies, to stop the evil eye, to have love. She can make bad medicine as well if she's angry. She's a strong lady even though she looks weak.'

'Fatima would never agree to take any love potion for Farouk.'

'My mum can find a way. The situation is a big problem for my family. Maybe it can solve the problem.'

Addy's blood rushes to her face and her cheeks burn. 'You can't trick Fatima into marrying Farouk.'

'Adi, it's enough, please.' Omar throws his arm across his face. 'My head is crushing me.'

Addy stares at Omar. Her head spins with confusion. Where did Fatima get her father's Polaroid of Aicha with her three young children? Why does Omar have her father's Shakespeare book? The mystery of what happened to Hanane and the baby is like a puzzle with missing pieces. Omar knows something he's not telling her. And Fatima said her mother had given her the Polaroid, so Aicha's hiding something as well. It's like the puzzle pieces are hanging in the air, just out of her reach. She can't leave Morocco until she knows what happened in Zitoune back in 1984.

Addy climbs off the bed and pads over to the chest of drawers. She pulls open the bottom drawer and unwraps her white tagelmust.

'Omar?' Addy rests her hand on the arm he's thrown over his eyes. 'Omar?'

A soft snore escapes from between his lips.

She sits on the bed with the Shakespeare book in her lap. Soon. Soon, she'll know what's going on.

She wraps the thin white cotton of her tagelmust around the book. It's like her father's out there on the other side, throwing out silken threads like a spider to catch her and weave her into his story. No longer just her father's story. Or Hanane's story. It's her story now. Hers and Omar's.

# Chapter Forty-One

**Zitoune, Morocco – May 2009**

Omar strides up the path, crunching through the gravel, his baseball cap low over his forehead to shield his eyes from the bright noon sun. The rooster runs across his path and lets rip with a strident crow as it dodges Omar's feet.

'You're fine, Adi?' He leans over to kiss her, then he drags a chair up to the table and flops into it, rubbing his bloodshot eyes.

Addy saves the paragraph she'd been writing on her laptop and sits back in her chair on the veranda. 'You look terrible.'

'I have a headache.'

She pushes a basket of Fatima's bread across the table. 'I've just made tea. Do you want some?'

Omar reaches for the bread and tears off a large chunk. 'Mint tea?'

'Yes, Fatima taught me.'

Addy raises the teapot high over an empty tea glass. Her arm wavers. A spray of tea shoots over the glass and drenches the bread.

'Darling, what are you doing? Fatima must teach you how to pour the tea well.'

Omar sifts through the bread and tosses the soggy bits over the railing to the rooster. He pours himself a stream of hot tea and gulps it down like a man dying of a ravenous thirst.

'How did it go with Farouk and Rachid?'

Omar exhales a tired sigh. 'It's a big situation, darling. Farouk insists to marry Fatima quick. I told him he has to wait until after Ramadan at least. It gives me time to think about the situation well.'

'When's Ramadan?'

'The end of August for one month.'

'No final decision has been made yet?'

'Not yet. They left now. Farouk didn't want to stay because he doesn't like my situation with you.' He leans back in the chair and scrutinises Addy. A smile teases the corner of his mouth. 'We argued like a normal couple last night.'

Omar reaches into his jeans pocket and hands Addy her passport.

'My passport? Good grief, I'd forgotten to get it back from you.'

'Don't worry. It was safe anyway. I had to bring it to the policeman. He has to know all the foreigners who stay in Zitoune. He insisted to make a copy of your passport.'

'What?'

'It's normal. He must do it for the government.'

'He has to do it for every tourist?'

'Yes, if they stay with a family here, or stay many nights. It's regulation. He was upset I didn't give it to him before. Don't worry, darling. I waited for him to make the copy so it didn't get lost.'

Omar rolls up a piece of bread and dips it in honey. He gets up and stretches. 'I must go and check on the tourists. The driver is unhappy I couldn't go this morning. I must make sure everything is well. I sent Amine to guide them. He can practise his English.' He heads towards the steps as he licks the dripping honey off his fingers.

'I'll go over to your mother's later and make us all a nice tagine for supper. I'll get Fatima to help me. Maybe it'll cheer her up.'

247

He lopes over to Addy and plants a kiss on her lips. 'I made a mistake, *habibati*. I must kiss you before I go.'

'Promise me you won't make Fatima marry Farouk.'

'I promise. Fatima can make her own mind for that. I am not the police of her, except I tell her she's forbidden to see Amine again.'

Addy takes a deep breath. 'Omar?'

'Yes?'

'There's something I need to talk to you about.'

'No problem. Later. Tonight.'

'Okay. It's important.'

'Nothing is important except for us to be together, *habibati*.'

He jogs down the stairs to the path. The rooster hops out of his way in a flurry of brown feathers, a wad of soggy bread in its beak.

# Chapter Forty-Two

**Zitoune, Morocco – March 1984**

Hanane drags a wooden stool over to the small window in the olive hut and climbs onto it. The rain thuds on the compacted earth roof like Gnaoua drumming and the tinny ping of water dripping into the pots she's set under the leaking ceiling adds to the noise.

She eases open the window and clutches onto the metal grille to steady herself. Not more than thirty metres away, the brown river pushes through the olive grove like a hungry serpent, devouring the new trees the farmers had planted among the old ones in February, groaning as it gorges itself on the valley's lifeblood.

There was no way for her to get home now. The bridge would be flooded. She'd just have to wait here and pray to Allah that the river wouldn't rise any further. Later, she'd need to ask Jedda to cover for her again. Explain to her father that she'd stayed with Jedda and Aicha and the children after her medicine lesson, safely out of the storm's reach.

She shuts the window and eases herself down off the stool. The battered steel brazier, blackened with years of use, sits on the hard earth floor in a corner of the room behind the huge wooden olive press. The coals burn red as they disintegrate to a fine grey ash and Hanane squats down beside it, holding her hands over the heat.

She knows she shouldn't be here. She'd tried to stay away from him after their visit to the cave. But, when they'd seen each other at the market a week later, it was like the veil that had separated them was lifted. Yes, she accepted that they'd never marry, but she'd steal what little time that was left them, until one day she'd find that he'd gone.

If she were discovered alone in the hut with Gus – she could hear them: *A foreign man! In the place he slept!* – her honour would be destroyed. No one would believe that she was still pure. All foreign men were devils, that's what she'd always heard when the village women gossiped over tea and biscuits with her stepmother. They could make a girl pregnant just by holding her hand, they'd say. Hanane smiles. If that were true, she'd have a hundred children by now.

How full her heart was for Gus's smile, his touch, his voice, the flash of humour in his sky-blue eyes. How she dreamed of becoming his wife. But it was impossible. He was a Catholic. He could only marry her if he embraced Islam and that was something he couldn't do. Not even for her.

But she was like a bee drawn to honey. She slipped away from her father's house as often as she dared, sometimes just to glimpse Gus teaching Omar and Momo English in the clearing by the olive hut, or to spy on him as he wandered through the market buying food for the strange meals he'd cook her on the rare days when her father was in Azaghar and Mohammed and Bouchra were at Bouchra's parents' house in Beni Mellal. Chicken in dumplings. Irish stew. Like lamb tagine without the spice.

Her father and Mohammed had nothing to worry about. As much as she wished for it, Gus never touched her. He'd feed her his odd food and tell her stories about his travels. He made her laugh. She'd read her poems to him while he held her hand.

When she was with him she felt happier than she'd ever believed possible.

She was a good woman. Honest, pure. Gus respected that and she loved him for it. She prayed five times a day, even *Salat Al-Fajr* before dawn, which wasn't so easy sometimes. She cherished the freedom she'd been allowed, and thanked Allah in her prayers for giving her the mountains and river as her playground. So much better than some cramped, dark home in a crowded city medina.

It'd been so much easier to slip out of the house after she'd turned thirteen and her father was occupied with his new wife, the slow-moving, dull-eyed Hind. If it hadn't been for Hind's father's restaurant on a prime spot by the waterfalls, Hanane doubted her father would've given the girl a second look. Now, Hind and her baby were long dead from a complicated birth, the restaurant was her father's and Mohammed's, and the family wanted for nothing.

She was sixteen when Hind died, and everything changed. Her days became tedious with washing and cooking. When she tried to slip out to hike into the mountain fields, her father or Mohammed would grill her to know where she was going, who she was seeing. Finally, Jedda stepped in and offered to teach her the mysteries of herbs and flowers to become a healer. It was like Jedda had known that she was trapped. But, of course, Jedda had the gift.

Now, her father was determined to marry her off to the cousin from Tafraout miles away near Agadir. The wedding was set for May, before Ramadan. But Allah had brought this Irishman, Gus, to Zitoune. To her. What was her fate to be?

251

# Chapter Forty-Three

## Zitoune, Morocco – June 2009

Addy taps on the bamboo rails of the birdcage and slips her finger between the bars. Fatima's green-feathered budgerigar flies off its perch and comes to rest on her knuckle. Its claws cling to her skin like ivy fronds.

'Do you think he's lonely, Fatima? Do you think that's why he doesn't sing?'

'It might be.'

Fatima slumps out of the kitchen carrying two bowls of wet green henna. Sighing heavily, she squats down on a stool and sets the bowls on the ground.

'Maybe I should ask Omar to buy it a companion.'

Fatima shrugs. 'As you like.'

Addy wiggles her finger and watches the bird fly back over to its perch. Poor bird. You're meant to fly, not watch the world go by. She casts her eye over at Fatima. Another lonely bird. If only she could help her to fly . . .

She rolls up the sleeves of her white top and sits on a stool beside Fatima, who lays Addy's right arm across her knees. Fatima removes a large plastic syringe from her pocket and takes out the

252

plunger. The door to the stable yard creaks open and Aicha enters the courtyard with Jedda.

'Ah! Henna. *Zwina*.'

Aicha guides the grumbling Jedda to an empty stool and squats beside Fatima. She pulls off Jedda's sandals and smears the pungent green mud over the soles of Jedda's feet. Scraping the dregs out of the bowl, Aicha coats her own palms and soles, rubbing the last bits of henna into her fingernails as a final flourish. She waves at Addy as she heads back out to the stable yard.

Fatima scoops up a handful of henna from the second bowl and presses it into the syringe with her fingertips. She pushes the plunger into the top of the syringe and squeezes thin trails of henna into sweeping vines and stylised flowers over the back of Addy's hand.

'Where did your mother go?' Addy asks as she watches Fatima embellish the design with dots and curlicues.

'She goes to visit a lady who will have a baby soon. She helps the babies to be born.'

'Oh, really? Did she always do that?'

'Yes. She learn from Jedda. She goes to all the ladies in the mountains here. Many children call her *tata*. It means auntie.'

Was that how Aicha had met Gus? Had she been Hanane's midwife? But if she had been, why did she deny knowing who Hanane was when Addy had shown her the Polaroid? Another puzzle piece hanging in the air. How did they all fit together?

Addy lifts her hand and admires Fatima's handiwork. '*C'est belle*.'

Fatima shrugs. '*Mashi mushkil*.'

A clatter of hoof beats, car horns and the burble of voices filters into the courtyard. Addy looks towards the door. 'What day is it?'

Fatima looks up from refilling the syringe. 'The day of the market.'

'Why don't we go to the market? I'll take some pictures.' Addy glances over at Jedda, who's watching Fatima like an old cat spying on a nervous mouse. 'Jedda can come, too.'

Fatima drops the syringe on the table and claps her hands, her face suddenly alight. 'Oh, yes. I want some new shoes and Omar doesn't choose well.'

Addy waves her naked arm at Fatima. 'After you finish my henna tattoo.'

Fatima pulls Addy's arm over her lap. 'Which hijab should I wear, Adi? The pink or the blue?'

'It's only the market, Fatima. Wear whatever you like.'

Jedda knocks her stick against Fatima's leg and mumbles to her. A smile lights up Fatima's face.

'Jedda says we must to buy you a hijab so you will be a good Muslim wife for Omar.'

'Let's not talk about that.' She looks over at Jedda. 'How did your grandmother know we were talking about hijabs? She doesn't speak French.'

'Jedda understands every language even if she doesn't speak them. She's a *shawafa*.'

'A *shawafa*?'

'Yes. A djinni came to her when she was a girl. Since then she can see the future and hear the thoughts of people. It doesn't matter what language.'

'You believe that?'

'Yes. You don't believe in *shawafas* in England?'

'Well, some people do. My sister does. They're called witches. Or psychics. It's all a bit hocus-pocus for me.'

Fatima frowns. 'Hocus-pocus?'

'Umm, magic. Make believe. It's hard to believe it.'

'When you know Jedda well, you will believe in *shawafas*.' Fatima drops the empty syringe into the henna bowl. 'I think I'll wear the pink hijab today.'

*

Fatima and Addy each hold one of Jedda's arms as she waves her stick in front of her like an orchestra conductor to clear the way through the crowded market.

'Adi, what are you doing here?'

Addy turns towards Omar's voice. He's standing with Yassine and Amine in front of a stall selling bootleg CDs.

'Omar? I thought you said you were guiding tourists today.'

'It was only a small group today. I gave it to another guy since it's better to come to the market.' He frowns. 'You bring everybody. They know I can buy everything they need. They don't have to come here.'

Addy squints up at the clear blue sky. 'It's such a lovely day, I thought it'd be nice for Fatima and Jedda to get out of the house.'

'The ladies visit each other all the time in their houses. They're not in prison.'

Addy juts out her chin in defiance. 'Exactly. That's why I thought it would be nice to come over to the market. Jedda wants me to buy a hijab. She thinks you'll marry me if I wear one.'

'You don't have to have a hijab for me, Adi. I like you as you are.' He sighs and shakes his head. 'Anyway, it's nice to see you with my sister and my grandmother. Everybody is looking at you.'

Yassine greets Jedda like she's a beautiful young girl, telling her she's *zwina*, and the old woman grins back at him toothlessly. Fatima chews her bottom lip as she concentrates on the men slicing open watermelons on the back of a truck, the bright pink flesh dripping water over the rusty green fenders.

Addy catches Yassine's eye.

'You are well, my sister?'

'Yes, thank you. And you?'

'I am well now that my sun has come to the market of Zitoune.'

Omar jabs at Yassine's shoulder. 'It's my sun, not your sun, Yassine.'

'But the sun, it shines on all of us. It's true, my friend?'

Addy rolls her eyes. 'I think I'll go and look for the shoe stall with Fatima and Jedda. Fatima wants some new shoes.'

'*Mashi mushkil*, darling. I'll come in a while.' Omar peels several notes off a roll of dirhams and hands them to Amine. 'Here. You go with them, but don't talk to Fatima or I will beat you like a gorilla. If the ladies like some shoes, buy them, but make a good negotiation for their honour.'

As they wander through the market, people call out greetings to Jedda, some of the younger women stopping to kiss the old woman's gnarled hand.

'Jedda's very popular,' Addy says.

Fatima nods. 'When she was young she did the Hajj to Mecca with my grandfather, so she is a Hajjah. It's a big honour. *Inshallah* I will go one day with my husband.'

Addy bends over and kisses Jedda's hand. '*Hajjah* Jedda.'

The old woman pats Addy's cheek and says something in Tamazight. Addy raises a questioning eyebrow at Fatima.

'She says you and Omar must marry soon because she is an old lady. She wants to see her grandchild before she goes to Paradise. *Inshallah*, Adi.'

Marriage? A child? Why can't they just let things be? Addy opens her mouth to speak, but the words refuse to form. She takes hold of Jedda's hand and follows Amine through the crowd.

Progress to the shoe stall is slow, as the villagers greet Jedda, and Addy photographs the abundance of vegetables on display – shiny green and red peppers, fat courgettes, tomatoes so ripe they look about to burst, and ropes of garlic and onions hanging off the bamboo struts of the lashed-together stalls. Fragrant green herbs spill over tabletops and stacks of silvery tin teapots glisten in the sun. They pass a stall where thick ripe watermelons drip pink juice onto the tabletop and Addy urges Amine to buy them all wedges.

On the shoe stall, men's, women's and children's shoes tumble over a blue plastic sheet spread over the dry earth. Addy collects the watermelon rinds from Jedda and Fatima, and hands them to Amine.

'Can you find a stool for Jedda to sit on, Amine? I think she's getting tired.'

Amine cups the dripping rinds in his hands. '*Mashi mushkil.*'

Fatima holds up a pair of high-heeled black plastic shoes with large gold buckles. 'You like, Adi?'

Addy grimaces. '*Non. Pas bien.*' She roots through the bizarre selection of second-hand shoes, sandals and trainers and finds a flat black leather shoe. Jedda nods her approval. Fatima pushes out her lower lip and grabs a purple faux-suede platform shoe with gold leather straps, which she dangles in front of Addy like an exotic fruit.

Addy waggles her finger in a circle at her temple. 'You're crazy, Fatima.'

Jedda knocks Addy's arm with her stick and copies Addy's gesture. Fatima and Addy break into giggles. Suddenly, Fatima slams her mouth shut as she stares over Addy's shoulder. Addy turns around. She's face-to-face with Zaina.

Addy extends her hand. '*Bonjour*, Zaina.'

Zaina scowls at Addy's splayed fingers. She spits into the palm of her hand and wipes it against her djellaba.

A screech from the shoe stall. The purple shoe flies from Fatima's hand past Zaina's ear. Zaina screams and ducks. Another shoe sails past and popcorn shoots out in all directions from a direct hit on the popcorn stand. The popcorn seller throws up his hands and bellows out his objections. Jedda whacks Zaina on her bottom with her stick as the two girls shriek at each other. Villagers and stallholders push towards the mêlée. Amine squeezes through the crowd, carrying a battered wooden stool. 'What's happen?'

Addy looks over at him. 'Zaina showed up and all hell broke loose.'

Omar breaks through the wall of djellabas. 'What goes on here?'

The popcorn seller pulls at Omar's arm, protesting as he jabs at the popcorn littered over the earth like fat grubs.

'Amine, what happened? You were responsible.'

'I'm so, so sorry, Omar. I get a chair for Jedda and when I come back, everybody is fighting.' His eyes dart over to Fatima, who blushes and looks quickly away.

Zaina's eyes flick from Fatima to Amine.

Jedda pokes her stick into Zaina's side and gabbles something that causes the crowd to suck in its breath.

'Adi, take Fatima and Jedda to the house,' Omar says. 'I'll come soon.'

When she's by the roadside, Addy casts a quick look back. Zaina clutches Omar's arm as he bends to listen to her.

'What did she say?'

'What?'

Addy turns over in the bed as Omar enters her bedroom. 'Zaina.'

Omar pushes the mosquito net aside and sits on the foot of the bed, bending over to untie his trainers.

'Don't mind, Adi. She's jealous of you. It's her problem.'

'Why? What did she say?'

'She said you insulted her.'

Addy sits up against the pillows. 'I insulted her! How?'

Omar's face is outlined in the moonlight streaming in from the window.

'You didn't kiss her on the cheeks when she said hello.'

'What? I held out my hand to her and she stared at it like I was carrying some infectious disease. Then she spit in her hand and rubbed it on her djellaba. It was pretty insulting. Did she tell you that?'

Omar rubs Addy's naked arm with his knuckles. 'Never mind, *habibati*. It's no problem for me if you insulted her. It's her problem.'

Addy slaps the mattress. 'But I didn't insult her. I tried to be polite.'

'She said Fatima tried to kill her.'

Addy grunts. 'Well, that's true. Shame Fatima's aim wasn't better.'

'For sure, darling. I have to pay the popcorn seller two hundred dirhams because he is so angry. I made a punishment for Amine.'

'Amine had nothing to do with it.'

'I left Amine to be in charge. I was going to pay him to be your bodyguard. But now I won't pay him. It's his problem. I have to punish him.'

Addy falls back on the pillow and scowls at the outline of a ceiling beam. The faint lace of a spider's web drapes from the beam to a corner. Spiders everywhere.

'I don't need a bodyguard. I can take care of myself.'

Omar pulls off his baseball hat and T-shirt and tosses them onto the rug. He yawns. 'I must make sure you're fine even when I'm away.'

Addy squints at the web, trying to make out where the spider is. Is Omar her spider? Is she a fly caught in his web?

'Why weren't you at dinner, Omar? I helped to make a tagine.'

'I had to make things well in the market.'

'All night?'

'Never mind for that. I'm so, so tired.'

The book. The Polaroids. Tomorrow. It has to be tomorrow.

Omar pulls back the sheet and climbs into the bed. Kissing Addy quickly, he turns onto his side and settles into the pillow. Addy gazes at the brown expanse of his back.

'Omar?'

'Yes?'

Addy runs her hand along his shoulder. 'What did your grandmother say to Zaina?'

'She cursed her.'

'Really?'

'She said Zaina will never have a baby.'

Out of the corner of Addy's eye, a large black spot springs to life. It scurries across the web to the beam.

'What did Zaina do?'

Omar turns over in the bed. 'She cursed Fatima and she cursed you. Don't worry, *habibati*. Nobody can hurt you if Omar Chouhad breathes on this earth. Even the djinn.'

# Chapter Forty-Four

**Zitoune, Morocco – June 2009**

Omar sits up in Addy's bed and rubs his hand over his face as he blinks at the bedroom door. '*Chkoun?*'

'Mohammed.'

'Mohammed?'

'*Naam.*'

Addy props herself against her pillow. 'How did he get in?'

'He knows where the key is. He hid it there.' Omar throws off the sheet and reaches for his jeans.

'What do you think he wants?'

'I'll see.' Shoving his feet into his trainers, he picks up his T-shirt and his tagelmust from the floor. 'I'll come soon. It's early yet. You can sleep.'

Addy burrows under the covers. The bed's warm from Omar's body. Her mind grasps for the thread of sleep, but the thoughts that have been niggling at her for the past few weeks spin around her head. Only a few more weeks before her visa runs out. What then? What's going to happen with Omar and her? Then there was Nigel. What would she do about him when she went back to London? And Hanane and the child. And Omar. What was going on there? How did he get her father's book? Then there

261

was the question of how the photos from her father's Polaroid camera ended up in Fatima's photo album. It's like she's splashing through murky water that closes over her head every forward stroke she makes.

The window shutters slam against the bedroom wall. Addy jolts upright and blinks at the sharp morning light. Omar stands outside, his turbaned head and shoulders silhouetted against the sunlight.

'Adi, you must come quick. Somebody looks for you. Come to the house.'

'Who's looking for me?'

But Omar's already gone.

The blue metal door to the house is ajar when Addy arrives. It groans like an old man when Addy pushes it open.

'*Chkoun*?' Aicha calls from the kitchen.

'Adi.'

Omar's mother pops her head around the kitchen door and points to the living room as she wishes her good morning. Addy enters the living room, squinting as her eyes adjust to the darkness from the courtyard's bright sunlight.

'Philippa?'

Her half-sister perches on a banquette in neatly pressed cotton chinos, grimacing at the tea glass she holds delicately in her long fingers. She's knotted an Hermès scarf over her striped Ralph Lauren shirt, and a cream Prada handbag sits beside her on the banquette like a pet. Her expensive leather loafers are splattered with something that looks like donkey manure.

'Pippa? What on earth are you doing here?'

'That's hardly the friendliest greeting for the sister who's trekked out into the middle of nowhere to find you.'

Addy stumbles over to Philippa and kisses her on the cheeks. 'Why did you come? I'm fine.'

Philippa brushes a strand of hair off her forehead. 'You've hardly been peppering me with missives about your Moroccan adventure. After the phone incident with this Omar person, I had no option but to come out here myself to see that you were all right.' Philippa's expression stiffens as she clocks the plastic matting, the nylon damask upholstery, the plastic flowers, the rolled-up prayer mats in the corner, the flat-screen TV on the wall beside the door. She swats at a fly. 'Quite frankly, I'm not sure you're in your right mind.'

Aicha enters the room carrying a tray full of plates of olives and dates, a basket of fresh bread, and bowls of olive oil and honey. The bread fills the room with delicious yeastiness. Fatima follows close behind with a plate stacked with *msemen* and a bowl of small triangular cheeses wrapped in foil.

Jedda shuffles into the room behind them. The ageless black-and-white cat's at her feet, winding itself around her cane. Jedda stops abruptly to peer at Philippa with her good eye and stamps her stick on the plastic mat as she mumbles under her breath. She teeters across the room and eases herself onto the banquette as far away from Philippa as she can manage. The cat curls against her feet.

Addy points at her half-sister with a piece of bread. '*Watnasse Adi*, Philippa,' she says to Aicha. My sister, Philippa.

Aicha claps her hands together. '*Marhaba. Yamma* Phileepa.'

'Omar's mother welcomes you. She says she's your mother.'

'That would be a biological impossibility.'

Aicha drags a stool up beside Addy and tears off a hunk of bread, dipping it into honey. She offers Philippa the sticky bread. '*Marhaba. Eeesh lafdoure.*'

'This is Omar's sister, Fatima,' Addy says to Philippa. 'You should take it. She'll only insist until you do. She'll be offended if you don't eat it.'

Philippa picks the pancake out of Fatima's hand and tears off a small bite. She nibbles at it like it's a piece of wet cardboard.

'Delicious. Just like mother used to make.'

Addy nods towards Jedda. 'That's Omar's grandmother. Everyone calls her Jedda, which means grandmother. You're meant to kiss her head.'

'I'm meant to *what*?'

'Kiss the top of her head. It's a sign of respect. You should do it. Otherwise you might get the bad eye and, take it from me, you want to avoid that at all costs.'

'Oh, for heaven's sake.'

Philippa sets down the pancake and edges towards Jedda. The cat yowls and darts out of the room. Philippa kisses the scowling woman on the top of her bandana. Jedda waves her away as she babbles something to her in Tamazight.

Fatima laughs. '*Laa*, Jedda. *Wallo* Tamazight.'

Addy wipes the honey off her fingers with a small towel that Aicha hands her. 'So, you can see I'm all in one piece. And a few pounds heavier. What else do you need to know?'

Philippa dabs at her fingers with a handkerchief. 'After that last phone call, I wanted to see for myself that you weren't the star attraction in some sex slavery ring.'

'Pippa!'

'I've convinced my Russian clients that they want a Moroccan-themed cinema room, so I'm officially on a buying trip. Those white Moroccan rugs with the zigzags are all the rage in London. I'll buy them cheap and sell them to the Russians for a killing.' Philippa's eyes dart around the room. 'I had no idea you were living in a hovel.'

'Don't be rude. It's perfectly comfortable here.'

'Addy . . .' Philippa dabs at her fuchsia lips with her handkerchief.

'What?'

'There's something you should know.'

The metal door slams against the clay wall in the courtyard. Omar steps into the living room, his face a blank mask under his blue turban.

'Omar?'

Omar moves aside. Her ex-fiancé, Nigel, stands in the doorway. He runs his hand through his expensively cut brown hair in the familiar nervous gesture. His hazel eyes have the look of a pet dog who knows he's disappointed his owner.

'Hi, Della. Surprise.'

'Nigel?' Addy glances at Omar. 'He's a friend of mine from London.'

'I know. I saw his photo before.' Omar gestures for Nigel to sit on the banquette. 'You might be hungry. My mother made a good breakfast, so enjoy.'

'Thanks, mate.'

Nigel pats Omar on his arm and sits on the sofa beside Addy. A whiff of sweat, perfumed with sandalwood. He rests his hand on her knee. Addy sees Omar's eyes dart to Nigel's hand. His jaw's tight and the vein jumps in his temple. She shifts her knee and edges away from Nigel.

'I put the luggage in your house, Adi,' Omar says flatly.

'Omar, I—'

'I must go to work. I'm a professional guide and there are many tourists here. I must earn well for my family. So, you should enjoy *your* family.'

265

# Chapter Forty-Five

**Zitoune, Morocco – June 2009**

'Pippa, what were you thinking?' Addy paces the polished concrete floor in her cottage, clutching a striped cushion to her chest.

Philippa sits on the banquette under the front window, her legs neatly crossed. A dew of sweat gleams on her forehead.

'You've no idea how much Nigel's been suffering since the incident.'

'The *incident*? He cheated on me. When I was having chemo.'

'Addy, please. Nigel will be back from the service station at any moment. You've said yourself that he was in a state of shock about your cancer diagnosis. He feels terrible about everything. He really wants to make it up to you.'

Addy throws herself onto the banquette. 'Since when have you become Nigel's best friend?'

'Look, he contacted me. Me! The woman who'd made his life a living hell after he left you. He blocked up my bloody inbox with his messages. Nigel's turned his life around. He's been made an associate at the law firm. He's quit drinking. He's going places, which is more that you can say for—'

'Which is more than you can say for . . .?'

'You can't be serious about this Omar person.'

266

'Why not?'

'He lives in a bloody mud hut. Have you seen the toilet? I mean, honestly.' Philippa gets up and strides across the concrete floor to the kitchen.

Addy watches her sister stamp around the tiny kitchen. If she chooses to be with Omar, she may damage her relationship with her only living relative. But then, does she even have a relationship with Philippa to ruin?

'Damn it, Addy.' Philippa slams closed a cupboard door. 'What do I have to do to get a proper cup of tea in this godforsaken place?'

A clink of ice on glass. 'Here, Della.'

A sluggish breeze wafts up to the veranda from the river, doing little to take the edge off the evening's heat. Addy looks up from her notebook at Nigel.

'Where's Pippa?'

'Off to bed. I think the shock of breakfast in a mud hut was too much for her, not to mention fending the monkeys off dinner at the restaurant.' Nigel offers Addy the cold glass. 'A G & T. Ice and all. God bless duty-free.'

Addy eyes the fizzy drink. A fat green lime slice bobs among the ice.

'C'mon, enjoy it, Del. It'll take the edge off this ruddy heat.'

'Where'd you get ice?'

'Froze some of your bottled water this morning in a plastic bag, then mashed up the ice with my shoe.'

'Huh. Very resourceful.' She takes the glass. 'Thanks.'

Nigel flops into a chair and props his feet on the railing. Pristine beige suede loafers. No socks. White linen shirt and trousers. Has somebody been polishing him up?

'Pippa said you've quit drinking.'

'Yes, indeed.' He jiggles the ice against the glass. 'It's soda. I've turned over a new leaf. I promise you, I'm a much-improved model.'

Addy sips her drink. 'Nice shoes.'

Nigel knocks the toes of his loafers together. 'Tod's.'

'Who chose them for you?'

'Del, c'mon. Life's good. Alistair's made me an associate at the firm.'

'So Pippa said.'

'Aren't you going to congratulate me?'

'A wolf in sheep's clothing is still a wolf.'

Nigel swings his legs off the railing. 'You look great, Della. I like your hair short like that. It suits you. You look about twenty-five.'

His tan brings out the green in his eyes. Handsome. She grits her teeth until an ache spreads along her jaw. Why is her heart jumping around in her chest like a circus acrobat?

'What are you doing here, Nigel?'

He reaches over and cups his hand over hers. 'I miss you. I thought, maybe, you could give me another chance. I probably don't deserve it, I know. I'm sorry, Del. I'm really sorry about what happened.'

Addy pushes her drink away and rises, moving to a corner of the veranda, where she plants her bare feet on the stone terrace like a soldier defending her territory.

'What about your girlfriend? Did she finally suss you out? Is that why you're back?'

'We're no longer together.'

'Did you screw around on her, too?'

'Del . . .' He rubs his eyes. 'No, I didn't. Oddly enough, she seemed to think I still had a thing for you.' His eyes are pleading. A dog begging for forgiveness. 'The thing is, she was right.'

'Stop it, Nigel. I'm not doing this with you any more. It's over.'

Nigel sets down his glass and crosses the stone terrace. He reaches out and brushes a wisp of hair out of Addy's eyes. She bats away his hand.

'I said stop it.'

'Sorry. You've every right to think I'm a wanker.'

'Too right. So, why *are* you here?'

He leans against the railing and contemplates the star-filled sky. 'I fell apart when you were going through chemo. I didn't know how to help you. I thought you could die and there was nothing I could do about it. I felt helpless. Like I'd failed you somehow. Like I . . . I don't know. I couldn't cope. So I ran away.'

'Just when I needed you.'

'I'm sorry, Della. I love you. I've always loved you. I'll do anything to make it up to you. I should've married you years ago.'

Her heart cartwheels. She had loved Nigel. She'd been committed. Forever. That's all she'd ever wanted. To love someone and be loved back. To be 'the one' for someone. She'd thought Nigel was the one. Until she'd discovered forever isn't always forever.

Her father's marriage to Essie had ended in divorce. His marriage to her mother, Hazel, had ended with her mother's death. Love always ends. Someone's always abandoned. Maybe that's why she's so obsessed with Gus and Hanane's story. Maybe she wants proof that somehow, against all odds, their love lasted. Even if they were separated by oceans and continents, she wants to know that it didn't matter. Her father couldn't have abandoned Hanane and the baby. She wants to believe in love. She wants proof. Maybe then she can believe in a future with Omar.

'Del? What is it?'

She stares at Nigel as the truth she's been hiding from herself faces her like a reflection. *I don't trust I have a future with Omar.* She's been deserted so often that she's ready to bolt rather than be left behind again. That's why she's been hiding her infertility from him. It's her get-out clause. Her excuse to extricate herself from the relationship when it becomes too real, too complicated. Abandon Omar before he abandons her. Don't let herself be hurt again.

'Sit down, Del. I'll get you some water.'

'No. I'm fine.' Addy gulps down a breath of the warm night air. 'Look, Nigel. There's no point to this. You've wasted your time coming here.'

'C'mon. We're a pair. Like socks and shoes. Laurel and Hardy. Charles and Diana. No, wait. That's not a good example.' He runs his hand along Addy's arm. 'We've had some fun, haven't we? We could still have fun.'

'Fun? What fun? If you weren't at work, you were glued to your laptop in the spare room. I don't call the occasional game of Chinese Checkers a laugh riot.'

'I thought you liked Chinese Checkers.'

Addy rolls her eyes. 'You know what I mean. You were busy climbing the career ladder, and I was busy trying to get my photo studio off the ground. Sure, when we first got together we had fun. But, over time our life changed and I didn't notice. Not until I had cancer. Then I noticed, especially when you went AWOL when I was having chemo. *And* there was the drinking.' Addy shakes her head. 'No, Nigel, I'm done. The cancer changed me. I've realised I'm mortal.'

'We're all mortal.'

'But I *know* I'm mortal. I don't trust that I'm going to live to a hundred any more. I've got things I want to do. Write this travel book. Exhibit my pictures in a gallery. Find a way to make a living as a travel photographer. Embrace new experiences. Isn't it time you got on with your own life?'

Leaning over, Nigel kisses her. She pushes against his chest. 'No.'

He holds up his hands in surrender. 'Sorry. I thought—'

'You thought what? That you could just walk back into my life? I'm sorry you had a hard time when I was sick. Poor you. My heart bleeds. But you made a big mistake walking out on me when I needed you most. No, wait, cheating on me and then walking out. It tore me apart. There's no going back. I could never trust you again. We're done.'

270

'I'm sure my showing up like this is a shock, so I'll forgive you for not welcoming me with open arms.'

'What do you mean, you'll *forgive* me?'

'Calm down, Del.'

'How dare you speak to me like that!'

'Look, I'm sorry. I'm an ass. I didn't mean what I just said.' He reaches for Addy's hand, but she wraps her arms across her body. 'It's not too late, hun. Let's try again. We can make it work. I know you better than anyone, Del. I know what makes you tick. Look, I need you. You complete me. We complete each other.'

'I don't want to complete you. I don't want to complete anybody. I just want to be my own person and figure out my life in my own way. Anyway, things have changed. I love Omar.'

'Oh, really? The guy with the turban?'

'Yes, really.'

The light from the living room filters through the sheer draperies, casting a glow over Nigel's white linen shirt and trousers.

Nigel rubs his forehead. 'Right. So, what do you suggest we do about the flat?'

The flat. Buying it together had seemed like such a good idea four years ago.

'We'll have to sell it.'

'There's the thing, Del. This recession has killed the market. We'd be lucky to break even if we sell now. Lose money, more like. People are caught up in negative equity all over Britain. That's if we could even find a buyer. I'm up to my neck in debt. The clothes, the car . . . it's all on credit. It's bloody expensive keeping up appearances now that I'm a partner. And because of this bloody recession I got the promotion but no raise. Still on my associate salary which doesn't cut much mustard in London, I can tell you. I need to make as much money out of the flat as I can. No doubt you do, too. It doesn't look like your Moroccan friend's rolling in dough.'

'What are you saying, Nigel?'

271

'I've moved back into the flat.'

'You *what*?'

'I own half of it. I've every right to live there.'

'Are you suggesting that we live together until the market recovers? That could be years.'

'Del, we don't have a choice. Look, we own the place together. Why don't we just try to work things out? It'd be easier all around.'

How could he think this was even an option? Nigel hadn't come to Zitoune to declare his undying love to her. He was here because he was desperate – he didn't know how to live without a woman to shore him up, and in his mind she was the easiest target. The flat was the link that kept them chained together. The flat and the past. But the past was dead and the flat could burn down for all she cared. She'd happily be the one to light the match.

'You're sweeping me off my feet.'

Nigel sighs and runs his hand through his hair. 'Well, you could always buy me out.'

'You know I don't have the money to do that.'

Nigel looks at Addy and shakes his head. He strolls over to the table and picks up Addy's drink. He swivels it in his hand, the ice clinking against the glass. 'So, what are you going to do? Ask your mountain guide friend for the money? Doesn't it usually work the other way around?'

'That's enough!'

Nigel drains the glass and sets it down on the table. 'At least you've been getting some. No harm to have a little diversion every once in a while. But it's time to get back to reality now, don't you think? C'mon. It's me, Nigel. Nigel and Addy. We belong together.'

Addy feels the heat rise in her face. 'You should go. Find a hotel. Better yet, go back to London. We'll deal with everything when I'm back.'

He looks at her, his eyes hard green stones. 'He's a pretty boy at least. You haven't changed that much, Del. You've always been a sucker for a pretty face.'

In the morning, Addy wanders out of her bedroom towards the kitchen. A jumble of sheets on the thick multicoloured rug, an empty gin bottle, a dirty glass and a note on the table are the only signs left of Nigel's recent presence. She pads barefoot across the cold concrete floor and picks up the note:

*You win, Del. For now.*
*PS: I'll warm up your side of the bed.*
*N xxx*

# Chapter Forty-Six

**Zitoune, Morocco – June 2009**

The June day is hot and dry. Addy spends the morning in the Zitoune souk with Philippa, watching her sister haggle with the shop sellers for rugs and trinkets for her clients. They stop at Mohammed's restaurant for lunch.

'Has Omar been here with the tour group?' she asks Mohammed when he comes over to collect their empty plates.

'No, nobody see him today.'

'Where's Amine? Has he gone missing, too?'

Mohammed grunts. 'Maybe he went to swim in the pools by the gorge. Sometimes he's a bad boy like that when the weather is hot.'

'Ah, the delights of playing hooky,' Philippa says.

Mohammed cocks his head towards Philippa. 'Hooky?'

'Running away from your responsibilities.' Philippa glances over at Addy. 'Something my sister's very good at.'

Mohammed pockets the dirhams Philippa hands him. 'I wish I could remember the day when I had no responsibilities. It's many, many years ago when I was very young and handsome.'

'Still very handsome,' Philippa says as she dabs at her lips with a paper napkin.

Addy raises an eyebrow as she looks over at her sister. Mohammed smiles broadly, his gold teeth shining in the sunlight.

'You are most kind, madame.'

'Philippa. I'm Addy's sister.'

'Phileepa. It's a beautiful name. Welcome in Morocco. You have a big welcome here.'

'Thank you. Uh, I think you owe me a bit of change, twenty-five dirhams.'

Mohammed shakes his head sadly. 'So sorry. No change.'

'It's only about two pounds, Philippa,' Addy says as she watches Mohammed retreat through a blue swing door into the kitchen. 'Consider it a tip.'

'But I'd left a tip. It was the bloody same in Marrakech. No one has change. Who's hoarding all the change in Morocco?'

'Still very handsome?'

'Well, he is. Reminds me of Telly Savalas in his *Kojak* days.'

'He's married.'

'Aren't they all?'

Addy sighs. 'When did you say your plane was leaving?'

'I didn't. I'm having such a fun time buying all this tat for my clients that I think I'll stay around a while longer. The whole trip'll be tax deductible. My accountant'll love me.' She fans her face with the end of her Hermès scarf. 'It's bloody hot. I think I'll have a lie-down when we get back to the house. I'm absolutely bloody knackered.'

Addy approaches the building site. She needs to ask Omar about her father's book. Explain about Nigel. Understand what's going on.

She spies him sitting on the concrete block wall staring at the foundations, his blue turban a stab of colour amid the dull green of the olive trees and the piles of grey gravel and concrete blocks. Her shoes crunch on the gravel. Omar turns and watches her as she weaves around the mounds of stones and sand towards him.

275

'I missed you at breakfast at your mum's this morning, *habibi*.'

'I been busy.'

Addy sits beside him on the concrete block wall. 'I'm really sorry about Nigel. It's a crazy situation.'

'I can see the situation well. Be well with your boyfriend, Adi. I'm just a rubbish Berber guy to fuck, full stop.'

'Don't say that! Nothing's going on with Nigel. I didn't invite him here. It's over with him. I told you that.'

'You have to know you are like the white flower I waited for in my garden. One day it came and I'm so happy for that. It made my heart be as big as the sun. Then somebody came and stole it, and now it's finished for me.' He presses his lips together and stares at the olive grove.

Everything is stacked against them. Their ages, their cultures, their religions, the fact they live on different continents. How could their relationship possibly last? Then again, it hardly mattered. It was enough that they loved each other now. Isn't now all anyone has? Why hasn't she ever said the words?

'Omar, I . . . I love you.'

Omar jolts his head around and looks at Addy. 'You never said it before. I notice it well.'

'I was afraid. I'm still afraid.'

Omar reaches for her hand and holds it in his like a precious gift. 'Why are you afraid, *habibati*? I would never hurt you.'

'I'm afraid that you'll regret being with me. Maybe not now, but one day. You'll look at me and think "she's old", or "I made a mistake", or . . . "I don't love her any more". That would destroy me. I'm not able to give little pieces of my heart away. I give all of my heart. That's not always a good thing. It tears me apart when things go wrong.'

'It would never happen like that for us. I'm not a rubbish English guy.' Omar swears under his breath in Tamazight. 'You are in my heart and I gave you the key.' He sighs heavily and rests his head on her shoulder.

She enfolds him in her embrace. 'Omar, there's something I need to talk—'

He sits back. The crease deepens between his eyes. 'I don't like that your boyfriend is in your house.'

'He's not my boyfriend. I told him to leave. I told him I was with you, full stop.'

'I saw you kiss him last night. It crushed me like I fell over the waterfalls.'

'You saw that?'

'I followed you. I been jealous, you have to know about it.'

'I pushed him away.'

Omar nods. 'It's true.'

'I told him it's over. I told him I love somebody else.'

'Who do you love?'

'You. I love you.'

Omar pulls Addy against him and kisses her again. 'I love you, Adi. There is no one else for me in this life. You have to know about it.'

Her father's book will wait.

# Chapter Forty-Seven

**Zitoune, Morocco – June 2009**

The shutters crash against the wall of Addy's bedroom.

'*Habibati*! Come to breakfast at my mother's house. Be quick with your sister. We're going to the desert.'

She squints through the sharp sunlight at Omar's blue-turbaned head, framed in the window like a portrait.

'What? Today?'

'Yes, with Yassine and Mohammed. You said you want to go to the Sahara, so I arrange it. Yassine will drive and Mohammed will be like the father between me and Yassine.'

Addy throws off the covers and walks over to the mirror in the Beatles T-shirt Philippa had brought her from London. She grimaces in the mirror, pressing her fingers down on a spike of unruly hair.

'Isn't Mohammed busy with the hotel and the restaurant? Amine's been playing hooky.'

'I know what this means, hooky. Mohammed tell me. *Mashi mushkil.* Mohammed gave Amine the responsibility to be the manager of the restaurant when he's in the desert. Amine is so, so happy for that. He love the responsibility. Mohammed loves to go to the desert. He makes good animation with the tourists and

278

he tells them to come to his hotel in Zitoune. It's good business for him, and for me, as well.'

'I need a shower and we need to pack. And I have to show Fatima how to use the new washing machine.'

'*Mashi mushkil*. Be quick. We'll go for three nights. Don't take so much luggage. The plumber is coming this morning for the washing machine. It's a big honour for my family that you bought it. My mother loves you for it.'

'I didn't do it to *buy* her love.'

'She loves you anyway. Now she loves you even bigger.'

'I did it to help your mother and Fatima save time. It takes them two days to wash and dry all the laundry by hand, did you know that?'

'*Que sera sera.*'

Addy pulls off the T-shirt and heads towards her bathroom.

'*Habss*. I hope your sister leaves soon. I been like a bachelor again.'

Addy sticks her head around the bathroom door. 'Can you imagine the bad eye if you were sleeping in the same house with me and my sister? Anyway, I thought you'd be used to me by now and would appreciate a rest.'

'I'll never be used to you, *habibati*. Even if I live one hundred years.'

Omar, Yassine and Mohammed are in Aicha's courtyard huddled around the new white washing machine with two other men when Addy and Philippa arrive at Aicha's house. The bamboo birdcage with its silent green-feathered occupant has been set on an old table next to the kitchen door. Aicha, Fatima, Jedda, Lamia and several of the village women sit on cushions and stools around the low wooden table in the courtyard. They sip tea and munch on *msemen* and sugar cookies as they chatter and watch the installation.

Omar looks over at her as she comes in. 'Adi. How do you fix it?'

A soggy pile of paper mashed into a muddy puddle catches Addy's eye. She picks up the wad of paper and waves it in the air.

'It would help if you read the instructions.'

'Nobody in Zitoune has a washing machine,' Omar says. 'It's a new situation.'

'All the more reason to read the instructions. I'm not a plumber. I've never installed a washing machine.'

Omar nods at the paper in Addy's hands. 'You can read the instructions and be our manager.'

'They're in Arabic.'

Omar grabs the wad of paper and hands it to the scrawny man with a wrench standing next to him. The man shoves it into the back pocket of his grey flannel trousers and says something to Omar as he heads out of the front door. The barrel-chested electrician kneels down in the puddle of water and unscrews a wall socket. In his dirty black trousers and a thick yellow-and-black wool jumper he resembles a fat, mustachioed bee. Pulling out the electrical wires with the screwdriver, he fiddles with joining up the washing machine cables to the electricity supply.

'He's going to electrocute himself, Omar. Tell him to get out of the water.'

The front door bangs open. The scrawny plumber enters dragging a long hose, a cigarette dangling from his mouth.

'*Mashi mushkil*. The plumber will fix the situation.'

Omar points with a piece of bread to the washing machine as he and the men head out of the front door. The plumber has connected one end of the hose to the back of the washing machine and the other to the courtyard tap.

'Show Fatima how to use the machine of washing, darling. We'll get the gasoline for the car in Azaghar.'

Lamia and the other women take their leave, piled down with bags of fresh bread and cookies. Aicha follows Fatima and Jedda into her bedroom.

Philippa turns to Addy. Her straw hat and oversized Jackie O sunglasses leave only the tip of her white nose and chin visible over the slash of vivid lipstick.

'Where did they go?' she asks Addy.

'They went to pray in her room.'

'Oh.' Philippa's lips twitch.

'They're very devout Muslims.'

'And you're okay with that?'

'Of course. It's a Muslim country.'

'Yes, of course. It's just that . . . I've never been around Muslims so . . . so intimately before.'

'For heaven's sake, Pippa. We're all just people. We all want the same things. Food, a home, an income, love, happiness. We just have different points of view. The road would be very crowded if we all took the same journey.'

'What are you now? A philosopher?'

Fatima emerges from Aicha's bedroom dragging two over-flowing pink laundry baskets.

'*Viens*, Adi. *Nous faisons le washing.*'

Addy helps her to sift through the clothes, showing Fatima how to separate the whites from the colours. She loads the coloured clothes into the machine and fills the dispenser with washing powder. After crossing the courtyard, she twists open the tap and shouts at Fatima.

'*Pousses le bouton!*'

Fatima presses the button. The washing machine jumps and rattles violently. Fatima leaps back. '*Ooh, la la.*'

'Bloody hell, Addy. It sounds like it's going to bore a hole down to China.'

Addy rushes over to the washing machine and lifts the lid. She gives Fatima a thumbs-up. '*Mashy mushkey.*'

'Are you sure buying them a washing machine was wise?'

'I only did it to help lighten some of their workload. You wouldn't believe how much time they spend washing clothes by hand. They do it in the river. It takes ages. I've done it with them. In fact, it almost finished me off, but that's another story.'

Aicha emerges from her bedroom carrying an old wicker basket stacked with towels and sheets. Addy gestures to the washing machine, but Aicha smiles and shakes her head, pointing towards the river as she crosses the courtyard to the front door.

'What is it, Fatima? Your mother doesn't like the washing machine?'

'No, no, Adi. She love the machine of washing. It's a big honour. But she like to go to the river to wash the clothes to see her friends.'

Addy stares at Fatima. She's been a fool. She's taken away Fatima's day of socialising with the women at the river. She's closed down one of Fatima's few escapes from the house. Fatima's a caged bird, just like Farouk's poor, silent present.

'Would you prefer to go to the river to wash the clothes, too?'

'*Laa!*' Fatima shakes her head so vigorously that a black curl escapes from her hijab. 'I will go with my mother to talk with the ladies, but I will wash my clothes in the machine of washing. I am a modern woman because of my sister Adi.'

'*Marhaba*, Fatima.'

It's okay. This time it's okay. But she has to be careful. Beware of good intentions. Every action has a reaction. Uncle Rachid had warned her.

282

# Chapter Forty-Eight

**Todra Gorge, Morocco – June 2009**

Philippa opens up her cream Prada handbag. 'What? Why are you looking at me like that?' She roots outs a tube of lipstick and a compact.

'I'm just wondering if the Sahara Desert's ready for you.'

'What choice do I have?' She peers into the mirror and dabs fuchsia lipstick on her lips. 'Stay here and peel vegetables with Granny until you get back?'

'You could always catch a tour bus back to Marrakech and hole up in the Mamounia Hotel. You could give Nigel a call, now that you're best mates.'

'Don't tempt me. I've heard the Churchill Bar is divine. But, I'm here to visit you, darling sister. So visit you I shall, even if it kills me.' She snaps the compact closed and drops it into her handbag with her lipstick.

'It's not you I'm worried about. I hope *I* survive the visit. The Nigel surprise almost gave me a heart attack.'

Philippa peers over the top of her sunglasses. 'I'm sorry about that. He'd given me such a sob story. I felt sorry for him. Can you believe it? I'm usually such a hard nut.'

'Omar was furious. I've had a lot of explaining to do. Don't you dare tell Omar that Nigel and I own a flat together.'

'My lips are sealed. I haven't told Nigel a thing about our desert jaunt.'

'You've been talking to Nigel? Since he left Zitoune?'

'Well . . . uh . . . he rang me.'

'You didn't have to answer.'

'What would you have me do? Delete his number?'

'There's an idea.'

'For your information, I've told him that my loyalties lie with you. Blood is thicker than water and all that rubbish. As far as I know, he's been chatting up German tourists at the Club Med in Marrakech.'

The wheels of a car crunch to a stop outside the front door. A horn blasts. Philippa loops the strap of her Prada bag over her shoulder and picks up the pull handle of her Louis Vuitton suitcase. 'The desert. God give me strength.'

A valley of palm trees twists far below the unpaved track of mountain road like a green river. Yassine steers the car towards a cluster of mud houses springing from the mountainside like anthills, weaving the battered Renault around tables jutting into the road. Fossils, straw hats, and pieces of cloth embroidered with neon zigzags and silver sequins, are on offer, but there's no other sign of life.

'Where is everyone?'

'It's Friday,' Mohammed says. 'It might be they are at the mosque.'

The road narrows as they exit the village. It becomes a single track lane rutted with potholes clinging to the side of the mountain's red sandstone face. A tour bus rockets around a blind corner towards them like a heat-seeking missile. Yassine steers hard against the mountainside, flipping his side mirror into the car with his hand just before the tour bus tears by.

'Jesus Christ!' Philippa and Addy exclaim in unison.

Yassine tosses the mirror over to Omar. '*Mashi mushkil*. It's Moroccan driver. He don't mind.'

'Well, I bloody mind.' Philippa roots around her handbag and pulls out a jar of Tiger Balm. She dabs a shiny smear on each temple. 'Aren't there any safer roads?'

Omar frowns at Philippa in the rear-view mirror. 'You think it's easy to go to the Sahara? It's far away. We must go over many mountains. It's not like New York City.'

'Phileepa, you must not worry,' Mohammed assures her. 'Yassine is a very safe driver. He is like the Ayrton Senna of Morocco.'

'Didn't Ayrton Senna die in a car crash?'

Mohammed shrugs. 'It was his fate.'

'Fate is fate.' Omar rifles through the CDs spilling out of the glove compartment. 'If it's your fate to die today, Phileepa, nothing can stop it. So, enjoy.'

Philippa scoops out another thick dollop of Tiger Balm. 'Bloody hell.'

Yassine steers the car through a slit in the mountain face. The road disappears into dark shadow.

'Where are we, Omar?'

'Todra Gorge, *habibati*. Many people come to do mountain climbing here.' Omar taps on his window. 'Many years ago, a big river made this canyon. The river made the green palm trees in the valley we passed, even though everywhere else is dry.'

The crevice opens up, revealing a concrete car park crammed with tour buses and jeeps. A hotel constructed of peach-rendered concrete, crowned with Berberesque crenulations, squats next to the stream. Brown goat hair and wool tents cluster in front of the canyon walls, and candy-coloured tagelmusts hang like bunting from rope strung against the orange sandstone mountainsides.

Yassine parks the car beside a white tour van. Omar points to two specks of white high up on the side of the canyon.

'It's climbers there. You see?'

'They're idiots.' Philippa adjusts her sunglasses and loops her handbag over her arm. 'I need the loo. I'm desperate. I'll see you inside.'

Addy squints at the climbers. 'I'd never be brave enough to do that.'

'I can do it.'

'You're a mountain climber?'

'I had to do it for my mountain guide qualification. I have many secrets, honey. One day, maybe you will learn them all, just like I learn about you.'

Philippa waves from a rustic wooden table set with napkins folded into the shape of chef's hats. The room is painted bright orange, and red patterned rugs cover the concrete floor. Banquettes upholstered in a chaotic mix of vibrant stripes and florals line three of the walls.

Addy picks up a menu as she shuffles along the banquette next to Philippa. 'Nothing to your taste, Pips? You've got that face on you again.'

Philippa tosses the menu onto the tablecloth. 'It's hardly Nobu's black cod. I could kill for black cod. And a glass of wine.'

Addy scans the menu. *Salade Marocaine, Tagine d'Agneau, Tagine de Poulet, Tagine de Dinde, Brochette d'Agneau, Brochette de Poulet, Frites.*

'Never mind about black cod. I'm starting to obsess about spaghetti.'

Omar takes Addy's menu. 'It's not Italia here, darling.'

'Don't you ever get tired of eating the same thing?'

'It's Morocco, so you eat Moroccan food. It's normal.'

Philippa hands him her menu. 'Salad for me. No dressing. And water. In a bottle.'

'Me too. But I'll have dressing. Lots of it. I've reached my tagine tipping point.'

'As you like. You'll be hungry later for sure.'

'Where are the others?'

'They went in the back to eat with the drivers. They know many guys from Marrakech and Casa.' Omar tucks the two menus under his arm. 'I'll make the order with the waiter and I'll go eat with them as well. It's good for me to talk to the drivers. I might get some business.'

'What time will we get to the desert?'

'Not today. Tonight we'll stay at a hotel in the mountains and tomorrow we'll go to the desert.'

'Bloody hell.' The brim of Philippa's straw hat flaps about her head like a bird attempting flight. 'You mean we have another day in that car?'

'Tourists always want to make a plan. It's good to be natural. *Que sera sera.*'

'Ignore her, Omar. Go and eat with your friends. After lunch, I'll get my camera and you can guide Philippa and me through the gorge.'

'*Mashi mushkil.*' He holds up his hand and rubs his thumb and forefinger together and looks at Philippa. 'I hope you're rich. I'm a very expensive guide.'

Omar tugs a turquoise tagelmust off a line of tagelmusts wafting in the breeze like long, graceful flags. He twists the fabric around Addy's head and drapes the tail end around her neck in an elegant swag. She catches his gaze and his cheek dimples.

'The colour makes your eyes turquoise. You know I love it.'

Addy rubs the fabric between her fingers. Less than three months ago, Omar was a stranger to her, but now this man in a blue turban is her lover. Their lives are entwining and even though they're from different worlds, it feels preordained. Like they're two pieces of a puzzle locking together. Is it synergy? Fate? Random chance? Why does she feel her father is somehow involved? Then there's the question of why Omar has her father's book, and why Hanane was wearing her mother's Claddagh wedding ring in the photo. Not to mention where Fatima got the old Polaroids of her family. Why does everyone she asks deny knowing anything about Hanane? Even the policeman in Zitoune looked at her like she was crazy, asking about a woman in a twenty-five-year-old photo. Something's going on, and she needs to find out what it is.

She's returning to London soon and she's no closer to finding out about Hanane and the baby. Enough is enough. Tonight she has to ask Omar how he got hold of her father's Shakespeare book. No more hesitations. No more delays. If he has secrets, it's time to find out what they are. No matter what the cost.

# Chapter Forty-Nine

**High Atlas Mountains, Morocco – June 2009**

In the town, the shop sellers have re-emerged to flag down the passing traffic with their offerings of fossils and trinkets. Yassine leans on the horn as he inches the car through the village, following a narrow road newly paved with pungent asphalt down the mountainside into the desert valley spotted with date palms. Despite Philippa's huffing, Yassine stops regularly for Addy to capture pictures of the mud-walled houses clinging to the mountainside, the ancient castle-like kasbahs tattooed with Amazigh symbols, or a flash of vivid colour where someone's hung a rug from a window to air in the breeze.

The sun's throwing its last rays over the valley when they reach the hotel, another concrete new build, painted in orange render and stamped with zigzags and crosses. It perches on an outcrop of orange limestone, which drops away to the arid skeleton of a river far below. A concrete mixer sits next to a newly poured path covered by wooden planks. Yassine parks on the roadside behind two white tour buses and wanders with Mohammed to join the drivers, who lean, smoking, against one of the buses.

'You couldn't have found us a finished hotel, could you, Omar?' Philippa complains as she lumbers with her luggage over the wooden planks to the entrance doors. She stops short in the doorway. 'Bloody hell. It's like Buckingham Palace during the Changing of the Guard.'

A dozen Japanese tourists mill about the lobby dragging suitcases across the terrazzo floor. At the reception desk, a Japanese woman in the smart navy suit of a foreign tour guide flaps a piece of paper, protesting in broken English to the receptionist, who shakes his head and lifts his hands in incomprehension.

Omar sets down his knapsack and Addy's tripod bag. 'I'll go to fix the situation.'

Philippa parks her Louis Vuitton suitcase next to Addy's feet. 'Watch this for me, would you? I'm going to have a nosy around while Omar saves the world.'

Addy watches her sister wander over to a seating area and pick up a sequinned *handira* wedding blanket to inspect the large silver sequins. The room is large and its orange polished plaster walls, still bare of any pictures or wall hangings, echo with the Japanese voices. The only concessions to sound dampening are the upholstered banquette and thick black-and-white Beni Ourain wool rug in the seating area.

Omar waves a room key above his head and shouts to Addy over the Japanese tourists. 'Come for the keys.'

Shifting the camera bag onto her shoulder, Addy grabs the handles of the two suitcases and wades through the sea of tourists to the front desk.

Omar hands Addy the keys. 'It's a nice room, honey. It's for the honeymoon.'

Philippa pushes her way through the tour group. 'Why on earth didn't you come over to us with the keys, instead of making us fight through this lot? It would've been the intelligent thing to do.'

Addy frowns at her sister. 'Pippa. Be nice.'

'I'm hot and I'm tired, and every bone in my body's been rattled out of alignment. My osteopath will have a miracle to perform when I get home to civilisation.'

'It's better to come to the desk, Phileepa.' The vein in Omar's temple is pulsing. 'It's more intelligent.'

Philippa plucks her sunglasses from her face and tucks them into the top of her wrinkled linen shirt. 'Whatever. Thank God I have alcohol. I'll bring the vodka to dinner and we can all have a drink. I think we deserve it.'

Omar purses his lips. 'I don't drink alcohol. I'm Muslim.'

'Fine. All the more for Addy and me.'

'She doesn't drink also.'

'That's news to me.'

Addy holds up her hands. 'Calm down. Both of you. Please. It's been a long day and we're all tired. Omar, if I want a drink, I'll have a drink. We're far enough from your family for no one to get upset.'

'It's not good to be drunk, Adi.'

'Since when did you ever see me drunk?'

Philippa grabs her suitcase handle. 'Enough already. The last thing I need is to be dragged into a domestic. I'm bringing vodka to the table and I'm more than happy to drink it all myself.'

Omar presses a light switch in the dark hallway, but nothing happens. He peers into an ornate lantern protruding from the wall.

'There's no light inside.'

'*Quel surprise,*' Philippa says.

Omar takes out his cell phone and shines its light on the room numbers until he finds Philippa's room. He unlocks the door and presses the light switch. A small lamp by the bed lights up.

'At least there's electricity, Pippa,' Addy says.

Philippa tosses her straw hat onto the bed. 'Thank heaven for small mercies.' She shivers and rubs her hands together. 'It's bloody cold in here.'

'It's the High Atlas Mountains, Phileepa,' Omar says. 'It's colder here, especially in the night-time.'

Omar opens the bathroom door. He flicks the light switch.

291

Nothing. He runs the tap and re-enters the bedroom, wiping his wet hands on his jeans.

Philippa throws herself on top of the large bed, which is strewn with embroidered cushions. 'Oh, bliss. I'm just going to lie here and let my bones settle back into place. Knock on my door when you're going to supper. Till then I think I'll pass out.'

Omar glances around the dark hallway. He grabs Addy's shoulders and kisses her hard on her mouth.

'I miss you, *habibati*. I been patient, but your sister gave me a headache.'

'Join the club. She's not an easy woman.'

'I must be polite because she's your sister, but it's not so easy sometimes. I apologise for that. You have to know it upset me a lot she brought your boyfriend here.'

'Yeah. I wasn't happy about that either. Don't worry, I told her.'

He checks the number on the door across from Philippa's with the light from his phone and unlocks the door. When he flicks the light switch, ornate iron lanterns on the bedside tables switch on, casting coloured light into the vast room.

'Lovely,' Addy says. 'Two bulbs even.'

Omar takes Addy's hand and guides her towards the bed. 'Come, darling. I been patient. But I'm not patient any more.'

'I should take a shower. I'm sweaty from the trip.'

Omar pulls Addy down onto the bed. The golden light from the lantern turns his eyes a clear amber. 'Don't mind for a shower. There's no hot water.'

Addy slides out of bed and pulls on her kaftan top as she pads across the thick red wool rug to the bathroom.

'I guess there aren't any showers in the desert, are there?'

'No, darling. No showers or no toilets.'

'No toilets?'

292

'It's the desert, darling. It's camels and it's tents. Full stop.'

'Philippa's not going to like that. She packed her hairdryer.'

'She's a crazy lady. I told you to pack simple stuff only. Why did you bring your suitcase? You should bring your bag only. It's a problem, darling.'

'The electrical tape came off. Things would just fall out. My underwear would be all over the desert.'

Omar grabs his knapsack and tosses it up onto the bed.

'You think I'm a crazy lady too sometimes, don't you, Omar?'

He looks up at her, a toothbrush and tube of toothpaste in his hand. 'What do you mean?'

Addy sits on the tumble of blankets and sheets beside Omar. 'I know I'm not always the easiest person. I can be moody.' She sighs. 'Maybe . . . maybe you'd be better off with someone else. Someone younger.'

Omar frowns, the crease between his eyes deepening. 'Why do you say that? You must stop it, darling. I'm a serious guy. I made my decision. Maybe you think I'm a rubbish guy like Yassine who has a foreigner lady from Holland even though he's married. The shit guy from England thinks I'm a rubbish guy. Your sister thinks I'm a rubbish guy for sure.'

'No, she doesn't.'

'They think I'm a kidnapper.'

'Philippa was just joking when she said that.'

'It's not a funny joke for me, darling. I made a mistake to do that phone call before, one hundred per cent. I'm so sorry for that.' He looks at Addy, his eyes shining like polished marble in the dim light. 'What about your boyfriend?'

'He's not my boyfriend.'

'Why did he come here? You invited him?'

'I had no idea he was coming. It was Philippa.'

Omar rubs his temples. 'I don't like the situation at all. It makes me want to hurt him. For sure I could do it easy.'

'Nigel's not worth fighting. He means nothing to me any more.'

293

'It might be. But I know you been with him before. It makes me jealous like a lion.'

Addy stares at Omar. She's been so selfish. She'd never considered Omar's feelings about her relationship with Nigel. It was shaking him off his foundations as much as it was jolting and jarring hers. Rachid's words come to her again. She's the pebble thrown in the pond and the ripples are becoming waves. More than waves. A tsunami.

It was time. She treads across the rug to her suitcase. Unzipping it, she takes out her father's Shakespeare book. She clutches the red book to her chest.

'Where did you get this book, Omar?'

A shadow crosses Omar's face. 'Where did you find it?'

'On your desk. I was resting in your room one day and I wanted to read something. I found this.'

She sits on the bed and opens up the book to the inside cover. '"*To my darling Augustus from Nanny Percival, Christmas 1945*". This was my father's book. You knew my father, didn't you? Why did you lie to me when I showed you the photograph?' She slides the fading Polaroid of Gus and Hanane out from the pages of *Othello*.

Omar takes the photograph. He stares at the grainy image and rubs his thumb across the faces of Addy's father and the young Moroccan woman.

'He did a big mistake, Adi. It's better not to talk about it. It's a long time ago.'

'So, you did know him?'

'Yes.'

'What happened? I never knew he'd come to Morocco until I found the photo after he died. I didn't come to Morocco just to take photos and write. I came to Zitoune to see if I could find Hanane. To find the baby, who must be about twenty-four by now. Or find out what happened to them.'

Omar lets the Polaroid fall onto the blanket. 'Many people will be angry if they know he was your father.'

Addy thinks of her father, laughing and rolling around the grass with their collie, Kip, while she swings in old tyre from a branch of the oak tree in their Nanaimo garden.

'I don't understand that. He was a wonderful father to me. Well, he was when he was at home.'

'You were lucky, darling. He was a bad man in Zitoune.'

Addy's heart jumps. A bad man? Her father? Had he done something terrible? Perhaps that was why he'd never mentioned Hanane and the baby. And why Mohammed, the policeman, Aicha and Jedda all denied recognising Hanane. Maybe there was a scandal.

'What did he do? What happened to Hanane and the baby?'

Omar scans Addy's face like he's looking for clues to a puzzle he's trying to solve.

'I was young, just a boy when he came here. Maybe I don't understand the situation well.'

Addy sits up against the pillows beside Omar. 'Tell me. Tell me everything. Even if it's bad, I want to know.'

# Chapter Fifty

**High Atlas Mountains, Morocco – June 2009**

'One day a man came to the village. He was a hiker, with a backpack and a tent, and he had a strange camera which made pictures in your hand. He was older, like forty years, and taller. He had black hair and blue eyes, like you, darling. I was a boy, maybe seven years. Even so, I made a good business with the figs and the tourists with my brother, Momo, who had ten years. I had eyes everywhere in my head to know what's going on in the village.'

Omar picks up the Shakespeare book and flips through the pages. Closing the cover, he sets it down gently on the blanket.

'The man made a camp near the source of the waterfalls.'

'I've been there. With Amine and Fatima.'

Omar raises his eyebrows. 'When were you there with them?'

'Fatima and I went for a walk to the source one day. Amine followed us because he said you wanted him to keep an eye on me.'

'There are many eyes in Zitoune. It's good he followed you. You always have to move, to go, to do stuff. It's hard for you to be quiet in a house like the ladies here. I'm sorry if I don't understand you well sometimes, Adi. This is a new situation for me. It's like you want to be free like a man.'

296

'Of course I want to be free, like anybody should be – man or woman. Free like a bird. Not like Fatima's poor caged budgie.'

'You remind me of that man. You have the same energy. He told us his name is Gus. So we called him Mister Gus. I followed him. I showed him the waterfalls, and the cave with the carvings, and the footsteps of dinosaurs.'

'Dinosaur footprints. I'd like to see those. My father had a photo of them. I'd like to photograph them for my book.'

'*Mashi mushkil.* I will show you one time. Anyway, he paid me money for it, so I was proud for that. It made Yassine and his brother, Driss, very jealous. My brother, Momo, he don't mind. He was always a good boy. He went to school. He was polite. Not like me.'

'Fatima showed me a photo of your mother with you, Momo and Fatima as a baby. She said your brother died in a flood.'

Omar nods. 'It was his fate.'

'I'm sorry. That must've been hard for all of you.'

Omar presses his fingers against his eyes. 'It happens like that sometimes. Life is short.'

Addy brushes her hand across her left breast. 'Yes. I know.' Addy looks at the smiling faces of her father and Hanane in the photograph. 'Fatima had several Polaroids. I recognised my father's writing on the back. How did she get them?'

'Mister Gus took many photos with the magic camera. It was incredible to see them come out of the mouth, like it's spitting. He gave some to my mum. Me too, I have one.'

He reaches into his back pocket and takes out his wallet. Flipping it open, he pulls out a Polaroid that's been cut down to fit into the wallet. The edges are frayed and the gloss cracked, but the image is still clear, though the colours are fading and reddening. Omar as a young boy in the branches of an olive tree with a young, laughing woman. Hanane.

'You knew her.'

'Yes. She was a good lady.'

297

'And your mother knew my father and Hanane, too.'

'Yes.'

'And Jedda?'

'Yes. Everybody.'

'Everybody lied to me. You lied to me.'

Omar shakes his head. 'We only did it to protect your honour. We don't want you to be ashamed for your father.'

'I could never be ashamed of my father.'

Omar smiles sadly. 'I hope so.' He runs his thumb across her cheek. 'We must go to dinner soon, *habibati*. Your sister will be hungry.'

'I need to know about Hanane.'

'You're sure?'

'It's why I came to Morocco.'

'You told me you came here to take pictures for your book.'

'Yes, that's true. But, honestly, I could've done that anywhere. I came to Morocco because of my father's photos. Especially the photo of him with Hanane in front of the waterfalls. I came to find out what happened to her and the baby. And why my father was here. Why he'd kept it a secret. He started to write me a letter about Hanane, but he never sent it. I want to know why.'

'You came to be a detective of Zitoune like *Columbo*.'

Addy picks up the Polaroid and wraps the bed blanket around herself.

'I guess. So, how did you get my father's book?'

Omar sits on the end of the large bed.

'Mister Gus taught me English very well. Sometimes Momo came, too. He was a good student. Mister Gus gave us the book of Shakespeare one time and said one day we should read the stories. I tried, darling, but it's hard.' Omar shakes his head. 'I told you before I was a bad boy. I was always running away from school to make business with the tourists. I wanted to be businessman to make money. Mister Gus told me if I could speak English I could make good business with the tourists. He was a clever teacher to me. He gave me motivation.'

'So he wasn't a bad man at all.'

'Not then. He was kind then. Momo liked the book a lot. He loved the stories. After he die, I took it. I tried to be good like Momo, to go to school, to be polite. I think to become a teacher to honour Momo. I studied for one year at the university in Beni Mellal. This is true, I swear it. But it's hard for me to be in a room with the books. It wasn't my cup of tea, you have to know about it. I tried to be Momo, but I'm Omar. So I came back to Zitoune to be a tour guide. And then, when I had money, I went to Marrakech to study one year to be a professional mountain guide.'

'I see.'

'Your sister will be angry to wait for us, Adi. We should go.'

'I know, I know. Who was Hanane? I need to know.'

'She was a beautiful lady who was the youngest sister of Mohammed Demsiri.'

Addy's eyes widen. 'Mohammed is Amine's uncle. You told me Amine's parents weren't married. That means . . .'

'Yes, darling. Amine is the son of Hanane.'

Addy's eyes widen. 'And Amine's father?'

'Mister Gus.'

Addy's mind spins with the revelation.

'My father? Are you sure?'

Amine is her half-brother. Why hadn't she been able to see that? The dark eyes, the full lips are Hanane's, but the wide smile – yes, her father is in Amine's smile. The same smile her father would greet her with after his long absences on his travels. And Amine has Gus's long, straight nose. Slightly too large for his face. Just like hers and Philippa's. And Gus's straight black hair. Black Irish hair.

'Yes, *habibati*. One hundred per cent.'

Addy looks at the Polaroid in her hand and runs her finger over Hanane's pregnant belly. 'It's incredible.'

'One time, Mister Gus paid me to put a picnic for them in the cave of the drawings, like Yassine did for us. I helped them to be together. Momo said I'm a bad boy to help them, but I didn't mind. I do what I like. They went everywhere in secret. Sometimes they went to the building of the olive oil. Always it was a secret. Hanane was a good Amazigh lady. She didn't want people to say bad things. She was afraid of the evil eye.'

'The evil eye seems to follow the Percivals everywhere.'

'You have to be careful for it, darling. There is much bad stuff like that in the mountains. Jealousy. Bad feelings. People go to *shawafas* to make potions for badness. Many people come to my grandmother for this because she is a very powerful *shawafa*. But she never does badness, even though she can. She only makes good medicine for people. She teach my mother to do good medicine only. Some people say my grandmother have a djinni to do stuff for her.' He shrugs. 'But it's just ladies talking.' He taps the Polaroid in Addy's hand. 'I was the photographer of this picture.'

'You took this picture?'

'Yes.'

'Really?'

'It's our fate to be together, Adi.'

Her reality slips. She's in a space that aligns, but not in a way she'd ever considered possible.

'What happened to Hanane? Mohammed said Amine's mother died.'

Omar rubs his eyes. 'It's hard to talk about it, darling. It's better I don't tell you. It will hurt you.'

'Tell me. I need to know what my father did. Maybe that's why I'm here. Maybe I'm here to fix it.'

'There's no way to fix the situation, *habibati*.' He sighs. 'Okay, I will tell you the story.'

# Chapter Fifty-One

**Zitoune, Morocco – March 1984**

The metal door swings open, blowing Gus into the room on a blast of wind and rain.

'The bridge is washed out,' he says in French. 'The shops are all flooded.'

'What about the houses by the shops?' Hanane frowns. Omar's family lived by the shops.

Gus shrugs out of Hanane's father's old brown wool djellaba. 'They're stuffing rugs by the doors, but that's not going to help much. The water's rising too fast. I've been telling people to leave for higher ground, but they won't listen to me.'

'Will we be all right here? We're so close to the river.'

'It's high enough. We'll be fine.'

Hanane lifts the kettle off the brazier and pours the steaming water into a teapot stuffed with green tea, fresh mint and lumps of sugar. As she pours the tea into tea glasses, the spicy freshness of the mint wafts through the room. She hands a glass to Gus.

'Thank you, my darling.'

Hanane blushes. She sips at the steaming tea. '*Marhaba.*'

Gus grabs the stool from underneath the window and sets it down beside the brazier.

'Please, sit down, Hanane. It's more comfortable than squatting.'

Hanane dips her chin shyly. 'Thank you.'

He settles cross-legged on the striped cushions and watches Hanane silently as she sips the tea.

'I know something's on your mind,' he says. 'You can tell me.'

How can she tell him of her guilt? Of the dishonour she'd bring upon herself and her family if her relationship with him was discovered. Even though he'd never touched her. They'd never believe her. Gus would never understand the way people were here.

She shakes her head. 'It's nothing.'

Gus sets down the tea glass and squeezes her hand. 'I don't believe that for a minute, Hanane.'

'It's just—'

A pounding on the door. 'M-M-Mister Gus! Come quick!' A boy's voice.

The door jumps on its hinges as the boy jiggles the locked handle.

Gus throws open the door. 'Yassine? What's going on?'

'A c-c-cow. They tried to r-r-rescue it.' The boy shivers in his soaking ski jacket and jeans. 'They're in the river on the b-b-big rock. The one near the b-b-bridge.'

Hanane grabs a towel and wraps it around the boy's quivering shoulders. 'Who, Yassine? Who's on the rock?'

'It's the c-c-cow of Momo and Omar's m-m-mother. It ran away from the w-w-water. We tried to c-c-catch it but it went in the river. It got stuck on the r-r-rock. Omar said we must to r-r-rescue it. They went on a b-b-branch to get to the r-r-rock.'

Gus throws his brown djellaba over his head. 'Who went on the branch?'

'My brother and Omar and D-D-Driss.'

'Holy Mother of God. Stay here with Hanane. I'll get help.'

'No, Mister Gus. I must come. It's my b-b-brother. I don't want him to go over the w-w-waterfalls.'

302

Hanane grabs her djellaba from the olive press. 'I'm coming too.'

Gus and Hanane push through the villagers clustered in the thick red paste of the muddy riverbank, following Yassine as he dodges through the chattering crowd.

'There, they're there.' Yassine points to the three boys clinging to a large rock in the middle of the swollen river.

The sodden cow is wedged in a crack in the rock, its tin bell clanging forlornly as it wrestles to free itself.

'Mister Gus!' Omar, Momo and Driss wave from the top of the wet rock as they struggle to keep hold of the cow's rope.

Hanane slips in the slick mud and grabs onto Gus's arm to steady herself. 'Momo! Omar! Driss! Be careful. We'll help you.'

'Jesus Mother of God.' Gus grasps hold of the branch the boys have used as a bridge to the rock and leans his full weight against it. 'Hold on, boys. Stay where you are.' He looks around at the men, their deep-lined faces shadowed by their hooded djellabas. 'Come on, you have to help us.' Gus spots the green plastic raincoat and peaked cap of the village's new young policeman shrinking back through the wall of brown wool djellabas. '*Monsieur Le Police*. Help us! Get some rope.'

Hanane pushes through the men and grabs the arm of the policeman. 'Please. You have to help them.'

The policeman thrusts Hanane's hand away. 'I'm not going to help the Irishman's whore.'

Hanane gasps. 'What did you say?'

The man's eyes stare at Hanane in contempt. 'I know you're fucking the foreigner. I've been watching you. You came here today with him from the olive hut.' He spits into the mud at Hanane's feet. 'You should do your family a favour and go spread your legs in Marrakech. At least you'll make some money there instead of throwing yourself away on that filthy foreigner.'

The slap sends the policeman's hat flying into the mud. Hanane stares at her smarting palm and clutches it to her chest.

'I am a good woman. The day will come when you will regret this insult.'

The policeman picks up his hat and slaps it against his raincoat. 'What are you going to do? You'll be finished in Zitoune when I tell your family. How will you stop me? Send a djinni after me?' He sweeps his flat brown eyes over her. 'Maybe we can make a better arrangement.'

Anger spins through Hanane's body. 'A djinni? I will do much worse than that. Remember me. Because I will remember you.'

A hand grasps Hanane's arm and yanks her around. 'Hanane. What are you doing here?'

Her brother stands in front of her, his eyes flicking between her and the policeman.

'Mohammed! You have to help. The boys are on the rock in the river. They tried to rescue Aicha's cow. Mister Gu— the foreigner is trying to help them. Can you get a rope? Anything?' She pulls at Mohammed's arm. 'Come, Mohammed. Please.' Mohammed spies the policeman sliding into the screen of the olive grove. He looks at the frantic face of his sister. So what the police told him is true. He glances towards the river.

'Please, Mohammed. I beg you. The rope from the washing line. We can use that. I'll go with Yassine to get it. We have to hurry. The boys could drown.'

'Yes. Fine. Bring the rope. I'll help.'

Hanane grasps her brother's hand and kisses it. 'Thank you, Mohammed.'

He pulls his hand away. 'We'll talk later, Hanane. This situation is not finished.'

Gus tugs at the yellow nylon rope around his waist linking him to the thick trunk of an olive tree. Mohammed leans his weight onto the branch that rests precariously against the boys' rock.

'Hurry,' he says to Gus in French. 'The river is pushing the branch. We don't have much time.'

Hanane scans the faces of the village men.

'Anyone? Please. Help us. How can you just stand there? It's not for me. It's for the boys.'

'Please,' Yassine weeps as he runs from man to man, clutching at sleeves and the loose djellabas. 'Help my brother.'

Hanane glares at the men. 'May Allah forgive you all.'

Aicha pushes through the crowd. 'Hanane, what's happening? Jedda told me the boys are in trouble. She's looking for her key to call her djinni to help.'

Hanane points to the river. 'The boys . . .'

Aicha holds her hand up to her mouth. She screams and slides through the mud to the riverbank.'Boys! Momo! Omar! Hold on!'

'The cow, Mama!' Omar yells over the rushing water. 'We have to save the cow. How will you sell milk and butter if she drowns?'

'Never mind, Omar, hold on! We're coming for you.'

Gus launches himself into the freezing current. The water pushes his feet out from under him and he fumbles for the branch.

'Jesus wept,' he curses under his breath.

Mohammed reaches over the branch and grabs hold of Gus's hand, pulling him to his feet.

'Be careful. I will hold the branch still.'

Hanane reaches her arms around Aicha and the shivering Yassine, hugging them to her as they watch. Clutching the branch to steady himself, Gus inches through the current towards the wailing boys until the rope jerks him to a halt halfway across.

Gus beckons to Omar. 'Come on, Omar. Show them how easy it is.'

'Go, Omar,' Momo says to his brother. 'You are the best climber. Go on the branch. Mister Gus will help you.'

'But the cow.'

'Never mind the cow. Go on the branch.'

Omar sits on the slick rock and inches over to the branch. He reaches over and grasps the grey trunk, then slowly shimmies across to Gus.

Gus holds out a hand. 'I've got you, Omar. Grab hold.'

Omar reaches over and clutches Gus around his shoulders. Gus grasps hold of the boy's small body and wades back to the riverbank. Mohammed grabs hold of Omar's sodden ski jacket and pulls him over to safety. Aicha runs over to her son and wails as she presses him against her body.

'I'm fine, *Yamma*,' he says as he squirms out of her grasp. 'It's no problem. Yassine, come on.'

The two boys hurry to the riverbank and yell across to the others. 'It's easy, Momo! Driss! Come on. You can do it.'

Gus wades back out into the river.

'Come on, Momo,' he says, beckoning to the boy. 'Just do what your brother did. Pretend you're one of the monkeys by the waterfalls.'

'Don't go, Momo!' Driss cries. 'Don't leave me by myself. I'm afraid.'

'Don't worry, Driss,' Momo says. 'You go first. It's fine. It's a strong branch.'

'I'm afraid, Momo.'

'Mister Gus will help you. It will be fine.'

'Okay, Momo. I'll try.' Driss crawls onto the branch and begins to whimper. 'I can't do it, Momo.'

'You can. You can. Look, Mister Gus is close.'

'The cow!' Omar screams.

The cow emits a terrified bellow as it suddenly frees itself from the rock and crashes into the raging current. The tin bell's ring is swallowed by water as the cow thrashes against the current propelling it towards the waterfalls.

Driss throws his body onto the branch and clings to it like a baby macaque on its mother's back. 'Momo! I'm afraid!'

'I'm right behind you, Driss,' Momo calls to him. 'Don't worry. I'll help you.'

'Hold on, Driss!' Omar yells from the riverbank. 'Mister Gus is coming.'

A crack like a gunshot rings out across the river as the branch splinters. The boys fall into the pushing current. The black-haired heads slip under the water. They bob up just under the bridge, and disappear again under the rushing current. Mohammed and the men run along the riverbank, Omar and Yassine chasing after them. Aicha screams. Gus stands in the churning river, his face a mask of shock. Hanane puts her hand to her throat. Her voice is broken, silenced by her cries.

# Chapter Fifty-Two

**High Atlas Mountains, Morocco – June 2009**

Addy hugs Omar against her. His shoulders shake with emotion.

'I'm so sorry, Omar. That's terrible. Your poor mother.'

Omar sits back and presses his fingers against his eyes. 'It was their fate.'

'You don't have to tell me any more right now. We can talk about Hanane and my father another time.'

'No, *habibati*. You must know the whole story. After the flood, Yassine told everybody Hanane was with Mister Gus in the olive hut. It was a big scandal. Like Mount Everest.'

'Just because she was in the hut with my father?'

'You don't understand, Adi. This was *haram*. She dishonoured herself. Nobody could trust her after that. The family of Hanane tried to force her to marry a cousin in Tafraout. There was a big argument with Mister Gus and the family of Hanane. They didn't talk to her any more after that. Somebody put the bad eye on Mister Gus and Hanane for bringing bad honour to Zitoune. It was a hard situation for Hanane. Her heart was broken for losing her family.

'Mister Gus took her to Marrakech because the situation became very bad in Zitoune. They were gone for many months. Then one day they came back to talk to her family. I took the photo of them at the waterfalls when they came back. Everybody could see that Hanane is pregnant. Mister Gus insist to talk to her father and Mohammed, but no way. They refuse. So, again Mister Gus and Hanane left. Hanane cried so much.

'Many months later, Hanane came by herself in a *grand taxi* from Marrakech. She is close to have the baby. She went to her family to help her. Her brother, Mohammed, sent his wife to get my mother to help, but my mum was afraid. But my grandmother helped her. Jedda doesn't mind what people think.'

'You're like your grandmother.'

'She's better than me. She's Hajjah. One hundred per cent she will go to Paradise one day.'

'So Jedda delivered Hanane's baby?'

'Yes, I insist to help my grandmother. Hanane was very sick. In the night-time, Amine was born. Mister Gus came in a *grand taxi* soon after, but Hanane she died before he came. He didn't see her. When somebody dies here, they must be buried quick. It was *haram* for him to go to the cemetery because he is Christian.'

'What about Amine? Did he see Amine?'

Omar shifts his gaze away. 'No.'

'No?'

'Mohammed took Amine away.'

'Why? My father could've brought Amine back to Canada. I would've had a half-brother. I might even have come here with Amine one day. And met you.'

'Mohammed didn't want Mister Gus to take Amine because he wanted the baby to be Muslim and he was angry for how Mister Gus had shamed Hanane.' Omar looks at Addy. 'It's hard for me to tell you this, darling.'

'Tell me what?'

Omar looks away, unable to meet Addy's gaze. 'Mohammed paid my mother to lie to Mister Gus.'

It's like a slap. 'Your mother lied? But how? She doesn't speak English.'

'Yes, she lied. She told him Amine died as well.' He inhales a deep breath. 'She told me to tell Mister Gus for her. In English.'

Omar had lied to my father. Gus never knew he'd had a son. A son who'd lived.

Omar looks at Addy. 'After that, Mister Gus left Zitoune. The story became history. And then you came and you showed people the picture, and the story is alive again.'

# Chapter Fifty-Three

## Zitoune, Morocco – March 1984

'How can you do this to me, Hanane? How can you do this to your family?' Hanane's father tosses his soaking djellaba over the strident floral upholstery of a living room banquette.

'I'm sorry, sir. I don't speak Tamazight,' Gus says in French. 'Your daughter didn't do anything wrong. Blame me, by all means, but she's entirely innocent.'

'How can you say that?' Mohammed says in French as he pulls his djellaba over his head and throws it on top of his father's. He jabs a finger at Gus. 'I saw with my own eyes the situation by the river.' He turns to his sister, who stands as still and lifeless as a statue in the doorway. 'The police saw you go in the olive house to meet this man, Hanane. Yassine found you there today. You can't say this is not true.'

Hanane looks at her father's angry face. The lines seem to have etched themselves more deeply in his face since the morning. The pain she's caused. How can she ever forgive herself?

Mohammed's wife, Bouchra, shuffles out of the kitchen, the baby swaddled across her broad back with a scarf. She flicks her eyes from Gus to her sister-in-law.

'I told you you should have married her to Mehdi last year,

311

Mohammed,' she says to her husband in Tamazight. 'This would never have happened. Now, our child will be stained by her sins.' She steps across the plastic mat and pushes Hanane's shoulder, throwing her off balance against a table.

Gus reaches out and catches Hanane before she falls. 'Hold on. That's not necessary.'

Mohammed barks at his wife, who retreats sullenly back into the kitchen.

Hanane's father opens his arms out in a gesture of despair. 'What am I to do now, Hanane?' he asks her in Tamazight. 'The only solution is to marry you immediately to Mustapha in Tafraout, if he will still have you.'

'No, *Baba*! Please! I don't want to go there. It's so far away. I'll know no one there.'

Gus sees the distress in Hanane's face. He reaches for her hand, but she steps away, shaking her head.

'No, Gus. Don't touch me here. It will upset them.'

'Hanane, what did your father just say? What's this about Tafraout?'

'We have a cousin there,' Mohammed says to him. 'He's older. His wife hasn't given him any children, so he looks for a second wife. He asked to marry Hanane last year, but we were looking for her to be the first wife for someone. But now, this is the only solution for her honour. She can't stay here. She is finished in Zitoune.'

'That's crazy. You can't marry her off to some stranger.'

'Tell the man this is none of his business, Mohammed,' Hanane's father says. 'Tell him he must leave here. He makes my house a dirty place.'

'*Baba*, he's a good man. He never touched me, I swear it by Allah's angels.'

'Hanane, go to your room. Tomorrow, we will take a taxi to Marrakech and take the bus to Agadir. I will call Mustapha to meet us there to bring us to Tafraout for the marriage. *Inshallah* you will be married as soon as we have the papers.'

Hanane gasps and runs over to her father. She pulls at his sleeve and sinks to her knees.

'Please, *Baba*, I'll be good. We must stay for the funeral of Momo and Driss tomorrow. I promise I won't see this man again. Just let me stay here in Zitoune. Please.'

Gus steps forwards, but Mohammed bars his path to Hanane.

'Hanane, please, tell me what's going on,' Gus pleads.

Her father shakes her off his arm. 'Tell this devil to leave my house at once before I kill him.'

Hanane rises and turns to Gus, her face streaked with tears.

'He told me we must leave tomorrow to journey to Tafraout. He says I must become the second wife of my cousin, Mustapha.'

Gus steps towards her, but she holds up a hand to stop him.

'You can't let them do that to you, Hanane.' He reaches out his hand to her. 'Come with me. Come with me and be my wife.'

'Your wife?'

'Yes. I mean it. I love you. I won't have you treated like this. Come with me and we'll make a new life in Canada. We'll find a way.'

Hanane looks over at her beloved father's face. How could she have caused him such pain? How can she cause him even more pain? She glances over at her brother. With her shame, she's shamed them both. But she wouldn't marry a man she didn't love.

She walks over to Gus and takes his hand. She turns to her father.

'Goodbye, *Baba*. I'm going with him. He's asked me to marry him. I love him. I'll be his wife.'

Her father's face contorts into a mask of pain. 'You're a Muslimah. You can't marry this man. If you step out of that door with this devil, you are no longer my daughter. You can both go and live with Shaytan Iblis. He will be happy to have you.'

# Chapter Fifty-Four

**High Atlas Mountains, Morocco – June 2009**

The dining room is loud with conversations, the scrape of chairs on the terrazzo floor, the clink of glasses all echoing around the crowded room. Only the banquette seating, upholstered in garish orange-and-gold embroidered damask, softens the unfinished austerity of the room. Omar points at one of the long rows of tables. Mohammed waves, beckoning them over. The sleek-haired woman sitting beside Yassine turns around.

'Addy. *Finally.*'

'Sorry, Pippa.'

Mohammed pushes the table out and pats the firm upholstery. 'Come, Madame Adi. It's comfortable on the cushions.'

'Be careful, *habibati*,' Omar says. 'Maybe Mohammed looks for another wife.'

Mohammed grins, the light from a wall-mounted lantern glinting on his gold teeth.

'*Inshallah.* If it's my fate.'

Omar taps Addy's arm. 'It's better for me to sit next to Mohammed. He's a handsome man yet. I don't trust him.'

Mohammed chuckles. He's wearing a thick brown wool djellaba

over his clothes, but even the rustic simplicity of the djellaba cannot conceal his air of self-confidence and prosperity.

Addy settles onto the banquette cushions beside Omar, squishing him up against Mohammed. Across from her, Yassine leans back in his chair. His left arm rests across the back of Philippa's chair as he smokes a roll-up cigarette. A soft pressure on Addy's ankle. She jerks her foot away. She catches Yassine's eye and his mouth twitches. He picks up a wine bottle labelled with a picture of a dromedary and fills Philippa's glass with yellow wine.

'Where'd the wine come from?' Addy asks.

Philippa wags a finger at her sister. 'Guilty.' She picks up a corkscrew. 'I came prepared.'

'I thought you said you had vodka.'

She puts down the corkscrew and reaches over for Addy's empty water glass. 'Vodka, wine. Why do you think my suitcase is so heavy? I'm on holiday. Well, a working holiday, at least.'

Omar places his hand over Addy's glass. 'Maybe you are alcoholic, Phileepa. Adi doesn't want wine.'

Addy lifts Omar's hand off her glass. 'Hold on, Omar. I'd like a glass of wine tonight if it's all the same to you.'

Omar looks at Addy, the crease deepening between his eyes. 'As you like.'

A pair of double doors at the far end of the room, shining with the same high gloss as the rest of the woodwork, swing open, and three young Moroccan men in blue gowns and tagelmusts enter carrying trays of soup. A slender waiter of no more than twenty, his blue gown hanging off his lanky frame like a sheet, sets thick clay bowls of fragrant soup in front of Addy and Philippa. Readjusting the load on his tray, he moves on to the next table.

'*Khoya, stana,*' Mohammed calls after him.

The waiter turns around and responds sharply in Arabic. Mohammed levers himself off the banquette and stabs at the waiter with his finger as he fills the air with an angry rant. Yassine joins

315

in the argument, jumping out of his chair and jabbing the waiter on the shoulder, sending the tray of soup into a dangerous tilt. The other two waiters set down their trays and rush over.

Omar rises and waves his tour guide card at the waiters. Balancing the tray on his hip, the waiter picks the card out of Omar's hand, turning it over again and again as he squints at the identification.

'*Je suis un guide professionel*,' Omar says, thumping his chest. '*Je suis le patron de les autres*.'

The waiter thrusts the card at his colleagues, who peer at the photo and back at Omar as they confer heatedly. The waiter returns the card to Omar with a shrug and sets three more bowls of soup onto the table.

Omar nods and sits down. '*Shukran bezzef*.'

'*Mashi mushkil. Marhaba*.'

The waiters wander away, still arguing.

'What was that all about?' Addy asks.

'He say the dinner is not for Moroccans,' Mohammed says as he splashes wine into his water glass.

'Not for Moroccans?'

Yassine blows out a smoke ring. 'They say we must go to the kitchen to eat with the drivers.'

Omar waves away Yassine's smoke ring. 'I said I'm the tour guide for the group. I showed him my licence. It's permitted for the tour guide to eat with the tourists because he does the animation for everybody. I spoke in French, so he knew I'm serious. I said Mohammed and Yassine are tour guides as well and I'm their boss.'

'*Mahbool*.' Yassine pushes out his chair and leaps to his feet. He waves the cigarette at Omar. 'You are not the boss of me.'

'*Allah i naal dine omok*.' Omar stands and jabs his finger at Yassine. 'If I want to be the boss of you, I will be the boss of you.'

Yassine flicks his chin with the back of his hand. '*Moss zebbi!*'

Omar shifts back and forth behind the barrier of the table like a caged tiger. 'I'll kill you, Yassine. *Nknshih fik bla dfal*.'

Laughing, Yassine backs out of the room. 'You can fuck, Omar.

316

Go well to the desert, my friend. Go find yourself a donkey.' He presses his hand against his lips and blows a kiss at Addy. 'You go well, Turquoise. When you look for a good man, come to Yassine. I know you fuck well. I saw you with Omar in the cave.'

'*Mchi thawa!*'

Yassine makes a fist and slaps his bicep with his right hand. '*Houi omok!*' He ducks out of the room just as Omar's soup bowl smashes against the shiny wooden archway, sending shards of clay shooting across the terrazzo floor.

'Where's Omar?' Addy asks when she returns from the ladies' room.

Mohammed raises his shoulders, puffing out a cloud of tobacco smoke. The butt ends of five cigarettes lie like fat grubs in the orange peels and mutton bones on his plate.

Philippa reaches into her shoulder bag and pulls out a second bottle of Moroccan wine. 'He went to sort out the hot-water situation. I wasn't about to stop him.'

Addy tugs at the heavy chair, wincing as it scrapes along the terrazzo. She flops into the chair and yawns. Her head throbs from Omar's revelations and the two – or was it three? – large glasses of wine Philippa's plied her with.

'I should go. Omar said it's a long journey tomorrow. I know he's still upset about Yassine.'

Philippa peels the metallic cover off the top of the wine bottle. 'The desert? How do you think we're going to get there? Our ride's buggered off.' She glances at Mohammed. 'Excuse my French, Mo.'

Mohammed raises his eyebrows. 'What?'

'Oh, never mind.'

'Mo, Pippa?'

'So much easier than Mohammed.' Philippa picks up the corkscrew and stabs it into the cork.

'I'm sure Omar will figure something out.'

Philippa eases the cork out of the bottle with a soft *thunk*. She clicks her fingers at Addy. 'Glass.'

'I should go and find Omar.'

Philippa grabs Mohammed's wrist and reads the face of his fake Rolex. 'For heaven's sake. It's only ten. I hardly ever get to have fun any more. Besides, it looks like the Japanese tourists are just getting warmed up.'

Addy glances over to the front of the room, where two Japanese women are singing Kylie Minogue's 'Can't Get You Out of My Head' to the accompaniment of the waiters on African drums.

Philippa fills Addy's glass with the yellow wine. 'I never knew you were such a stick-in-the-mud. No wonder Nigel left you. Have some more wine. You need to chill out.'

'Philippa. No, really.'

Philippa thrusts the glass at Addy. 'One more glass. We don't need to tell Omar. Right, Mo? No telling Omar.'

Mohammed's head lolls against the wall as he grins crookedly at Philippa. '*Mashi mushkil*, Phileepa. I am at your service.'

Addy exhales an exhausted sigh. Her mind was still struggling to process everything Omar'd told her about her father and Hanane. Maybe the wine would help her sleep.

She expels a tired sigh. 'Fine. One glass.'

'Good girl. You've got some of Dad's Irish blood in you, after all.'

'Pippa, you don't know the half of it.'

Philippa raises her glass. 'Chin-chin.'

'Why you say that?' Mohammed squints at them through his drooping eyelids.

'It means cheers, Mo darling. It's Italian. Come on. Have a go.' Philippa raises her glass. 'Chin-chin! Down the hatch and over the tongue, look out, liver, here I come!'

Addy stares at her sister, her wine glass halfway to her lips.

Philippa dabs at her mouth with her napkin, leaving a fuchsia streak on the white cotton. 'What?'

'I've never seen this side of you before.'

'You thought I was a boring old fart, didn't you?'

'Well . . .'

'Well, you're right. I am *now*. Must keep up appearances in London. Can't risk alienating my nouveau riche clientele. All these people with new money are so conservative, Addy. Where are those mad old English aristocrats? "Let's build a house shaped like a pineapple." Oh, to have been an interior designer in the eighteenth century.'

Mohammed laughs. 'You are funny lady.' He stubs out his cigarette in the orange peel and raises his glass. 'Tell me again.'

'Chin-chin!' Philippa and Addy exclaim in unison. They raise their glasses, and take a large swig of wine. Before Addy knows what's happened, Philippa's sloshing more of the fruity yellow liquid into her glass.

'Addy, you need more wine.'

Addy's head is floating. She's drunk too much already. She blinks hard to focus on her sister, whose face has become fuzzy around the edges.

'I really shouldn't.'

'Oh, do loosen up. Have some fun.'

'It's the last one, Pippa. Seriously. Then I really have to go.'

'I know, I know. I've got an idea. Let's do a drinking game. Have you ever done that, Mo? Do what I do. One, two, three, drink.'

Addy gulps down the wine.

Mohammed slams his empty glass on the table. 'Again.'

Philippa points to the front of the room. 'Oh, look, someone's doing acrobatics.'

Addy follows the direction of Philippa's finger to see a man lying on the terrazzo floor, balancing a dreadlocked blonde woman on his raised hands.

A hand on Addy's shoulder. His face spins as she turns around.

'I'll bet you didn't know chin-chin means penis in Japanese.'

'Nigel?'

After that, Addy goes blank.

319

# Chapter Fifty-Five

**Essaouira, Morocco – May 1984**

'Stand there, darling. By the cannon. Please let me take your picture. I promise it won't hurt.'

Hanane runs her hand along the cold black iron of the cannon on the rampart as she looks out over the noisy waves crashing and foaming against the rocks far below.

'No, *habibi*. If somebody takes the photo from you they could do magic on me.'

'You let me take your photo the first time I met you. Up in the tree with Omar.'

'Yes, it's true. Maybe it was a mistake. What happened to the photo, *habibi*?'

'Omar insisted I give it to him.'

Hanane turns around and brushes her wind-whipped hair out of her eyes. Her new turquoise scarf flutters around her, threatening to fly out over the Atlantic. She grabs at the flapping fabric and ties it into a knot around her neck.

'That boy. He has such a strong will. He gets what he wants. He'll be rich one day.' She frowns. 'I hope he didn't lose the photo. Somebody could give us the bad eye.'

'I'd never let anyone give you the bad eye, Hanane.'

She smiles as Gus aims the camera at a round hole in the rampart that frames a view of the ancient whitewashed city.

'I think someone's already done magic on me, anyway. Why else would I be here by the sea with you? A girl from the mountains. I only wish . . .'

'What?' Gus walks over to Hanane and hugs her. 'That we'd met sooner? When I was a younger, more handsome version of myself?'

Hanane laughs. 'No, of course not. No, I only wish that my family could accept my happiness. I'm so sorry for what happened after the flood, *habibi*. What my father and Mohammed did, it was terrible. How can I ever go back?'

'Would you like to go back?'

She looks at Gus's broad face, the white skin turning tan from the hot May sun. The eyes as blue as the sky overhead. The long nose and the small lines tracing out from the corners of his eyes. The straight black hair she loved to comb with her fingers when they were in bed at night.

She sighs. 'I miss the olive trees and the waterfalls. I miss how the sun makes the mountains shine red as it sets. I even miss silly Omar. I miss my home.'

'We'll make a new home.' Gus runs up the steps to a corner turret and sweeps his hand across the view to the town, shimmering like a mirage in the May sun. 'Why not here? In Essaouira?'

'It's a lovely place, my love. But it's so far from the mountains.'

'There are a lot of places we could live in Morocco, Hanane. I know you didn't like Marrakech—'

Hanane grimaces. 'Too noisy. Too many people.'

'We can go up to Casablanca. Fes. The Rif Mountains are up there. Maybe you'll like Fes. I'll take you to the Sahara if you like. We could even go to Canada and start a life together there. You'd meet my daughter, Addy. She'd visit us when she's back from university. I know you'll like each other. It's all possible. We can stop in London on our way to Canada so you can meet my other

321

daughter, Philippa. I want them both to know you. We'll go wherever you want, Hanane.'

'Canada? It's very cold there, isn't it?'

'Not all the time. Not so much on Vancouver Island. Just rainy in the winter.'

Hanane frowns as she looks over the rampart out at the horizon. 'It's very, very far.'

Gus reaches out his hand. The sun glints off his thick gold Irish ring. 'My darling, we don't have to decide right now. There's no rush.' He leans on the cold stone wall beside her and watches a ship plough through the waves in the distance. 'I've made a lot of mistakes in my life. I've been selfish. I haven't been there for people. For Hazel, or for my daughters. Not the way a father's supposed to be. I was better with Addy, I tried. But poor Philippa.' He shakes his head. 'I don't think she'll ever forgive me for divorcing her mother and leaving for Canada without her.' He sighs. 'I thought she'd be better with her mother. Happier in England. I didn't understand until recently how unhappy she'd been growing up. I think there are times that she hates me.'

Hanane cups his cheek with her hand, her Irish wedding ring still a strange sight on her finger. 'No, *habibi*. She could never hate you. You have a loving heart. You must reach out to both of your daughters. I want to know them. They'll be my family now.'

Gus leans his forehead against Hanane's. 'Let's go for a walk in the souk, my darling. Then we can go and eat some fish by the harbour.' He nods towards the cluster of blue-and-white buildings by the harbour front. 'Judging by how fat the cats are here, the fish must be good.'

Hanane runs her thumb over the sapphire heart of her wedding ring. The pair to her husband's. Rings designed by an Irishman in Morocco so very long ago, Gus had told her. Made as he'd worked as a slave for a goldsmith in Tangier while his lover waited so patiently for him to return to her back in a place called Galway. Twelve long years she'd waited until he was finally released. A man

322

named Richard Joyce. Gus's great-great-great-grandfather. And now Gus was here. Fate kept sending his family to Morocco. This time it had sent him to her. He was now her fate, too.

'You slide the bottom back, slide this slat to the left, pull out this little peg and shake out the key. Then you slide the fourth vertical slat downwards and you'll see the keyhole. Now all you have to do is unlock the box.' The old shop seller inserts the tiny key into the keyhole, twists it twice clockwise and opens the lid, revealing a compact compartment. He grins widely, revealing his three remaining teeth, as he hands the wooden box to Hanane. 'It's easy once you know how.' The man's Darija is odd and Hanane strains her ear to process his inflections.

'It's very clever,' Hanane says as she turns the wooden box, decorated with intricate mother-of-pearl inlay, over in her hands.

'It has a place for you to hide your secrets,' the old man says.

Hanane glances at the man. A white turban sits on top of his head, the loose tail tucked around his dark wrinkled face.

'I have no secrets.'

The man grins even more broadly as his eyes flick from Gus back to her. 'Everyone has secrets.'

Gus takes the box from Hanane and turns it over, examining the workmanship.

'How much?'

'Three hundred dirhams.'

'Fine.'

'No, *habibi*. It's too much.'

'It's fine, darling. I'm happy to pay it.'

Gus hands the box back to the shop seller and pulls out his leather wallet from his back pocket. He flips open the well-worn leather flap and counts out three dirty dirham notes.

'He's thieving you, my love.'

Gus hands the shop seller the notes, who quickly pockets the cash. The old man closes the box's lid then slides the slats and key back into place. Gus takes the box and tosses it from one hand to the other, testing its weight.

'It's perfect. Just big enough. Even Omar wouldn't be able to figure it out.'

Hanane laughs. 'Omar would figure it out. Even if it took him thirty years.'

# Chapter Fifty-Six

**High Atlas Mountains, Morocco – June 2009**

*She's floating on a yellow sea. The sky above her is a hot blue. There's nothing around her but the shimmering yellow water. Not yellow from the sun. More like melted butter. Yes, the colour of melted butter. She trails her hand through the liquid. Cold. Cold melted butter. Is that possible?*

*Looking down, she sees that she's lying on a carpet of white wool with black zigzags. She wears a white wedding dress, full and lacy. Meringue. Who chose that? Must have been Philippa. The tail end of a white tagelmust floats out to the horizon, lapping against the waves. She lifts her wet hand and touches her fingers to her lips. Wine. She's floating on wine.*

*She closes her eyes. The sun pins her to the carpet. She lets the waves take her wherever they wish. A bird cries somewhere far above. She opens her eyes and scans the blue sky. Blue like Omar's tagelmust.*

*A couple of birds circle above, looping and darting like two aerobatic planes. They pick up speed and aim for each other, spinning out of each other's path just as it seems they'll collide. They fly closer to her. The larger bird is as blue as the sky; the other has red and green and yellow feathers, as colourful as . . . as . . . something she*

325

*can't remember. No, she remembers. A planet. A tie-dyed planet. The tie-dyed bird dive-bombs in to peck at the larger bird before it swoops away, laughing. Laughing? How can birds laugh?*

*The blue bird loops around in an arc, picking up speed as it descends. Thrusting out its feet, its black talons gleaming in the sunlight, it catches the smaller bird. The small bird screams. The blue bird's descending too fast. They're too close to the water. The yellow sea splashes upwards like a geyser as the birds make impact. The water closes over them. Everything's quiet. Even the lapping waves make no sound.*

The dark room is empty. Addy rubs her throbbing head. Her T-shirt has ridden up over her bra. She rolls her tongue around her mouth and swallows. Stale wine and mutton grease. The shower's running in the bathroom. Omar must have got the hot water fixed. She needs a shower. Something to blow the cobwebs out of her mind. And orange juice. She needs a lot of orange juice.

She swings her bare feet off the bed. She stumbles over her jeans on the thick white rug on her way to the banquette, where she'd left her suitcase. It isn't there. Nor is her straw hat or her sunglasses, which she remembers tossing onto the low brass table. She looks around the room. Something's different.

The bathroom door opens. 'Omar, I—'

'Omar?' Nigel stands in the doorway, a towel around his waist, drying his hair with a facecloth. 'I could be offended by that.'

'Pippa. Open up.' Addy pounds on Philippa's door.

'Who is it?' Philippa's voice is thick with sleep and alcohol.

'Addy. Who else? Let me in.'

The key jiggles in the lock and the door swings open. Philippa's in her Ralph Lauren striped pyjamas, a purple satin eye mask pushed up over her matted hair.

'God, Addy. Do you know what time it is? Six fucking fifteen. I haven't even reached REM yet.'

Addy pushes past her. 'Have you seen Omar?'

Shutting the door, Philippa pads across the room to the bed. 'Why would I have seen Omar? He's *your* boyfriend.' She climbs on top of the bed, and pulls the mound of sheets and blankets up to her chin.

'Pippa, it's a disaster.'

Philippa opens an eye, its blueness sharpened by the red veins threading over her eyeball. 'Don't be a drama queen. It's hardly the end of the world. So you slept with your ex-fiancé. That was probably a good thing.'

The blood rushes to Addy's face. 'What?'

'You heard me. I saw you leave with Nigel last night. Now let me get some sleep.' Philippa tugs the eye mask over her eyes. 'Breakfast isn't until eight. We can talk then.'

Addy pulls off Philippa's eye mask. 'How did Nigel know we were here? Did you call him?'

Philippa sits up against pillows. 'He texted me yesterday morning. He said he's worried about you. He doesn't trust Omar. There's one thing we agree on, at least. He wants another chance.'

'You said you hadn't told him we were going to the desert.'

'Well, I didn't *tell* him, did I? Not literally.' Philippa shrugs. 'It was a text.'

Addy sinks onto Philippa's bed and covers her face with her hands. 'Oh my God.'

'Look. You and Omar? It's never going to work.'

She glares at her sister through her fingers. 'No thanks to you.' She drops her hands and picks at a loose thread of embroidery on a blanket.

'I only expedited the inevitable, Adela. I did you a favour.'

'Just like what happened to Dad.'

'What do you mean?'

'Why is it that people who claim to love you hate to see you love someone different?'

'What *are* you talking about?'

Addy looks at her sister. 'Our father and his Moroccan lover, Hanane. Her family didn't approve of their relationship, either. Even when she got pregnant. Especially after that.'

'What are you talking about?'

'When Hanane's family found out about her pregnancy, they refused to have anything to do with her. She and Gus left Zitoune. But she couldn't stay away from her family. She travelled back from Marrakech on her own just before the baby was due. She had the baby that night. She died before Dad got to Zitoune.'

'Who told you this?'

'Omar. But everyone in Zitoune knows.'

'What happened to the baby?'

'We have a Moroccan half-brother, Pippa.'

'We what?'

'You've met him. His name's Amine. He was the boy waiting on us in Mohammed's restaurant. He's Mohammed's nephew. Everybody calls him a bastard. He has no status in Morocco.'

'Amine's our brother?'

'Yes.'

'And Dad hid this all these years?'

'He didn't know. They lied to him. They told him the baby had died. They thought it was the best thing, you see. Wouldn't it have been better if Dad and Hanane had been allowed to love each other? To live their lives together? Our lives would've been different. Amine's life would've been different. Maybe Hanane wouldn't have died. Love needs to breathe. Love needs to be allowed to live.'

# Chapter Fifty-Seven

**Casablanca, Morocco – May 1984**

Hanane raises her face to the sun and closes her eyes. The warmth pricks at her skin like tiny drops of hot rain. The wind whips off the Atlantic and across the Corniche boardwalk, stirring up the waves, which crash onto the long sandy beach. She opens her eyes and reaches up to brush wayward strands of hair from her face.

She glances over to the ice-cream stall, where Gus is engaged in a lively discussion with the ice-cream vendor. No pistachio, she guesses. Why does she crave pistachio so much?

She rubs her hand across the blue cotton of her djellaba. Unless . . . She frowns. She'd thought the nausea was from all the travel. The crowded *grands taxis*, the decrepit buses, the interminable twists of the roads. She counts back the months. She hasn't bled since March – two months. And she's always been regular.

'Here you go, darling.' Gus lopes across the boardwalk licking a chocolate ice-cream cone. He holds out a cone of pink ice cream. 'I've got you strawberry. No pistachio, I'm afraid. I hope it's all right.'

Hanane smiles. 'I've never eaten strawberry before.'

'No? You're in for a treat. They love strawberries in England. Strawberries and cream.'

Gus holds out his hand and Hanane slips her hands into his warm grasp. They stroll along the boardwalk as they lick their ice cream, past boys playing football on the sand by the seaside and old men in djellabas, who glance at her and frown as they pass by. Her stomach suddenly flutters and she feels her blood rush down to her feet.

'Can we sit? I'm feeling a little tired. I think it's the heat.'

'Of course, darling. There's a bench just over there. There's a nice view of the ocean.'

They sit and the nausea subsides. The pink ice cream is dripping onto her wrist and she licks at the sticky drops.

'That's where they're going to build the king's mosque.' Gus points along the beach in the direction of the city centre. 'Nothing much there now. I expect they'll start digging the foundations soon. Well, as soon as he raises the money. It's going to cost a fortune.'

'His men have already come to Zitoune for money. My father was very unhappy about it. So was Mohammed. It was money to make the restaurant bigger. My brother is impatient to be rich.'

'Your brother's a clever man. I'm sure he'll be the king of Zitoune one day.'

Hanane leans her head against Gus's shoulder as she chews the sweet biscuit of the cone.

'Do you wish for another child, *habibi*?'

'I'd be delighted if we had a child.'

She sits up and looks into his clear blue eyes, at the fine lines tracing out from the corners as he smiles at her. She takes his hand and guides it to her stomach. 'I'm happy for that.' She rests her hand over Gus's. 'Because our child is coming.'

'Our child?' He looks down at her stomach, still flat under her djellaba. 'You're pregnant?'

'Yes, I think so. I must go to a doctor when we are back in Marrakech, but I think so.'

Gus wraps his arms around her and hugs her close to him. 'Oh, my darling. Our baby. Our future's just beginning and it'll be a grand future, I promise you.'

Hanane squirms in his embrace. 'My ice cream! It's melting all over you.'

'I don't care. Let it melt. Mine's all over my hand. Let it rain ice cream!' He releases her and they lick the melting treats. 'Do you want to tell your family?'

'I don't want to talk about my family.'

'But they're your family, Hanane. I know you miss them.'

'I miss Zitoune. Not them. Not after . . . what happened.'

'Maybe when you tell them about the baby—'

Hanane looks at Gus. 'It will be worse. The baby will only be proof of my disgrace in their eyes.'

'I can explain everything to them. They'll see they've made a mistake. We're married, for Heaven's sake.'

'There is no point, *habibi*. They'll never approve of our relationship. Not after what the policeman said. Even if we show them the marriage paper, they'll think the baby was conceived in Zitoune. They'll believe it's not legitimate.' Hanane shakes her head. 'No, my love. You're my family now. It is only for us to find our home.'

# Chapter Fifty-Eight

**High Atlas Mountains, Morocco – June 2009**

Omar stands beside one of the vans talking to the driver, his baseball cap pulled down low to shield his eyes from the sun. He glances at Addy as she approaches, then he turns his back and continues his conversation.

Addy holds out some wedges of an orange. '*Limoun*?'

The driver smiles. He takes two wedges. '*Shukran, madame*.'

Omar ignores the offering. Addy rests her hand on his arm. His muscle tenses under her fingers.

'Could I talk to you when you're finished with the driver?'

'You can talk to me now.'

She clears her throat. 'No, not here. I'll wait for you on the terrace.'

She steps over the wooden boards and sucks on a sweet orange wedge as her world shakes like an earth tremor under her feet.

'Yes?'

Addy looks at Omar from her perch on the ledge. She raises her hand to shield her bloodshot eyes from the bright morning sun.

'I'm so sorry, Omar.'

'*Mashi mushkil*.'

'I should've come back to the room after supper.'

Omar stands like an unbending tree on the grey concrete floor of the terrace. He folds his arms across his chest.

'Yes.'

'I made a mistake. I was just going to have one glass of wine, then . . . I don't know what happened.'

'Your sister made you drunk.'

'It wasn't her fault. She's on holiday. She wants to have some fun. I got carried away.'

'Where did you sleep last night?'

Addy squints at the winding riverbed far below and moistens her lips. 'In Philippa's room. She thought you'd be mad at her if I turned up drunk in our room last night.'

'For sure I would be angry. I'm angry yet.'

'I know. I'm sorry.'

'You made an embarrassment for yourself to be drunk, Adi.' He shrugs. 'I don't mind about your sister, but it's very bad for Moroccans to see my girlfriend drunk. They will think you're a bad lady.'

'I'm sorry.' Addy wraps her arms around her knees and balances on the edge of the concrete ledge.

Omar takes her hands and steadies her. 'Be careful, darling. You might fall.'

'I was counting on the fact you wouldn't let me.'

Omar hoists himself onto the ledge. 'You made me angry, *habibati.*'

'I know.'

'You were so, so drunk last night. Mohammed told me this morning.'

'He's one to talk.'

'It's true what you say. Mohammed is sick this morning. He has a headache.'

In the sunlight, Omar's eyes are bloodshot. He squints at the light. 'Your sister made a bad honour for you.'

'It's not her fault.' Addy sighs. Her head throbs and her tongue is like glue. 'Sometimes I feel so . . . constrained here. I mustn't do this and I mustn't do that. Just because I'm a woman. It's making me crazy.' She drops her head into her hands and presses her fingers against her temples.

'You have a headache?'

'Yes.'

'I'll tell the driver to stop at a pharmacy in Erfoud.'

Addy blinks against the strong morning light. 'The driver?'

'I made an arrangement to be the tour guide on a tour bus. I promised my wife we would go to the desert.'

'Your wife?'

He leans over and brushes Addy's lips with a kiss. 'You're my wife even though you make me disturbed sometimes. I must learn to understand you well.'

'I'm not your wife.'

Omar wraps his arms around her. He rocks back and forth, gaining momentum. 'So will you be my wife, Adi?'

'Omar, stop!'

'If we die, it's our fate. Will you be my wife, *habibati*?'

'Yes. Fine. Stop it!'

Omar stops the rocking and hugs her to him. 'You make my mind crazy, darling. I'm always thinking of you, you have to know about it. You're in my blood. I want to make a family with you. It's our fate to be together ever since your father came to Zitoune. We'll make a big wedding celebration after Ramadan. I will buy you a beautiful kaftan of turquoise silk so you will be the most beautiful *rosa* of Zitoune.'

'There's no rush. We barely know each other.'

'I know you well enough.'

Addy looks at Omar. 'I can't have children.'

Omar stares at her. He drops his arms. 'One child even, *habibati*. A boy or a girl, it doesn't matter.'

The scar on her breast throbs. Addy rubs it with the flat of her hand. She's on a roller coaster, spinning out of control. Whatever happens, she has to tell Omar the truth.

'I had cancer.' She touches her breast. 'It's why I have this scar. It's why I can't have children. None at all. The cancer medicine stopped that.'

They're surrounded by the hum of the tour bus engines, the chatter of the drivers and the clatter of tourists dragging their luggage across the wooden boards. But on the ledge it's like a vacuum has descended. No sound. No air. No future.

Omar presses a kiss into Addy's palms. When he looks at her, his eyes are wet.

'If I could have cancer for you, I would do it. You're the angel of my life, Adi. It's our fate to be together in this life. *Inshallah*, we will find a way.'

# Chapter Fifty-Nine

**Merzouga, Sahara Desert, Morocco – June 2009**

It's late afternoon when the tour bus reaches the Sahara Desert. The sand slides over the roads and into the yards of the few squat dull yellow houses and hotels of Merzouga. The waning sun streaks the sky red, casting a pink glow on the towering dunes behind the town.

The driver parks beside a half-dozen tour buses, in front of a sprawling single-storey adobe building that wouldn't look out of place in an old John Wayne Western. Almost on cue, a tall brown-skinned man in a blue gown and turban pushes through the swing doors. Yelling in Arabic, he waves at the bottleneck of tourists on the covered porch, who are pulling clothes out of suitcases and jamming necessities into knapsacks.

Omar claps his hands for attention. 'Okay, everybody. You see the big sand dunes of the Sahara? It's called the Erg Chebbi. It's very, very famous in the world. It's one hundred fifty metres tall in some places and fifty kilometres long. On the other side in fifty kilometres is *Algérie*. We must be careful in the desert, because there are some mines near *Algérie*. Anyway, it's nicer in Morocco, so we won't go close to *Algérie*. So no problem.'

'Mines?' Philippa looks up from the compact mirror. 'You don't mean land mines?'

'For sure, land mines. They make a big boom when they explode. It happens sometimes.' He shrugs. 'Don't worry. Be happy. You'll be fine, Phileepa. The Tuareg guides know the desert well. They're the blue men of the desert. The sand is in their blood.'

'Good God, Addy, where have you brought me?'

Addy squints at the blazing sun through her sunglasses. 'The Sahara Desert. You said you wanted to come to the desert.'

Philippa pushes her oversized sunglasses up her nose. 'Yes, well, when you said Sahara, I didn't think you meant the *actual* Sahara desert. Isn't that in Arabia or something?'

'Africa. It's in Africa. We're standing on it.'

'Bloody hell.'

Philippa scans the dunes pushing up against the reddening sky behind the hotel. She turns to Addy, the bug-like sunglasses reflecting back Addy's hot, sweaty face.

Philippa lowers her voice. 'So, what happened with Nigel?'

'Shhh. Don't talk about him here.'

'Omar's not here. I saw him go off with Mohammed and the driver. Did you actually sleep with him?'

'Pippa!'

'Well?'

'I don't think so.'

'You don't think so?'

'I had my clothes on when I woke up. Well, most of them. I don't remember.'

'You don't remember? What did Nigel say when you woke up?'

'Nothing. Not much. He came out of the bathroom in a towel. He seemed pretty amused by it all, actually. I ran back to my room, but Omar wasn't there so I woke you up. If Omar asks, tell him I slept in your room. That's what I told him.'

337

Philippa nods, the brim of her hat flapping around her face. 'Where's Nigel now?'

'I don't know and I don't care.'

'You're going to need to deal with him, Addy. He's living in your flat.'

'I know. When I get back to London it's top of the list. Don't you dare say anything about him to Omar.'

Philippa makes a twisting motion in front of her pink lips with her fingers. 'My lips are sealed.'

A metal door clatters against the far side of the bus. The ground resonates with soft thunks as luggage hits the sand. As Philippa repairs her make-up in the wing mirror, Addy walks around the bus. Omar and Mohammed are pulling out the tourists' luggage and stacking it into piles in the sand. Omar points to Addy's and Philippa's bags and suitcases.

'Too many for the camels, darling. I told you before.' He thrusts the handle of Addy's suitcase towards her. 'Hurry, put your clothes and your sister's in my knapsack. Take one camera only. We'll leave everything else in the hotel.'

Addy looks over at the crowd sifting through their suitcases in front of the hotel. 'So *that's* what everyone's doing.' She wipes the sweat off her forehead with the back of her hand. 'I need all of my lenses and the tripod. I'm not going to leave them here. Anybody could take them.'

Omar frowns at her. 'We're not thieves here.'

The tension between them snaps in the dry heat of the desert air.

'Okay. Fine. I'll pick out just what I need from the suitcase and tell Philippa to do the same. But I'm taking all of my camera equipment.'

'You must be quick, darling. The camels go soon. The guides don't wait.' Omar hoists her camera bags over his shoulders with his knapsack and heads off towards the hotel porch. 'Come quick with your sister.'

338

Addy drags the luggage over the sandy ground to Philippa. Her sister's huddled in the shade of the bus, holding a tiny battery-operated fan up against her face.

'We've got to unload, Pippa. There's no room on the camels for the suitcases.'

'You're joking.'

'You've got to hurry. Omar said the camels are leaving any minute. I don't want to be left behind on account of you.'

'Oh, stop being such an ass.'

'Don't you dare start, too.' Addy presses a hand to her throbbing forehead. 'I'm sorry. I'm just hungover. And this heat . . .' Addy takes off her straw hat and fans her face. 'Everything's getting on my nerves.'

'Everything's getting on *your* nerves?' Philippa huffs. The fan emits a buzz like a cloud of mosquitoes. 'Join the club.'

The hotel lobby is a circus. People tossing clothes in and out of suitcases, haggling over the overpriced tagelmusts on sale at the front desk, elbowing each other for the few remaining packets of tissues and bottles of water for sale on a table next to the door to the only toilet. A half-dozen Tuareg guides spin through the crowd. '*Yalla*! *Yalla*!' they shout, their blue gowns flapping as they herd the tourists towards the exit at the rear of the hotel.

Addy unzips her suitcase as Philippa joins the queue of women in front of the toilet. She sorts out piles of necessities and non-necessities on the terrazzo floor.

Omar leans over and grabs a handful of her underwear, stuffing it into his knapsack. 'It's fine, Adi. You don't need anything else.'

Addy grabs at his knapsack and yanks out the jumbled mix of underwear. 'Don't tell me what I need.'

Omar rolls his eyes. '*Yalla*, Adi. You have to hurry. The camels are going.'

Addy scans the crowded lobby and frowns. 'Where are they going to put our suitcases?'

Omar waves his hands at her in frustration. 'It's a room here. Lots of people have to put their suitcase here. Don't worry.'

The back of Addy's neck prickles and heat flushes her face. 'Just give me a minute. I won't be long if you leave me alone.'

Omar slaps his hands together impatiently. 'Darling. Hurry. *Yalla.*'

The words tumble out before Addy can stop them. 'Fuck off with the *yalla.*'

Omar drops the knapsack on the floor. Addy watches in silent fury as he storms off, her camera bags over his shoulders, until he's lost among the blue gowns of the Tuareg guides.

Philippa and Addy join the other tourists behind the hotel. Addy scans the group for Omar, and recognises an American tourist with a heavily botoxed face and floppy hat from their bus. She's being pushed by two Tuareg guides onto the top of a kneeling dromedary that groans every time she stabs it with the heels of her designer shoes. The woman's elderly mother, dressed in vibrant floral prints topped by a large yellow hat, is already sitting on top of a dromedary like a wizened parrot. She pets the face of the bemused young guide sitting behind like he's a favoured chick.

'Madame!' A guide holding the rope lead of a kneeling dromedary beckons to Philippa.

'Bloody hell. These things reek.' Philippa reaches into her purse and pulls out a white handkerchief, pressing it against her nose.

'Better get used to it, Pippa. They're going to be part of our lives for the next twenty-four hours.'

Philippa staggers over the sand towards the kneeling beast. 'I'm going to need to fumigate myself when I get back to England. And burn my clothes.'

A young Tuareg guide taps Addy on the shoulder and points towards a dromedary at the front of the caravan. '*Yalla.*'

Addy follows him, her feet sinking into the fine sand with each step. She hands him Omar's knapsack and, grabbing a hunk of the dromedary's hair, she throws her leg over the rough brown blanket. The guide slaps the animal on its rear and Addy lurches forwards as the groaning dromedary jerks up onto its rear legs. As it straightens its front legs, Addy shoots backwards, almost tumbling over its rump.

'*Labass*?' The guide smiles as he hands her Omar's knapsack. He has a friendly face. There's something about him that reminds her of Amine. Her brother, Amine.

'*Bikher*.'

'*Hamdullah*.' He takes hold of the long rope lead and clicks his tongue. The dromedary moves forwards in a slow, bobbing motion.

Addy turns around in her seat and sees the caravan unfurl behind her, the dromedaries attached to each other with ropes. Philippa's perched on the rough brown wool saddle, stiff-backed and unamused, blowing air onto her flushed cheeks with her fan. Following behind her are the two American women, the two young acrobats from the hotel and a Japanese man wearing a surgical mask, who's attempting to record the caravan while he clasps a large suitcase against his chest. A couple more riders catch up to the rear of the caravan.

In his coarse brown djellaba with the hood pulled over his bald head, Mohammed looks like Obi-Wan Kenobi. He's drinking a can of beer and smoking something that Addy suspects is a spliff. Omar follows close behind, the blue of his clothes a dot of vivid colour in the sandy landscape, her camera bags strapped across him bandolier-style.

Seeing Addy watching him, Omar pulls the ring off his beer can and throws back his head, pouring the beer down his throat. He swings his arms out wide and drops the can into the sand. He pulls two more beers out of a plastic bag slung across the dromedary's saddle and starts to sing, loud and slightly off-key. He urges his animal up next to Mohammed's and offers Mohammed a beer. Mohammed tosses his empty can into the

341

sand and takes the beer from Omar. He takes a swig and joins Omar in the drunken singing.

A gust of wind catches the brim of Addy's straw hat and sends it flying. It skims over the dunes like a stone skipping across a pond.

'My hat!'

Omar holds out his can of beer towards the flying hat. 'It's gone on the wind to *Algérie*.'

Addy spins around and stares out over the blue tagelmust of her guide at the darkening desert. Soon, Omar has the two young acrobats and the Japanese man singing along to his song. Even the American woman's mother joins in with an enthusiastic 'Mama Africa' whenever the chorus comes around.

Addy's never felt more alone, although she takes some solace in the knowledge that Philippa's probably as miserable as she is. The desert spreads out before her, a sea of sand burned red with the last light of dusk.

They trek across the desert for over an hour, the heat of the day quickly dissipating as the sky turns to night. Eventually, they reach a cluster of brown tents nestled at the foot of the dunes. Another group has already arrived, their dromedaries standing like sentries around the fringes of the camp. Several dune buggies sit like giant black beetles at the foot of a large dune. A pair of Tuareg guides in blue gowns and tagelmusts hover over a campfire and pyramids of tagine pots, feeding the fire with sticks to keep the dinner cooking.

Addy's guide leads the caravan to the edge of the encampment. The two guides from the campfire come over and join him, clucking at the dromedaries and slapping their hindquarters. Groaning and spitting, the animals lumber down onto their knees, shrinking like deflating bellows. Addy slides off the animal onto the soft beige sand. She clutches onto the blanket-covered hump as her balance recalibrates from the dromedary's slow undulations. She looks around for Omar, but he and Mohammed have disappeared.

She joins Philippa and they follow the others past the campfire into the largest tent. Inside, long wooden tables and benches have been set up on pink-and-yellow plastic mats. A group of German tourists has claimed several of the tables and are pulling cans of Heineken out of their knapsacks.

The two acrobats wave at them from a table. Philippa and Addy edge past the others and join them on the bench. The girl has blonde dreadlocks down to her waist, and wears green army pants and a sleeveless T-shirt with *Je Me Souviens* printed across it in bright blue letters. The boy has a shadow of regrowth where he's recently shaved his head and a skull earring piercing his left ear.

He holds out a hand to Addy. '*Bonsoir*. I'm Dominique. But everybody call me Dom.'

Addy shakes his hand. 'Hi, I'm Addy.'

The girl waves her hand. 'I'm Dominique, too.' She makes a pinching gesture with her fingers. 'I speak English only a leetle.'

'Dom and Dominique, that's easy to remember.' Addy nods at the girl's T-shirt. 'Are you from Québec?'

'From Montréal,' the girl says. 'We meet you last night in the hotel.'

Philippa laughs. 'I'm afraid my sister was pissed out of her gills last night so she doesn't remember a thing.'

Addy smiles wanly and nods towards her sister. 'Philippa. My sister.'

Philippa reaches for the plastic basket full of bread and offers it around. 'That was a marvellous show you put on in the hotel last night.'

'Thank you,' Dom says. 'We are with the *Cirque Magique de Montréal*.'

'How marvellous.' Philippa tears a hunk from the bread. 'I saw the show in London last year. Tell me, how do you keep from vomiting when you do those bungee head spins?'

Addy chews on the bread as she listens to the laughter and

343

chatter. Why is it that, now, when she should be enjoying a once-in-a-lifetime experience with the man she loves, she's sabotaged it with her bad mood? She sinks deeper into a funk of unhappiness as the answer slowly materialises.

Because she's a coward and she's afraid.

# Chapter Sixty

**Zitoune, Morocco – October 1984**

The waterfalls crash over the orange clay cliffs, bouncing from one sandstone ledge to another into the green pond at its base. A couple of tourist rafts, their pink and yellow plastic flowers a jolt of colour in the landscape, paddle into the spray. The shrieks of the drenched tourists waft up to the lookout.

'I've always loved this view,' Hanane says as she surveys the scene. 'The waterfalls have a magic, don't you think?'

'I know what you mean, my darling. Pictures don't do it justice. You can't capture the way it *feels* in a photo.' Gus looks through the viewfinder of his Polaroid camera but then shakes his head and lets it fall against his chest.

'Give me the camera, Mister Gus,' Omar says. He slurps the dregs of his orange juice and reaches for the camera. 'I can make a good picture of the waterfalls. You will feel all the magic.'

'Oh, really, Mister Boss? And how much is that going to cost me? You've already had two glasses of orange juice.'

'I make it complimentary for you and Hanane, for the memories.'

'Really?' Hanane laughs. 'Are you going soft, Omar?'

'Never. You must be strong to be a businessman.' He takes the

345

camera from Gus and loops the strap around his neck. 'I'm so happy to see you again, Hanane. I want to make a memory for you and Mister Gus. Each time you look at the picture, you will remember me as well.'

Omar peers through the viewfinder and waves at them to move together until they're framed by the streaming white water in the distance behind them. Gus puts an arm around Hanane's shoulders and she leans into him, smiling. She turns to look at Omar, who clicks the photo. The camera spews out the glossy grey-and-white card.

Omar waves the Polaroid in the air. 'I got it!'

'Omar, I wasn't ready!' Hanane objects.

'It's better like that. More natural. Can I go show Yassine?'

'Sure, Mister Boss.' Gus reaches into his pocket and pulls out some loose change. 'Here, get us a couple of orange juices, okay? Get one for Yassine and another one for you, if you want.'

Hanane watches Omar scamper over to the bar Yassine's father's constructed of old watermelon crates. Yassine runs around the bar to watch as Omar unveils the photo.

Gus rests his hand on Hanane's growing bump. 'Would you like a girl or a boy?'

'I don't mind, *habibi*. I just wish for it to be healthy.' Her eyes cloud over. 'And for our baby to know their grandfather and uncle before we go to Canada.'

'I know. Let's have our orange juice and we'll go there now.'

Hanane pounds on the door to her father's house. 'Please, *Baba*! Please talk to me!'

Gus reaches for Hanane's hand. 'Hanane, please. Let me.'

Hanane wipes the tears from her cheeks and nods. Gus pounds on the door.

'Mohammed! Mr Demsiri! Please, open up. We need to talk to you.'

A bolt scratches against the metal and the door creaks open.

346

Mohammed's wife, Bouchra, steps onto the concrete porch. She eyes Hanane's pregnant stomach.

'How can you come here to shame us again, you filthy woman?'

'Please, Bouchra, let me see my father. It's not what you think at all. We're married. We have the paper. Is Mohammed here? We can show him the paper.'

'Show *me* the paper.'

'But, Bouchra . . .'

She clicks her fingers in Hanane's face. 'Show me the paper.'

Hanane looks at Gus. 'Show her the paper, *habibi*. She's insisting.'

Gus takes out his wallet and removes a piece of paper folded into many squares. He unfolds the document and hands it to Bouchra.

Bouchra frowns. The scribbles jump before her eyes. She thrusts the document back at Gus. 'This could be anything. How do I know it's what you say?'

'Please, Bouchra, just get Mohammed or *Baba*. They can read it. They'll know what I say is true.'

Bouchra sneers at her sister-in-law. 'You're not welcome in this house, Hanane. You've destroyed us. Go back to Marrakech with your devil.'

She steps back into the house and the door slams. Its tinny echo stabs into Hanane's heart.

# Chapter Sixty-One

**The Sahara Desert, Morocco – June 2009**

Addy's peeling an orange at the long dining table when she spies Omar slipping into the tent with Mohammed. The two men edge around the tables and head towards a group of drivers and guides eating lamb tagine at a wooden table at the back of the tent. A trio of young blonde German women waves at them as they squeeze past the women's table. The women call out '*Kommen sitzen*' with an enthusiasm that darkens Addy's mood still further. The giggling tourists cluster around Omar and pose for photos as Mohammed makes a show of pouring out hot mint tea into their tea glasses.

'You don't mind if I join you, do you?'

Addy freezes, her fingernails embedded in the orange rind.

Nigel squeezes onto the bench between Addy and Philippa.

'Fancy meeting you here, girls. Small world.'

Nigel's tanned and rested in khaki shorts and a loose white linen shirt.

'What the . . . How on earth . . .?' Addy glares at her sister. 'Did you do this?'

Levering herself off the bench, Philippa grabs her hat and loops her Prada purse over her arm.

'If ever there was a cue to find the loo, this is it. And no, Addy, this has nothing to do with me.' Philippa grimaces at Nigel, who's grinning at them like it's all a great joke. 'You're starting to look desperate, Nigel. It's not becoming.'

Nigel's grin deepens. 'I've had a good teacher. If anyone knows about desperation, it's you, Philippa.'

Philippa sets her fuchsia mouth into a hard line and leans over to Nigel's ear.

'Bastard.'

'I know, I know, words can't express the joy you feel at seeing me again, Del.'

Nigel grabs a water bottle and a tea glass from the middle of the table. He splashes the water into the glass and drinks it down in thirsty gulps.

Addy glances over at Omar. His amber eyes are fixed on her like those of an injured hawk.

'What are you doing here, Nigel?'

'I couldn't very well leave things the way they were when you ran out this morning.' Nigel tears off a hunk of bread and dips it into the greasy gravy congealing in the clay tagine pot. 'I didn't even have a chance to tell you what a lovely time I'd had.'

'What do you mean?'

'You know, last night.' He pops the gravy-soaked bread in his mouth. 'It was just like old times. Magical.'

Addy buries her face in her hands. How will she ever explain this to Omar? What must it look like? Like she's a liar, and a cheat and a two-timer. She drops her hands and glares at Nigel's amused face.

'You're lying. Nothing happened.'

Nigel raises his eyebrows. 'How can you say that, Del? I'm genuinely hurt. Don't you remember? You seemed to be enjoying yourself last night. I know I did.'

Out of the corner of her eye, Addy glimpses Omar's blue gown as he moves along the edge of the tables, out into the night.

*

'Addy, for God's sake, come on. You can't just go to bed and mope. To hell with men.'

Philippa holds back the flap of the tent and peers into the darkness. Addy's huddled, fully dressed, under a layer of blankets against the chill of the desert night. The beat of African drums and sound of off-key singing filter into the tent from the campfire.

'How can I possibly go out there, Pippa? My life's a mess.'

'Oh, forget about them. Life's too short for shit. That's my philosophy, anyway.'

'You're not exactly what I'd call a mentor.'

'Look, they're not out here. Mohammed isn't around, either. Probably passed out in a sand dune somewhere.' Philippa waves a bottle of vodka. 'Come on. Fuck the lot of them.'

The light from an outside lantern traces a gold outline around Philippa's shadowed body. Maybe she's right. Fretting here in the tent is doing her no good. Every time she closes her eyes, she's haunted by Omar's wounded look. She kicks off the blankets and sits up on the lumpy mat.

'You're right. Give me a minute. I'll meet you at the campfire.'

Addy stumbles over to the tent flap and out into the chilly night air. A yellow glow emanates from the campfire out near the dromedaries. Black shadows of bodies huddle around the fire, swaying and clapping to the rhythm of the drums. The mournful voice of a Tuareg guide sings a lament into the desert night.

As she approaches the campfire, she glimpses Philippa's face reflected in the glow, where she sits beside Addy's caravan guide. Philippa grips an animal skin drum between her knees and she mimics the guide's movements as he drums in accompaniment to the singer. Addy edges around the group and kneels in the sand beside her sister. Then she sees him, on the other side of the fire, his face glowing yellow in the firelight.

'Vodka's just there.' Philippa nods towards a bottle of Absolut Vodka sticking out of the sand. 'There's a can of Coke, too.'

'I thought you said he wasn't here.'

Philippa looks across the campfire to Nigel, his head wrapped in a turban, who's sharing cans of Heineken with the German women.

'He's just arrived. I think he's drunk.'

Addy catches Nigel's eye. He lifts up the can of lager in a salute. 'I can't do this.'

Addy makes a move to get up, but Philippa grabs the sleeve of her denim jacket and pulls her back.

'Just ignore him.'

Addy sinks into the sand. 'I feel so tired, Pips. I'm tired of my life. I want a new one.'

'Oh, do me a favour, Addy. Get some booze down you.'

'No, no alcohol. I'm still paying for last night.'

'Have the Coke. Then go, if you want to wallow in misery.'

Addy takes the can of Coke out of the sand. The flat, warm liquid rasps along her throat.

Philippa sets the drum in the sand in front of Addy. 'Have a go on the drum, Addy. Abdul will help you. It's easier if you wrap your legs around it so it doesn't fall over.'

'I don't think . . .'

Philippa grabs the Coke out of Addy's hand. 'Exactly. Don't think. Just do.'

Abdul shifts behind Addy. She's enveloped by his warmth and a light scent of sweat as he reaches his arms around her body to the drum. His blue gown flashes through the air as he beats out a hypnotic rhythm.

'You put your hands on mine,' he says into Addy's ear. 'You follow me.'

'I'm not sure—'

'For God's sake, Addy,' Philippa says. 'Just do it. Relax.'

Addy glances at Philippa then rests her fingertips on Abdul's and closes her eyes. Her hands fly across the drum skin on top of Abdul's. His breath brushes her cheek like a feather. He's careful not to touch her body, although she sits within the circle of his arms. They're connected only by her fingertips on his hands. His skin is smooth and warm. She smells the musky scent of his skin. Her heart beats in her ears. But as Abdul leans over her, all she can think about is Omar.

'Ah, there's your handsome landlord.' Philippa waves at Mohammed and beckons him over.

Addy makes out Mohammed's bald head lit by the moon's silver light. He waves at Philippa and picks his way around the huddled tourists towards them.

'You know he's married, Pippa.'

'Yes, Addy. He has two wives, actually. He told me all about them at supper last night. "They don't understand me" and all that rot. Don't worry. I have no intention of becoming Mrs Demsiri the Third.'

'I don't know how you can even speak to him, knowing how he treated Hanane.'

'We weren't there, Addy. You have the word of someone who was a child at the time. Maybe Hanane was . . . Oh, I don't know.'

'Maybe Hanane was what? Loose? A gold-digger?'

'Well, why else would the whole village want to cover it up? She was obviously an embarrassment to them.'

'I can't believe you're saying this. She's our brother's mother. Our father loved her.'

Mohammed sweeps his arms towards the full moon. 'Phileepa, the moon of the universe shines on the desert where you sit.'

'Hi, Mo. Have a seat. Shove over, Addy.'

Addy sticks the empty Coke can into the sand. 'I think I'll call it a night.'

'Already? The party's just getting started.'

Addy glances across the campfire, but there's no sign of Nigel. No sign of Omar either. She sighs and rubs her aching forehead. She'd come to Morocco to escape her problems, but she just seems to have created more. Her whole life is a disaster.

*

'Addy.'

Addy turns towards the voice. The drums and singing murmur in the desert behind her. A shadow emerges from behind one of the tents, the moonlight throwing silver highlights over the folds of the turban.

'Nigel?'

Her ex-boyfriend moves towards her, his feet unsteady in the sand.

'Looks like your goatherd has dumped you, Del.'

'Can't you leave me alone?'

Nigel sighs. 'Oh, Delly, Delly. Can't you see? I love you, hun. I want you back.' He thrusts his hand at the black dunes beyond the tents. 'I've hauled my ass all the way to the bloody Sahara for you. Isn't that proof that I'm serious?'

'I don't know what to think, Nigel. It's like you've become my stalker. It's creeping me out.' Addy shifts her feet in the sand.

Nigel's in front of her now. Taller than she remembers. Or is it just the shadows making him seem taller?

'You're imagining things, hun.' He reaches out his hand and brushes his fingers against her cheek. She pushes his hand away. 'Del, what's the matter? You seemed to like it well enough the other night.'

'Nothing happened.'

He drops his hand onto Addy's shoulder. 'But you're not really sure, are you? I'm truly hurt and sorry you can't remember. If you did, we'd be back in Marrakech by now, having a grand old time at the Mamounia Hotel on my expense account. You see, I've seen the error of my ways. You're absolutely right. I got caught up with my work and I neglected you.' He gives her shoulder a squeeze. 'Let me make it up to you. We can start over. Clean slate. What do you say?'

Addy steps away from him and folds her arms across her body. 'You've got a great imagination, I'll give you that.'

'Del, I feel sorry for you. I really do. This Omar wanker doesn't

353

love you. He's buggered off with one of the tourist girls. I saw him. He's playing you.'

Pain slices into Addy's gut as real as if Nigel had stabbed her. 'I don't believe you.'

Nigel leans towards her. She smells his hot, beery breath.

'It's true. Cross my heart and hope to die.' He staggers in the sand as he runs his finger across his chest and pats his heart.

Addy backs away. Her foot catches on a tent peg and she stumbles. Nigel reaches out and grabs her arm.

She brushes Nigel's hand away. 'You're drunk, Nigel. You don't know what you're saying.'

Addy's heart pounds in her chest. Bile rises in her throat and she swallows, the bitterness burning into her stomach.

Nigel rubs her arm. 'I understand. You're upset. He probably does this kind of thing all the time. Just forget about him.'

Addy looks Nigel square in his eyes. 'Okay, tell me what really happened the other night. We need to be honest with each other, don't you think? If there's any chance.'

'Nothing happened, Del. I swear.' He holds up his right hand like a Boy Scout. 'You passed out and I let you sleep. That's it.' He brushes her cheek with his knuckles. 'More's the pity.'

Nigel grins and pushes her against a tent post. He leans into her and kisses her neck.

Addy pushes against his chest. 'No, Nigel.'

'You don't really mean that.'

She tries to twist her head away, but he digs his fingers into her hair, anchoring her against his body. 'Come on, Del. I know you want it. I know you.'

Addy forces herself to relax into his embrace until she feels his hold relax. Stepping back, she lifts her foot and stamps down hard on his instep with the heel of her shoe.

Nigel grasps at his foot. 'Del! You bloody bitch.'

'You don't say that to her.'

Omar stands beside the tent, his body outlined by the moonlight. The tail end of his tagelmust is drawn across his face, only his eyes visible.

'Omar!' Addy stumbles across the sand and wraps her arms around him, but Omar makes no effort to hug her. She steps back, confused.

'So, Addy beats you well. She's a strong lady.'

Nigel rubs his lips. 'She tastes nice, too.'

The words are barely out of Nigel's mouth before he's lying on the sand, black blood streaming out of his nose. Groaning, he presses his hands against his face.

'You bloody bastard!'

Omar moves towards Addy like a silver spectre in his gown and tagelmust. He grabs her hand. 'Come.' He pulls her along behind him, past Nigel writhing in the sand, past the tents and the dromedaries, out into the vast desert.

She stumbles after him up a towering dune. 'Where are we going?' she pants. But he says nothing.

When they reach the top of the dune, he tears the tagelmust from his face.

'Why is he here?' His words come out like nails driving into a wall. 'You invited him?'

'No.' She gasps for breath from the climb. 'I had no idea Nigel was here.'

'You love him?'

'No!'

'How do I know you're telling the truth? He say you been with him in the hotel. You told me you were with your sister that night.'

Addy's feet sink into the sand. She's drowning. But she won't go without a fight.

'I love you, Omar. Only you. Nothing happened, I swear it. You heard him. He admitted the same thing. You can believe me or not. I'm telling you the truth. I didn't tell you because . . . because I was a coward. I was afraid you wouldn't understand. I barely understand it!' She rubs her forehead. 'You always said it was fate that brought us together. Maybe it did. Can't you see it? We're both part of a bigger story. A story that started the day my father met Hanane. Only God, or Allah, or the universe knows what the bigger picture is. Our story isn't finished, *habibi*. It's only beginning. Unless you end it. If you think I'm a liar, end it. I won't.'

Omar stands on the dune, his eyes boring into her. 'I won't. I can't, *habibati*.'

Addy flings her arms around his neck and kisses him. They're alone on a desert island in a sea of sand. The moon hangs in the diamond sky above them in their desert Eden.

Omar pushes Addy into the sand. He kisses her until her lips burn. She pulls his body hard against hers. Wanting all of him in a frenzy of arms, lips and legs. She yanks at his jeans and he thrusts into her. The sand is cold and the moon is an enormous white orb above his head. She wraps her legs around his body and opens herself up to him.

When they're finished, Addy watches him as he kneels astride her, rearranging her clothes. He glows above her in the moonlight like a ghost. She's calm. All the dust and debris of doubt has been sucked away, until there's nothing left but stillness.

They lie side by side on top of the dune. Addy stares at the luminous moon. Omar's hand is warm against hers and she feels the pressure of his foot where it rests across her ankle. They drift on top of the dune as if they're the only living souls in the sea of sand.

'It's a strange world that brought us together, *habibati*.'

Addy turns her head. Omar's also staring up at the moon. 'Sometimes it feels like a dream.'

'But it's not a dream, is it? It's our life.'

She gazes up at the star-sprinkled sky, seeking out the familiar shadows of the Man in the Moon. 'How do you feel about that, *habibi*?'

'I'm happy for it, darling. Sometimes I'm sad for it, too.'

'Why are you sad?'

He reaches for Addy's hand and plays with her fingers. 'You gave me the key to a big world. I want to be in the world with you beside me and me beside you.' He slides his fingers between hers, closing them around her hand. 'But sometimes I'm lonely for my life before I met you.'

Addy's heart sinks in her chest. How can she tell him she understands? That she feels the same way? 'Chalk and cheese' her mother would call them, in her practical Canadian way. She wants to wrap them in a blanket of hope, here on this island in the sandy sea. But with every movement, the sand shifts and she sinks deeper into its cold depths. She wonders if their relationship is, ultimately, doomed.

'My life was more simple before I knew you, Adi. I knew my path well. I made a plan to find a lady to marry, to have children, to do guiding well, to save money, to make a tour business. Only I couldn't find the lady.' There's an edge of regret in his voice.

Addy looks over at his strong profile, illuminated against the black sky by the moonlight.

'I never meant to complicate your life, Omar. I never meant for anything to happen.'

Omar looks over at her. 'What about this man from England? He came to Morocco for you. He must love you yet.' His eyes watch her, searching for the truth. 'Maybe you love him still.'

Addy rolls her head from side to side in the sand. 'No. I told you, it's over with him.' She takes a deep breath and steels herself to tell the full truth. 'We own a flat together in London.' Her mouth is bone dry. 'He thinks it'll be more . . . more financially convenient if I move back with him. But I won't. I've told him that.'

She leans on her elbow. 'I need to go back to England soon. My Moroccan visa's almost up. I'm going to move in with Philippa for a while. I have to convince Nigel to sell the flat. Then I'll be free of him for good.'

'Maybe you'll forget about me. It's hard for me to know that he'll be there close to you.'

'I'll never forget about you, *habibi*. I need the money from the flat if I'm going to move to Morocco. I spent what my father left me to pay off my debts, buy the new camera equipment and fund this trip to Morocco. Philippa thought I was mad. But I had to come. Not just to find Hanane and Amine. But for me. To find me.'

'You would move to Morocco?'

'Why not? Maybe not right away. But I can look into it. There's nothing for me in London. I can be a photographer anywhere. Maybe I'll teach photography to tourists. Write a blog. Maybe I can write more travel books. Who knows?'

Omar nods. 'The doors are closed in England.'

'Everything for me is here in Morocco.'

'What do you mean?'

'Well, your mother and your sister and your grandmother are here, of course.'

'That's it?'

'It's a wonderful place for me to take pictures to sell to travel magazines. It's so photogenic.'

'And?'

'Well, the weather's very nice.'

He grabs Addy and rolls her on top of him. 'That's everything? You're sure?'

She smiles down at his face, lit silver by the moon. 'I almost forgot. There's a guy called Omar. He's kind of okay.'

He pulls her tight against him. 'Okay only?'

'Omar, I can't breathe.'

'Okay only?'

Addy relaxes her body against his and he loosens his hold. They stay like that until their breathing synchronises.

'He's the man I love.'

Omar rolls her off him and sits up in the sand.

'*Habibati*, I must tell you something.'

A prickle of unease chases over Addy's shoulders. 'Yes?'

'There was a lady before I met you. Her family made the papers for marriage. They wait for me to sign them.'

'A lady?'

'Yes.'

'Do I know her?'

'Yes.'

'Who is it?'

He looks over at Addy. 'Zaina.'

It's like a stab to her heart. 'That's why Zaina hates me.'

'I don't mind for Zaina. It's why I didn't sign the papers yet, even before you came. I went to the judge two times to do it and I left. It makes her parents angry. My mother doesn't understand. My mother wants grandchildren. Even me, I want children, too. It's normal.'

Normal. Something she'll never be again.

'Then you came to Zitoune. I knew you are the lady I been waiting for. I'm happy even when you make me angry. I want to tell you everything. I never had a relationship with a lady like it before. Even though sometimes we don't understand each other well. I'm so sorry for that.'

Omar reaches out to brush the fringe out of Addy's eyes, but she leans back out of his reach. He drops his hand.

'I brought you to my family and everybody loves you a lot. My mother says you're like an Amazigh lady. She loves that you bought a washing machine. It's a big honour for her. She says to me why can't Adi be like the Dutch lady of Yassine and I marry Zaina. This is a good way in her mind. But I don't want that situation at all, one hundred per cent. I want you to be my wife, full stop.'

'Is that how everyone sees me? Like Yassine's Dutch girlfriend?'

The line between Omar's eyebrows deepens. 'They know I love you like my wife. I'm clear about that with everybody. They don't have permission to think about you in a bad way.'

Addy clutches a handful of the cold sand and watches it run through her fingers.

'I couldn't stay with you if you married Zaina.'

'I know it. I think sometimes I must stop it with you. I think in the desert today to stop it with you. But I can't. You got me. I'm finished. I want us to be all together. I want to make the *dar* with you. With you I see the possibility of the kasbah hotel and the tour agency. Before it was a big dream that is in outer space. But you make me believe in myself.

'I'll rent a café by the river this summer to earn more money. I'll do guiding two times a day. I'll work very harder because now I work for two people. For you and for me.'

'What about Zaina?'

'I'll tell her family I won't marry her. They'll be angry, but that's not my problem.' He shrugs. 'My mum will have to accept it.'

She's the stone thrown into the pond and the ripples are turning into waves. It feels unreal, like she's an actor in a movie she's created in her dreams. But even as she's living it, it's like she's sitting in a cinema, watching the story unfold in front of her. Why is it that a person can spend so much of their life waiting for it to happen, and then when it does, everything happens so fast that it feels like the events spin by without touching them? That sometime later, when everything has settled down again, they look back at the big events and it's like a dream that's happened to someone else?

# Chapter Sixty-Two

### The Sahara Desert, Morocco – June 2009

Addy wakes up beside Omar under a pile of blankets in a small tent. Moroccan wool rugs in red-and-black geometric patterns hang over the tent's brown walls and cover the sand. Leaning on her elbow, she examines Omar's sleeping face. He smiles.

'So, you're awake, *habibi*.'

'I can feel you watching me.'

She traces the outline of his lips with her fingertip. 'I'm allowed.'

Omar opens his eyes. 'For sure you're allowed, darling. Nobody can stop you.'

She moves her fingertip along the curve of his cheekbone. 'I didn't know they had private tents.'

'It's for special clients. VIP. I made a plan for us to have it. But then we were fighting, so you went in the big tent with your sister.'

She lies back and squints at the pattern of the rug hanging over the tent's ceiling. 'I'm sorry about all that.'

'What happened to you yesterday, darling? You been moody. It cut me like a knife.'

'I was tired and hot, and I had a hangover.' Addy rubs her eyes. It's only half the truth. She's been worried that she'd slept with Nigel. 'And I lost my hat.'

'I'm sorry for that. I will buy you a new hat. Anyway, you have to know I opened the door for you in Morocco. You are welcome in Morocco and in my heart.'

'I know. But I think Philippa has you pegged as a slave trader who's after what's left of my flimsy virtue.'

'A Barbary corsair?'

Addy laughs. 'A Barbary corsair. Yes, that suits you.'

Omar rolls over on top of her. 'For sure I would sail the world to find you and take you to be with me. Nobody can stop me.'

'What about me?'

Omar buries his head against Addy's shoulder and kisses her neck. He leans over her ear and whispers. 'You want me to stop it?'

The tent flap flies open. Mohammed stands in the entrance pounding on a drum. '*Yalla*! *Yalla*! *Lafdoure*! Breakfast!'

'*Allah I naal dine omok*,' Omar swears as he rolls off Addy.

Mohammed laughs. '*Yalla*! *Yalla*!' The tent flap falls behind him.

Addy hears him enter the next tent to the shrieks of the German women.

'If he says *yalla* to me one more time, I'll make him yellow,' she says grumpily.

Omar rolls back on top of her. 'You're a strong lady. I love it.'

Mohammed sticks his head through the entrance flap again. '*Yalla*! *Yalla*!'

'*An nhwik*.'

Mohammed ducks his head out of the tent just as Omar's Nike trainer slams against a rug on the wall.

'If he comes again, I'll kill him.' Omar runs his hand along Addy's bare arm.

'What about breakfast?'

'We eat later, *habibati*. First, I'll make you hungry.'

Somewhere in the distance, Mohammed bangs the drum. '*Yalla*! *Yalla*! We go. Come on. Fab. Mama Africa.'

*

362

Addy's just mounted her seated dromedary and is adjusting her camera strap, when Omar grabs her around her waist and launches himself onto the blanket saddle behind her. He clucks his tongue and kicks the sides of the animal with his heels. The dromedary groans and lumbers to its feet.

Philippa clambers onto the dromedary behind them. 'Looks like Paradise has been regained.'

Mohammed grabs her waist and settles onto the saddle behind her.

Addy frowns at her sister, still angry about the aspersions Philippa had cast on Hanane.

'It looks like I'm not the only one who's found Paradise in the desert.'

Philippa slides her sunglasses down her nose and peers down the line of dromedaries.

'What's happened to Nigel?'

'The English? He's gone,' Mohammed says. 'He go with a German lady in a dune buggy this morning. He don't drive well. It might be he go to *Algérie*.'

'I hope he goes to Antarctica,' Omar mumbles.

The Tuareg guides walk along the rank of the dromedaries, checking the ropes. The young guide Abdul grabs the rope hanging from Addy's dromedary's bridle.

He smiles at Addy. '*Labass?*'

'*Bikher. Shukran.*'

Omar barks at Abdul in Arabic. The guide's smile dissolves. He grips the rope behind his back and leads the caravan out towards the dunes.

'What did you say to him?'

'You have to know I saw him last night teaching you the drumming. He sat behind you and he put his arms around you. I been jealous. I told him I will fight with him like a lion if he talks to you again.'

Mohammed laughs behind them. Addy looks over at her sister,

glamorous in her white capri trousers, purple kaftan top, floppy hat and huge sunglasses. Mohammed reaches around Philippa and pulls her against him.

'The foreigner ladies is so nicer. I think it might be I will marry another wife.'

'*Wife?*' Philippa adjusts the tagelmust she's looped around her neck like a scarf. 'Mo, we need to talk.'

As the caravan reaches the base of the first large dune, the German tourists are led off on their dromedaries in another direction by one of the guides. Abdul leads Addy's caravan up the side of the dune until they're trekking along the top of a long ridge of sand.

'Where are the others going?'

Omar points over to the ridge of a dune where the other caravan is silhouetted in a long, graceful line against the blue sky.

'It's for making pictures. It looks nice for the tourists.'

Addy raises her camera and focuses her lens on the silhouetted caravan, the riders' tagelmusts bright dots of colour against the blue sky.

'Look!' Philippa shouts as she points to the opposite side. 'The acrobats.'

Addy looks around and sees Dom standing on top of his dromedary, his arms outstretched. He reaches down onto the blanket saddle and unfolds his body into a handstand. Behind him, Dominique moulds herself into bizarre contortions on top of her dromedary. Addy flicks the 'continuous' switch and the shutter clicks furiously as she captures their acrobatics. From the crest of the other sand dune, the German tourists clap and whistle.

'It takes pictures quick, darling.'

'Yes.' She lowers the camera and turns around to face him. 'I've just had an idea. I've taken so many pictures since I've been in Morocco that aren't right for the travel book. As soon as I get back to London, I'm going to talk to a gallery about doing a show of my Moroccan images. The quirkier ones, like the acrobats here in the desert. Amine in his dreadlock hat. The monkey stealing food from the tables in Zitoune. It'll be amazing.'

'You'll be in London a long time.'

Addy chews her lip. So much of her life is still in London. Moving to Morocco might not be so easy.

'Just for a while. I'll be back soon. I promise.'

'You have to.'

'I'll come back. Don't worry.'

'When?'

'Soon. As soon as I can. I'm going to need to earn some money first.'

'Darling, you must come back. I gave you my heart. I will die if you take it away.'

The dromedaries plod along in the sand. Addy leans back against Omar, anchored into place by his arm across her body. She sways with the rocking movement of the animal. The desert is quiet. All around, she sees nothing but a vast sea of sand and dunes and the blue, blue sky. The other caravan has disappeared behind the dunes. It's like they're the only people left on earth. The dromedaries' feet thud softly in the sand. She closes her eyes and dozes.

# Chapter Sixty-Three

**Zitoune, Morocco – December 1984**

A pounding on the front door. Mohammed glances away from the television on top of a corner table in the living room – the grey concrete block walls still unplastered and unpainted – to the new silver watch on his left wrist.

'Bouchra, what kind of time do you call this? It's almost midnight. Bouchra!'

More pounding. His young wife appears in the doorway, her face dull with sleep.

'You'll wake the baby with all your noise.' She wipes at her eyes with her fingers. 'Why don't you just answer the door yourself? I had to come all the way from the kitchen.'

'I'm busy.' He points to the football match on the television. 'Argentina has just scored against Liverpool. It's an important match.'

Mohammed hears Bouchra shuffle over to the door, her carpet slippers catching on the rough concrete.

'Mohammed.'

'What?' He waves his hand at the television. 'What's Liverpool's problem? C'mon! C'mon! Watch that guy Barberon.'

'Mohammed, come quick.'

Slapping his hands on the banquette, Mohammed rises and heads for the hallway.

'What? Don't they know the Intercontinental Cup . . .?' His mouth falls open.

His sister, Hanane, clings to the doorframe, her pregnant belly announcing her shame.

'Hanane, what are you doing here? Where's your Englishman?'

His sister looks at him, her brown eyes full of fear.

'Please, Mohammed. Help me. I'm not well. The baby's coming soon.'

He watches as his sister's eyes roll back and her knees give way. He rushes forwards and thrusts out his arms. The weight of her pregnant body pulls them down into the mud outside the door.

Bouchra grimaces as Hanane writhes on the bed. A groan escapes her sister-in-law's mouth.

'What are we going to do with her? She can't stay here.'

'She's my sister. Look at the state of her. Where else is she supposed to go? Get her some blankets.'

'It'd be better if the bastard dies. It would repay your father's death.'

His hand makes contact with his wife's face. She gasps and raises a hand to her reddening cheek.

'Get Aicha. Once the baby comes, we'll decide what to do.'

Bouchra sidles out of the room. The front door slams. Mohammed sits on the foot of the bed, watching his sister pant and moan. Her feet kick off the sheet, and her djellaba, filthy from the mud, rides up over her naked legs. Leaning over, he tucks in the sheet. Women's work. It's not for a man to be present here.

'Look what you've done to us, Hanane.'

Hanane, panting softly in a momentary rest from the pains of labour, holds out her hand to him.

'I'm so sorry to disturb you, Mohammed. Please. It's not what you think.' She drops her hand. 'I married Gus in Marrakech in the spring. I'm not a bad woman.' Her forehead drips beads of sweat down her temples into the flowered pillowcase. 'Where's *Baba*? We tried so hard to speak to you both in October. It's why we came. But . . .' Her breath catches on a sob.

'You were already dead to him, Hanane.'

'If only he would have listened to us. Gus wanted so much to speak to him. I've done nothing wrong, Mohammed. But I want to beg *Baba*'s forgiveness for causing him so much pain.'

'You broke *Baba*'s heart, Hanane. You were always his favourite. He's in Paradise now.'

'*Baba*'s dead?'

'He couldn't bear the shame of your dishonour.' Mohammed lifts a corner of the sheet and wipes the dampness off her forehead. 'If you're married, where's your husband? You should be with him.'

Hanane closes her eyes. A tear slips from under her lashes down her cheek. She wipes it away and looks up at her brother.

'I know. We planned it that way, but . . . I had to come home. To be with my family. Do you understand?'

She grits her teeth and clutches at the sheet as a contraction takes hold, panting until the pain subsides.

'You left him?'

'No. Never. My husband had to go to Rabat for my visa. We're going to start a new life in Canada. He has a house on a beautiful island by the ocean. He has a daughter there from his wife who died. He has another daughter in England. A new famil—' Hanane groans and clutches her swollen belly.

She reaches out again for Mohammed. He stands at the foot of the bed, unable to take her hand.

'I'll get you some water.'

'Yes, Mohammed. Please.'

She gulps down the water he brings from the kitchen.

'Thank you. The baby wasn't supposed to come for two more weeks. Then the pains started. I was alone. I was afraid.'

'So you came back to Zitoune.'

'Yes. My husband will be back in Marrakech tomorrow evening. I left him a note. He'll come for me and for our baby. *Inshallah*.'

Her body is gripped with another labour pain. This time she screams. In the depths of the house, Mohammed's baby wails.

Mohammed presses his palms to his forehead. His sister has married a *kitabi*. A Christian. But the marriage doesn't matter. It's *haram*. Forbidden for a Muslimah to marry a Christian man. With or without the marriage, she's made herself a prostitute. A *zaaniyah*. An adulteress.

'Will Hanane be okay, *Yamma*?'

'Omar, I told you to stay home with your sister.'

Omar grips the doorframe, peeking his head into the bedroom, where Hanane lies panting on the bed.

'Fatima's fine. Jedda's there.'

'This is no place for a boy.'

Hanane arches her back, biting her lips in vain as another scream slides up her throat. Mohammed grimaces. 'Can you help her, Aicha?'

Aicha stands at the foot of the bed beside Mohammed and Bouchra. She longs to reach out to Hanane, wipe the sweat from her face, calm the girl's panic, guide the infant into the world. But . . . What has this beautiful girl done? What djinni has been sent to defile her, to bring his child into the world? She has no husband. She's ruined herself.

Aicha turns away from the bed. She shakes her head. Her gold coin earrings dangle in her earlobes. She can have no part in this badness. She'd turned her back on her mother's spells and magic potions long ago. She was in the world to help, not to disturb the djinn. To bring only good. She could not bring a djinni's child into the world.

'I can't. I'm sorry. Hanane must live her fate. It is not for me to interfere in Allah's will. Come, Omar. We must go home.'

# Chapter Sixty-Four

**Zitoune, Morocco – June 2009**

Amine enters the courtyard of Aicha's house. He's had his hair cut very short, highlighting his dark eyes and long, straight nose. The white patch glows against his brown skin, which has tanned darker from the summer sun. He glances at the faces of the family group sitting around the tagine pot.

'Mohammed told me Omar call him to tell me to come here fast. It's a problem?'

'Amine, come and sit.' Addy gestures for him to sit on the stool between her and Philippa. 'Have some lamb tagine. It's delicious.'

Amine sits on the stool and smiles at Fatima as she hands him the basket of bread.

'I been nervous to come. I thought it's a problem.'

'For one time it's no problem,' Omar says as he scoops up a chunk of meat with his bread. 'Addy have some big news for you.'

'Big news?' Amine looks over at Addy. 'Which news?'

Addy darts her eyes at Philippa. 'You know that Philippa and I are sisters? We have the same father but different mothers.'

Amine nods.

'Our father came here to Zitoune many years ago after my mother went to Paradise. He met a lady here and they fell in love.'

She glances over at Aicha, who's busy sucking the marrow out of a mutton bone. It's just as well she doesn't understand English. Probably a good thing that Fatima doesn't, either. She looks at Jedda, who's peering at her with her good eye. Can Jedda really understand her? No, that's impossible. Just another mountain superstition.

'My father and the lady had a baby. The baby was born on December the ninth. Almost twenty-five years ago.'

Amine chews on a piece of mutton. 'The same day like me. That's nice.'

Philippa tuts. 'No, no. You're not getting it. You're the baby. You.'

Amine chokes on the meat and swallows hard.

Fatima thrusts the water bottle at him. 'What's happening, Adi?' she asks in French.

'In a minute, Fatima. I'll tell you soon.'

Addy reaches over and rests her hand on Amine's knee.

'You're our brother, Amine. Philippa and me, we're your sisters. Your mother was the lady who my father loved. They loved each other.'

Amine's eyes fill with tears. He presses his fingers against his eyes. 'Serious?'

'Yes, serious. You're a Percival, just like us.'

Amine's shoulders begin to shake. Addy reaches over and hugs him against her as Philippa pats him on the back.

'You give me the biggest gift in the world, Adi,' Amine says, emotion strangling his words. 'You give me my father.'

Addy turns over in her bed and watches Omar on his cell phone. Omar finishes the call and sets the phone down on the bedside table.

'Omar?'

'Yes, *habibati*.' Omar sits on the bed beside Addy.

'Have you spoken to Zaina's parents yet? To tell them your engagement is off.'

The crease forms between Omar's eyebrows. 'Soon, darling. When the time is better.'

'Why wait? It's not fair on Zaina to string her along.'

Omar sighs. 'Don't mind about Zaina. She's young yet. Her father will find her another husband quick.'

'Maybe she doesn't want another husband.'

'It's her problem. Don't mind for the situation, darling. It's not your business.'

'Not my business?' The blood rises in her cheeks.

He reaches over and turns off the switch on the bedside lantern. 'Darling, I'm so, so tired. I must sleep. I have a lot to do tomorrow. I have to find someone to manage the café of Yassine near the waterfalls. Yassine's gone with the wind. Even his wife don't know where, so I'm taking his café to make a business. Soon I'll have enough money for the architect for *Dar Adi* with the money you give me as well.'

Addy picks at the bedcover. 'At least Fatima seems to be happier when Zaina's around. Have you noticed how much Fatima and your mother are arguing? Even Philippa's noticed. What do you think that's all about?'

'My mum insists Fatima marry Farouk. She's telling her all the time to do it, but Fatima says no. She insist to marry Amine.'

'You know she loves Amine. She told me.'

'It's impossible for Amine to marry Fatima. He's a bastard.'

'My father's his father.'

'Even so, Mister Gus didn't marry Amine's mother. I'm so sorry for this situation, darling, you know this is true. So, he's still a bastard.'

'Don't say that. It's not a nice word. He's illegitimate.'

Omar sits up and turns on the light. 'Adi, when Mister Gus thought Amine die as well as Hanane, he left Zitoune. He never came back after that. The policeman came to take away Amine because he was bast . . . illegitimate. The policeman say Amine must go to a special house in Beni Mellal.

'Mohammed paid the policeman to be quiet and for Amine to stay with him and his wife, even though she was very angry about the situation. Even yet, Mohammed pays the policeman so he doesn't make trouble for Amine. I cannot permit Fatima to marry into this situation. She'll suffer.'

'If Fatima and Amine want to marry, we have to help them. He's my half-brother.'

'No, darling. It's impossible.'

'Why? Maybe it's their fate to be together. Have you thought about that?'

'I swear I'll help Amine for his future because he's your brother. It's incredible that Mister Gus is the father of you and your sister and Amine. Even so, it is impossible to fix this problem. Amine is illegitimate, as you say. That's his fate, *habibati*. He can never marry Fatima. You must accept it.'

373

# Chapter Sixty-Five

**Zitoune, Morocco – June 2009**

Zaina enters the courtyard of Aicha's house carrying a basket covered with a red-and-white striped cloth. She nods at Addy and Aicha, kisses Jedda on top of her head and sits on a stool beside Fatima, who's bent over Philippa's hands applying intricate henna patterns. She sets the basket down and unwraps the striped cloth. The sweet, cakey aroma of freshly baked cookies wafts into the air.

'*Shukran*,' Aicha says. She waves her hands at Zaina, her palms wet with pungent green henna.

A motorbike whines into the lane. The engine idles in front of the house, then the motorbike roars off again. The front door swings open and Omar strides into the courtyard swinging a straw hat in his fingers. He taps at the birdcage and coos at Fatima's little green budgie, then he walks over to Addy and sets the hat on her head.

'Thank you, *habibi*.'

'I told you I would buy you a new hat since your other one flew to *Algérie*.'

Omar bends over his grandmother and kisses the top of her head. Addy watches Zaina follow him with her eyes.

Omar grabs a handful of cookies and stuffs three into his mouth. He wipes the crumbs from his lips.

'There is some lunch, honey? I'm so hungry.'

'No. We've been doing the henna.'

He frowns and strides into the kitchen, emerging with a cold brochette, Jedda's black-and-white cat at his heels. He drags a stool beside Jedda and bites into the cold mutton.

'We should have tagine for lunch. There is a problem with Fatima.'

'She's still upset about Amine.'

'Still?'

'Yes. She loves him. You can't just turn that off like a tap.'

He tosses a chunk of mutton to the cat and licks the mutton grease off his fingers.

'It doesn't matter about love, *habibati*. It matters about security. Amine doesn't have papers because his parents didn't marry. So, I tell him he must be rich to make Fatima secure. Then he can pay for the doctor and for the education of his children. To be Fatima's husband he must be able to support his family well.' He nods towards his sister. 'Fatima understands this requirement.'

'He's a waiter in his uncle's restaurant. How's he supposed to get rich?'

'This is not my problem. It's the problem of Amine.'

'Amine's my brother. If it's his problem, it's my problem, too.'

'And mine.' Philippa waves her hennaed hands in the air. 'Maybe we can get him a job in London.'

'As you like, Phileepa. Even so, it will take a long time, and Farouk is impatient to marry Fatima.'

'I thought that was over. Fatima doesn't want to marry him.'

Omar tugs the last chunk of mutton off the skewer and pops it into his mouth. He chews as he looks at Addy. He swallows and wipes his mouth with his fingers.

'My mum and my uncle and my aunt insist to make a wedding

for Fatima and Farouk. They love it for the honour of the family. They want to do it soon. Even before Ramadan.'

'But you're not going to let that happen, right?'

'Family is very, very important in Morocco. It's a bad situation to disturb the honour of a family.'

Addy looks down at the twisting curlicues of henna on her feet.

'But you promised that Fatima could choose her own husband.'

'Yes, I know. I don't know the answer for this situation.'

Someone pounds on the metal door and shouts Omar's name. Omar drops the skewer onto the low table and goes over to open the door. Mohammed shoves past him, waving a crumpled piece of paper.

'You're happy, Omar? You make him to do it.'

'What happened? What are you talking about?'

'Amine. He's gone. He said he will go to Europe.'

Fatima looks over at Addy, her dark eyes wide. 'What's happening?'

Mohammed waves the crumpled paper at Omar. 'You told Amine he can't marry Fatima because he's a bastard. You said he must be rich, but you know this is an impossibility for him. He said Omar insists that Fatima must marry an old uncle for the honour of her family. It's true, isn't it? *Mahbool.*'

The green budgie jumps off its perch and flaps around the bamboo cage.

'Mohammed, it's true I told him he had to be rich to marry Fatima, but I never told him about Farouk. This was not his business.'

Philippa draws her pencilled eyebrows together. 'If you didn't tell him, then who did?'

Mohammed pounds his chest with his fist and points a finger at Omar. 'You think Amine is bastard rubbish. You think he's the son of a whore. My poor sister who die.'

Fatima tugs urgently at Addy's sleeve. 'What's he saying about Amine?'

Mohammed waves Amine's letter at Addy. 'It's the fault of you.

When you showed me the photo of Hanane and your father by the waterfalls, I felt the bad eye happening again. Your father brought big shame to my family. Then everybody forgot the situation until you told Amine he's the son of your father. You made big problems since you came here.'

'Mohammed, I had no idea . . .'

Omar pats the older man on his shoulder. 'Adi didn't mean to make problems.'

Mohammed shoves Omar's hand away. 'Amine is my blood, even if his father was an evil man. He said he will go on a boat to Europe to be rich. He said it's finished for him in Morocco if Fatima marries Farouk.' He presses his fists against his eyes. 'Amine, Amine.'

'What, Adi?' Fatima asks, her voice shrill with anxiety. 'What did Mohammed say?'

Addy takes hold of Fatima's hand. 'Amine wrote a letter to Mohammed. Someone told him that Omar was forcing you to marry Farouk. He said he couldn't stay in Morocco if you couldn't be his wife.'

Her eyes widen. 'Where's Amine?'

'Oh, Fatima. He's gone to Europe.'

Fatima clutches Addy's hand to her chest. 'Who told Amine this? Only our family knew that my uncle wished to marry me. My family and . . .' Fatima slowly turns to face Zaina.

'*Laa*!' Zaina shakes her head wildly. 'I only told Amine maybe. Maybe you will marry your uncle. Maybe!'

'Liar!' Fatima lunges for the basket of cookies and launches it at Zaina, showering her with shortbread. She picks up the broken cookies and hurls them at Zaina's face.

Aicha and Philippa leap off their stools and pull at the two girls as they kick and scream at each other.

'It's enough, Fatima.' Omar points to Aicha's bedroom. 'Go.'

Fatima runs into Aicha's room, her wails resonating around the courtyard. Zaina mumbles something apologetic to Omar.

He shouts at her harshly. Then she's on her knees, begging. Crying.

Addy stares at the wailing girl. At the devastated uncle. At her shocked lover.

She's a pebble thrown into a pond. Mohammed, Omar, Zaina, Fatima and Amine are floating leaves dragged under by the ripples.

# Chapter Sixty-Six

**Zitoune, Morocco – June 2009**

'Is it true?'

'What?' Omar stands at the open window of Addy's bedroom, staring out over the tops of the olive trees to the mountains beyond.

She tosses her T-shirts into her suitcase. 'Did you tell Fatima she has to marry Farouk?'

Omar turns around, his eyes narrowing. 'Why do you say that?'

'Why else would Amine have left like this? He was so excited to find out about his father. He wanted to know everything about him. He said he wanted to marry Fatima and make a life in England with her. We could've helped them. They could've had a wonderful future there. They could've had the chance for a life together that my father and Hanane never did.'

'If you think it, then it must be so.'

'You told me Fatima could make her own decision. You promised.' Addy's chest constricts as anger takes hold. She slams down the lid of the suitcase. 'Look where your honour's got you now. Your sister's life destroyed. Amine on a dangerous journey to Europe. Mohammed breaking his heart over his nephew. Are you happy now? Are you happy to marry off your sister to an old man as a brood mare? All for the sake of your family's bloody honour.'

'You don't understand how it is to be Amazigh.'

'You're right, Omar. I don't understand it, and I'll never understand you.'

Addy finds Fatima lying on a banquette in Aicha's living room, her breath catching on tearless sobs. Aicha sits beside her, rubbing Fatima's head, while Jedda perches on the opposite banquette like a protective owl, tapping the floor with her stick, the cat curled at her feet. Tea is set out on the low table, but no one's touched it.

Addy kisses Fatima on her cheek. Fatima reaches her arms around Addy and hugs her. The front door of the house slams against the clay wall. Its tinny reverberations echo around the courtyard. Omar enters the living room. He picks up the teapot and pours a stream of tea into a glass. Between sips, he answers Aicha's strident questions.

Jedda slaps her stick on the wooden table and rises to her feet. Grumbling under her breath, she pushes past Aicha and Omar and out to the courtyard, the cat following at her heels.

Addy whispers to Fatima that she's sorry, that she'd believed Omar when he'd told her that Fatima was free to make her own decision about marrying Farouk. That she never would've believed he'd go back on his word.

Fatima sits up, her face puffy and wet. 'No, Adi. It's not Omar's fault. He gave us a chance. He told Amine he must earn ten thousand dirhams and then we could have a wedding. Amine and I discussed it many times. He tried to earn more money in the restaurant and working for Omar. He even was doing some guiding around the waterfalls. But the money came slow – ten thousand dirhams was an impossibility, I could see it.' She sighs heavily. '*I* made the decision to marry Farouk. It was me, not Omar.'

Addy jerks her head around to Omar. He's watching her, his face inscrutable. She turns back to Fatima.

'But why?'

Fatima's brown eyes are dark with tears.

'I must be secure in my life, Adi. My children must be secure. I love Amine. Even more since I know he is your brother. He has taken my liver. But he wouldn't be a good husband for me. He is poor and he have no papers. I would be old before he have ten thousand dirhams to marry me, and I want to have a family. Farouk is my aunt's brother. My family will have a good honour if I marry him.'

'I don't understand.'

'After Farouk left I think about the situation all the time. I think maybe it might be possible to be the wife of Amine, but . . .' She shakes her head sadly. 'I think about having a baby with no name. It's not possible for me to do that. I think about it so, so much. It is much better for me to marry my aunt's brother, Farouk. I will have a better life with him. I will be with Uncle Rachid and Aunt Nadia, and I will have his children to look after. I will love that.'

Addy sits back against the cushions. 'So, you've been trying to decide between Amine and Farouk. That's why you and your mother have been arguing.'

Fatima nods. 'I only tell Zaina my decision two days ago. I didn't even tell Amine or my mother or Omar my decision yet, because then it would be final. This is how I know Zaina told Amine.' She smiles a thin, bitter smile. 'Sometimes I think Zaina have a djinni in her. She makes mischief for people. I'm sure she told Amine Omar was forcing me to marry Farouk.'

'So why are you so upset that Amine's left if you've decided not to marry him?'

A sob wrenches from her throat. 'Because I didn't know I love him so much until he is gone!'

Addy's eyes dart over to Omar. He's looking at her like someone who's opened a much-anticipated gift only to be disappointed once the layers of colourful paper and ribbons have been stripped away.

'You think I would force my sister to marry Farouk?'

'I'm sorry, Omar. I thought . . .'

'Fatima is free to decide for herself. I told you this before. I would never make her marry somebody she don't want.' He rises from the banquette and strides out into the courtyard. The front door reverberates like a thunderclap.

Jedda hobbles into the room, a wooden box under her arm. She holds out the box to Addy and says something in Tamazight.

Addy looks over at Fatima. 'What's she saying?'

Fatima wipes her wet cheeks with the back of her hand. 'She want you to open it. She say it's for you.'

'For me?'

'Yes, she insist for it.'

Addy takes the box and turns it over in her hands. The highly polished orange wood has a burred grain on the top and bottom with inlays of mother of pearl, and the front is faced with curved vertical slats. Just like the box Hanane's holding on the boardwalk in Casablanca in her father's Polaroid. She tugs at the lid but it doesn't budge. She holds it up to her ear and shakes it. Something rattles inside.

'I don't know how to open it.'

'Maybe you need a key.'

'But there's no keyhole.'

Aicha leans over the table and takes the box from Addy. She shakes the box and fingers the vertical slats as she questions the old woman. She suddenly drops the box onto the banquette, her hand to her mouth.

'*Laa*, Jedda.'

'What is it?' Addy picks up the box as Aicha rushes out of the room. 'What's going on?'

Fatima glances over at her grandmother, who leans on her stick studying Addy with her good blue eye.

'Jedda said that your father give Omar this box when he came here to find Hanane and the baby. He tell Omar to give it to Jedda. He said it has his heart. Jedda give it to you since you are the daughter of Mister Gus.'

382

'This was my father's?'

'Yes. My mother is upset for that. She think it has bad magic.'

Addy shakes the box. 'His heart. What does that mean?'

'You must open it.'

'I don't know how.'

Fatima hugs Addy and whispers in her ear. 'Omar.'

# Chapter Sixty-Seven

**Zitoune, Morocco – June 2009**

Addy's feet crunch on the gravel. Omar looks over his shoulder. Addy sits beside him on the concrete wall at the building site. She sets the wooden box wrapped in one of Fatima's scarves in her lap. The air is heavy with all the things she wants to unsay.

'I'm sorry. I should never have doubted you, Omar.'

Omar exhales as if he's carrying a large weight. 'Yes.'

Beyond the mounds of earth and stacks of cement blocks, the dense leaves of the olive trees meld into inky blackness in the waning light.

'I've made a lot of mistakes since I've been in Zitoune.'

'It is true.'

She's ruined everything. But she can't let it end like this. She can't let him hate her.

'Morocco's so different from Canada and England. I'm always putting my foot in it here.'

Omar frowns at her. 'What do you mean?'

'It's an expression. Putting your foot in your mouth. Putting your foot where it shouldn't go and it makes things worse.'

Omar grunts. 'It's true. Many times you put your foot in it. You're not an Amazigh lady.'

The shadows of the trees are lengthening and the chirp of the cicadas fills the cooling air.

'You'd like me to be Amazigh, wouldn't you? You say it often enough.'

Omar stares past the building site into the dense olive grove.

'It would be more easy, one hundred per cent.'

'But I'm not.'

'No.'

'I feel awful about the whole Fatima and Amine situation. I feel like I'm to blame. I'd get Fatima to come with me on my walks when you were having Amine following me. I made it easy for them to talk to each other. I shouldn't have interfered.'

Omar rubs his temple. 'Adi, don't mind. Even if you didn't come to Zitoune, somehow it would be the same result. It's their fate. Just as it's Fatima's fate to marry Farouk. Even though you have to know I don't like this situation. But she made her decision.'

Fate. What is *their* fate? She unwraps the scarf and holds the box out to Omar.

Omar takes the box from Addy.

'I know this box. I remember it. Mister Gus wanted Jedda to bury it in Hanane's grave. She didn't do it. She must know you would come one day.'

'She didn't know my father had other children.'

'Jedda knows.'

'Do you know how to open it? I can't figure it out.'

He holds it up to his ear and shakes it.

'Something's inside.'

He twists it around in his hands, prodding and pulling until the bottom slides back. A slat loosens under his fingers and he pulls out a peg. A small brass key drops into his hand. He runs his fingers along the other slats until one shifts downwards, revealing a keyhole. He gives Addy the key.

'You do it.'

She takes the box and inserts the tiny key. She twists it

clockwise until it stops and opens the lid. She looks into the compartment.

'Oh, my goodness.'

'What is it?'

Addy reaches into the box and picks out a ring. Gold. The crowned heart held between a pair of hands. She turns it over and examines the back. The gold mark – twenty-four carat. And her father's initials: AJP – Augustus Joyce Percival. Such a strange middle name for a man. The surname of some Irish ancestor, he'd once told her. A wanderer, he'd said. It's in their blood.

'So, that's what he meant by his heart being in the box.'

'There's some papers in there as well, Adi.'

Addy places the ring back in the box and takes out the sheets of paper. Another ring rolls out of the papers and onto the dirt. Omar leans over and picks it up.

'It's like the other ring, but more smaller.'

Addy takes the ring. 'It's my mother's. I saw a photo of Hanane wearing it. I never thought I'd see it again.' She places it gently into the box beside her father's ring. In between the yellowing pages, she spies a sheet of thin blue paper. She slides it out and scans the familiar handwriting. She looks up at Omar.

'It's the rest of my father's letter to me.'

She takes the Polaroid out of her pocket and unwraps the unfinished letter, marrying it to the blue sheet from the box:

> 3rd March, 1984
> Zitoune, Morocco

*My darling Addy,*

> *I'm sorry it's taken me so long to write. You know how crazy things can be when I'm over in Nigeria. I loved your letter about your initiation week at Concordia, but please tell me*

*that was a purple wig, and that you didn't dye your lovely titian hair. Just like your mother's.*

*Well, I'm not in Nigeria any more. Things are still unsettled here with the politics and all that, and with the glut of oil on the market right now, they terminated my contract early. No need to have a petroleum geologist searching for oil when they have more of it than they can sell!*

*The job down in Peru doesn't start till May, so I've headed up to North Africa for a bit before going there. It's dinosaur land up here, so I thought I'd do a little independent oil prospecting. Remember what I used to tell you when you were little? Where there were dinosaurs, there's probably oil. I might try to stop by Montréal to see you when I get back before flying back to Nanaimo. Is The Old Dublin still there? They do a cracking pint of Guinness.*

*Addy, my darling, I've been doing a lot of thinking up here in the mountains. It's a beautiful place – you must come here one day. I know how much you love the Rockies. There's something about mountains, isn't there? Solid and reassuring. A good place to come when life wears you down.*

*I know it hasn't been easy for you since your mother died. You know there was no option but the boarding school, what with me having to travel so much for work. You made a good fist of it, though. Honour student. I never told you how proud you made me. I'm sorry for that. I'm sorry for a lot of things . . . I hope you know how much I love you and your sister.*

*There's something I need to tell you. I'm not sure how you'll feel about it. I've met someone here. Up here in a tiny village in the Morocco mountains. You know they talk of thunderbolts? It was like that. I can't explain it. Maybe you'll feel it yourself one day. I hope you do.*

*She's a lovely young woman from the village. She writes poetry. She has such spirit. She's only twenty-three,*

387

*Addy – nineteen years younger. I only hope that she feels the same way. I think she does – she comes over to a little olive oil hut I've discovered and she's kind enough to eat the meals I make for her. She likes my Irish stew. Just like you do. She writes lovely poems, which she reads to me in French, though she's just begun writing some in English. I've been practising her English with her.*

*She's not the only one I've been teaching English. There's a funny little boy who's become my shadow. He can't be more than seven, but he already acts like he's the king of Zitoune. His name's Omar. He has an older brother called Momo, who's a properly serious boy. Good in school, polite, studious. They couldn't be more opposite. Funny how siblings can be so different, isn't it? But brothers and sisters are important. Remember that, Addy. Do go and visit Philippa when you can. It would be wonderful for the two of you to meet and be friends.*

*The weather's been beautiful since I've come. You should see the fields here in the spring. As green as Ireland, would you believe that? And red poppies everywhere. You'd love it. I'm going to plant some field poppies in the grass back home when I'm back . . .*

*I don't know what to do about Hanane. That's her name. Hanane Demsiri. How can it ever work? She's Muslim and I'm Catholic. Muslim women aren't allowed to marry outside their faith. I'd have to convert if we were ever to marry – did I just say that? Marry. Yes, I'd marry her if I could. I'd stay in Morocco to make a life with her. You don't need me there in Canada now that you're at university. You can visit me here. You'd love it. You're a wanderer like me. Not like Philippa. She's a real city girl. I wish I could find a way to connect with her, but I know she blames me for leaving her and Essie. I just couldn't stay. Not in that situation. I tried to get Philippa over to Nanaimo when I married your mother, but Essie wouldn't have it.*

*Must sign off for now. It's pouring with rain – has been for the past two days. I hope it stops soon, or the river may flood. I hear it happens in the mountains here from time to time.*

*I just wanted you to know that I love you. I'm proud to be your father.*

*Love*
*Dad*

'Look, there are poems here. They're in English. These must be some of Hanane's.' Addy shuffles through the papers. 'There's something else. It's in Arabic.'

Omar takes the document and squints at it in the fading light. He looks over at Addy.

'They been married.'

'Married?'

'It says here. Augustus Joyce Percival. And here. Hanane Demsiri. They been married 22 March 1984 in Marrakech.'

'Do you know what that means? Amine isn't illegitimate.'

'It depend.'

'What do you mean?'

'They need to have the paper of Shahada for the marriage to be proper.'

'What's that?'

'The paper to prove your father became Muslim so he can marry her.' Omar flips through the papers. 'There's no Shahada paper here.'

'My father had to become Muslim for this marriage to be legal?'

'Yes. Unless he paid somebody well.'

Addy looks at Omar. Her father's faith had been important to him. The one constant in his life. It was hard to imagine him converting.

'Surely this marriage certificate should be enough for Amine to get his identity papers, shouldn't it? Then Fatima and Amine can marry.'

'But Amine is gone.'

'My father and I should never have come here. It's like we're cursed.'

'Never say that, habibati. It's your fate to come here, just as it was your father's.'

# Chapter Sixty-Eight

**Zitoune, Morocco – December 1984**

Omar follows his grandmother into the bedroom.

'Will she be okay, Jedda?'

The old woman looks at the beautiful girl panting on the bed as she clutches at the damp sheet shielding her swollen stomach.

'Go home, Omar. You're not needed here.'

'I can help. I can get water.' He unwraps the tagelmust he's tied around his neck and rushes to Hanane's side, wiping her sweat-drenched face. 'I can help. I'm not afraid. She's my friend.'

'The baby's at home. You should go.'

'But *Yamma's* there.' He pours out a glass of water from the pitcher Jedda's put on the bedside table and sits on the bed beside Hanane. 'Here, Hanane. Drink. It will help.'

Jedda reaches inside herself. *Great Dihya, what is to become of this girl?*

A face appears in her mind's eye, the red hair of the Kahina, the Amazigh queen, streaming in the wind around the woman's face.

*You must do all you can to save them both,* the great queen answers. *He must live. The future requires it.*

*And this boy, Omar. What of him?*

*He has his part to play, Fadma. Let him stay. He must know the*

391

*truth of the events of this night, even though it will be many years before the truth will be revealed to the one who comes in search of it.*

*And what is my role in this?*

*Without you, the woman and the child would surely die. It is in your power to save them, Fadma.*

*The baby comes early and the girl is so ill. There are some here who would prefer to let them die. If I do what I can, will they live?*

The Kahina shakes her head, her long hair sweeping around her like a red cloud. *I cannot say this. It is fate that shall decide this. You have a kind heart, Fadma, and you have a great gift. I have given you my ring and my djinni. Use them wisely. You will live a long life. I will keep you on the earth until you find the one to whom my ring must pass.*

*How will I know them?*

*You will know, Fadma. You will know it in your heart.*

Bouchra reaches over the sleeping girl and lifts the swaddled baby out of her arms.

'What are we are going to do with them? They can't stay here. Look at this brat. He has the mark of Shaytan Iblis on his face.'

Jedda folds up the soiled sheets and stacks them into a plastic basket.

'Go home, Omar. You've been a big help. It's been a long night. Tell your mother I'll be back soon.'

Omar yawns and follows Bouchra and his grandmother out of the room. He reaches across Bouchra's arm and pats the baby on its head. Black hair. Straight like Mister Gus's. But its face – brown and white. Part Hanane and part Mister Gus. He stands on his toes and kisses his grandmother on her headscarf.

'Thank you for letting me stay, Jedda. I knew you could help Hanane.'

'Omar, you must never tell anyone of this night. Do you understand?'

Omar stares at Mohammed's wife. 'Why?'

'This is our family matter, do you understand? Why your

grandmother let you stay, I'll never understand. This is our private business. If I hear anything about this in the village, I'll have the biggest djinni in all of Morocco come and sit on your chest when you sleep. Every time you wake you will see his ugly face and be afraid. Do you want that?'

'No.'

'Good.'

Jedda sets down the basket of laundry and straightens her back as she waves Omar out of the door. When he's gone, she turns to Mohammed's wife.

'Why do you scare the boy, Bouchra? He's done nothing but help tonight.'

'Fadma, I know you're a powerful *shawafa*. But you know, this situation is not your business. Let my husband deal with his sister and her brat. He will do whatever he must to save our honour. I will not let this *zaaniyah* ruin my own children's future.'

Aicha sweeps her eyes over the Englishman. His clothes are creased and rumpled and dark shadows rim his blue eyes. This man, this Mister Gus, has brought nothing but shame to Zitoune. To poor Hanane and her family. It is as well that Mohammed's taken the baby to Bouchra's parents in Beni Mellal. Now she, Aicha, must atone for leaving Hanane on the birthing bed. This man must leave Zitoune, and she must be the one to ensure it. She fingers the coins in her apron pocket. Enough for a new cow. She beckons to Omar, who she's spied eyeing them from behind the stable yard door.

'Omar, come here. You need to talk to this man for me.'

Omar creeps around the heavy wooden door.

'Tell this man that Hanane died after the baby came.'

Omar's eyes widen. 'Hanane died?'

Aicha looks at her son. At his eyes filling with tears. Her heart wrenches and she reaches out and enfolds him in her arms.

'After Jedda left with you, Hanane became very sick in the night. I'm sorry, Omar. I didn't want to tell you. Mohammed insisted she be buried right away so nobody could disturb her resting place. You know, some people would not like that she had a baby without being married. We couldn't let them disturb her, could we? No one must know where she rests.'

Omar rushes into his mother's arms weeping. '*Yamma*, she was so happy. Jedda helped her well.'

'Omar?' Gus asks. 'What's your mother saying?'

'Oh, Mister Gus. Hanane died! She was sick after the baby came and she died!'

The man's haggard face blanches, as if all his blood's being sucked into the earth. 'That's not possible. Where is she? Where's the baby? Omar, ask your mother.'

Aicha feels pity rise inside her, but she squashes it like an insect. This man doesn't deserve her pity. This man has ruined Hanane and fathered a child marked by Shaytan Iblis.

She pats Omar's wiry black hair. 'Omar, you must tell him the baby died as well and that they have both been buried.'

Omar pushes out of her hold. 'The baby died?'

'No. Mohammed brought him to Bouchra's parents in Beni Mellal. The baby will grow up here, with Mohammed's family. It makes sense, doesn't it? Mohammed is the baby's uncle. The baby will be like his own son.'

'But, *Yamma*, Mister Gus is the baby's *baba*.'

'He is not a proper father, Omar. The baby can't stay with him. You understand this, don't you? Don't you think it's better for Hanane's baby to be raised by Hanane's blood family? You can be like his big brother. You'd like that, wouldn't you?'

Omar wipes his eyes and nods. 'I miss having a brother.'

'Then tell him, Omar. Tell him the baby died.'

# Chapter Sixty-Nine

**Zitoune, Morocco – December 1984**

Jedda unlocks the door to her room behind the stable and slips the key back into the pocket of her full skirt. She pushes open the door and enters the small, dark room. Dull white light filters through the grimy window, throwing highlights onto the jars and bottles lined up on wooden shelves lining the clay walls, and the bundles of herbs and flowers drying on strings nailed to the ceiling beam. The cat runs between her feet and jumps onto a stool by the window.

Jedda closes the door and limps over to the wide wooden shelf under the window, the cloth bag banging against her sore hip. The rheumatism is taking hold. How is it that she can help others, but her potions are useless on her own body?

Setting the cloth bag onto the shelf, she takes out the wooden box. She fumbles with the wooden slats with her arthritic fingers until the small brass key drops into her palm. She opens the lid. One by one, she unfolds the sheets of paper, running her fingers over the unintelligible words:

> *Sky-riding swift*
> *Make your feathers a pen*
> *And write my love in the sky.*

395

*My heart is a harp*
*Silent until your fingers*
*Strum its silent song.*

*Settled by your side*
*We are like cats*
*In warm sun*
*Content in silence.*

Carefully folding the papers, she places them back in the box. She reaches into the box and takes out a heavy gold ring, holding it up to the light from the window. Golden hands encircling a heart topped with a crown.

'It's a beautiful ring, Fadma.'

Jedda looks over at the tall black woman sitting on the stool.

'Isn't it, Lamia. It belongs to the foreign man. Hanane had one like it.' She reaches into her apron pocket and holds up the delicate gold ring with the sapphire heart. 'She told me it was her wedding ring. She didn't want Bouchra to take it when she slept. She asked me to put it in a safe place until she returned to Marrakech.' She turns the ring over in her arthritic fingers, then she drops it in the box. 'I will give the box to Amine when he marries.'

'Why did Aicha lie to this man? Why did Mohammed take the child away?' The tall, broad-shouldered shepherd rises from the stool and leans on his freshly peeled wooden staff.

'Mohammed felt it would be best. If the stranger believed the baby had died with his mother, he would leave. There would be no reason for him to stay, would there?' Jedda limps past the shepherd and eases herself down on the stool.

'I do not understand why I was called to Oushane the morning after Amine's birth. If I had been here when the stranger called on Aicha, I would have told him the truth, that Amine was alive.'

'Perhaps this is why you were called away, Fadma,' Lamia says. 'It was fate.'

396

'Fate! There is no such thing. Our selfish actions create great waves until the dams burst and we are flooded with the pain and chaos we have caused. People cause all the misery in this world. Not fate.'

Jedda rises and reaches for the box. The rings sit shining on their bed of papers. She shuts the lid and locks the box.

# Chapter Seventy

**Zitoune, Morocco – June 2009**

'Pippa, where on earth have you been? The tour bus to Marrakech is leaving in an hour. Omar's had to call in favours to get us seats.' Addy fastens the zipper on her tripod bag and adds it to the pile of luggage on the concrete floor.

Philippa sets a large package covered in an orange cloth on the kitchen table. 'I took a taxi into Azaghar. I couldn't deal with all the drama going on here. Did you know they have the most amazing market there? Everything's as cheap as chips. I'm having a stack of rugs and lanterns shipped back to London. I'll make a mint back in England.'

'Great. Fine. I'm ecstatic for you.' Addy takes her phone out of her pocket and presses her messages. She thrusts the phone at her sister. 'What do you make of this?'

Philippa scans the message: *Del - A bird in the hand is worth two in the bush. See you at our flat. Let me show you what a reformed character I am. Or pay me my share and the flat's all yours. Your call. Nx'*

She hands the phone back. 'Looks like you're going to have your hands full when you're back home.'

Addy pockets her phone. 'Tell me about it. I wish I never had to go back.'

'Maybe you'll feel differently once you're back in London. Nigel has his good points.'

Addy glares at her sister. 'Don't even go there. We agreed I could camp out in your spare room until I can convince Nigel to sell the flat. You're going to have to get used to me.' She rubs her neck and looks at the stack of luggage. 'Do you have anything else?'

'Don't you dare think I'm sentimental when I show you this.'

'Show me what?'

'It's a gift for Omar's family. For feeding and watering me, because Lord knows I would've starved if I'd relied on you.'

Philippa pulls the orange cloth off the package on the table. A flash of bright blue as the bird flutters around the bamboo cage.

'A budgie?'

'The other one looked so lonely.'

'*You* thought Fatima's bird looked lonely? Are you going soft?'

Philippa points a fuchsia-tipped finger at her sister. 'Don't you dare go there. I have a reputation to maintain.'

'Fatima'll love it. Maybe it'll cheer her up.'

Philippa drapes the cloth back over the birdcage. 'Poor girl. The first heartbreak is always so hard.'

'I hope she doesn't go through with marrying Farouk. Omar's told her she doesn't have to. She doesn't know whether to wait for Amine or do what she thinks is right, which is marry Farouk. Aicha's all for the marriage, which is making it really hard. And there's still the question about Amine's legitimacy. The marriage wouldn't have been legal if Dad hadn't converted to Islam. But there's no proof he did. Maybe he just bribed someone to marry them.'

Philippa taps a polished fingernail on the tabletop. 'Just a minute. Just one minute.'

'What?'

Philippa hurries past the kitchen and into her room. A moment later she returns clutching a manila envelope. She thrusts the envelope at Addy.

'Here, I totally forgot, what with everything that's been going on. The solicitor sent me another pile of papers from Canada just before I came here. One of them was in Arabic.'

Addy flips open the seal and pulls out a sheet of yellowing paper.

'I need to find Omar.'

# Chapter Seventy-One

**Zitoune, Morocco – June 2009**

'*Mesdames, attendez!*' Mohammed runs across the car park, his beige djellaba flapping.

'There's a turn up for the books,' Philippa says as she passes her luggage to Omar to load into the tour bus. 'Mo's obviously missing me.'

Addy laughs. 'He hasn't realised yet the bullet he's dodged.'

'You're starting to sound like me.'

'Please, God, no.'

'Madame Perceeval, Phileepa, *ma gazelle*, please to wait one minute.'

Omar slams shut the luggage door on the tour bus. 'What do you want, Mohammed? There's a problem?'

'*Mashi mushkil.* I must make a big apology. Since Omar show me the Shahada paper of your father, my heart is so full. It is the best gift of the world for me. My sister and my family have a good honour now. I only wish Amine could know about it yet.'

'Me too, Mohammed. Philippa and I'll do everything we can to find him once he gets to Europe. He's family.'

'If Amine's our half-brother, what's that make you, Mo? My

step-uncle?' Philippa holds out a manicured hand. 'It's been fun, but I think it's goodbye.'

Mohammed presses his hand against his chest. 'You will always live close to my heart, *ma gazelle*.' He reaches into the pocket of his djellaba and hands Philippa a thin white envelope. 'Since you are going to Marrakech, please can you deliver this for me? I have some business there but it's hard to go now because it's many tourists in the hotel and the restaurant. And since Amine is gone, I must work very hard. The post in Morocco is not so good sometimes. It will be more faster if you can give it personally.'

Philippa tucks the letter into her handbag. 'That's fine, Mo. Consider it done.'

Omar takes hold of Addy's hand. 'Come with me.'

He leads her behind a crumbling stone watermill above the waterfalls. A low stone wall is the only barrier to the water crashing over the cliff into the pool below. He leans into her and curls his fingers around hers.

'Maybe your sister can go and you stay here with me, *habibati*.'

'My visa runs out tomorrow. I have to go, *habibi*. I'll be back. You're not going to get rid of me that easily. I wish you could come to Marrakech with us.'

'I wish it as well, darling. But I must take my grandmother to the doctor in Azaghar because her hip it's hurting a lot, and the doctor is only there certain days in the month. My mother insists for it.'

'I understand.'

Omar reaches into his jeans pocket. He holds out a ring in the palm of his hand. Jedda's silver ring with the zigzags and triangles carved into the band. He slides it onto Addy's finger. He taps the heavy ring.

'You must come back to me. It's our fate. Allah said it to you in your dream the first day.'

Addy stares at the ring. 'You know I can't have children.'

'I thought about it a lot. It's hard for me not to have children. But if it's our fate, it's our fate. *Inshallah* Allah will find a way.'

'Omar . . .' Addy sighs. 'I'm not ready to get married. I need to stand on my own two feet.'

'What you mean? You have two feet.'

Addy laughs. 'It's just an expression. I need to be more self-reliant.'

'Darling, you can stand on two feet or one foot, I don't mind. I can wait. You know Omar always get what he wants.'

'So I've been told. Maybe you can visit me in England. See what I'm like when I'm . . . not here. Maybe you won't like me.'

'I will like you, be sure about it. You make me feel my life, *habibati*. Before you, I was sleeping. Before you, it was darkness. And now you bring me the sunlight. I love you, one hundred per cent.' He kisses her.

She buries her fingers into the folds of his tagelmust. The waterfalls thrum as he covers her face with kisses. Sweet kisses. The only kisses she's ever wanted.


The gears of the tour bus grind and the driver reverses out of the car park.

Philippa leans out of a window and waves. 'Hurry up! He's leaving.'

Omar grabs Addy's hand and they run across the car park. The bus shudders to a stop in a cloud of pink dust. The door flings open.

Omar hugs Addy tight against his chest.

'People will see, Omar.'

'I don't mind.'

'*Yalla!*' the driver shouts. '*Yalla! Yalla!*'

Addy steps up into the bus. The door slams shut behind her. She stumbles down the aisle and slides into an empty seat behind Philippa. Through the window, she watches Omar grow smaller, in his blue gown and tagelmust, in the middle of the car park. He raises his hand in the air, fingers spread. She holds up her hand. As if they're touching through glass.

The bus rumbles past the service station at the crossroads. The donkey's tethered to the old petrol pump. The Coca-Cola sign swings from the hook above the window. Addy's phone buzzes in her pocket. A text from Omar: *I don't know what happened to me. I am destroyed.*

# Chapter Seventy-Two

**Marrakech, Morocco – June 2009**

'It's here.' The boy points to the green-painted wooden door studded with back nail heads.

Addy looks down the narrow alley lined with the faded terra-cotta walls of the old Marrakech medina and checks the address on the envelope. Aside from an ancient bicycle leaning against a wall, there's no other sign of life.

'You're sure? Mohammed said it was a business.'

The boy taps on the door. 'It's here – one hundred per cent.'

'Fine, fine.' Philippa reaches into her purse and pulls out a coin. 'Here you go. Thank you very much.'

The boy turns the coin over in his hands. 'It must be fifty dirhams.'

'Fifty dirhams?'

'It's a good price. It's very complicated to come here.'

Addy fishes into her bag and pulls out her wallet.

'What do you think you're doing? Put that away.' Philippa takes a twenty dirham note out of her purse and waves it at the boy. 'Twenty dirhams, take it or leave it.'

The boy's eyes follow the waving note. He snatches it from Philippa's hand and runs back down the alley, calling out as he disappears around a corner. 'Abdel! M'hamid! *Yalla! Yalla!*'

'Do you think we overpaid him?'

Philippa rolls her eyes. 'Do you think? Five dirhams would've been plenty.' She shrugs. 'But he can probably do more with twenty dirhams than I can with it in London.'

'You *are* going soft. First the bird, now the boy.'

'Oh, do be quiet.' She glances at her watch. 'Come on, let's get this done. I want to get some shopping in before dinner.'

Philippa bangs the large iron door knocker against the door. They stare at the green door in silence. She's about to knock again, when the door creaks open. A plump, middle-aged woman in an apron stands in the doorway clutching a dripping mop.

Addy holds out the white envelope. 'Hello,' she says in French. 'I have a letter from Monsieur Mohammed Demsiri. Can I leave it with you?'

The woman takes the envelope. '*Shukran.*'

The door creaks closed.

'Right. Duty done,' Philippa says. 'Let's go shopping.'

They're halfway down the alley, when the door creaks open behind them.

'*Mesdames, attendez.*'

The woman's beckoning from the doorway.

'What do you suppose she wants?'

Philippa frowns. 'Money, of course. It's effort to take delivery of an envelope.'

'You're such a cynic.'

'No, just experienced.'

They walk back along the alleyway. When they reach the doorway, the door's open. A woman steps into view. She smiles and reaches out a slender hand.

'Hello. I am Hanane.'

# *Epilogue*

Omar walks through the frosted glass doors into the Arrivals Hall at Gatwick Airport. Scaffolding and canvas sheets cover half of the large hall, hiding the shouting labourers from view. His heart thumps, but he walks slowly, his knapsack casually over his shoulder pulling the new suitcase from the Azaghar market, determined to show Adi that this is nothing for him. That he is a man of the world, just as she is a woman of it.

It's been two months since he's seen Adi on her last visit to Zitoune, though he's carried her in his mind – her low, warm voice teasing, laughing, reassuring him as he laboured on the guest house between his tours around the waterfalls. It was her face that he struggled to draw. Her blue eyes, the long, straight nose, the thrust of her lower lip when she was unhappy, the shock of thick copper hair falling into her eyes. He could conjure up each element easily enough, but when he tried to paint the final picture of her face, the edges blurred and melted away until all he was left with was a feeling. The feeling of Adi.

His eyes search the crowd waiting behind the shiny metal railing. His stomach feels empty, despite the two toasted cheese sandwiches he's eaten on the plane. Everything is grey. The airplane was grey, the sky is grey, this room is grey. The people are all dressed in black and grey. It'd been his first time in an airplane. He'd prayed to Allah for the plane not to crash. Then to fly above the clouds like a bird. It was incredible. Everything was incredible.

A few months ago, he was a mountain guide in Zitoune with a dream of a guest house and no money to build it. With a mother pleading with him to marry Zaina and get on with having children. With a simple life in Zitoune mapped out by fate. Then Adi arrived on the Marrakech tour bus and everything changed. Here he is now, in England. Maybe he'll move here with Adi after they marry. Earn money to build his guest house; have a travel business to the desert. Why not? He can earn well in England. Then he'll build a big house for Adi and his family in Zitoune. We can never guess our fate, he thinks. We can only follow it.

'Omar!'

He finds her face. The blurred edges of his memory coalesce into a finished picture. The red hair longer around her white face. The eyes still as blue as the sky. The nose, long and straight and noble. 'The nose of a queen,' as his mother says. Adi, with her fiery hair and her bright green jacket, is a jolt of colour in the sea of greyness. He fingers his bright blue cotton tagelmust, wrapped around his neck like a scarf. He's brought the colour of Morocco with him.

He walks alongside the railing. Adi follows him, on her side of the barrier, weaving around waiting relatives and drivers holding misspelt signs. Then she is standing in front of him. He smells her scent – light, fresh, like the cedars in Ifrane. He leans over to kiss her cheek. Then her arms are around his neck and she is kissing him. His arms fold around her body. They are an island of colour in a grey sea.

'Adi, I came for you.'

# Acknowledgements

Thank you to Richard Skinner and the Faber Academy class of 2011 for their encouragement and feedback on the first rough draft, to Judith Chinn and Carolyn Chinn for helping me keep the faith, to Melvyn Fickling for his astute comments on the many drafts, Jane Johnson for her encouragement, Vicky Seton for being a beta reading star, Carolyn Gillis for pointing me to Avon Books, my wonderful editor Molly Walker-Sharp who opened the door, my agent Jo Swainson for taking a chance on me, and my friends in Morocco who've welcomed me into this beautiful country. Shukran from the bottom of my heart.